The Goddess

OTHER VALANCOURT BOOKS TITLES OF INTEREST:

By Richard Marsh

THE BEETLE: A MYSTERY
THE DATCHET DIAMONDS
THE JOSS: A REVERSION
PHILIP BENNION'S DEATH
THE SEEN AND THE UNSEEN
CURIOS: SOME STRANGE ADVENTURES OF TWO BACHELORS
BOTH SIDES OF THE VEIL
A SPOILER OF MEN
THE GODDESS: A DEMON
A SILENT WITNESS AND OTHER STORIES
BETWEEN THE DARK AND THE DAYLIGHT *(forthcoming)*

By Bram Stoker

THE SNAKE'S PASS
LADY ATHLYNE
THE MYSTERY OF THE SEA
THE LADY OF THE SHROUD *(forthcoming)*

By Bertram Mitford

THE WEIRD OF DEADLY HOLLOW
RENSHAW FANNING'S QUEST
THE SIGN OF THE SPIDER
THE KING'S ASSEGAI
THE INDUNA'S WIFE
THE WHITE SHIELD

VALANCOURT CLASSICS

The Goddess

A Demon

BY

RICHARD MARSH

AUTHOR OF "THE BEETLE: A MYSTERY," "THE JOSS: A REVERSION," "A
SPOILER OF MEN," "BOTH SIDES OF THE VEIL," &C.

Edited with an introduction and notes by
Minna Vuohelainen

Kansas City:
VALANCOURT BOOKS
2010

The Goddess: A Demon by Richard Marsh
First published by F. V. White in 1900
First Valancourt Books edition 2010

Introduction and notes © 2010 by Minna Vuohelainen
This edition © 2010 by Valancourt Books

ISBN 978-1-934555-06-4

Composition by James D. Jenkins
Published by Valancourt Books
Kansas City, Missouri
http://www.valancourtbooks.com

CONTENTS

INTRODUCTION

Richard Marsh, professional author

IN November 1900, an article in the high-culture review *Academy* considered the rising fortunes of what its anonymous author termed the "Yarning School." Characterized by the "faculty of beginning a story anywhere and continuing without art or insight, but with reckless invention," the Yarning School was responsible for "romances which will beguile a railway journey, or even form the stay-at-home pabulum of millions." While reluctantly admitting "the innate genius for telling a story" which defined the Yarning School to be "a fine gift," the reviewer regretfully concluded that "these are fat years for the yarners." The writer attributed their success to the millions of new readers who had entered the market in the years following the 1870 Education Act and were demanding cheap, light reading. These readers were the target audience of the Yarning School, for "it is precisely the prevalence of shallow learning that multiplies novelists and ensures readers. [...] [T]housands [...] are satisfied [... with] the crude literary fare which is supplied to them so lavishly."

The author of the indignant exposé of the Yarning School was not afraid of naming names. Among the Yarners named and shamed were Guy Boothby, William Le Queux, Fergus Hume, Hume Nisbet, and George Manville Fenn, all writers of fair popularity. Above all, however,

> There is Mr. Richard Marsh: he is prodigious. The tradition current in the receiving department of this office that he publishes a new novel every Tuesday is an exaggeration. We do not believe that, working at top pressure, Mr. Marsh writes one novel a month. But [...] he comes near to this figure.

In "a year of unexampled depression in the book trade," the writer states, "Mr. Marsh has got into his stride and he throws off a story with an abandon—we might add, an abandonment—that is refreshing." Among the popular texts torn apart by the reviewer was

Marsh's gothic novel *The Goddess: A Demon*, which, the reviewer notes, "relies on [its] sub-title to secure immediate attention to certain weird happenings in Imperial-mansions." The critic scornfully suggests that such "delectable plot[lines] probably flashed upon Mr. Marsh while his ticket was being punched on the top of a 'bus," and goes on to quote the *dénouement* to *The Goddess*, stating that "The public who will accept the solution of this story will accept anything." *The Goddess*, he observes, "is scrumptious dormitory yarning; but is it anything else?" Nonetheless, the reviewer is forced to admit that "Mr. Marsh is [...] on terms with his readers; for him the rest is mechanics, and for them it is excitement."[1]

The conservative review of the fiction produced by the "Yarners" was published in 1900, Marsh's *anno mirabilis*. Since 1897, Marsh had steadily built on the promise of his bestseller, *The Beetle: A Mystery*, culminating in an impressive show of energy in 1900, a year in which he did indeed come near to producing one novel a month with his eight volumes of fiction, totaling over half a million words. In 1901, Marsh defended his production rates in a letter to the *Academy*:

> During the last year or two work of mine which appeared in print twelve years ago has been brought out as new. The impression has consequently grown up that I flood the market with books turned out by machinery. As a matter of fact, since I finished *The Beetle* in the spring of 1896, I have not written, on an average, one novel a year. An author can have no reasonable objection to the production of fresh editions of his books, but he has every right to protest against his old work being issued by owners of copyright as if it were new.[2]

Marsh had earlier explained that "Simultaneous publication is not equivalent to simultaneous production. [...] I assure you I had no wish that my books should be treading on each other's heels." In fact, Marsh claimed, it was his custom to "produce slowly. Kneading a story, mentally, is a delight, setting it forth on paper is about as bad as a surgical operation."[3] In 1900 Marsh did come dangerously

---

[1] "The Yarning School," *Academy* 59 (3 November 1900): 423-424.

[2] "Mr. Richard Marsh's Stories," *Academy* 60 (9 February 1901): 131.

[3] "Mr. Marsh Explains," *Academy* 52 (30 October 1897): 358.

close to flooding the market. However, his eight volumes—which included gothic and supernatural fiction, a novel of stage life, an episodic narrative in which Christ returns to contemporary London, a schoolboy adventure, and detective and mystery stories—also guaranteed him plenty of attention and many readers. After 1900, Marsh's reputation as a popular author was firmly established, his production levels stabilized at three volumes a year, and reviews of his work became increasingly appreciative of the craftsmanship and innovativeness displayed in his novels.

Marsh's career was intimately connected to the conditions which characterized the turn of the century, a potential golden age for the popular novelist. This transitional period in British print culture witnessed a number of significant developments: beneficial changes in taxation, the introduction of cheaper and quicker printing methods, advances in distribution and communication, the emergence of magazines specializing in fiction, increasingly aggressive marketing, the introduction of state education and, consequently, near-universal literacy amongst the urban lower middle classes. From the 1880s, the publishing industry responded to the challenge of catering for these newly-literate consumers by providing them with cheap, light reading, particularly fiction, in the shape of the six-shilling one-volume first edition, weekly penny papers such as *Tit-Bits* and *Answers*, and sixpenny illustrated monthlies such as *Strand*, *Windsor*, and *Idler*.[1] This new audience, it was acknowledged, consisted of working men and women who had had limited educational opportunities and now had limited leisure time. This, Helen Bosanquet argued in the conservative *Contemporary Review*, was "a tired public, craving to forget its weariness, and eagerly seizing upon any mental distraction which will help." As Bosanquet contemptuously recognized, peculiar qualities were required of writers catering for the newly literate:

> [A]uthors who are to fulfil this function must write under very
> difficult conditions. For one thing, they cannot look for more

---

[1] Richard D. Altick, *The English Common Reader: A Social History of the Mass Reading Public, 1800-1900*. 2nd edn (Columbus: Ohio State University Press, 1998), 306-17; Joseph McAleer, *Popular Reading and Publishing in Britain, 1914-1950* (Oxford: Clarendon Press, 1992), 3-25.

than the minimum of intellectual exertion on the part of their
readers […]. Indeed, it is doubtful how far the necessary con-
centration is possible in the detached and interrupted moments
which they can give. In the second place, the physical conditions
under which the stories are to be read involve a style which
must be difficult to acquire, and very difficult to handle well. […]
[T]he story must march straight to its end with as little impedi-
menta as possible. […] The conditions of the stories are, then,
that they must be interesting, easily read, concise, and purely
narrative.[1]

Newly literate workers, reading fiction on the public transport and
after work, "prefer[red] to be excited and interested," one writer
asserted in the veteran *Blackwood's Edinburgh Magazine*, "Hence
the popularity of the sensational novel, taking horrors for its subjects and criminals for its heroes, and leading the reader onwards
from surprise to surprise to the dramatic *dénouement* which should
be enveloped in mystery."[2]

Marsh's career can be seen as a continuous attempt to provide
"interesting, easily read, concise, and purely narrative" fiction for
readers who "prefer[red] to be excited and interested." From the
time that the first work attributed to "Richard Marsh" appeared in
Belgravia in 1888, Marsh accurately gauged the mood and tastes of
the fin-de-siècle public. His early work mostly falls into the gothic
and crime genres, but by the end of the century, he had branched
out into the sensation, thriller, and romance genres which were
to remain his standard fare from then on. Apart from 76 volumes
issued by 16 different publishers, Marsh published short and serial
fiction in a number of magazines, including *Belgravia*, *Household
Words*, *Cornhill Magazine*, *Gentleman's Magazine*, *Home Chimes*,
Blackwood's Edinburgh Magazine, *Longman's Magazine*, *All the Year
Round*, *Answers*, *Idler Magazine*, *Harmsworth Magazine* (later *London
Magazine*), *Pearson's Weekly*, *Pearson's Magazine*, *Windsor Magazine*,
Cassell's Magazine, and, most importantly, *Strand Magazine*. As
noted below, he also issued short stories and serial novels in the
regional newspaper press, for example the *Manchester Weekly*

---

[1] Helen Bosanquet, "Cheap Literature," *Contemporary Review* 79 (1901):
674-675.
[2] "Crime in Fiction," *Blackwood's Edinburgh Magazine* 148 (August 1890): 172.

Times where *The Goddess* was serialized. Marsh was clearly aware of current developments in publishing and tailored his literary production to suit a growing but increasingly diversified market of lower-middle-class and female readers. Among them, he built up a solid reputation as a provider of entertaining and up-to-date popular fiction.

Bernard Heldmann, *alias* "Richard Marsh"

So who was "Richard Marsh," this "universal literary provider?"[1] Marsh was born Richard Bernard Heldmann in London on 12 October, 1857. His father, lace merchant Joseph Heldmann, was of German Jewish origin, and his mother Emma, née Marsh, was a lace-manufacturer's daughter from Nottinghamshire. Bernard (his preferred name), or "Bertie," was born just before his father became embroiled in bankruptcy proceedings which revealed that he had been defrauding his employers, who also happened to be his in-laws, to the tune of £16,000 by selling goods below cost value. His career as lace merchant over, Joseph Heldmann took to private tutoring, teaching German, English Literature and the Classics at various London schools before running his own school in Hammersmith, West London. The Heldmanns had at least three further children: Henry (Harry, 1858-1932); Sophia Alice (Alice, 1860-1938); and John Whitworth, who died in his infancy (1870-71).

Young Bernard appears to have taken after his father in his unscrupulousness. His grandson Robert Aickman, himself a fine gothic author, states that Heldmann was expelled from Eton and Oxford (though there is no evidence that he attended either) "owing to incidents with women,"[2] and implies that his lifestyle was unconventional and flashy. By 1880, Heldmann had deserted his family background in trade and education for journalism, then a semi-intellectual career on the borders of respectable society. He first began to publish fiction under his given name at the youthful age of 22 in the devotional publications *Quiver* and *Young England* and the boys' paper *Union Jack*. The weekly *Union Jack*, associated with two favorite boys' writers of the time, W.H.G. Kingston

---

[1] Robert Aickman, *The Attempted Rescue* (London: Victor Gollancz, 1966), 11.
[2] Aickman, *Attempted Rescue*, 11.

(1814-1880) and G.A. Henty (1832-1902), provided Heldmann with his initiation into the literary life. Under Henty's editorship, he quickly became a trusted contributor of short and serial school and adventure stories before being promoted to co-editor in October 1882. However, in spring 1883 Heldmann's contribution to the paper began to flag, the serial he was publishing was interrupted in March, and his editorship was abruptly terminated by Henty in June. Speculation has long surrounded the abrupt end to Heldmann's career in spring 1883. While the exact circumstances of Heldmann's breach with Henty remain unclear, a partial record of his activities in the aftermath of his dismissal in 1883 can now be offered.[1] However, while we now know the reason for the gap in his literary production in the mid-1880s and for his subsequent adoption of the pseudonym "Richard Marsh" in 1888, it must be stressed that we still have no information on what caused Heldmann's journalistic career to falter in early spring 1883: did he suffer a nervous breakdown? Did he get into debt? Were women involved? Or did he steal from Henty?

On 12 February, 1884, the Cardiff *Western Mail* reported on the capture of a forger at the seaside town of Tenby in South Wales: "On Saturday night the Tenby police succeeded in capturing a person who has been for some time wanted in connection with the frauds on the Acton Branch of the London and North-Western Bank," the paper reported: "The name of the person is Bernard Heldman, *alias* Captain Roberts, *alias* Dr. Wilson. He is described as a journalist, and formerly of Acton; and is required at Tunbridge Wells in connection with several frauds on the above bank."[2] The *Kent and Sussex Courier and Southern Counties Herald* supplies further detail on the charges at Tunbridge Wells:

---

[1] See also Minna Vuohelainen, *Richard Marsh: Victorian Fiction Research Guide* 35 (October 2009), http://www.canterbury.ac.uk/arts-humanities/Media/victorian-research-fiction/StockList/35-Richard-Marsh.aspx; Callum James, "Callum James's Literary Detective Agency, Case #1: Why Was Richard Marsh?," *Front Free Endpaper*, 30 November 2009, http://callumjames.blogspot.com/2009/11/callum-jamess-literary-detective-agency.html; Robert Kirkpatrick, *The Three Lives of Bernard Heldmann* (London: Children's Books History Society, 2010), pp. 17-19.

[2] "Capture of a Forger at Tenby," *Western Mail*, 12 February 1884, 4.

Bernard Heldmann, alias *Capt. George Roberts*, a journalist, pleaded guilty to two indictments charging him with having, at Tunbridge Wells, obtained by false pretences from Emma Thrift food and lodgings, value £3, with intent to defraud.— Mr. Stone, who prosecuted, said that the prisoner went to the house of Mrs. Thrift and obtained board and lodging, representing himself to be Capt. Roberts. Whilst he was staying there he went to Mr. Oliver, a butcher, to pay for something he had there, giving him a cheque for £15, here also representing himself as Capt. Roberts. When the cheque was presented it was dishonoured.[1]

Heldmann was, accordingly, sentenced to eighteen months' hard labor at the West Kent Quarter Sessions on 9 April, 1884 for obtaining board and lodgings ("food pudding tea coals") by false pretences from Emma Thrift, and for obtaining money (£10 15*s*.) by false pretences from William Oliver.[2] He served his sentence in full at Maidstone Jail, which can now be identified as the original of Marsh's fictional Canterstone Jail, and was released on 8 October, 1885. The Maidstone Prison Nominal Roll tells us that he was considered well-educated, declared his occupation as journalist, had brown hair, and was 5 foot 5 inches tall.[3]

These, then, are the facts of the case. However, the press reportage can also give us an insight into Heldmann's mindset and self-fashioning. The case revolved around fraud and Heldmann's careless financial dealings:

Mr. Stone, who prosecuted, said that the prisoner [...] had obtained from the bank a cheque book in the name of his brother, and drew cheques to a large amount, which were all dishonoured.—Mr. Dickens, for the defence, said the prisoner

[1] "False Pretences at Tunbridge Wells," *Kent and Sussex Courier and Southern Counties Herald*, 11 April 1884, 8.
[2] *West Kent Quarter Sessions*, Wednesday 9 April 1884, 72. See also *County of Kent: Criminal Register: England and Wales 1884*, 284: "Return of all persons Committed, or Bailed to appear for Trial, or Indicted at the General Quarter Sessions held at Maidstone on the ninth day of April 1884, showing the nature of their offences, and the result of the proceedings."
[3] *Maidstone Prison Nominal Roll*, November 1883-November 1884, no. 2100: "Hildmann, Bernard."

did not get the cheque book in his brother's name but in his own, as he had a sum of from £300 to £400 in the bank, but he considerably overdrew, thinking that he would have some money paid into his account.[1]

Indeed, Arthur Charles Bocking, also referred to as Brocking, "a bank clerk at the Acton Branch of the London and South Western Bank," deposed that Heldmann had "opened an account at his branch bank in March" 1883 under his own name. Bocking "had not known prisoner before, but had an introduction from his brother who had an account and was very respectable." Heldmann "received a cheque book containing 100 forms" but as early as 21 May, 1883, Bocking had cause to write to Heldmann "calling his attention to the irregular way in which the account had been kept." Heldmann failed to respond, and Bocking closed the account.[2] Bocking explained that the "first cheque to which he refused payment had come in on the 16th May" 1883. After May 1883, Heldmann had gone from bad to worse and was "believed to be wanted at various parts of the kingdom for various frauds." When captured, his possessions included the telltale "cheque book [...], a gold watch and chain, some bills, and £2 5s. in money [...]. In one of the letters were three cheques taken from the prisoner's cheque book, filled in for various amounts in different names."[3] These findings told a story of fraud: "all the recent counterfoils, from which the cheques were torn had not been filled up," and the "original accounts seem to have ended in May" 1883, when Heldmann's connection with *Union Jack* was terminated by Henty.[4] Bocking explained that

> Since he wrote to prisoner, 13 cheques had been presented, bearing prisoner's signature or some other name in the writing of the prisoner which he recognized for a total sum of £271 3s. Eight of the cheques were in prisoner's own signature. The 13

[1] "False Pretences at Tunbridge Wells," 8.
[2] "'Captain Roberts' Sent for Trial," *Kent and Sussex Courier*, 20 February 1884, 3.
[3] "Systematic Frauds by a 'Captain,'" *Maidstone and Kentish Journal*, 21 February 1884, 3.
[4] "Important Capture of an Alleged Swindler," *Kent and Sussex Courier*, 13 February 1884, 3.

cheques were inclusive up to January 22nd. The eight cheques
amounted to £1,198 1s. [...] It was a handwriting easily detected.[1]

The press reports tell a story of a man living on his wits in
France, the Channel Islands and Britain:

> Supt. Embery, of Tunbridge Wells, said he had found out that
> the prisoner had been to Guernsey, where he passed a cheque
> for £200, from thence he went to France, where he passed under
> the name of Dr. Wilson. He passed a cheque at Folkestone in
> the same name, and from thence went to different places in
> England under different *noms de plume*, passing cheques wher-
> ever he went. There were several warrants out against him.[2]

Heldmann "was known to have crossed the Channel" on 7
December, 1883,[3] and had, since then, been staying at various British
watering places until his capture at Tenby just over two months
later. It seems, then, that he had left Britain earlier in 1883 and had
been living the life of a fraudster for some time before his capture.

The newspaper reports reveal that Heldmann was living under
a host of false names, including Captain Roberts, Captain Martyn,
Henderson, and Dr. Wilson, and affecting a cultivated gentlemanly
manner. He was, here, playing on the class prejudices of late-nine-
teenth-century British society. Heldmann, "a stylish person, aged
25,"[4] is repeatedly described as having "the appearance of a well-to-
do gentleman"[5] and as "a well dressed individual."[6] Heldmann's stay
at the Thrifts at Tunbridge Wells establishes his demanding habits:

> He ordered a good dinner when he came in. [...] During that
> week she supplied him with puddings, &c., from her own stores,
> as well as tea and sugar and coals. He ordered his own wines,
> &c. [...] He stated that he was a Captain and that he must have

---

[1] "'Captain Roberts' Sent for Trial," 3.
[2] "False Pretences at Tunbridge Wells," 8.
[3] "Important Capture of an Alleged Swindler," 3.
[4] "An Alleged Swindler," *Maidstone and Kentish Journal, Rochester and
Chatham Journal, and South Eastern Advertiser*, 18 February 1884, 8.
[5] "Capture of a Forger at Tenby," 4.
[6] "Systematic Frauds by a 'Captain,'" 3.

a hard bed, as military men did not like soft beds. [...] She did
not volunteer sweets, as he asked for them.[1]

The most comprehensive of these accounts of "the adventures
of a swindler of the 'high-toned' sort" comes from the *North Wales
Chronicle*, which reported on Heldmann's exploits at Llandudno:
the "fashionably-dressed, good-looking" fraudster, with his
"manly, open countenance" here took on the identity of "Captain
George Martyn, of the Indian Army" and "put on the airs of a
gentleman" both "by general deportment" and by his "elaborate
get-up." The paper reported on the Captain's upper-class accent
("aw, and please give the portah this shilling"), his request for the
"best wines," his parties, his breakfasts at 11am, and his dinners at
6:30pm. This "'awistoquatic' stranger" had spoken of his weekly
£12 allowance from his father, cashed in the remittance when it
"arrived," paid his £4 bill, and moved on with his £8 change, only
for the townspeople to find out that "the Captain and his cheque
[were] entirely a fraud."[2] It is, then, apparent that Heldmann was
here creating a convincing alter ego for himself. Such dual existences and criminal transactions would later form the mainstay
of Richard Marsh's literary production (indeed, they feature
prominently in *The Goddess*), and this "lost" period in Heldmann/
Marsh's life was, thus, clearly formative. It is, also, probable that
Heldmann was writing during his adventures. The *Kent and Sussex
Courier* reported on the insistent enquiries by Heldmann's solicitor
for "a list of the papers, &c., found on the prisoner," including "a
number of private papers having no bearing on the case."[3] Could
these papers, which Heldmann was so eager to retrieve, have been
manuscripts?

After his ignominious demise, Heldmann vanished from the
literary scene for some time. We do not know what Heldmann
did immediately upon his release from prison on 8 October, 1885.
However, within a year, he had settled with a woman called Ada
Kate Abbey. A number of Marsh's later novels portray an essentially

---

[1] "'Captain Roberts' Sent for Trial," 3.
[2] "'Captain George Martyn, of the Indian Army,'" *North Wales Chronicle*,
23 February 1884, 6.
[3] "Important Capture of an Alleged Swindler," 3.

good man coming out of prison and taking lodgings at a troubled household, the daughter of which he eventually marries: could this be how Heldmann met Ada? The couple's first child, Alice Kate, was born in July 1887 when Ada was only twenty years old and Heldmann working as a journalist for an unidentified paper or magazine; however, Alice died in her infancy in March 1888. Five further children, Harry, Mabel, Madge, Conrad, and Bertram, followed in rapid succession between July 1888 and January 1895.

Such a large family would have been hard for a young man with no expectations to support, and Heldmann may have resorted to producing fiction to supplement his income from journalism. He is likely to have been aware of his mother's will, dated 15 June 1888, which to all intents and purposes disinherited him by leaving him £25, plus a list of religious exhortations, out of an estate valued in 1911 at nearly £3000. By summer 1888 Heldmann was again producing fiction—now under the pseudonym "Richard Marsh," a combination of his own first name and his mother's maiden name, as well as the name of his maternal grandfather and, accidentally, of the trainer of the Prince of Wales's racehorses. Heldmann's burst of productivity coincided with the birth of his children and led to the growing prosperity of the family, as testified by their frequent relocations in West London and Sussex. Eventually, the family settled at Haywards Heath, Sussex, where Heldmann died of heart failure and heart disease at the age of 57 on 9 August 1915.

The Goddess: A Demon (1900)

The Goddess: A Demon was published in 1900, a busy year for Marsh. The novel was initially serialized in the Manchester Weekly Times and Salford Weekly News, a regional penny weekly, in twelve installments between 12 January and 30 March, 1900. The paper regularly carried fiction, which was designed to be entertaining, to supply readers with leisure pursuits, and, in the case of serial fiction, to ensure continued sales. Marsh published in the Manchester Weekly Times on a regular basis in this period: in 1898, the paper had run his novella The Woman with One Hand (1899) in a serial format under the title "Something to his Advantage." This was followed by "In Full Cry" in 1899 (In Full Cry, 1899), "The Strange Fortune of

Pollie Blythe: The Story of a Chinese 'God'" in 1900-01 (*The Joss: A Reversion*, 1901), and "The Man in the Glass Cage; or The Strange Story of the Twickenham Peerage" in 1901 (*The Twickenham Peerage*, 1902). In addition to these serials, three of Marsh's short stories also appeared in the *Manchester Weekly Times* in the 1890s.

The serial was advertised prominently, and Marsh's name featured both in the advertisements and at the top of each installment. The *Manchester Weekly Times* "boomed" the "brilliant" and "sensational" new serial as "a modern story of crime, love, and mystery" with "a remarkable opening." The readers were told about the charms of the "extremely popular" Mr. Marsh:

> His success is not far to seek. He brings to his work gifts of a very rare order; he is a delightfully unconventional writer, and tells a story in quite a unique way. Combining something of the sensationalism of Wilkie Collins with a humorous insight reminding one of Charles Dickens, his style exhibits qualities which it owes to neither of these famous novelists, no[r] to any other. It is characterised by a peculiar directness and vigour which invest the narrative with fascinating interest. As for plot and incident, it is sufficient to say that in all Mr. Marsh's stories the movement is very rapid, and the reader is hurried forward with breathless interest.[1]

The weekly installments varied in length from 4500 to 6600 words, averaging 5500 words over two pages in the *Manchester Weekly Times*'s eight-page fiction supplement, and concluded on a cliffhanger: Bessie's bloody cloak, the hesitation of Inspector Symonds, the Goddess's laughter. The first seven installments were illustrated by "Dean" with some rather crude black-and-white drawings which depicted the most dramatic scenes in the novel: Ferguson confronting the woman who came through the window from his bed; the discovery of the body (albeit with no sign of blood!); Dr. Hume pointing a revolver at Ferguson; and Ferguson's assault on Bernstein. Intriguingly, the Goddess herself is not portrayed at all, perhaps because of her implied nudity or because of the obviously limited abilities of the artist.

The novel was brought out in volume form by F.V. White, a

---

[1] "Fiction for the New Year," *Manchester Weekly Times*, 22 December 1899, 9.

publisher of popular fiction, who also issued Marsh's occult novels *The House of Mystery* (1898), *In Full Cry* (1899), and *The Joss: A Reversion* (1901). *The Goddess* was published at the standard price of 6s. in striking pictorial boards, reproduced with this edition. As noted by the *Academy*'s review of the "Yarners," the title and the cover were designed to sell in a market where purchasing decisions could be made very quickly on the basis of first, often visual, impressions. The volume itself was not illustrated, and, indeed, the *Manchester Weekly Times* drawings were not of high enough a quality to appear in a 6s. volume.

The critical reception of the novel, charted in Appendix A, was mixed. As noted at the beginning of this introduction, critics were by autumn 1900 exhausted with Marsh's work. "Mr. Marsh exhales novels; no pun or offence intended,"[1] the reviewer of the *Academy* joked, "We do our best to keep up with Mr. Marsh. [...] We have begun to take quite a sporting interest in Mr. Marsh, and ask ourselves anxiously—'Can he manage twelve in the year?'"[2] The reviewer of *Judy* also criticized Marsh's prolificacy:

> The book trade is pretty dull just now; but there are some writers whose activity nothing under the sun avails to quell. [...] if you would keep pace with Mr. Marsh it must be to the exclusion of most other people. I regret, however, that personally I had never any desire to keep pace with Mr. Marsh. I can, therefore, do no more than chronicle the appearance—I am much too wary to commit myself by calling it the latest—of another novel from his pen.[3]

The *Academy* branded the novel "red-hot melodrama" and "capital reading for Margate," a scathing comment from this high-culture review.[4] The *Athenaeum* was more encouraging, admitting that the novel "reflects credit on the imagination of the author," "has merit as a shocker, and [...] is fairly well written." Its "solution

---

[1] "Notes on Novels," *Academy* 59 (13 October 1900): 310.

[2] "Notes on Novels," *Academy* 59 (17 November 1900): 468.

[3] H. Lush, "Scribes and Pharisees," *Judy, or the London Serio-Comic Journal* 60 (September 1900): 430.

[4] "Notes on Novels," *Academy* 59 (11 August 1900): 112.

[...] is postponed with a skill that is equally creditable. There is a good deal of naïve humour about Ferguson and his narrative."[1] The *Graphic* compared *The Goddess* to Poe's "Murders in the Rue Morgue" (1841), a clear influence on the novel, stating that Marsh had "evidently made up his mind to go one better than" Poe:

> [I]ts combination of ghastliness and ingenuity is completely in harmony with the methods of the Master, of whom its conception is by no means unworthy. In producing the requisite reality of effect he is less successful; he is without Poe's appreciation of the value of little details, and of the still greater value of the art of omission. It is something, however, that such a comparison should be favourably suggested.[2]

The novel was moderately successful, remaining in print on Methuen's lists in the early twentieth century after the copyright changed hands. However, it cannot be said to have matched the popularity of Marsh's 1897 bestseller, *The Beetle: A Mystery*. In fact, the two novels have a good deal in common. Both are urban gothic texts set in a menacing, contemporary London which has suffered a supernatural foreign invasion by a female monster with apparent powers of mind control.

Fog and violence: Marsh's London

In *The Goddess*, an Indian sacrificial idol (the eponymous Goddess, an iron maiden with apparent supernatural powers) exerts an uncanny influence over an imperial adventurer-gone-wrong, the novel's villain Edwin Lawrence, seemingly precipitating him to alcoholism, insanity, fratricide, and, eventually, a gruesome suicide. Although we hear little of the imperial exploits which have brought Lawrence into contact with the Goddess, the novel is rooted in India, and the Goddess represents a set of alien morals and practices introduced into contemporary London: "Some queer things still take place in India,"[3] the novel's first-person

---

[1] "New Novels," *Athenaeum* 3798 (11 August 1900): 179.

[2] "New Novels," *Graphic*, 15 September 1900, 401.

[3] Richard Marsh, *The Goddess: A Demon* (London: F.V. White, 1900), 294. All further references to the novel will be placed within the text.

narrator John Ferguson, "an adventurer from the four corners of the world, soiled with something of the grime from each of them" (142), explains. The Indian backdrop, associated with the traumatic Uprising of 1857, would still have provoked unease at the end of the century. In nineteenth-century fiction, notably the stories by Kipling which we are told Lawrence is reading, India was also known as a place for young men to "go wrong." Imperialism conditions the behavior of the novel's male characters and affects the shape of their London scene. Ferguson, for example, explains that he is "a hard man" whose "life has been lived, for the most part, in odd corners of the world" (141), and he has a tendency to resort to violence when under pressure. The emphasis on Britain's imperial legacy is particularly strong at the beginning of *The Goddess*, which sees Ferguson and Lawrence visit the *Empire* Theatre before proceeding to their rooms in *Imperial* Mansions. Here, Ferguson sees "Lawrence *juggle* with the [card] pack" (1, my italics). These references bring the Empire and its twin legacies of imperial guilt and threat of colonial rebellion or revenge into the very heart of London.

While India forms a backdrop to the novel's plotline, the text itself is set in modern London, a troubled city that was the centre of a national debate on social inequality and urban decay at the fin de siècle. London had grown at an uncomfortable pace in the nineteenth century, expanding from four million inhabitants in 1881 to seven million by 1911, resulting in overcrowding in the slums of the East End. *The Goddess* contains some remarkable crowd scenes, where the "hustling throng" gathers as out of nowhere to "h[a]ng round" the protagonists "like a fringe," "growing, both in numbers and in impudence" in preparation for "an ugly rush" (240, 252-253). In keeping with contemporary fears of the lower orders swamping respectable London, the crowd is dangerous and predatory. Such depictions of social divisions were common at the fin de siècle, when London was typically portrayed as a city divided along geographical and class boundaries into a wealthy West and a poor East. In Marsh's novel, the divisions in London are reflected in the doubling of characters: the crooked Edwin Lawrence murders his respectable brother Philip, and the divine Bessie Moore's degenerate brother Tom is responsible for her impending downfall.

Respectable London is here threatened from within by the unscrupulousness of degenerate middle-class men.

The attendant concerns over social disorder, national degeneration, and urban criminality were translated at the fin de siècle
into a distinct sub-genre of the gothic mode, urban gothic, which
focused on the decaying city as a site of corruption, degeneration,
and transgression. An imagery of darkness, fog, and unknow-
ability conveyed a sense of the city as a place of danger.[1] In *The
Goddess*, the famous London fog, some contemporary descriptions
of which are given in Appendix B, contributes quite remarkably
to this disorientating and confining effect, turning day into night
and preventing the characters from seeing clearly: "It was between
three and four o'clock in the afternoon. Already the lamps were
lighted. The fog still hung over the city. From the appearance of
things it might have been night" (215). In a device typical of detective fiction, the fog appears to gather more tightly as the characters grow increasingly puzzled at the mystery of the Goddess:
"Through the mist, out there in the Fulham Road, there came the
sound of a woman's laughter [...]—soft, low, musical; yet within
it, indefinable, yet not to be mistaken, a quality which was pregnant with horrible suggestion" (229). The fog associated with the
Goddess is symbolic both of the characters' mental perturbation
and of the anonymity and menace of London.

In turn-of-the-century literature and social discourse, London
is depicted as the site both of erotic opportunity and of sexual
danger. This "period of 'sexual anarchy'"[2] witnessed heated
debates over non-reproductive urban sexualities, particularly
demands for sexual equality by outspoken New Women and scan-
dals, most notoriously the trials in 1895 of Oscar Wilde, caused
by the discovery of a homosexual subculture in the metropolis.
While Marsh's novel contains examples both of female indepen-
dence and of homoerotic innuendo, it notably draws on the widely

---

[1] Fred Botting, *Gothic* (London and New York: Routledge, 2006), 1-13;
Robert Mighall, *A Geography of Victorian Gothic Fiction: Mapping History's
Nightmares* (Oxford: Oxford University Press, 1999), 30-33.
[2] Elaine Showalter, *Sexual Anarchy: Gender and Culture at the Fin de Siècle*
(London: Virago, 2001), 3.

reported debates over prostitution and public morality at the fin de siècle. The 1880s witnessed the campaigns against the Contagious Diseases Acts, which had given the police powers to examine suspected prostitutes while making no provision for similar treatment of their male customers. The Acts were suspended in 1883 and repealed in 1886, the year when legislation was introduced to protect young girls from predatory men. The amendment to existing age-of-consent regulations was at least partly due to the influence of the crusading New Journalist W.T. Stead, whose *Maiden Tribute of Modern Babylon* appeared in the *Pall Mall Gazette* in 1885. Stead's dark, distorted narrative portrayed London as a labyrinth where sexual corruption was a common fate. This was also the era of Mrs. Ormiston Chant's campaign against visible prostitution in the West End, particularly at the Empire Theatre frequented by Lawrence and Ferguson, where prostitutes openly paraded. Chant wished to reclaim the streets of the West End for middle-class women who were beginning to frequent the area as shoppers, and in 1894 succeeded in briefly shutting the Empire down. In the autumn of 1888, the unsolved Jack the Ripper murders, charted in Appendix C, had brought public interest in the vice trade to a sensational pitch. A number of prostitutes had been brutally murdered within a very small geographical area in Whitechapel in the East End of London, their bodies and faces slashed beyond recognition. In contemporary reportage, the Jack the Ripper case, like Stead's narrative, acquired a nightmarish gothic dimension, with a focus on the torn, mutilated and disemboweled bodies of the Ripper's victims. Speaking of the "superfluous brutality" of the murders, the "stains and pools of blood" that the murderer left behind him, the *East London Advertiser* sensationally compared the Ripper to "a murderous lunatic concealed in the slums of Whitechapel, who issues forth at night like another Hyde, to prey upon the defenceless women of the 'unfortunate' class."[1] The murders, like some "weird and terrible story of the supernatural," the paper added, had "excited the imagination of London to a degree without

---

[1] "The Whitechapel Murder," *East London Advertiser* (8 September 1888). *Casebook: Jack the Ripper*. http://www.casebook.org/press_reports/east_london_advertiser/ela880908.html (accessed April 13, 2010).

parallel" as "the mind turns as it were instinctively to some theory of occult force" and "[g]houls, vampires, [and] bloodsuckers [...] seize hold of the excited fancy."[1] The Ripper was gothicized as a "man monster," a "ghoul whose midnight murders have roused all London and frightened decent citizens in their beds."[2] "Yet," the *East London Advertiser* continued, "the most morbid imagination can conceive nothing worse than this terrible reality [...] that there is a being in human shape stealthily moving about a great city, burning with the thirst for human blood" and a "fiendish lust."[3] "The number of interesting, though blood-curdling theories," the paper concluded, could "form the material for a score of 'shilling dreadfuls.'"[4]

The Goddess, Marsh's "six-shilling dreadful" recalls contemporary accounts of sexual desire and corruption in fin-de-siècle London. The beginning of the novel promotes this notion of the Goddess as a lady of terrible pleasure. At the beginning of the novel, narrator John Ferguson, a former imperialist who confesses to having had little to do with women, experiences "a vision of the night." He has "no recollection of putting anything on in the shape of clothes" when he feels "an uncontrollable impulse to go to Lawrence," the neighbor with whom he is "on terms of intimacy" (4-5). In the other man's rooms, Ferguson witnesses a heavily charged scene involving "some wild beast [...] beside itself with fury. Yelling, snarling, screeching—a horrid, gasping noise— these sounds seemed to follow hard upon each other." Uttering "faint cries [...] of both pain and terror," Lawrence is seen "struggling frantically with some strange creature" which assails him

---

[1] "A Thirst for Blood," *East London Advertiser* (6 October 1888). *Casebook: Jack the Ripper*. http://www.casebook.org/press_reports/east_london_advertiser/ela881006.html (accessed April 13, 2010).

[2] "The Whitechapel Murders and the Police," *East London Advertiser* (15 September 1888). *Casebook: Jack the Ripper*. http://www.casebook.org/press_reports/east_london_advertiser/ela880915.html (accessed April 13, 2010).

[3] "A Thirst for Blood."

[4] "Homicidal Mania," *East London Advertiser* (6 October 1888). *Casebook: Jack the Ripper*. http://www.casebook.org/press_reports/east_london_advertiser/ela881006.html (accessed April 13, 2010).

"with its whole force," "rain[ing] on to his motionless body a hail
of blows, making all the time that horrid, gasping noise" before
breaking into "a woman's laughter" (6-7). Lawrence, the reader
knows by this stage, is not quite the gentleman he seems, and the
scene may be interpreted as Ferguson engaging in homoerotic
voyeurism by peeping in on his friend's nocturnal pleasures. Like a
common prostitute, the Goddess, the "strange creature" emitting
the "horrid, gasping noise," is always "ready" and "willing," "well
worth looking at," and "only needs a touch to fill her with impassioned frenzy. It is for that touch that she waits and watches" (279-
280, 289-290). Her life-size figure is "of a brilliant scarlet," the color
of blood, sexuality, violence, and anger, with "a curious suggestion
of life" (289), and her "performance" mimics sexual intercourse:

> As Lawrence sprang forward, the figure rose to its feet, and
> in an instant was alive. It opened its arms; from its finger-tips
> came knives. Stepping forward it gripped Lawrence with its
> steel-clad hands, with a grip from which there was no escap-
> ing. From every part of its frame gleaming blades had sprung;
> against this *cheval-de-frise* it pressed him again and again, twirl-
> ing him round and round, moving him up and down, so that
> the weapons pierced and hacked back and front. Even from its
> eyes, mouth, and nostrils had sprung knives. It kept jerking its
> head backwards and forwards, so that it could stab with them at
> his face and head. And, all the while, from somewhere came the
> sound of a woman's laughter [...]. A sharp-pointed blade, more
> than eighteen inches long, which proceeded from its stomach,
> had pierced him through and through. The writhing, gibber-
> ing puppet held him skewered in a dozen places. [...] Down he
> came, with his assailant sticking to him like a limpet. Pinning
> him on the floor, it continued its extraordinary contortions, lac-
> erating its victim with every movement in a hundred different
> places. It was difficult to believe that it was not alive. [...] As if
> its lust for blood was glutted, it rolled over, lethargically, upon
> its side, leaving its handiwork exposed—a horrible spectacle. A
> grin—as it were a smile, born of repletion—was on the crea-
> ture's face. (291-293)

The extraordinary sadism of this bizarre torture ritual equates
sex with pain, death, and humiliation. For Kelly Hurley, the

Goddess's "repletion" is connected with unnatural foreign female desire.[1] However, the idol's "handiwork" must surely have put contemporary readers in mind of the Jack the Ripper murders of 1888, which had presented the public with the spectacle of torn and mutilated female bodies. *The Goddess* displaces some of the horror of the murders, with their slashed and disfigured corpses, onto the novel's eponymous mechanical puppet and her "lust for blood". Like the Ripper, the "Goddess of the Scarlet Hands" (291) mutilates her victims beyond recognition: "his face and head had been cut and hacked to pieces. [...] His flesh had been ripped and rent so that not one recognisable feature was left. Indeed, it might not have been a man we were looking upon, but some thing of horror" (33). The monster's "mutilated" (296) victims, "all cut and slashed and sliced into ribbons" (262), present "a horrible spectacle" that recalls the Ripper's trail of blood. Interestingly, however, it is a female figure that here slashes men, as if in some strange inversion of the original murders in Whitechapel. Indeed, the Goddess's *"cheval-de-frise"* leads to a complete reversal of gender roles: it is the male who is here penetrated by the multiple knives which spring from the Goddess's supple body, recalling the mouths of female vampires in contemporary gothic fiction which similarly reveal an unexpected box of tools.

Modernity and mental health

The size, anonymity and social divisions of London are essential to the plot of the novel in allowing Edwin Lawrence to commit his crimes and vanish into the vast city. The beginning of *The Goddess* sees Lawrence and Ferguson in the comfort of the West End. A man of fastidious tastes and a liking for comfort, the urbanite Lawrence is described as "one of the most finical men [...] on the subject of draughts. A properly ventilated apartment set him shivering, even in the middle of summer. The faintest suspicion of a healthy current of air made him turn up the collar of his coat. No room could be too stuffy for him" (111). Such sensitivity sets Lawrence up as suspect, since healthy Anglo-Saxon manhood

[1] Kelly Hurley, *The Gothic Body: Sexuality, Materialism, and Degeneration at the Fin de Siècle* (Cambridge: Cambridge University Press, 1996), 185.

should surely not shiver at the thought of fresh air, and by the end of the first chapter, we share Ferguson's suspicions over his integrity. Lawrence's lack of financial foresight and an innate tendency towards criminality send him on his downward journey. For much of the novel, the reader must suppose Lawrence dead, but towards its end we learn that he has, in fact, abandoned his snug bachelor pad for a "large, bare, barn-like room" (266) in residential Pimlico in "a building which, outwardly, was more like a warehouse than a private residence" (253). Inside,

> The floor was bare. [...] The furniture was scanty. In one corner was a camp bedstead, the bedclothes in disorder. [...] Bottles, indeed, were everywhere; designed, too, to contain all sorts of liquids—wines, spirits, beers. Champagne appeared to have been drunk by the gallon. On the floor, in the corner, opposite the bedstead, were at least seven or eight dozen unopened bottles, of all sizes, sorts, and shapes. (266).

Lawrence has, then, gone from extreme comfort to extreme squalor. This social transgression is equated in the novel with Lawrence's mental breakdown, attributed to his obsession with the Goddess, his "demon" (245).

Marsh's novel insistently questions the mental health not only of Lawrence but of everybody. Interest in the study of the mind had increased in the course of the nineteenth century, and insanity was essentially seen as a disease of the highly civilized and industrialized: as Appendices D and E testify, the hectic excitement of urban life, the increased competitiveness of the business world, the use of alcohol and drugs, a new ease of access to education, and the reading of exciting fiction were all seen as conducive to mental illness. As Andrew Wynter bleakly concluded in 1875, "That there is an immense amount of latent brain disease in the community, only awaiting a sufficient exciting cause to make itself patent to the world, there can be no manner of doubt."[1] The "fearful progress of this moral avalanche"[2] was particularly noticeable in cities,

---

[1] Andrew Wynter, "The Borderlands of Insanity," in *The Borderlands of Insanity and Other Allied Papers* (London: Robert Hardwicke, 1875), 1.
[2] Forbes Winslow, *On Obscure Diseases of the Brain, and Disorders of the*

where "neuropathic brains which do not offer normal resistance to nervous currents" were likely to "find themselves in a state of constant excitation and irritation"[1] and "obsessed by fear." This, supposedly, resulted in "the chronic condition" of "nerve exhaustion" which the sufferer was "inclined to relieve [...] by imbibing alcohol with the result that the more he drinks the more he wants, until such imbibing becomes habitual."[2] As noted in Appendices D, E and F, these psychological theories challenged the notion of a stable personality by suggesting that identity, memory and thought could be disrupted by traumatic experiences, artificial agents, and suppressed drives. This notion was most famously articulated at the fin de siècle by Sigmund Freud, whose dynamic psychiatry maintained that whenever unconscious psychic drives, particularly erotic urges, were repressed, their energy inevitably appeared elsewhere, typically in hysterical or obsessive behavior.

The Goddess is a text obsessed with nervous maladies connected with modernity, including instances of hysteria, hallucination, irrationality, paranoia, persecution complex, delirium tremens, and dementia. The text abounds with medical terminology connected to mental health: "imbecile[s]" (12), "idiots" (86), "raving lunatic[s]" (96) and "maniac[s]" (257) feature prominently in this novel populated by characters who are "stark mad" (63), "off [their] mental balance" (73) and "mentally incapable" (129). Although Marsh mostly uses these terms in a non-medical sense, the frequency with which they occur marks the paranoia over mental health that characterizes the novel. The discussion is firmly situated within contemporary medical debates by the introduction of the character of Dr. Hume, "an authority on madness" (262), who "is a student of what he calls obscure diseases of the brain; insisting that we have all of us a screw loose somewhere, and that out of every countenance insanity peeps" (35). The sanity of Ferguson and Bessie is constantly in doubt, Bessie's brother Tom is portrayed

---

Mind: *Their Incipient Symptoms, Pathology, Diagnosis, Treatment, and Prophylaxis* (London: John Churchill, 1860), 174.

[1] Josiah Morse, *The Psychology and Neurology of Fear* (Worcester, Massachusetts: Clark University Press, 1907), 44.

[2] Frederick William Alexander, "'Claustrophobia': Cause and Cure" ([n.p.]: [n.p.], 1925), 1-2.

as a degenerate criminal, and Dr. Hume himself suffers from obsessions and paranoia. The most notable example of mental breakdown in the novel is, however, Edwin Lawrence. Lawrence's descent into madness is partly hereditary, partly self-acquired, and partly linked to the experience of modernity. Like Tom, Lawrence was "born with a twist in [him]; a moral malformation; a trend in the grain which, as [he] got [his] growth, gave a natural inclination in a particular direction" (271). Marsh is here referencing fin-de-siècle theories of degeneration, which saw hereditary degenerate tendencies as symptomatic of the modern world, and, particularly, or urban life. Lawrence is a creature of the city and, in contemporary medical parlance, predisposed to nervous ailments.

However, Lawrence exacerbates these tendencies by "the life of dissipation" (282) he leads and, in particular, his alcohol consumption, which, as Appendix E testifies, was seen at the time as a cause of mental breakdown. Alcohol abuse, leading to delirium tremens, accentuates Lawrence's inherent tendencies towards paranoia and persecution complex. In particular, Lawrence now begins to dread spatial confinement, a key characteristic of the modern city, refusing to enter public transport: "I'll have none of your cabs," he explains, "I'll walk. I'm cribb'd, cabined, and confined out in the open; in a cab I'd stifle" (245). The fear of being forced to enter a cab provokes "a fit of maniacal fury" and a "crescendo" threat of bodily violence (246). Lawrence associates his condition with psychic persecution by the Goddess and is haunted by auditory hallucinations of the Goddess's laughter: "There's a hand upon my heart, a grip upon my throat, a weight upon my head;" Lawrence explains, "they make it hard to breathe" (245). In an interesting conflation of the gothic register with medical terminology, Lawrence believes himself to be haunted by the Goddess, his "demon" (245), but Ferguson describes Lawrence's increasing *insanity* as his "demon:" "He was not mad, as yet, but on the border line, where men fight with demons. He had been drinking, to drive them back; but they had come the more, threatening, on every hand, to shut him in for ever" (243). As Appendices D and E testify, such language was commonly used in medical discourse at the time, and Marsh here offers us a particularly striking example of such discursive overlap.

Though mental disorders affected both sexes, mental problems were typically seen as "a female malady" in the nineteenth century.[1] Victorian medicine defined female sexuality in essentially biological terms, with respectable female sexuality linked to the reproductive function. Paradoxically, while women were held to be paragons of virtue, innocence, and morality, theories of female mental disorders were inextricably linked to female sexuality and the supposed instability of the female reproductive system at the "critical periods" of the female life—puberty, pregnancy, childbirth, and menopause.[2] Attempts were made to control female sexuality especially at these points, lest previously chaste women should suddenly go wrong and damage the patriarchal family unit, the cornerstone of Victorian society. The concept of "moral" insanity, as opposed to "intellectual" insanity, is key to the definition of female mental health in this period. One doctor defined moral insanity as "a morbid perversion of the natural feelings, affections, inclinations, tempers, habits, moral dispositions, and natural impulses, without any remarkable disorder or defect of the intellect, or knowing and reasoning faculties, and particularly without any insane illusion or hallucination."[3] This definition blurs the boundaries of eccentricity, vice, crime and insanity, and according to it almost any socially disruptive behavior could be classified as moral insanity requiring patriarchal "moral management" of the patient. Sexual rebelliousness and erotic excitement in women were prime factors in the attribution of moral insanity.[4] The end of the century also witnessed interest in hysteria as an essentially feminine illness. At the Salpêtrière Clinic in Paris, Jean-Martin Charcot offered highly charged demonstrations with his hysterical female patients, which popularized the image of the hysterical fit or contortion, where the patient's body would be convulsed with seemingly uncontrollable, often sexually suggestive, movements.

---

[1] Elaine Showalter, *The Female Malady: Women, Madness and English Culture, 1830-1980* (London: Virago, 2001), 3.

[2] Showalter, *Female Malady*, 55-59.

[3] Edgar Sheppard, *Lectures on Madness in its Medical, Legal, and Social Aspects* (London: J. & A. Churchill, 1873), 87.

[4] Showalter, *Female Malady*, 29-30.

Appendix F charts contemporary medical and fictional responses to hysteria and female sexuality.

Bessie Moore, the heroine of Marsh's novel, is characterized as "an angel" (143) and "the gentlest, sweetest soul" (94) in keeping with the Victorian cult of the Angel in the House, the chaste, passive, domestic woman. Her "wondrous beauty" (142) is emphasized alongside her innocence and domestic virtues. Importantly, Bessie resides away from the buzz of the frantic city, in a reassuringly "nice, wide, clean, old-fashioned street." Her "nice, clean, old-fashioned house" is described in terms that reflect the character of its occupant:

> It was not large, but the impression which its exterior made upon me was a distinctly pleasant one. It was detached; it stood back, behind railings, at a little distance from the pavement; in the sunshine it looked as white as snow; there was a flower-bed in front, and flowers made the window-sills resplendent (88).

Bessie's home possesses all the feminine virtues: it is clean, old-fashioned, pure in its whiteness, decked in flowers and, crucially, modest, standing some distance from the pavement. However, Bessie's sanity and innocence are suspect for much of the novel. Her association with the theatre, the apparent degeneracy and criminality of her brother, and her relationship with the masculine, aggressively possessive Miss Adair all point to a nervous weakness hidden by her beauty. Her confrontation with the Goddess accentuates this weakness, precipitating her into a state of semi-imbecility for much of the novel. It is, however, apparent that she has played some part in the strange orgy that Ferguson has witnessed in Lawrence's rooms. Her entry into his bedroom, too, puts her in a vulnerable position: it is clear from Ferguson's narrative that he expects to confront either a burglar or a prostitute. Tellingly, her appeal to Ferguson, who subscribes to the contemporary notion of women's moral superiority, is at its strongest when she is at her most vulnerable: this childlike, passive, helpless figure, Ferguson seems to suggest, is his ideal woman.

Bessie's part in the murder leaves her in a state approximating an automaton. This links Bessie, "the idol of the town" (142), to the Goddess, a mechanical sacrificial "idol; apparently a Hindoo goddess" (289). The nocturnal wanderings of Bessie, the primary suspect for the murder in Imperial Mansions, coincide with the activities of the Goddess, and their moonlight setting directs the reader to the perceived link between female sexuality, the menstrual cycle and insanity. While Bessie's sexuality appears thoroughly subdued, even repressed, it is also important to note that she is an actress who performs on stage in front of audiences, and the way in which men fall at her feet bears witness to her sex appeal. This suggests that Bessie is able to perform femininity, and, indeed, her appearances in this novel saturated with theatrical references are essentially dramatic, even "stagey" (271), characterized by effective entrances and melodramatic lines: "I had never before seen such acting as hers" (86), Ferguson admits, and now Bessie "depict[s] herself as playing a leading part in a hideous tragedy" (115). The Goddess's "unrivalled performances" (286), similarly, take place on a dais in front of a male audience. These "extraordinary contortions" closely mirror the hysterical fits showcased by Charcot's patients at the Salpêtrière. The gruesome performances of the Goddess, however, leave *Bessie* in a hysterical state and "all covered with blood," a symbol of violence but also of sexuality: "She had smeared her countenance with her fingers; all down one side of her face was a crimson stain" (15). In a text obsessed with hidden mental disease, this doubling of Bessie and the Goddess cannot be ignored. "It is as if I were two persons, and each keeps losing the other," Bessie wails, "Can there be two persons in one body? My brain seems blurred—as if it were in two parts. When I am using one part, the other—the other's all confused" (118). Bessie and the Goddess mirror each other in their associations with blood, in their sexual allure, and in their anger: the chaste Englishwoman with her melodic laughter and legitimate cause for anger has her evil foreign double, whose laughter is sinister and rage excessive. The Goddess may look harmless but her embrace is deadly; could Bessie, too, be "playing [the] part" of the Victorian angel (20)?

At the end of the novel, Bessie reassuringly marries Ferguson, a "prodigy of bone and muscle" (147), who will have the stamina to keep her on the straight. The Goddess is dismantled and, not entirely convincingly, explained to consist of a clockwork machinery and a phonograph containing a woman's laughter. Seemingly, then, our hero and heroine end the novel on a happy note. However, *The Goddess* is not a reassuring text. The novel discusses a great number of contemporary anxieties: the mental health of the modern city dweller, hysterical tendencies, duality, criminality, degeneration, illicit sex, alcoholism and extreme violence are the most prominent of these. The setting of the novel in a foggy, menacing London accentuates the fear of these social problems and seems to preclude any conclusive solution. Was the Goddess simply a mechanical puppet, or did she have supernatural powers? This Valancourt volume now makes this rich gothic novel available to contemporary readers in a reliable critical edition.

MINNA VUOHELAINEN

April 13, 2010

MINNA VUOHELAINEN is Senior Lecturer in English Literature at Edge Hill University. She studied International History at the London School of Economics and English Literature at King's College London before completing a Ph.D. on "The Popular Fiction of Richard Marsh: Literary Production, Genre, Audience" at Birkbeck, University of London. Her current research focuses on fin-de-siècle print culture, literary representations of London, and the discursive overlap between gothic fiction and factual discourses at the fin de siècle. She is the editor of Valancourt's 2008 edition of Richard Marsh's bestseller *The Beetle: A Mystery*, and is currently completing a study of Richard Marsh as a professional author.

A note on the edition

This edition is based on the first edition of *The Goddess: A Demon* (London: F.V. White, 1900), published at the price of 6s. in summer 1900. It reprints the cover of the first edition, the spelling and punctuation of which are here followed. Obvious printing errors have been silently corrected.

The Goddess was initially serialized in twelve installments in the *Manchester Weekly Times and Salford Weekly News* between 12 January and 30 March, 1900. Asterisks denote breaks between the original serial parts in the present text.

The text of the novel is here accompanied by a number of contextual appendices juxtaposing factual and fictional material from the period. The punctuation of the main text has been adopted and obvious printing errors silently corrected in the appendices.

A chronology of Richard Marsh

1854:   Joseph Heldmann arrives in London from Bavaria via Paris, and sets up as a lace merchant.

1856:   Marriage of Joseph Heldmann and Emma Marsh, daughter of lace manufacturer Richard Marsh, of Mansfield, Nottinghamshire, according to the rites and ceremonies of the Church of England (30 December).

1857:   Joseph Heldmann becomes a naturalized British citizen. Birth of Richard Bernard Heldmann at 23, Adelaide Road, St John's Wood, London (12 October). Joseph Heldmann becomes involved in bankruptcy proceedings following reckless trading (December).

1858:   Joseph Heldmann is branded a "German adventurer" and refused a bankruptcy certificate. Birth of Henry ("Harry") Heldmann at Railway Terrace, Mansfield, Nottinghamshire (28 October).

1860:   Birth of Sophia Alice ("Alice") Heldmann at 19 Scarsdale Terrace, Kensington, London (21 October).

1861:   Joseph Heldmann is working as classical and language tutor in London.

1867:   Birth of Ada Kate Abbey, daughter of journeyman stone carver Charles Abbey and his wife Hannah, in Walworth, Surrey (2 April).

1870:   Joseph Heldmann is in charge of Brunswick House School at 19 Mayland Road, Hammersmith, London. Birth of John Whitworth Heldmann (20 October).

1871:   Death of John Whitworth Heldmann (13 August). Edith Nesbit attends Brunswick House School together with her brother Alfred.

1880:   Bernard Heldmann publishes his first signed fiction in the devotional periodical *Quiver*, in the religious juvenile paper *Young England*, and in the secular boys' paper *Union Jack*.

1881:   Bernard Heldmann begins to publish serial school and adventure stories exclusively in G.A. Henty's *Union Jack*. His first volume-form novels, *Boxall School* and *Dorrincourt*, are issued by the religious publisher Nisbet.

1882:   Heldmann continues to work for *Union Jack* and becomes co-editor with Henty (October). Publication of *The Mutiny on*

Board the Ship "Leander" (Sampson Low); The Belton Scholarship (Griffith & Farran); Expelled (Nisbet).

1883:   Heldmann is living at Seaton House, The Vale, Acton, West London. Heldmann's serial "A Couple of Scamps" is dropped by Union Jack in March and only concluded in July. The co-editorship is abruptly and publicly terminated (5 June). Heldmann begins to live a fraudulent life, presenting checks on an account that has been closed. Publication of Daintree (Nisbet).

1884:   Heldmann continues to live on his wits until he is arrested at Tenby on 12 February. He is tried at Maidstone on 9 April and sentenced to eighteen months' hard labor at Maidstone Jail for obtaining money, food and lodging by false pretenses.

1885:   Heldmann is released from prison (8 October).

1887:   Birth of Alice Kate Heldmann, first child of Bernard Heldmann and Ada Kate Heldmann, née Abbey (14 July). No marriage certificate has been found for the Heldmanns, who are living at 21, Shaftesbury Road, Richmond, Surrey. Bernard Heldmann is working as a journalist.

1888:   "Richard Marsh" publishes his first signed short story, "Payment for a Life," in Belgravia (summer). Signed and unsigned stories follow in a number of weekly and monthly fiction papers. Death of Alice Kate Heldmann (24 March). Emma Heldmann disinherits Richard Bernard Heldmann in her will (15 June). Birth of Harry Randolph Heldmann (7 July).

1890:   Birth of Mabel Violet Heldmann (24 May). The Heldmanns are living at 4, Kempson Road, Fulham, London.

1891:   Birth of Madge Heldmann (5 August). The Heldmanns move from 2 Bedford Row, Worthing, West Sussex to Three Bridges, Sussex. Bernard Heldmann describes himself as "a professional author." Emma and Joseph Heldmann have given up Brunswick House School and are living at Worton Court, Isleworth, Middlesex, with Alice and Harry, now a stockbroker.

1892:   Birth of Conrad Heldmann (12 October). Publication of "A Vision of the Night," Marsh's first story in Strand Magazine (December).

1893:   "Richard Marsh" publishes his first novels, The Devil's Diamond and The Mahatma's Pupil (Henry).

1895:   Birth of Bertram Max Heldmann (9 January). Publication of Mrs Musgrave—and her Husband (Heinemann) and The Strange Wooing of Mary Bowler (Pearson).

1896:   Death of Joseph Heldmann (12 April).

1897:   Publication of *The Mystery of Philip Bennion's Death* (Ward,
         Lock); *The Duke and the Damsel* (Pearson); *The Crime and the
         Criminal* (Ward, Lock); *The Beetle: A Mystery* (Skeffington).
         Four impressions of *The Beetle* appear between September and
         December. Marsh is now signing all his magazine work.

1898:   Publication of *Tom Ossington's Ghost* (Bowden); *The Datchet
         Diamonds* (Ward, Lock); *Curios* (John Long); *The House of
         Mystery* (F.V. White); *Under One Cover: Eleven Stories by S. Baring-
         Gould, Richard Marsh, Ernest G. Henham, Fergus Hume, Andrew
         Merry and A. St John Adcock* (Skeffington).

1899:   Publication of *Frivolities: Especially Addressed to Those Who Are
         Tired of Being Serious* (Bowden); *In Full Cry* (F.V. White); *The
         Woman with One Hand and Mr Ely's Engagement* (Bowden).

1900:   Marsh issues eight volumes in the busiest year of his career:
         Marvels and Mysteries (Methuen); *A Second Coming* (Grant
         Richards); *Ada Vernham, Actress* (John Long); *The Goddess: A
         Demon* (F.V. White); *The Seen and the Unseen* (Methuen); *A Hero
         of Romance* (Ward, Lock); *An Aristocratic Detective* (Digby, Long);
         The Chase of the Ruby (Skeffington). Marsh begins to contribute
         to *Strand Magazine* annually.

1901:   Marsh's publication pattern settles to an average three volumes
         a year. Publication of *Amusement Only* (Hurst & Blackett); *Both
         Sides of the Veil* (Methuen); *The Joss: A Reversion* (F.V. White).
         The Heldmanns are living in New Street, Worth, East Sussex.
         Only the youngest child, Bertram Max, remains at home.

1902:   Publication of *The Adventures of Augustus Short: Things Which
         I Have Done for Others and Wish I Hadn't* (Anthony Treherne);
         Between the Dark and the Daylight (Digby, Long); *The Twickenham
         Peerage* (Methuen).

1903:   Publication of *The Magnetic Girl* (John Long); *The Death Whistle*
         (Anthony Treherne); *A Metamorphosis* (Methuen).

1904:   Publication of *A Duel* (Methuen); *Garnered* (Methuen); *Miss
         Arnott's Marriage* (John Long). Publication of "The Girl on the
         Sands," Marsh's first story featuring the lower-middle-class clerk
         Sam Briggs, in *Strand* (October).

1905:   Publication of *The Confessions of a Young Lady* (John Long);
         The Marquis of Putney (Methuen); *A Spoiler of Men* (Chatto &
         Windus).

1906:   Publication of *The Garden of Mystery* (John Long); *In the Service
         of Love* (Methuen); *Under One Flag* (John Long).

1907:   Publication of *The Girl and the Miracle* (Methuen); *The Romance of a Maid of Honour* (John Long); *A Woman Perfected* (John Long).

1908: Publication of a seemingly new Heldmann novel, *That Master of Ours* (Nisbet), "by the author of *Dorrincourt, Boxall School, Expelled*, etc." Marsh publishes *The Coward behind the Curtain* (Methuen) and *The Surprising Husband* (Methuen).

1909: Publication of *The Girl in the Blue Dress* (John Long); *The Interrupted Kiss* (Cassell); *A Royal Indiscretion* (Methuen).

1910: Publication of *Live Men's Shoes* (Methuen); *The Lovely Mrs Blake* (Cassell).

1911: Publication of *A Drama of the Telephone* (Digby, Long); *The Twin Sisters* (Cassell). Death of Emma Heldmann (11 July). Publication of "The Man Who Cut Off My Hair," Marsh's first story featuring the female detective and lip-reader Judith Lee, in *Strand* (August).

1912: Publication of *Judith Lee: Some Pages from Her Life* (Methuen); *Sam Briggs: His Book* (John Long); *Violet Forster's Lover* (Cassell).

1913: Publication of *If It Please You* (Methuen); *Justice—Suspended* (Chatto & Windus); *The Master of Deception* (Cassell).

1914: Publication of *Margot and her Judges* (Chatto & Windus), *Molly's Husband* (Cassell); *The Woman in the Car* (T. Fisher Unwin).

1915: Death of Richard Bernard Heldmann of heart failure and heart disease at The Ridge, Lucastes Avenue, Haywards Heath, Sussex (9 August). Funeral of Bernard Heldmann, St Wilfrid's Church, Haywards Heath (13 August). Heldmann's estate is valued at £453 14s. Death of Harry Heldmann in action (25 September). Publication of *The Flying Girl* (Ward, Lock); *His Love or his Life* (Chatto & Windus); *Love in Fetters* (Cassell); *The Man with Nine Lives* (Ward, Lock); *Sam Briggs, V.C.* (T. Fisher Unwin).

1916: Publication of *The Great Temptation* (T. Fisher Unwin); *Coming of Age* (John Long) and *The Adventures of Judith Lee* (Methuen).

1917: Publication of *The Deacon's Daughter* (John Long).

1918: Publication of *Orders to Marry* (John Long) and *On the Jury* (Methuen).

1919: Publication of *Outwitted* (John Long).

1920: Publication of *Apron-Strings* (John Long).

Further reading

Bernard Heldmann and Richard Marsh (biography and bibliography)

Aickman, Robert. *The Attempted Rescue*. London: Victor Gollancz, 1966.

Baker, William. "Introduction." In Richard Marsh, *The Beetle*, edited by William Baker. Stroud: Alan Sutton Publishing in association with the University of Luton, 1994: vii-x.

Dalby, Richard. "Introduction." In Richard Marsh, *The Haunted Chair and Other Stories*, edited by Richard Dalby. Ashcroft, British Columbia: Ash-Tree, 1997: ix-xxi.

---. "Richard Marsh: Novelist Extraordinaire." *Book and Magazine Collector* 163 (October 1997): 76-89.

---. "Unappreciated Authors: Richard Marsh and *The Beetle*." *Antiquarian Book Monthly Review* 144 (April 1986): 136-141.

Davies, David Stuart. "Introduction." In Richard Marsh, *The Beetle: A Mystery*, edited by David Stuart Davies. Ware: Wordsworth, 2007: vii-xii.

Greene, Hugh. "Introduction." In *(The Penguin Book of) Victorian Villainies*, edited by Hugh Greene and Graham Greene. London: Bloomsbury, 1991: 7-10.

Höglund, Johan. "Introduction." In Richard Marsh, *A Spoiler of Men*, edited by Johan Höglund. Kansas City: Valancourt, 2009: vi-xviii.

James, Callum. "Callum James's Literary Detective Agency, Case #1: Why Was Richard Marsh?" *Front Free Endpaper*, 30 November 2009. http://callumjames.blogspot.com/2009/11/callum-jamess-literary-detective-agency.html.

Kirkpatrick, Robert. *The Three Lives of Bernard Heldmann*. London: Children's Books History Society, 2010.

Pittard, Christopher. "'The Unknown! with a Capital U!:' Richard Marsh and Victorian Popular Fiction." *Clues: A Journal of Detection* 27.1 (2008): 99-103

Taylor, Michael Rupert. "G. A. Henty, Richard Marsh and Bernard

Heldmann." *Antiquarian Book Monthly Review* 277 (August/September 1997): 10-15.

Vuohelainen, Minna. "Richard Marsh." *Victorian Fiction Research Guide* 35 (October 2009). http://www.canterbury.ac.uk/arts-humanities/Media/victorian-research-fiction/StockList/35-Richard-Marsh.aspx.

---. "Introduction." In Richard Marsh, *The Beetle: A Mystery*, edited by Minna Vuohelainen. Kansas City: Valancourt, 2008: vii-xxx.

---. "The Popular Fiction of Richard Marsh: Literary Production, Genre, Audience." PhD dissertation, University of London, 2007.

---. "Richard Marsh's *The Beetle*: A Late-Victorian Popular Novel." *Working with English: Medieval and Modern Language, Literature and Drama* 2.1 (2006): 89-100.

Wolfreys, Julian. "Introduction." In Richard Marsh, *The Beetle*, edited by Julian Wolfreys. Peterborough, Ontario: Broadview Press, 2004: 9-34.

Bernard Heldmann and Richard Marsh (critical interpretations)

Bartlett, MacKenzie. "Laughing to Excess: Gothic Fiction and the Pathologisation of Laughter in Late Victorian Britain." PhD dissertation, University of London, 2009.

Garnett, Rhys. "*Dracula* and *The Beetle*: Imperial and Sexual Guilt and Fear in Late Victorian Fantasy." In *Science Fiction Roots and Branches: Contemporary Critical Approaches*, edited by Rhys Garnett and R.J. Ellis. Houndmills: MacMillan, 1990: 30-54.

Halberstam, Judith. "Gothic Nation: *The Beetle* by Richard Marsh." In *Fictions of Unease: The Gothic from "Otranto" to "The X-Files,"* edited by Andrew Smith, Diane Mason and William Hughes. Bath: Sulis Press, 2002: 100-118.

Höglund, Johan. "Introduction." In Richard Marsh, *A Spoiler of Men*, edited by Johan Höglund. Kansas City: Valancourt, 2009: vi-xviii.

---. "Apocalyptic London: the Construction and Destruction of the Heart of the Empire." *Literary London Journal* 5.2 (September 2007). http://www.literarylondon.org/london-journal/september2007/hoglund.html.

---. "Gothic Haunting Empire." In *Memory, Haunting, Discourse*, edited by Maria Holmgren Troy and Elisabeth Wennö. Karlstad, Sweden: University of Karlstad Press, 2005: 233-44.

Hurley, Kelly. "'The Inner Chambers of All Nameless Sin:' *The Beetle*, Gothic Female Sexuality, and Oriental Barbarism." In *Gothic: Critical Concepts in Literary and Cultural Studies*, edited by Fred Botting and Dale Townsend. 4 vols. London and New York: Routledge, 2004: III, 241-258.

---. *The Gothic Body: Sexuality, Materialism, and Degeneration at the Fin de Siècle*. Cambridge: Cambridge University Press, 1996.

---. "'The Inner Chambers of All Nameless Sin:' *The Beetle*, Gothic Female Sexuality, and Oriental Barbarism." In *Virginal Sexuality and Textuality in Victorian Literature*, edited by Lloyd Davis. Albany: State University of New York Press, 1993: 193-213.

Luckhurst, Roger. "Trance-Gothic, 1882-1897." In *Victorian Gothic: Literary and Cultural Manifestations in the Nineteenth Century*, edited by Ruth Robbins and Julian Wolfreys. Basingstoke: Palgrave, 2000: 148-167.

Margree, Victoria. "'Both in Men's Clothing:' Gender, Sovereignty and Insecurity in Richard Marsh's *The Beetle*." *Critical Survey* 19.2 (2007): 63-81.

Vuohelainen, Minna. "'Tales and Adventures:' G.A. Henty's *Union Jack* and the Competitive World of Publishing for Boys in the 1880s." *Journal of Popular Narrative Media* 1.2 (2008): 183-196.

---. "Introduction." In Richard Marsh, *The Beetle: A Mystery*, edited by Minna Vuohelainen. Kansas City: Valancourt, 2008: vii-xxx.

---. "The Popular Fiction of Richard Marsh: Literary Production, Genre, Audience." PhD dissertation, University of London, 2007.

---. "Distorting the Genre, Defining the Audience, Detecting the Author: Richard Marsh's 'For Debt' (1902)." *Clues: A Journal of Detection* 25.4 (Summer 2007): 17-26.

---. "'Oh to Get Out of That Room!': Outcast London and the Gothic Twist in the Popular Fiction of Richard Marsh." In *Victorian Space(s): Leeds Centre Working Papers in Victorian Studies* VIII, edited by Karen Sayer. Leeds: Trinity and All Saints, University of Leeds, 2006: 115-126.

---. "Richard Marsh's *The Beetle*: A Late-Victorian Popular Novel."

Working with English: Medieval and Modern Language, Literature and Drama 2.1 (2006): 89-100.

Wolfreys, Julian. *Writing London 3: Inventions of the City*. Basingstoke: Palgrave Macmillan, 2007.

---. "The Hieroglyphic Other: *The Beetle*, London, and the Abyssal Subject." In *A Mighty Mass of Brick and Smoke: Victorian and Edwardian Representations of London*, edited by Lawrence Phillips. Amsterdam and New York: Rodopi, 2007: 169-192.

---. "Introduction." In Richard Marsh, *The Beetle*, edited by Julian Wolfreys. Peterborough, Ontario: Broadview Press, 2004: 9-34.

Fin-de-siècle London, degeneration, crime

Beckson, Karl. *London in the 1890s: A Cultural History*. New York and London: Norton, 1992.

Fishman, W.J. *East End 1888: A Year in a London Borough among the Labouring Poor*. London: Duckworth, 1988.

Greenslade, William. *Degeneration, Culture and the Novel, 1880-1940*. Cambridge: Cambridge University Press, 1994.

Jones, Gareth Stedman. *Outcast London: A Study in the Relationship between Classes in Victorian Society*. Oxford: Clarendon Press, 1971.

Koven, Seth. *Slumming: Sexual and Social Politics in Victorian London*. Princeton: Princeton University Press, 2004.

Ledger, Sally. "In Darkest England: The Terror of Degeneration in *Fin-de-Siècle* Britain." *Literature and History* 4.2 (1995): 71-86.

McLaughlin, Joseph. *Writing the Urban Jungle: Reading Empire in London from Doyle to Eliot*. Charlottesville and London: University Press of Virginia, 2000.

Mighall, Robert. *A Geography of Victorian Gothic Fiction: Mapping History's Nightmares*. Oxford: Oxford University Press, 1999.

Pick, Daniel. *Faces of Degeneration: A European Disorder, c. 1848-1918*. Cambridge: Cambridge University Press, 1993.

Schneer, Jonathan. *London 1900: The Imperial Metropolis*. New Haven and London: Yale University Press, 2001.

Walkowitz, Judith R. *City of Dreadful Delight: Narratives of Sexual Danger in Late Victorian London*. London: Virago, 2000.

Wiener, Martin J. *Reconstructing the Criminal: Culture, Law, and*

Policy in England, 1830-1914. Cambridge: Cambridge University Press, 1994.

Sexuality, prostitution, Jack the Ripper

Begg, P. *Jack the Ripper: The Definitive History*. London: Longman, 2002.

Curtis, J.P. *Jack the Ripper and the London Press*. New Haven and London: Yale University Press, 2001.

Nord, Deborah. *Walking the Victorian Streets: Women, Representation, and the City*. Ithaca and London: Cornell University Press, 1995.

Parsons, D.L. *Streetwalking the Metropolis: Women, the City and Modernity*. Oxford: Oxford University Press, 2000.

Showalter, Elaine. *Sexual Anarchy: Gender and Culture at the Fin de Siècle*. London: Virago, 2001.

Stott, Rebecca. *The Fabrication of the Late-Victorian Femme Fatale: The Kiss of Death*. Basingstoke: Macmillan, 1992.

Walkowitz, Judith R. *City of Dreadful Delight: Narratives of Sexual Danger in Late Victorian London*. London: Virago, 2000.

Warwick, A. and Willis, M., eds. *Jack the Ripper: Media, Culture, History*. Manchester: Manchester University Press, 2007.

Modernity, mental health, hysteria

Ellenberger, Henri. *The Discovery of the Unconscious: The History and Evolution of Dynamic Psychiatry*. London: Fontana, 1994.

Gilbert, Sandra M. and Gubar, Susan. *The Madwoman in the Attic: The Woman Writer and the Nineteenth-Century Literary Imagination*. New Haven and London: Yale University Press, 1980.

Logan, P.M. *Nerves and Narratives: A Cultural History of Hysteria in Nineteenth-Century British Prose*. Berkeley: University of California Press, 1997.

Pykett, Lyn. *The Improper Feminine: The Women's Sensation Novel and the New Woman Writing*. London: Routledge, 1992.

Showalter, Elaine. *The Female Malady: Women, Madness and English Culture, 1830-1980*. London: Virago, 2001.

Small, Helen. *Love's Madness: Medicine, the Novel and Female Insanity, 1800-1865*. Oxford: Clarendon Press, 1996.

Smith, Andrew. *Victorian Demons: Medicine, Masculinity and the Gothic at the Fin de Siècle*. Manchester: Manchester University Press, 2004.

Trotter, David. *Paranoid Modernism: Literary Experiment, Psychosis, and the Professionalization of English Society*. Oxford: Oxford University Press, 2001.

The Goddess

A Demon

By Richard Marsh

Author of
"In Full Cry," "The Beetle: A Mystery," "Marvels and
Mysteries," "Ada Vernham, Actress," &c.

London:
F. V. White & Co.
14, Bedford Street, Strand, W.C.
1900

Contents

Contents

The Goddess

CHAPTER I

A VISION OF THE NIGHT

I WAS sure that I had seen Edwin Lawrence juggle with the pack. As I lay there wide awake in bed it all came back to me. I wondered how I could have been such an unspeakable idiot.[1] We had dined together at the Trocadero; then we had gone on to the Empire.[2] The big music hall was packed with people, the heat was insufferable.

"Let's get out of this," suggested Lawrence, almost as soon as we were in. "This crush, in this atmosphere, is not to be borne." I agreed with him. We left. "Come into my place for an hour," he said.

We both lived in Imperial Mansions,[3] on the same floor. His number was 64, mine was 79. You went out of his door, along the passage, round the corner to the right—the second door on the right was mine. I went in with him.

"What do you say to a little gamble?" he asked. "It will be better than nothing."

I agreed. We had a little gamble—at first for trivial stakes. I am an abstemious man. I had already drunk more than I was accustomed to. At his invitation I drank still more. We increased the stakes. I really do not know from whom the suggestion came, I know that I did not object. I had lost all my ready money. I kept on losing. He was dotting down, on a piece of paper, the extent of my indebtedness. Presently, when he announced the sum total, I was amazed to learn that it was very much more than I imagined—actually nearly a thousand pounds.[4] On the instant I was wide awake.

"Nine hundred and forty pounds, Lawrence! It can't be as much as that!"

"My dear chap, here are the figures; look for yourself."

He handed me the piece of paper. His manner of arranging the several amounts I found more than a little vague, but as I had been so foolish as not to have kept count of them myself, I was hardly in a position to dispute their accuracy; and, added together, they certainly did come to the sum he stated. Still I felt persuaded that there was a mistake somewhere, though in what it consisted I was unable at the moment to perceive.

"Look here," he said. "Be a sportsman for once in your life! I'll give you a chance—I'll cut you double or quits."

I did not want to. I would have very much rather not. Gambling on such a scale was altogether out of my way. But he urged me, and I yielded; I don't know why. I must have been very much more under the influence of drink than I imagined. We cut. I cut first— the knave of diamonds. As it was to be highest, not a bad card. I watched him as he cut, and saw that he dropped at least one card from the lot which he picked up; and that after he had had an opportunity of getting a shrewd guess at its value. The card which he faced was the queen of diamonds, exclaiming as he did so:

"That does you!"

"But that was not the card which you originally cut—you dropped one."

"I dropped one! What do you mean? I have not the slightest notion of having done anything of the kind, and, anyhow, it must have been by the sheerest accident. What are you looking at me like that for? Don't lose your temper because you happen to have lost."

The insinuation was as gratuitous as it was uncalled for. There was not the slightest danger of my losing my temper; but that I was right in what I had said I felt assured. But then the card might have been dropped by accident, and he might not have noticed what had happened. And, anyhow, in face of the fact that I had been with the man on terms of intimacy, and had never before had cause to suspect him of anything in the least dishonourable, having regard to his explicit denial, it was a delicate position to persist in. I got up from my chair, conceding the point.

"That makes eighteen hundred and eighty pounds you owe me. My sympathy, Ferguson; better luck next time."

I mentally resolved that I would not play cards again with Edwin Lawrence—at any rate, when we two were alone.

I was in a curious state of mind when I returned to my own chambers. The events of the evening buzzed in my head. It was not the money merely. Though I am very far from being a millionaire, and two thousand pounds, less one hundred and twenty, is not a sum to be lightly thrown away. The inquiry kept knocking at my brain—was the man whom already I was beginning to regard as a friend such a very poor creature after all? Was it possible that he had wilfully manipulated those figures to his own advantage, and, with intention, dropped that card? The more closely I followed the events of the evening, the less I liked the conclusion to which they led me.

When I went to bed my thoughts went with me. I could not shake them off. I tossed and tumbled in pursuit of sleep. And when, at last, slumber did come, my sleeping experiences were even more disturbing than my waking ones had been.

My repose is generally untroubled. I seldom am visited by dreams. But that night I had a most extraordinary dream; so extraordinary that I am haunted by it to this day, even in my waking hours. In appearance of reality it was little less than supernatural. Indeed, I do not mind admitting that I have been, and still am, at a loss to determine whether I was not—at least in part—an actual, sentient spectator, and not merely the subject of a vision of the night.

Of course, I am unable to say how long I had been to sleep, but it seemed to me that I had only just closed my eyes, when something, I knew not what, caused me to sit up in bed; and not only to sit up, but to get out of bed. I have no recollection of putting anything on in the shape of clothes; I am certain that I did not switch on the electric light,[5] I had a clear consciousness of the prevailing darkness. And, in the darkness, I had an uncontrollable impulse to go to Lawrence. I left the room, to the best of my belief, clad only in my pyjamas. In the passage was a light—it is kept burning all night,—and I distinctly remember noticing that it was burning as I passed along. Reaching Lawrence's door, I tapped at the panel. There was no answer. I hesitated before knocking again; and, as I did so, immediately became aware of a strange noise which proceeded from within.

A stranger noise I never heard. I experience a difficulty in describing it. It was as if some wild beast was inside the room, and was beside itself with fury. Yelling, snarling, screeching—a horrid, gasping noise—these sounds seemed to follow hard upon each other. And, mingled with them, were faint cries as of some one in extremity of both pain and terror. At that sound I ceased to hesitate. I turned the handle. I stepped inside. The sight I saw I am not likely to forget.

Lawrence was struggling frantically with some strange creature whose character I was not able to distinguish. From this creature proceeded those hideous sounds. It was a mass of whirling movement. I had never seen a being so instinct with frenzied action. Every part seemed to be in motion at once; and with its whole force it was assailing Lawrence. He seemed to be offering a feeble resistance, as, hauled this way and that, he staggered to and fro.

But, against such an attack, his efforts were vain. Presently he fell headlong to the floor. The creature, stooping, rained on to his motionless body a hail of blows, making all the time that horrid, gasping noise, and then was still.

I had been conscious all the time that there was something about the creature which was terribly human. It appeared to be covered with a flowing robe of some shining, silken stuff, whose voluminous skirts whirled hither and thither as it writhed and twisted. Now that it became motionless there broke on my ears the sound of a woman's laughter.

I am not a nervous subject. Nor am I, I believe, a physical coward. But I am compelled to own that, instead of attempting to interfere, or offering the assistance which I had only too good reason to suppose was urgently needed, at the sound of the laughter, like some frightened cur, I turned and fled. And not the least strange part of the whole business was that, as it seemed, immediately after, I woke up. Woke to find that, however it might appear to the contrary, I certainly had been asleep, for I was sitting up in bed covered with sweat and trembling in every limb.

I looked about me. The blind was up before the long French window. I remember drawing it up, as was my usual habit, before I got into bed. The moon was shining through. All at once a sound caught my anxious ear. I started forward to learn from whence it came. From the window! I stared with all my eyes. I was wide awake now, of that there could be no sort of doubt whatever. In the moonlight I could see that some one was standing on the other side of the pane—a faint, mysterious figure. The latch was raised; it was a little rusty, I could hear it creaking. The window was pushed open, as by an unaccustomed hand, with something of a jerk. Out of the moonbeams, like some spectral visitant, a woman stepped into the room.

CHAPTER II

THE WOMAN WHO CAME THROUGH THE WINDOW

I HELD my breath, staring in amazement. The figure was real, that was obvious. And yet, how could a woman have gained my window from without? Where had she come from at that hour of the night? What did she want, now that she was here?

A vague wonder passed through my mind as to whether her object might not be felony. She had left the window open—I could feel the cool night-air—and stood inside it, as if listening. Was she endeavouring to discover if her entrance had been discovered? She had but to use her eyes, and look straight in front of her, to see me sitting up in bed, staring. I was as visible as she was. So far as I could judge she remained motionless, looking neither to right nor left. Presently she sighed, as some tired child might do, a long-drawn sigh, as if the action brought relief to her breast. Then I was persuaded that she was at any rate no thief—there was something in the sound of that sustained respiration which was incompatible with the notion of a feminine burglar.

She came a little forward into the room, doubtfully, as if uncertain of her surroundings. She stumbled against a chair, the contact seeming to startle her. I saw her put her hand up to her head, with the gesture of one who was trying to collect her thoughts.

"I can't think where I am."

The words broke the silence in the oddest manner. The voice was sweet, soft, clear—unmistakably a lady's. It thrilled me strangely. Nothing which had gone before had disconcerted me so much—it was an utterance of such extreme simplicity. Was it possible that the lady was a somnambulist,[6] who, held in the thraldom of that curious disease, had woke to find herself in a stranger's bedroom? If that was the case, what was I to do? How could I explain the situation, without unduly startling her?

The question was answered for me. I must unconsciously have fidgeted. All at once her face was turned towards me. She exclaimed:

"Who's that?"

I arrived at an instant resolution—replying with the most matter-of-fact air of which I was capable.

"Do not be alarmed—it is I, John Ferguson. If you will allow me, I will turn on the light, so that we may see each other better."

I switched on the electric light. What it revealed again amazed me into speechlessness. At the foot of my bed stood the most beautiful woman I had ever seen; I thought so in that first astounded moment—I think so still. She was tall and she was slight. She looked at me out of the biggest and the sweetest pair of eyes I ever saw. But there was something in them which I did not understand. It was not only bewilderment, it was as if she was looking at the world out of a dream. She regarded me, as I sat, with my touzled head of hair, not, as I had feared, with signs of agitation and alarm, but rather with a curious sort of wonderment.

"I don't know who you are. Where am I? Have I ever seen you before?"

It was spoken as a child might speak, with a little tremulous intonation, as if she were on the verge of tears.

"I don't think you have. But don't be alarmed—you are quite safe. I think you have been walking in your sleep."

"Walking in my sleep?"

"I fancy you must have been."

"But—do I walk in my sleep?"

In spite of myself, I smiled at the simplicity of the inquiry.

"That is a matter on which you should know more than I do."

"But—where can I have walked from?"

"That also is a question to which you should be able to supply an answer. Do you live in the Mansions?"

"The Mansions?"

"These are the Imperial Mansions. Is your home here?"

"My home?" She shook her head solemnly. "I don't know where my home is."

"Not know? But you must know where your home is. Who are you? What is your name?"

"I don't know who I am or what is my name."

Was she an imbecile?[7] She did not look it. I never saw intellect more clearly marked upon a woman's face. But the more attentively I regarded her the more distinctly I began to realise that there was something peculiar in her expression. She seemed mazed, as if she had recently been roused from sleep and had not yet had time to acquire consciousness of her surroundings. My original surmise was correct; she had been walking in her sleep, and had not yet recovered sufficient consciousness to enable her to recognise the actualities of existence, and comprehend what it was she had been doing.

While I told myself this I had never removed my glance from off her. And now my gaze fastened on something which had for me a dreadful fascination.

She was covered from head to foot in a voluminous garment, which set off her face and figure to perfection. I took it to be some sort of opera-cloak, though, more than anything else, it resembled a domino[8] buttoned down the front. It was made of some bright plum-coloured material, which I afterwards learned was alpaca.[9] A hood, which was attached to the garment, was half off, half on, her dainty head. The whole affair, cloak and hood, was lined with green silk. The front of the cloak was decorated with voluminous green ribbons; one of these caught my eye. It was a broad sash-ribbon, some six or eight inches wide, reaching from her neck almost to her toes.

For quite half its length the vivid green was obscured by what seemed to be a stain of another colour. The stain was apparently of such recent occurrence that the ribbon was still sopping wet. But it was not the broad ribbon only which was stained; I perceived that, here and there, the bright hues of the knots of narrower ribbon were also dimmed. More, there were splashes on the cloak itself. She had her hand up to her head. I glanced at it. How could the fact have previously escaped my notice? There were stains upon her uplifted hand, and upon the other hand which dangled loosely at her side. They were half covered with something red—and wet.

All at once there came back to me the extraordinary vision I had had of the strange happening in Lawrence's room. I recalled the frenzied figure, clad in the woman's robe, with the whirling skirts. Woman's robe? Why, here it was in front of me, upon this woman, the very robe which I had seen. And here, too, now sufficiently quiescent, were the whirling skirts. I put my hand up to my eyes to shut out the horrid thought which seemed to rush at me; and I cried—

"Tell me who you are, and from where you come!"

There was silence. I repeated my inquiry. She answered with another.

"Why do you speak so strangely? And why do you put your hand before your eyes?"

The mere sound of her speaking soothed me. To my mind, one of the greatest charms of a woman should be her voice. Never did I hear a more comfortable voice than hers. It was impossible to imagine that a voice in which, to my ears, rang so unmistakably the accents of truth, could belong to one who was false. Removing my hands, I looked at her again.

She had smeared her countenance with her fingers; all down one side of her face was a crimson stain.

"Look," I cried, "at what you've done!"

"What have I done?"

"What's on your hands?"

"My hands? What is on my hands?"

She held out her hands in front of her, staring at them with the most innocent air in the world.

"It's blood."

"Blood? Where has it come from?"

She asked the question as a child might do. In spite of her

blood-stained face, the ring of truth which was in her voice, the unspoken appeal which was in her eyes, went to my heart.

"Try to think where you've come from, and what you have been doing?"

"Think? I can't think."

"But you must! Don't you see you're all covered with blood?"

"All covered with blood? Why, so I am! Oh!"

She gave a little cry which was more than half a sob. She swayed to and fro. Before I could reach her she had fallen to the ground. I found her lying as if she were dead. She had swooned.

This was a pretty plight which I was in. I have had but little experience of feminine society. My life, for the most part, has been lived in places where women are not. I knew as little of them as of the cuneiform character[10]—perhaps less. I, of course, had heard of women fainting, but never before had I seen one in such a pitiful predicament. What was I to do? I thought of Mrs. Peddar. She was the housekeeper at the Mansions—an excellent woman. Everything under her rule went by clockwork: she had been of more assistance to me in various matters than I had supposed that a person in her position could have been. But I scarcely felt that this was a case in which her interference might be altogether desirable.

As I looked at the lovely creature lying there so still, I felt this more and more. Her utter helplessness filled me with a curious sense of pity. A resolve was growing up within me to constitute myself her champion, if she would only avail herself of my services, in whatever circumstances of doubt and danger she might find herself. If she had something to conceal, by no action of mine should it be blazed to the world. Without her express sanction, neither Mrs. Peddar nor any one else, should be informed of her presence there. Yet how was I to restore her to consciousness?

While I hesitated I perceived that something was lying beside her on the floor. Where it had come from I could not tell; it was hardly the kind of thing to have fallen from a woman's pocket. I picked it up. It was a photograph of Edwin Lawrence; I could not help but recognise the likeness directly I raised it. Back and front it was smeared with blood. Actuated by an impulse for which I did not attempt to account, rising, I thrust it between the leaves of a book which was on the mantelshelf. She moved. Turning, I found that she had raised herself a little, and was looking at me with her eyes wide open.

"What is the matter with me? Have I been asleep?"

Her frank, fearless gaze, with, in it, that strange look of bewilderment, filled me with a sudden sense of confusion. I stammered a reply.

"You have not been very well. But you are better now. Let me help you to get up."

I held out my hand. Putting hers into it, she rose to her feet with a little spring. When she took her hand away, on mine there was a ruddy smirch. The condition of her plum-coloured garment, and of the bright green ribbons, seemed to have become more conspicuous even than before.

"Hadn't you better take off your cloak?"

She looked at me as if amazed.

"Take off my cloak? Why should I?"

"You will be more comfortable without it."

"Do you think so? Then of course I'll take it off."

She removed her cloak, with my assistance. I flung it over the back of a chair.

"You will find water there with which to wash your hands and face."

Again she eyed me with that suggestion of surprise.

"Why should I wash my hands and face?"

"There is blood upon them."

"Blood?" She held out her hands with her former gesture. "So there is. I had forgotten. I cannot think how it came there." Her cheeks assumed an added tinge of pallor. "Will it come off if I wash them?"

It seemed impossible to doubt that it was seriously asked; yet the apparent puerility[11] of the question stung me to a brusque response.

"We will hope that soap and water will at least, remove the outward and visible stain."

Turning, I went into my dressing-room, she following me with her eyes. There I hastily donned some more conventional attire. Thence, passing into the dining-room, I called to her through the bedroom door.

"When you are ready, may I ask you to come in here. We shall be more at our ease."

She did not keep me waiting, but appeared upon the instant, coming towards me holding out her hands as a child might do.

"I'm clean now. Aren't I clean?"

Her close propinquity filled with me wholly unreasonable agitation. I drew back. The removal of the cloak had disclosed a dark blue silk dress which fitted her, to my thinking, with the most marvellous perfection. There was a touch of white about her neck and wrists. Her beauty struck me more even than at first—it awed me. Yet at the back of my mind was born a dim fancy that somewhere in the flesh I had seen this enchanting vision before. I was at a loss as to the words with which I ought to address her, speaking at last, blunderingly enough.

"Have you any reason why you should wish to conceal your name?" She shook her head. "Then tell me what it is."

"But I don't know. Have I a name?"

"I presume that, with the rest of the world, you have. Pray do not suppose, however, that I wish to force myself into your confidence. I would only suggest that I think it might be better, for both our sakes, if you could give me some idea of where you came from before you entered my room."

"Did I enter your room? Oh yes, I remember; but—I don't remember anything more." She put her hand up to her head with the gesture which had previously struck me. "Where did I come from?"

"I don't know if you are intentionally trifling, but if you are unable to supply the information, I certainly cannot."

Something in my manner seemed to occasion her distress. She moved towards me anxiously, like a timid child who stands in fear of admonition.

"Why do you look like that? Are you angry?"

I knew not what to think or what to feel; but, at least, I was not angry. If she was playing a part, which I for one was disposed to doubt, she acted with such plausibility that I was conscious of my incapacity to discover in what the trick consisted. I perceived that, after all, this was a case for Mrs. Peddar.

"The housekeeper is a most superior person—a Mrs. Peddar.

She will be of more assistance to you than I can be. Will you allow me to tell her that you are here?"

"Why not? Of course you can tell her—if you like."

This was said with such an air of innocence, and with such an entire absence of suspicion that there could be anything dubious in her position, that I myself was conscious of a sense of shame at the thoughts which filled my mind. I moved towards the door. She stopped me.

"Who are you going to tell?"

"The housekeeper—Mrs. Peddar."

"Oh." This was with a little touch of doubt. "She's a woman. You're a man. I'm a woman." She said this with the utmost gravity, as if she were giving utterance to portentous facts which she had just discovered. She seemed to shiver. "Is she—nice? Will she—be kind to me?"

I registered a mental vow that she should be kind to her, or I would know the reason why; I said as much, though with less emphasis of language. Then I left the room.

But, before I actually went in search of Mrs. Peddar I returned into the bedroom, through the door which opened out of the passage. Using that plum-coloured cloak with scant ceremony, I rolled it up into a bundle and thrust it into a wardrobe behind a heap of clothes. Then, opening the window, I stood on the balcony and threw the water in which my visitor had washed her hands and face, as far as I could out into the street. I heard it fall with a splash on to the road below.

CHAPTER III

THE CONQUEST OF MRS. PEDDAR

Mrs. Peddar has her rooms at the top of the building—on the seventh floor. The lift runs all night.[12] It had been my intention, rather than summon it and attract the attention of the porter, to have climbed the endless flights of stairs; but, as luck had it, when I reached the staircase the lift was setting some one down. Since it was there I thought I might as well use it, to save time, and also my legs. I stepped inside.

"Up or down, sir?"

"I am going up to Mrs. Peddar."

The porter favoured me with a doubtful glance.

"Mrs. Peddar lives at the top of the building. She's in bed long ago."

"So I suppose. I'm afraid, however, that I shall have to wake her up again, as I am in urgent need of her assistance."

"Anything wrong, sir?"

"No. At least nothing in which you could be of service."

As we mounted I could see that Turner—the night porter's name is Turner—was wondering what possible business I could have with Mrs. Peddar that I should rouse her out of her warm bed at that hour of the night. It occurred to me to ask him a question or two.

"Has a lady come up lately?"

"Up where?"

"Up to the first floor—or anywhere?" He shook his head. "You're sure?"

"Certain. No lady's come into this building for a good two hours, at any rate. The last was Mrs. Sabin; she and her husband's on the fourth floor. They've been to the Gaiety Theatre:[13] I took 'em up in the lift. She was the last lady as came in, and that was just after eleven."

His words set me thinking. If my visitor had not come in through the doorway, how then had she gained access to my balcony, which is on the first floor, and between twenty and thirty feet above the ground. Turner volunteered a statement on his own account.

"And the last man who went out was Mr. Lawrence's brother."

I pricked up my ears at this.

"Mr. Lawrence's brother? Oh."

"Yes—Mr. Philip, I think his name is. He came down not three minutes before I saw you, just as I was going to take up Mr. Maynard—that was Mr. Maynard who got out as you got in. He seemed to be in a big hurry. I said good night as he went past, but he said nothing. He had a big parcel in his arms, almost as much as he could carry."

"You are sure it was Mr. Lawrence's brother?"

"It was him right enough. My cousin's his coachman—I ought to know him."

"You say he came down three minutes ago?"

"Not three minutes ago, I said."

Then, in that case, he must have been with his brother some time after my visitor had come to me. The knowledge occasioned me distinct relief.

Turner continued:

"He went up about an hour ago: perhaps a little more. He'd got no parcel then. I stared when I saw he'd got one when he came back. I shouldn't have thought he was the kind to carry a parcel, and especially such a one. I'd have called him a cab if he'd given me a chance, but I was just starting with Mr. Maynard, and he was off like a shot. Shall I wait for you, sir? The first door round the corner is Mrs. Peddar's."

I told him not to wait, feeling conscious that it might take me some time to explain to Mrs. Peddar what I desired of her. The lady must have been a light sleeper. Hardly had I saluted the panel of the door with my knuckles than a voice inquired who was there. When I informed her she made a prompt appearance in her dressing-gown.

"You, Mr. Ferguson! What do you want at this hour of the night?"

I immediately became conscious that it might be even more difficult to explain than I had supposed.

"I have a visitor downstairs, Mrs. Peddar."

"A visitor? Well? What has that to do with me? You can't have anything to eat at this time of night."

She said that, I take it, because in the Mansions meals are provided for residents, and she supposed that I had dragged her out of bed at that unholy hour in search of food.

"The visitor is a lady, and I wanted to know if you could give her a bed somewhere to-night."

"A bed? Who is the lady?"

"Well—the fact is, Mrs. Peddar, something very remarkable has taken place. I've come up to tell you all about it, and to ask your advice."

"You had better come in."

I went into her sitting-room, she, with an eye for the proprieties, leaving the door discreetly open. There was that in her bearing which made me wonder if she suspected me of having been guilty of some act of rakish impropriety, unworthy of my age and character. I was conscious that the course in front of me was not all smooth sailing.

"A young lady, Mrs. Peddar, has just entered my room through the window."

"Through the window! Mr. Ferguson! At this hour!"

"I'm afraid the poor thing is not quite right in her mind."

"I should think not. That is the best thing you can hope of her."

"She is quite a lady."

"Lady!" Mrs. Peddar tightened her lips. "Mr. Ferguson, are you laughing at me, sir?"

"I assure you I am perfectly serious; and I give you my word she is a lady. You have only to see her for yourself to find that. Wait a minute—let me finish! I thought at first that she was a somnambulist; that she had been walking in her sleep; and I am still of opinion that something strange has happened to her. She is unable to tell me her name, who she is, whence she comes, or anything about herself; she seemed as if she were mazed."

"Has she been drinking?"

"Come downstairs and speak to her; you will perceive for yourself that to connect her with such a notion would be worse than impertinence."

"No offence, sir, but when you tell me that a strange young woman comes through your window in the middle of the night, I can't help having my own thoughts."

"And I tell you, Mrs. Peddar, that the 'strange young woman,' as you call her, is a lady in every sense of the word, to whom, I am persuaded, something very serious has recently happened."

"Very good, Mr. Ferguson. I'm afraid that you're too soft-hearted, sir. Where is this young lady now?"

"She is in my dining-room."

"Alone?"

"Certainly she is alone."

"Then I should not be surprised if, by now, she's gone back through the window, taking something with her to help keep you in mind. You must excuse my saying that I don't think I ever did know quite so simple-minded a gentleman as you are, sir. One thing's sure—if we do want to find her we'd better hurry for all we're worth."

Urged by Mrs. Peddar I hastened with her down the stairs. But her forecast was not realised. My visitor had not gone. She was still in the dining-room, fast asleep in an armchair. The first thing which saluted our ears, as we entered the room, was the sound of her gentle breathing; she slept softly as a child. The sight which she presented touched the housekeeper's womanly heart.

"She does look a picture, that's certain! And quite the lady! And isn't she prettily dressed! My word, what lovely rings!"

The girl's hands were extended on her lap. I saw that on her fingers were what seemed to be two or three valuable rings. Now that Mrs. Peddar had started, her enthusiasm almost equalled mine.

"How pale she is—and how beautiful! It's plain that the poor thing's tired out and out. And you say that she came through the window! But however did she get there? and who is she? and where did she come from?"

"As I have told you, I have put those questions to her already, without success. As you can see for yourself, she appears to be worn out by fatigue. I think that if you could give her a bed for to-night—I, of course, will be responsible for all expenses—in the morning we may be able to obtain from her all the information we require."

"She shall have the bed all right, sir; I shouldn't be surprised if you're right for once. She looks a lady; and, anyhow, I never could be hard to any one so beautiful. But who's to wake her? She is so sound asleep, poor dear!"

"I will wake her."

I did—by laying my hand gently on her shoulder. She moved, turned, opened her eyes, and, when she saw who it was, sat upright in her chair.

"I've been asleep again; it seems as if my eyes would not keep open. Where have you been? I thought you never would come back. It was so quiet here, and this is such an easy chair, I had to go to sleep."

"I've been in search of Mrs. Peddar, of whom I told you. This is Mrs. Peddar."

The girl turned to her with a radiant smile; my conviction is that that smile won Mrs. Peddar's heart right off.

"Oh, Mrs. Peddar, I am so sleepy. I feel as if I wanted to sleep, sleep, sleep. I can't think what's the matter."

Mrs. Peddar was regarding her with inquisitive looks, in which, however, there was sympathy as well.

"You're tired, miss; that's what the matter is with you. A good night's rest will do you good; you shall have it if you'll come with me, and as comfortable a bed as you ever slept in."

"You'll be all right with Mrs. Peddar," I said; for the girl seemed to hesitate. "You could not be in safer keeping, or in kinder hands."

"Cannot I stay here?"

I looked at Mrs. Peddar; Mrs. Peddar looked at me. It was she who answered.

"I think, miss, you will be more comfortable if you come with me. You see, Mr. Ferguson lives alone."

"But where shall you be?"

The anxious tone in which the girl put the question, and the appealing gesture with which it was accompanied, afforded me an unreasonable amount of pleasure.

"I shall be here, not so very far away from you; and, the first thing in the morning, I will come to learn how you have slept."

"You promise?"

"I promise."

Never did I promise anything more willingly.

She was still reluctant to go. To appease her I accompanied her upstairs. When she reached Mrs. Peddar's own apartment she was still unwilling to suffer me to leave her, her unwillingness making me absurdly happy.

As I descended those interminable stairs it was as if I trod on air. It was ridiculous. Why should I be affected, one way or the other, by the whims, and airs, and fancies of an apparently half-witted woman, who had forced her way into my room at dead of night in a cloak all wet with blood.*

CHAPTER IV

DR. HUME

I WAS awoke next morning by Atkins bringing in my cup of coffee. He asked me a question as he arranged it on the small table beside my bed.

"Do you know, sir, if Mr. Lawrence slept in his rooms last night?"

He had aroused me from a dreamless slumber, and I was not yet sufficiently awake to catch the full drift of his inquiry.

"Slept in his rooms? What do you mean?"

"Because, sir, when I took him his coffee just now, as usual, I knocked four times and got no answer. And his door's locked; it's not his habit to lock his door when he's at home."

Atkins is one of the staff of servants attached to the Mansions, whose particular office it is to wait on the occupants of chambers on the first floor: a discreet man, who has a pretty intimate knowledge of the manners and customs of those on whom he attends.

"Mr. Lawrence was in his rooms last night. I was with him till rather late, and I believe he had a visitor after I had left."

This I said remembering what Turner had told me about his brother coming down the stairs, with the parcel in his arms.

"I think he must be out now—at least, I can't make him hear. And the door's locked; I never knew him have the door locked when he was in."

"Perhaps he's ill," I suggested. "I'll slip along the balcony and see. You wait here till I come back."

I do not know what induced me to make such a proposition, except that I was struck by the man's words, and impelled by a sudden impulse. On every floor a balcony runs right round the building. Lawrence and I had often made use of it to reach each other's rooms—his are the first set round the corner. I put on a pair of slippers and a dressing-gown, and started.

It was a chilly morning, with a touch of fog in the air, and it had been raining. I made what haste I could. The window of Lawrence's dining-room opened directly I turned the handle. I went inside, and I saw what I then instantly and clearly realised I had all along felt sure that I should see. I sprang back upon the balcony. Atkins was looking out of my window. I called to him.

"Come here! Quick! There's something wrong!"

He came running to me.

"What is it, sir?"

"I don't know what it is, but—it's something."

Atkins followed me into the room. Edwin Lawrence lay face foremost on the floor. All about him the carpet was stained with blood. His clothes were soaked. Had it not been for his clothes I should not have certainly known that it was Lawrence, because, when we turned him over, we found that his face and head had been cut and hacked to pieces. In my time I have seen men who have come to their death by violence, but never had I seen such an extraordinary sight as he presented. It was as if some savage thing, fastening upon him, had torn him to pieces with tooth and nail. His flesh had been ripped and rent so that not one recognisable feature was left. Indeed, it might not have been a man we were looking upon, but some thing of horror.

I spoke to Atkins. "Run and fetch Dr. Hume. I am afraid he will be of little use, but he must come. And the police!"

Off he sped to tell the ghastly tidings. So soon as he was gone I looked about me. On a chair close by was a pair of white kid gloves[14]—a woman's. I picked them up and put them in my pocket. Among the portraits on the mantelshelf was the face of one I knew. I put that in my pocket also with the gloves.

The room was in some disarray, but not in such disorder as to suggest that a desperate struggle had taken place. A chair or two and a table were not in the places in which I knew they generally stood; the table on which we had played that game of cards last night was pushed up against another, on which were some copper vases. A revolving bookcase had been driven up against the fire-place. On the woodwork were gouts of blood. There was a blotch on the back of one of the books—a volume of Rudyard Kipling's "Many Inventions."[15] On the edge of the white stone mantelpiece was the mark of where a hand had rested—a blood-stained hand.

Something lay on the carpet, perhaps two yards away from the dead man's feet. I took it up. It was a collar—a man's collar—shapeless and twisted and stiff with coagulated blood. As I stared at it a wild wonder began to take shape and to grow in my brain.

"Ferguson, what's the matter? What's this Atkins tells me about? Good God! is that Lawrence?"

It was Dr. Hume who spoke. He had come into the room while I was staring at the collar.

Graham Hume is a man who has taken high medical honours; but, having ample private means, he does not pretend to have anything in the shape of a regular practice. He has a hobby—madness. He is a student of what he calls obscure diseases of the brain; insisting that we have all of us a screw loose somewhere, and that out of every countenance insanity peeps[16]—even though, as a rule, thank goodness, it is only the shadow of a shade.

Some strange stories are told of experiments which he has made. His chambers are on the ground floor; and, though he has a plate on his door, his patients are few and far between—nor are they by any means always welcome even when they do appear. Probably the larger number of them are residents in the Mansions, and because that was so, any one living in the buildings being in sudden need of medical help used to rush at once to him. Lawrence used to chaffingly speak of him as "the Imperial Doctor."

Hume was still in the prime of life—perhaps forty, of medium height, sparely built, with clean-shaven face, high forehead, and coal-black hair. A good fellow, in his fashion; but with rather a too professional outlook on to the world. I always felt that he regarded every one with whom he came in contact—man, woman, or child—as a possible subject for experiment. Personally, I was conscious of feeling no dislike for him; but I had a sort of suspicion that he did not like me.

"Yes," I replied; "that's Lawrence—what's left of him."

He was kneeling by the dead man on the floor, his usually impassive face all alert and eager.

"How has this happened—and when?"

"That is what has to be discovered."

"Who found him?"

"Atkins and I."

"Was he lying in this position?"

"No; he was on his face. We turned him over."

"The man's been cut to pieces."

"It almost looks to me as if he had been scratched to pieces."

"I fancy these wounds are too deep for scratches—in the ordinary sense. It looks as if several narrow blades had been used, set in some kind of frame, or a row of spikes. The flesh has been torn open in regular layers. This is interesting—very." This was the kind of remark which I should have expected he would make; it came from him sotto voce.[17] "He's been dead some time, he's quite cold. Very curious indeed."

While he spoke he had been unfastening, with deft fingers, the dead man's clothes, laying bare his neck and chest. Now he called to me, with an accent of suspicion.

"Look at that!"

I looked. I saw that the body was almost as much disfigured as the head and face; that it was covered with gaping wounds.

"I see; enough violence has been used to kill the poor fellow a dozen times over."

"Is that all you see?" Hume spoke with more than a touch of impatience. "Don't you see that some sharp-pointed instrument has been thrust right through the man's body, from the back to the front, and from the front to the back, because he has been attacked from both back and front? If, then, a knife, or something of the kind, has been driven clean through him, as it has been, over and over again, how came it to miss his shirt, his coat, the whole of his clothes?"

"I don't quite see what you mean."

"Then, in that case, my dear Ferguson, I am afraid that you are even more dense than you usually are—which is unfortunate. If I were to stab you where you stand, the stabbing instrument would have to pass through your clothing, and, in doing so, would leave a mark of its passage. One would expect to find this man's clothing cut to pieces; but you can see for yourself that, with the exception of bloodstains, there is not a mark upon them; they are intact, without rent or tear. Are we to infer that the attacking weapon did not pass through them? In that case, was the man naked when he was attacked, and were his clothes put on him after he was dead?"

"I see, now, what you mean."

"I am glad of that; perhaps your mental faculties are beginning to move. I suppose these clothes are Lawrence's?"

"I can prove that; he was wearing them when I saw him last."

"Oh, he was, was he. When did you see him last?"

"Last night."

Hume glanced quickly up at me.

"Last night? At what time?"

I considered for a moment.

"I don't remember particularly noticing, but I should say that it was about half-past eleven when I left him, or perhaps a little after."

"Half-past eleven? Then I should say that within an hour of that time he was dead; perhaps within less than an hour. That's very odd."

"Why is it odd?"

"Was he alone when you left him?"

"He was."

"Did you part on friendly terms?"

The question took me somewhat aback; it was not one which it was easy to answer.

"May I ask why you inquire?"

"My dear Ferguson, it is a question which some one will put to you. You should be prepared with an answer. It seems rather unfortunate that you should have quarrelled with him within an hour of his being done to death."

"I did not quarrel with him."

"No? What did you do then? Your unwillingness to reply shows that it was not on the best of terms you parted."

"I shall be ready to give all necessary information to any one entitled to ask for it."

"So you are in a position to give information? I see? And you think I am not entitled to ask? Oh! What, to your mind, would constitute a title?—a magistrate's warrant? You don't happen to know if any one saw him after you did?"

"I believe that some one did."

Again he gave that quick glance upwards.

"Who was it?"

"I believe that his brother saw him."

"You believe! What makes you believe?"

"I was told by Turner, the night-porter."

"When?"

"Last night; or, rather, early this morning. I had occasion to use the lift. Turner told me that he had seen Mr. Lawrence's brother go up, and that he had just come down again."

"What time was that?"

"Between two and three."

"I fancy that before the clock struck two, or even one, this man was dead."

"I found this on the floor just before you came in."

I handed Hume the blood-grimed collar.

"What is it? A collar?" As he turned it over he saw what I had seen. "Here's a name—'Philip Lawrence.'"

"I believe that Philip is his brother's name."

He looked at me with an unfriendly something in his glance.

"What do you infer from that?"

"I do not attempt to draw an inference."

"But your tone suggests. Do you suggest that when Philip Lawrence came to see his brother he took off his collar and left it behind him on the floor? Why?"

"It must have been soaked with blood."

"Then you do suggest that Philip Lawrence left his collar behind because it was soaked with blood."

"I suggest nothing. I say that I saw it on the floor and picked it up; that's all."

Hume stood up.

"What else have you found?"

I fenced with the question. I did not propose to speak of the gloves or the photograph, being conscious that Hume was prepared to make himself extremely disagreeable if occasion offered.

"I have not looked. The collar lay staring at me on the floor; I could not help but see it."

"Then we will look together. In such a case as this, one never knows what 'trifles light as air' may prove 'confirmation strong as Holy Writ.'[18] Here's a waste-paper basket; let's see what's in it. More than one man has been sent to the gallows by a scrap of waste-paper. Here's what appears to be a letter—not too carefully written. Let's see what we can make of it. Hullo! what's this?" He read from the scrap of paper he was holding: "'Such men as you ought not to be allowed to live.' That's a strong assertion. And written by a woman, too, in a good, bold hand. I think I should recognise that caligraphy if I saw it again; wouldn't you?"

He handed me the fragment. The clear, characteristic writing was certainly a woman's. I felt that I should know it again if I saw it. The words were as he had stated them. He went on.

"If the intention of the person who tore up this letter was to conceal its purport, he did his work with very little skill. Here's another fragment which is plain enough. 'To-night I will give you a last chance.' To-night! I wonder if that was yesternight? If so he had his last chance—his very last. Here, on still another piece, is part of a signature. 'Bessie.' It certainly is Bessie. I know a Bessie." He smiled, not too pleasantly. "I wonder if—it's scarcely likely, though I shouldn't be surprised if this turns out to be the work of feminine fingers. I seem to scent a woman in it somewhere."

"It's incredible!" I cried. "How could such violence have been used by any woman?"

"How do you know that much violence has been used?— though there are women who are capable of as much violence as men. But, in this case, so far, there is nothing to show that much strength has been exerted. It is a question of what instrument has been employed. Obviously it is one of a most extraordinary and most deadly kind, and one which I should imagine would be as likely to be found in a woman's possession as a man's; indeed, I should say more likely, because I should expect to find a man preferring to trust to his own right hand. Let me tell you this, Ferguson. You are making a serious mistake in endeavouring to associate Philip Lawrence with this matter. I know him well. He is a man of high position and noble character; as incapable of such a deed as you. Indeed, I know him well enough to be aware that he is incapable; I have not sufficient knowledge of you to say, with certainty, of what you may be capable."

"Your language is quite unwarranted. I have made no endeavour of the kind."

"Are you perfectly candid? Are you sure that there is nothing at the back of your mind? My position here is quasi-official. It is my duty to ascertain how this man came to his death. Yet, while you refuse to answer my inquiries, questioning my right to make them, you volunteer some tittle-tattle about Philip Lawrence, and produce, with something very like a flourish of triumph, a collar with his name on, which, you say, you found upon the floor. I warn you again that, if you attempt to drag in Philip Lawrence's name, you will be guilty of a serious injustice, the consequences of which will inevitably recoil on your own head."

"Listen to me, Hume, in your turn. In the first place, I don't understand why you show me such an aggressive front. And, anyhow, you exaggerate the importance of your position. You merely happen to be the first doctor of whom I could think. Your business is to make a medical examination; so far, in that direction, I cannot say that I have seen you make any undue exertions. To suggest that your office is, in any sense, judicial, is sheer absurdity. We will stop at that. Some men would have regarded the questions which you have put to me as intentionally impertinent. I have enough acquaintance with you to know that it is your unfortunate manner which is to blame, and that your intention was innocuous.

"But let me add this: I know nothing of Mr. Philip Lawrence; I have never seen the man in my life. But, since he was seen to leave the building at an early hour this morning, in a somewhat curious fashion, exhibiting all the marks of haste; and since his brother has now been found here lying dead, I think, in spite of your ardent championship, he will be called upon to give some sort of explanation."

Why Hume behaved as he immediately did is beyond my comprehension. He came close up to me, looking me full in the face, in distinctly unfriendly fashion.

"Then I say you lie."

He said it quietly—it is not his custom to speak loudly—but he said it with unmistakable decision. While I was wondering whether or not I should knock the fellow down, Atkins came in with a policeman at his heels. It was time.

CHAPTER V

A CURIOUS CASE

I HAD only just returned to my own rooms when Mrs. Peddar appeared.

"The young lady is up, sir, and wishes to see you, if it would be quite convenient."

Her words, her tone, her manner, told me that the housekeeper had not yet heard of what had happened to the occupant of No. 64. Atkins had explained that he had experienced some difficulty in finding a constable, and, apparently, had said nothing of his errand to any one upon the way. The story of Edwin Lawrence's ending had not yet been told. I was not disposed to be the first to inform Mrs. Peddar.

"How is the young lady?" I asked.

"Well, sir, she seems all right, bodily, if I may say so, and she certainly has slept sound, and looks better than ever; but that there's something the matter with her mind, I feel sure."

"Have you found out her name, or anything about her?"

"No, sir, not a word. I looked at her linen when she was in bed, and it's marked 'E.M.'"

"'E.M.'?"

"Yes, sir, 'E.M.' And there's a purse in her pocket with eighteen shillings;[19] but that's all—no cards or anything. I was wondering if you wouldn't like Dr. Hume to see her. He's a clever gentleman, and might find out what's wrong with her; because, as I've said, that there's something wrong I'm sure."

I turned my back, being unwilling to let the woman see how strongly her reference to Hume had moved me. The idea that that man should have an opportunity to play any of the pranks, which he pretended were experiments, made in the interests of science, upon that helpless girl, made my blood boil.

"I don't think we will trouble Dr. Hume just yet, Mrs. Peddar."

"Very good, sir. I don't believe myself in doctors—not as a general rule; it's their bill they're thinking of, and not you, most of the time; but the young lady's seems such a curious case, and Dr. Hume has the reputation of being so clever, that I thought I'd just mention it."

"It's very kind of you, Mrs. Peddar. I cannot tell you how obliged I am to you for the interest you are taking in the matter; but then I know your good heart. Will you inform the young lady that I will come to her as soon as I have finished dressing?"

When I entered Mrs. Peddar's rooms the girl was standing by the window. As she turned to greet me I was positively startled by her loveliness. It filled me with a curious sense of exhilaration. Her face was illumined by that radiant smile which had struck me overnight as being one of her most striking characteristics. She extended both her hands.

"So it's you at last. I thought you were never coming."

"I have been detained, or I would have been here before. I hope you slept well, and that Mrs. Peddar's bed was as comfortable as she predicted."

"Slept! I seem to have slept all my cares away. Do you know, I think that something must have happened to me last night."

"What do you think it was?"

"That's just it—I can't think. I wonder if anything's the matter with my head."

"Perhaps you had some kind of a shock; try to remember."
She shook her head.

"I can't remember. And yet—I don't know. There's something in my head like a blot. It makes me feel so stupid."

"Can't you even remember your name?"

"No. I don't believe I have a name. Yet I suppose I ought to have a name, everybody does have a name; doesn't everybody have a name?"

She put this question with a little air of hesitation, as if she propounded a doubtful proposition.

"I should say so, as a general rule. It is rather an uncomfortable position for a young lady to be in—not to know her own name, nor the whereabouts of her home, nor who her friends are."

"Do you think so? Does it make me seem—silly?" She looked at me with a wistful expression, like a puzzled child. "I seem to remember people shouting; they were shouting at me. And clapping their hands—I can see them clapping their hands; then something happened."

"Where were the people—and why did they shout at you?"

"I can't think. I believe it's in my head somewhere, if I only knew where to find it; but I don't know where it is."

"Can't you remember what happened to you, and where you were just before you came to my room?"

"I remember coming through your window; I remember that quite well." A faint flush came to her cheeks. "But that is all. Everything seems to have begun then; nothing seems to have happened before."

I took a pair of white kid gloves out of my coat pocket.

"Are these your gloves?"

She eyed them askance.

"I don't know—are they? Where did you get them from?"

I did not care to tell her that I found them on a chair in the room in which Edwin Lawrence lay dead.

"You should know better than I, if they are yours."

"They may be—I can't tell. I'll try them on and see if they fit." She did try them on, and they did fit—to perfection. She held out her gloved hands. "They look as if they were mine—they must be; don't you think they are?"

"I have not a doubt that they are yours."

I turned my face away. A weight had become suddenly attached to my heart. There was a choking something in my throat. She was quick to perceive the alteration in my demeanour.

"Why do you turn your face away from me? Have I said or done anything wrong? Aren't the gloves mine?"

I replied to her with another question.

"Do you know any one named Lawrence?"

"Lawrence? Lawrence? I can't remember. Is it a woman's name?"

"No; it is not a woman's name, it's a man's name. Edwin Lawrence."

"Why do you ask? Do you know him?"

"I do; and so do you."

"I! How do you know I know him?"

"Because, last night, it was from his room you came to mine."

I regarded her with what quite possibly were accusatory glances; but if I expected my words to take her by surprise, or to cause her to betray signs of guilt, I was mistaken. She met my glances with serenely untroubled countenance, as if she were wondering what exactly my meaning might chance to be.

"I came to your room from his? What was I doing in his room?"

"Think! Try to think! You must remember what happened in Edwin Lawrence's room to cause you to fly through his window, taking refuge anyhow and anywhere."

"You say that I came from his room to yours; how did I come?"

"Along the balcony. You must have rushed through his window straight to mine; whether you tried other windows as you passed I cannot say. Perhaps mine was the first which you found open."

"Then his room is in this house?"

"Of course it is; it's on the same floor as mine."

"Then take me to it—now! At once! If I were to see the room, and to see Edwin Lawrence, it might all come back to me."

"Take you to see Edwin Lawrence?"

"Yes; why not?"

"Why should I not take you to see Edwin Lawrence? You know why!"

I gripped her roughly by the wrist. She gave a cry of pain. I loosed her, ashamed. She eyed me as if bewildered.

"Why did you take hold of me like that? You hurt me."

"You should not play with me."

"Play with you? I was not playing. I only asked you to take me to see this room, and this Edwin Lawrence, of whom you keep on speaking—that was all."

"Yes, that was all."

"Why do you look at me like that. You make me afraid of you. I thought you were my friend."

"How can I be your friend, to act a real friend's part, if you will not trust me?"

"Trust you? Don't I trust you? I thought I did."

She spoke like a child, and she was a lovely woman. I knew not what to make of her, what to answer. I had a hundred things to say, which, sooner or later, would have to be said. How was I to express them in words which would reach her understanding? Was she, naturally, mentally deficient? I could not believe it. Hers was not the face of an imbecile. Intellect, intelligence was writ large in every line. What then was the meaning of the cloud which had temporarily paralysed the active forces of her brain? Where was the key to the puzzle? As I hesitated she, coming closer, drawing up the sleeve of her dress, showed me her wrist, on which were the marks of my fingers.

"See how you have hurt me."

I was shocked; I had not supposed that I had used such force.

"I did not mean to do it—I beg your pardon. But this morning I'm afraid I am impatient; things have tried me."

"What things? Am I one of them? I am so sorry—please forgive me! I want you to be my friend, and more than my friend. You see how I am all alone."

"I see; I do see that."

The appeal which was in her eyes as they looked into mine stirred my pulses strangely. I know not what wild words were trembling on my lips; before they had a chance of getting spoken Mrs. Peddar put her head through the door and called to me—

"Mr. Ferguson, can I speak to you for a minute, please?"

I went to her at once. I perceived that the news had reached her. Her first words showed it.

"You have heard, sir, of the dreadful thing which has happened to Mr. Lawrence?"

"I have."

"From what I'm told"—we were in a small room which served her as a sort of ante-chamber; she looked about her furtively, as if she feared that walls had ears; the hand which she had laid upon my arm was trembling—"from what I'm told it seems that it must have been done just before the young lady—came—to your room."

"Such seems to be the case, from what I'm told."

"What shall we do?"

"At present, nothing. 'Sufficient,' Mrs. Peddar, 'unto the day is the evil thereof.'"[20]

"Do you think she knows?"

"Just now, I am sure that she does not."

She came closer, speaking almost in a whisper. Her lips were twitching. I have seldom seen a woman so disturbed.

"Do you think—she did it?"

"Mrs. Peddar! I have not yet found the key to the puzzle; but I am going to look for it, and I, or some one else, will find it soon. And of this I am certain now, that that child—she's little more than a child in years, and, at present, she's as helpless as any child could be—has had, of her own initiative, no hand or finger in this matter; she is as innocent, and as blameless, as you or I. She has suffered, but she has not sinned."

"I hope so, I am sure."

"Your hope is on a safe foundation. There is one thing which you might do—keep your own counsel. Don't tell all the world that you have a visitor; and, in particular, tell no one how that visitor came to you."

"I'd rather she never had come. I—I'm beginning to wish that I'd never taken her in."

"Don't say that, Mrs. Peddar. You will find that it was not the worst action of your life when you took that young girl, when she had just escaped, by the very skin of her teeth, unless I am mistaken—from things unspeakable, from the very gates of hell, under the shadow of your wing."

Mrs. Peddar shook her head and she sighed.

"Poor thing! Whatever happens, and I tremble when I think of what may be going to happen to her and to us, and to every one— poor young thing!"*

CHAPTER VI

THE DOCTOR ACCUSES

I FOUND it impossible to accept the conclusion to which it all pointed. I had locked the door of my bedroom, gone to the wardrobe, taken out that plum-coloured cloak. I had rolled it up as tightly as I could; the blood with which it was soaked, as it dried, had glued the folds together. I had difficulty in tearing it open. An undesirable garment it finally appeared as I spread it out in front of me upon the bed, discoloured, stiff as cardboard, creased with innumerable creases. And the stiffness was horrible. When one reflected with what it had been stiffened, and how, and when, and associated with the reflection that fair-faced girl, with truth in her voice and innocence in her eyes, one wondered.

That she had been in Edwin Lawrence's room at the very moment when the murder was taking place seemed clear. What had been her errand? What part had she played in the tragedy? Why, instead of giving an alarm, had she sought refuge in flight? In the answer to this latter question would, I felt persuaded, be found the key to the riddle. What she had witnessed had acted on her like a bolt from heaven; the shock of it had robbed her of her senses on the instant. With the scientific term which would describe her condition I was not acquainted; it was some sort of neurosis, involving, at least for the time, the entire loss of memory. If she could only describe what she had witnessed, her innocence would be established.

Such was my personal conviction; but, at present, it was my conviction only. The material evidence pointed the other way. Time pressed; danger threatened. If facts, as they were known to me, became known to others, an eager policeman, anxious to fasten guilt on some one, might arrest her on a capital charge. Apart from the question of contaminating hands, what might not be the effect, on one already in so pitiful a condition, of so hideous an accusation.

That she had witnessed something altogether out of the common way was plain. This had been no ordinary murder; the work of no everyday assassin. The presumption was that, taken wholly by surprise, she had seen enacted in front of her some spectacle of supreme horror; so close had she been standing as to have been actually drenched by the victim's blood. My vision—if it was a vision—might not have any legal value, but it was full of suggestion for me; and the impression was still strong upon me that some strange creature had been present in the room, by which the crime had been actually committed. I recalled Edgar Allan Poe's story of "The Murders in the Rue Morgue,"[21] in which the criminal was proved to have been a huge ape; but, though I had no notion what the creature I had really seen was, I was persuaded that it had had nothing in common with any member of the ape family.

In one respect my vision seemed to have fallen short. I had seen

Lawrence and his assailant; I had seen the whirling skirts—as, in this connection, I gazed at the plum-coloured cloak, I was conscious of an inward pang—I had heard the woman's laughter; but, though I had a clear recollection of looking around me, with a view of taking in the entire scene, I had seen no one else. Yet all the evidence went to show that, at any rate, two other persons had been present: my visitor of the night before, and the dead man's brother.

I will admit at once that I had little belief in the brother's guilt. I had heard something of Philip Lawrence; and, apart from the known integrity of the man's character, I could not conceive of any cause which could impel him to the commission of so unnatural a crime. Still, there was Turner's statement, quite unsuspiciously uttered, that he had seen him go up to his brother, and seen him come down again. As I had said to Hume, he would at least be called upon to explain.

But, as it seemed to me, what I had at present to ascertain was, what had been the nature of the errand which had taken a young girl, at that hour of the night, to Edwin Lawrence's chambers. And, as it chanced, I immediately came upon something which seemed to throw a light upon the matter. Turning over the cloak, with a view of returning it to its hiding-place—for I was aware that, at any moment, I might be interrupted, and I was resolved, at least until I saw my way more clearly, to keep the existence of so, apparently, criminatory a garment a secret locked in my own breast—I came upon a pocket in the green silk lining. There was something in it, which I took out.

It was an addressed envelope. The writing I instantly recognised; I had seen it on the scraps of paper which Hume had taken out of Lawrence's waste-paper basket. The envelope had been neither stamped nor posted. The address—it could hardly have been vaguer—was "George Withers, Esq., General Post-office, London." Without hesitation I tore the envelope open. I had reached a point at which I felt that, at any and every cost, I must get out of the darkness into the light.

The contents of the letter I give verbatim.

"DEAR TOM,
"I am going to see that scoundrel to-night. He had better take

care, or something will happen to him, of that I am sure. And he
will be sure before I have done with him. In any case, I'll write you
at length to-morrow."

                                                        "B."

Two points struck me about this odd epistle: it contained
neither a date nor an address, and, while "George Withers" was
on the envelope, the letter itself began "Dear Tom," the inference
being that "George Withers" was an assumed name, to which it
had been arranged that communications should be directed. The
"B." of the signature was, I had little doubt, the "Bessie" of the
scraps of paper; in which case the "E," which Mrs. Peddar had
discovered on the linen, stood for "Elizabeth." There still remained
the puzzle of the "M."

The letter had scarcely a reassuring effect. That the "scoundrel" alluded to was Lawrence, and that "to-night" was last night,
I thought was probable. If that were so, then it seemed that this
young girl had gone to Lawrence with anything but friendly intentions; and it was quite certain that something had happened to
him, as she had predicted. One could only hope that it was not the
something which she had in her mind's eye; and that, in any case,
she had had no hand in the happening. As a clue to the lady's identity the letter did not carry one much forwarder.

As I was wondering what was the next step which I should
take, a thought occurred to me—the photograph which I had
taken from Lawrence's mantelshelf. I had it in the pocket of my
coat. I took it out. It was an excellent likeness; the operator had
caught her in a characteristic pose, and made of her a really artistic
picture. But it was not with the likeness that I was at that moment
concerned. I looked at the back of the portrait, to see by whom it
had been taken. There was the name of one of the best London
photographers in London. Eureka! the thing was done. I had only
to go to the man's establishment to gain particulars of the original.
Surely, when he had been told the circumstances of the case, he
would not refuse to let me have them.

Filled with this idea I began to feverishly roll up the plum-
coloured cloak. As I did so there came a rapping at the door.

"Who's there?"

"I want to speak to you."

The voice was Hume's. Fortunately I had locked the door, or he would quite possibly have walked straight into the room.

"I will be with you directly."

I returned the cloak to the wardrobe, put the portrait into my pocket, and with it the letter, then went to Hume.

He stood with his back to the window, and his hands behind his back, regarding me, as I entered the room, with a keenness very like impertinence. There was something hawk-like in his attitude, as if he was ready to pounce on me the instant he could find an opening. I had never had much pleasure in the man's society; but this air of open resentment was new. It was as if out of Lawrence's murdered body there had come a malicious spirit, which had entered into him, and inspired him with a sudden and unreasoning desire to work me mischief. That he meant to be disagreeable his first words made plain. I immediately made up my mind that, to the best of my ability, his intention should be persistently ignored.

"No wonder, Ferguson, that you resented my inquiry as to the terms on which you parted last night with the dead man."

"Indeed? My dear chap, sit down. If you can manage it, don't wear quite such an air of gravity. This affair of poor Lawrence's seems to have affected you even more than it has me—which is odd."

"It is odd."

"Because I had always supposed that he was a more intimate acquaintance of mine than yours."

"Such seems to have been the case. How much did you owe him?"

"Owe him! Hume, you seem disposed to ask some very odd questions."

"You think so? When a person is suspected of a crime, the first thing one looks for is a motive; you understand?"

"I understand your bare words, but what is behind your bare words I do not understand."

"Presently you will. Before we part I will endeavour to make myself sufficiently plain. I repeat my question: How much did you owe him?"

"Nothing."

"You lie."

"Hume, that is the second time you have used such language to me this morning, and the second time I have refrained from knocking you down."

"That is true. Perhaps my turn will come to be knocked down. I am aware that you are the sort of person who, for less cause, will do much more than knock a man down." He inclined his head further towards me, his resemblance to a bird of prey becoming still more pronounced. "Ferguson, I'm a pathologist; a student of mental diseases.[22] As such I have regarded you for some time with growing interest. Unless I err you are the victim of a form of aberration which is not so unusual as some may suppose; you suffer from mnemonic intervals."[23]

"I have not the faintest notion what you mean."

Indeed, I was beginning to wonder if the doctor himself was not stark mad. He went on, in his quick, even tones, as if he were calculating what the effect of each word would be before he uttered it.

"If you were to kill me where I am standing, I believe that you would be capable of forgetting what you had done directly I was dead; and quite possibly the consciousness of your action might never visit you again. That is what I mean."

"Hume!"

For some cause his words seemed to penetrate to the very marrow of my bones, as if they had been daggers of ice.

"Now I will explain to you why I assert that, consciously or unconsciously, you lie in stating that you owed Edwin Lawrence nothing. You see this." He held out a small leather-covered volume, which was fastened by a lock. "I found it in his room after you had gone. It's a sort of diary—rather an unexpected volume for such a man to have—which statement is itself only another instance of the unwisdom of judging, on insufficient data, of the direction in which a man's tastes may be inclined. In it he appears to have made fairly regular entries, the last so lately as last night, after you had left him. Here it is:

"'Have been playing cards with Ferguson, and winning pretty heavily. Have long been conscious that F.'s an unusual type of man—dangerous. The sort you would rather not have a row with.

Felt it more than ever to-night; believe if he could have torn the heart clean out of me, without scandal, he would have done it then and there. A bad loser. He said some things, and looked more; as good as suggesting I had not played on the square. I did not break his head, but, though I only laughed, I did not love him any the more. It's eighteen hundred and eighty that he owes me. I suspect it will be like drawing his eye-teeth; but I'll have it. The money will be useful.'

"That is the last entry he made in his diary. He must have been killed before the ink had long been dry. It suggests the terms on which you parted. What have you to say to it? Do you still assert that you owed him nothing?"

I had listened to Hume's readings with feelings which I am unable to describe. In the rush of events I had, for the moment, forgotten the game of cards which we had played together. It was not pleasant to have it recalled in such a fashion, by such a man. The falsity of the conclusions which he drew from my temporary forgetfulness stung me not a little.

"I do still assert that I owed him nothing. One minute; let me finish. But the eighteen hundred and eighty pounds which I should have given to Edwin Lawrence will now be handed over to his estate."

"True. As he correctly perceived, you are an unusual type of man. Ferguson, you and I are alone together. What I am about to say will be said without prejudice. I shall not whisper a hint of it abroad without good and sufficient ground to go upon, but I tell you now, quite frankly, that it is my opinion that you used some means—what they were I do not pretend at present to under-stand—to compass Edwin Lawrence's death."

"Hume!"

"I know that you were in his room when he was being killed."

"You know that I was in his room!"

"I suspected it at first. Now I know it. I will tell you how. A girl, one of the servants of the place, just stopped me to say that, at an early hour this morning—so far as I can judge, within five minutes of the commission of the murder—she saw you running along the corridor, from Lawrence's room towards your own, as if you were flying for your life. My own impression is that you were flying from the life which you had taken."

"Hume! Some one saw me in the corridor! Who was it?"

"At this moment, never mind. The woman will be produced in due course. She says that the perspiration was pouring down your cheeks; which seems odd, considering that the morning was chilly, that you are not of a plethoric habit,[24] and that you were clad only in your pyjamas."

It was with difficulty that I retained my self-control. Was it possible that it had not been a vision after all, but that I had been the actual spectator of that awful tragedy?

As I was endeavouring to arrange in my mind the new aspect of the case suggested by Hume's words, the door opened and a man came in.

"Is one of you two gentlemen Mr. Ferguson?"

"I am."

"Then you're the gentleman they've sent me to as being Mr. Edwin's friend. The Lord forgive me, but I believe that my poor master's murdered him!"

CHAPTER VII

THE SUSPICIONS OF MR. MORLEY

THE newcomer was a man apparently about sixty years of age, short, and grey-haired, with old-fashioned, neatly-trimmed side whiskers. He was dressed entirely in black, even to black kid gloves; his hat he carried in his hand. He seemed to be in a state of considerable agitation, and stood looking from one to the other of us as if he was endeavouring to make up his mind as to who or what we were. Hume recognized him at once. He went striding towards him from across the room.

"Morley, you had better come with me. It is to me you wish to speak, not to this gentleman."

I interposed.

"He asked for Mr. Ferguson. I am Mr. Ferguson. It therefore seems that it is to me that he wishes to speak."

"Don't talk nonsense! You're a stranger to him; I tell you it's a mistake. You know me, Morley, don't you?"

The old gentleman looked at Hume with eyes which seemed half dazed.

"Yes, sir; oh yes. You're Dr. Hume. I know you very well."

"You hear? Stand aside!"

"I shall not stand aside. And, Hume, take my strong advice and don't attempt to interfere with any visitor of mine. You hear me?"

"I hear, but I shall not pay the least attention. Morley, I forbid you to say a word in this gentleman's presence. You have no right to speak of your master's private affairs in the presence of strangers. I am his friend; I will safeguard his interests. I tell you that by not keeping a strict watch over your tongue you may do him a serious mischief."

"Very good, Hume. Evidently to remonstrate with you is to waste one's breath. I will try another way." Taking him up in my arms I carried him towards the door. "I am going to put you outside my room, and, before you attempt to enter it again, I trust that you will have learnt at least the rudiments of decent manners. Out you go!"

And out he went. Depositing him on the floor in the corridor, I locked the door in his face. He banged against it with his fist.

"You shall pay for this!"

"Very good; render your account. I will render you such moneys as are due."

"Morley, I forbid you to say a word to him at your peril."

I turned to my visitor.

"I beg, Mr. Morley, that you will take a seat. Pray do not heed our excitable friend. Just now he can hardly be said to have the full control of his senses—as you yourself perceive. As you remarked, I am John Ferguson, the friend of Mr. Edwin Lawrence. You, I take it, are in the service of his brother, Mr. Philip."

Mr. Morley's calmness had not perceptibly increased. He seemed impressed by the way in which I had handled Hume; and, also, disposed to be influenced by the doctor's express commands to hold his tongue; he was like a man between two stools.

"Yes, sir, I'm in Mr. Philip's service; but I think that perhaps the doctor's right, and I oughtn't to talk about my master."

"Possibly, Mr. Morley; but you have spoken of him already. You have accused him of murder."

"No, sir, not that!"

"Just now, in the presence of Dr. Hume and myself, you expressed your belief that Mr. Philip had killed Mr. Edwin."

"Oh no, sir, not that; I didn't go so far as that. I didn't mean it if I did."

"What you meant is another question; that is what you said. I may tell you, Mr. Morley, that I am not of your opinion. I do not believe that Mr. Philip had any hand whatever in his brother's death."

"No, sir? I—I'm glad to hear it."

"Very soon you will receive from his own lips an explanation which will blow all your doubts away. I believe that he will clear the whole thing up at once, if you will take me to him."

Mr. Morley's jaw dropped open.

"Take you to him? But that—that's just it. I don't know where he is. Isn't he—here?"

He looked about him as if he half expected to discover Philip Lawrence hidden behind a curtain or under a table.

"Do I understand you to mean that your master has not returned all night?"

"Yes, sir; that's what I do mean, and that's what makes me so— concerned. He's a gentleman of regular habits—most regular; and I've never known him to stop out all night before without giving me warning."

I felt that, in that case, he must indeed be a gentleman of most regular habits.

"Where does Mr. Philip Lawrence live?"

"In Arlington Street;²⁵ that's his London address."

"When did he go out?"

"After midnight, in—in a towering rage."

"In a towering rage? With whom?"

"Well, sir,"—Mr. Morley came closer; he cast an anxious glance around him; he dropped his voice—"I'm not a talkative man, not as a rule, as any one who knows me will tell you; but I've got something to say which I feel I must say to some one, though you heard what Dr. Hume said. But, perhaps, sir, as you're Mr. Edwin's friend, you're Mr. Philip's too."

"Mr. Morley, in making any statement to me, you will be at least as safe as if you made it to Dr. Hume. I tell you that I believe your master's hands are clean. To prove it, we shall have to establish the truth. If you have anything to say which will go to make the darkness light, say it, like a man, before it's too late."

"You won't use it to do him a disservice? And you won't say that I talked about him in a way I didn't ought to have done?"

"I will do neither of these things."

"Well, sir, I like your looks; you look like the kind of gentleman one can trust, and I flatter myself I'm a pretty good judge of faces; and—and the way you handled Dr. Hume was"—he coughed behind his hand—"queer.[26] I'll make a clean breast of it."

The old gentleman's hesitation had its amusing side; I was conscious that something very unusual had happened to throw him, to such a degree, off his mental balance.

"That's right, Mr. Morley; we shall soon arrive at an understanding if we are frank with one another. Sit down."

He sat down on the edge of a chair. His hat he placed beside him on the floor, crown uppermost.

"Well, sir"—with his gloved fingers he stroked his chin, still regarding me with an air of dubitation—"I'm afraid that Mr. Edwin was not all that he ought to have been."

"I am afraid that something similar could be said of all of us."

"It was in money matters chiefly, though there were other things as well; but in money matters he was most irregular—quite unlike Mr. Philip. Mr. Philip has let him have thousands and thousands of pounds; what he did with it was a mystery. They quarrelled dreadfully."

"Brothers will quarrel, Mr. Morley. It's a way they have."

The old gentleman shook his head.

"Ah, but the fault was Mr. Edwin's. Mr. Philip is hot-tempered, but Mr. Edwin was always in the wrong."

Leaning towards me, Mr. Morley whispered, under cover of his hand, "Once Mr. Philip thrashed him—broke his stick across his back, he did; Mr. Edwin must have been black and blue with bruises. Mr. Philip's very quick when he's roused, and he's a better man than his brother. He was very sorry afterwards for what he had done—dear me! how sorry he was. He went to his brother and he asked him to forgive him, and Mr. Edwin did forgive him; I expect he got a good deal more money out of Mr. Philip, or he never would have done. He was unforgiving enough, was Mr. Edwin, unless it paid him to be otherwise; he'd wait for years for a chance of returning, with good thumping interest, what he thought was an injury; it was the only thing he ever did return with interest."

The expression on Mr. Morley's face as he said this did not itself suggest the charity which forgiveth all things.[27]

"So it went on, for soon they were quarrelling again. But lately it has been worse than ever."

Looking anxiously about him, Mr. Morley again resorted to the cover of his hand.

"There's been—there's been some trouble about some bills.[28] Mr. Edwin's been putting some bills on the market which weren't quite what they ought to have been, and getting money on them. I'm afraid he's been making an unauthorized use of his brother's name."

"Are you sure of what you say? At this point it is for me to follow Dr. Hume's lead and warn you to be careful."

"Oh, I'm sure enough. I've too much reason to be sure. Forgery, sir; that's what it was, rank forgery. In his rage Mr. Philip let it all come out, so that there's plenty of others who know of it, or I shouldn't be speaking of it now. Mr. Philip has gone on dreadfully since he found it out. I've sometimes wondered if he was going mad.

"Yesterday afternoon Mr. Edwin came to Arlington Street; there was an awful scene. I went into them; I didn't think they'd come to blows in front of me. Then Mr. Philip began at me. 'Morley,' he said, shouting so that you might have heard him in Pall Mall,[29] 'my brother's a thief! That's no news, you've heard it before; but he's been robbing me again, on fresh lines, and he'll keep on robbing me until, in spite of all I can do, he'll succeed in dragging an honoured name through the mire. But before then, Morley, I'll kill him, for the cur he is. If he's found with his neck broken you'll know who did it.'

"Then he turned to Mr. Edwin. 'So you've had fair warning.

And now, you blackguard, out of this house you go before I throw you through the window.' And out he did go, and it was about time he did, or I believe Mr. Philip would have thrown him through the window."

Mr. Morley passed a red silk handkerchief carefully to and fro across his brow. I thought of how Edwin Lawrence and I had spent the previous evening. He certainly had not worn his troubles where others could see them; he was generally something of a cynic, but I did not remember to have seen him more genially inclined, or apparently in a more careless mood. The man, as limned by Mr. Morley, was to me an entire revelation.

The old gentleman went on. "In the evening, about nine o'clock, some one came to see Mr. Philip. He was a big, portly party, very well dressed, with shiny black hair, and I noticed that his fingers were covered with rings. I set him down for a Jew.[30] He wouldn't give his name, and when I told him Mr. Philip wasn't in, he said he'd call again. He came again, about eleven. Mr. Philip hadn't returned; so he gave me a letter, and told me to give it to him directly he did. It was just past twelve when Mr. Philip did come in. I gave him the letter, though I was in two minds as to whether I hadn't better keep it till the morning, for I smelt that there was mischief in it; and now I wish I had, for directly he opened it Mr. Philip broke into the worst rage I ever saw him in. He was like a man stark mad. 'That brother of mine,' he screamed, 'is a more infernal scoundrel even than I thought he was; I'll kill him if I can find him!' And he tore out of the house before I could move to stop him."

Again the red silk handkerchief went across Mr. Morley's forehead. The mere recollection of the scene bedewed his brow with sweat.

"Well, sir, I sat up for him all night, and my wife, she sat up to keep me company; but he never came home. We listened to every sound, and we jumped at every footstep that came near the house, thinking it was him. Emma—that's Mrs. Morley—kept on snivelling pretty nearly all the time. 'Joe,' she kept on saying— my name's Joe, sir, leastways Joseph—'Joe, do you think that Mr. Philip's killing him?'

"To be asked such a question made one feel like killing her; for it was the very question which I kept putting to myself all through the night. My feeling was that Mr. Philip had been drinking more than he was used to, and that letter found him in an evil mood; and when he's in one of his rages he's not the good, kind-hearted, fair-minded gentleman he generally is, he's more like a raving lunatic,[31] although I say it, and capable of anything.

"When morning came, and there were still no signs of him, I couldn't stand it any longer. So I came round to see Mr. Edwin, and directly I came they told me he had been murdered. Murdered! Murdered!" He repeated the word again and again, as if he found a ghastly pleasure in the repetition.

I paced up and down, pondering the tale as he had told it. I perceived how, from his point of view, the case looked black against his master. Yet still I felt persuaded that there was something in the whole business which was beyond our comprehension, and that, when we learned what that something was, it would be conclusively shown that the deductions which he drew were erroneous.

"Do you think that Mr. Philip killed him?"

"No, Morley, I do not. But I think that, if you get a chance, you'll hang him."

"Hang Mr. Philip? Me? No, not—not if he'd killed Mr. Edwin a dozen times over."

"On the contrary, if you don't take care, you'll hang him, although he hasn't killed Mr. Edwin even once. If they were to put you into the witness-box, and you were to tell that tale, your evidence would need but the slenderest corroboration to send him to the gallows right away."

"Mr. Ferguson!"

"Morley, you must know that you had not the slightest right to tell me what you have done. Fortunately your information has been imparted to a person who will not make an injurious use of it; but, if you take my serious advice, you will not breathe a word of it to any other living soul. You will go straight home, and you will say nothing to any one; and you will know nothing either."

"But—but where is Mr. Philip, sir?"

"What business is that of yours? I take it that he is free to regulate his movements without consulting you. Whatever concern you may feel, you will not allow a hint of it to escape you—that is, if you have your master's interests at heart!"

There came an imperious rapping at the door.

"Who's there?"

"It's I—Inspector Symonds, of the Criminal Investigation Department. Be so good, Mr. Ferguson, as to open the door."

"There, Morley, is some one who will be glad to listen to what you have been telling me, but if you have the least regard for your master's reputation, not to mention his neck, you will see him further first. You're not forced to speak a word unless you choose; I shouldn't choose; and here's something to help you not to choose."

I handed him a wine-glass full of brandy. He swallowed it so fast that it set him coughing. There came the knocking at the door again.

"Open this door, Mr. Ferguson!"

"With pleasure. You seem to be in a hurry, sir. Possibly you are not aware that these rooms are private, and that it is not necessary that I should open to every person who takes it into his head to knock."

As, opening the door, I planted myself in the doorway, Mr. Symonds looked at me as if surprised. He was not a little man, but I was a good head taller, and I fancy that he had not expected to find me quite so big, or he would have hustled past me. As it was, he refrained.

"I am informed that you have some one in your rooms who can give important information in the matter of Mr. Edwin Lawrence's murder."

"Indeed. Who is your informant?"

"I am. You will find, Ferguson, that you cannot play with edged tools."

Hume was the speaker.

"So? Pray enter, Mr. Symonds." Hume tried to pass in after him. "If you don't mind, I would rather not. I think that edged tools are better outside."

I shut the door in his face; he taking my cavalier treatment of him more meekly than he was wont to do. Perhaps he remembered.

Mr. Symonds immediately assailed the lamblike Mr. Morley.

"I believe that your name is Morley; and that you are in the service of Mr. Philip Lawrence. What information have you to give with reference to the murder of his brother?"

"Mr. Morley has no information to give."

It was I who answered.

"Let Mr. Morley speak for himself."

"Permit me to repeat, Mr. Symonds, that these premises are private; and before I allow you, on these premises, to bully a guest of mine, I must request you to show me the authority on which you are acting."

Inspector Symonds looked me up and down, as if he did not know exactly what to make of me. He seemed to hesitate.*

CHAPTER VIII

THE RECOGNITION OF THE PHOTOGRAPH

WHEN I had succeeded in extricating Mr. Morley from the clutches of Inspector Symonds, after a considerable wordy warfare, during which I had difficulty in keeping the inspector's language within parliamentary bounds, I started on a little errand of my own.

The inspector appeared to be under the impression that, for some malevolent reason, I wished to interfere with the due and proper execution of the law; and he told me, quite frankly, that so soon as Mr. Morley was off my premises he would bring, not only the old gentleman, but, so far as I understood, myself also, to book. Therefore, feeling that, under such circumstances, two might be better than one, so soon as the interview was ended, I proceeded, since his way was mine, to escort Mr. Morley at least part of his way home.

The old gentleman was in a condition of great mental perturbation. He was sorry, for his master's sake, that he had said as much as he had done to the inspector, and he was also sorry, for his own sake, that he had not said more; for he was uncomfortably conscious that, by his comparative reticence, he had incurred the officer's resentment.

"Do you think, sir," he said, as we were parting—and I thought, as he was speaking, how old he seemed and tremulous—"that that Mr. Symonds will hunt me up, and worry me, as he as good as said he would? Because I know that I shan't be able to stand it, if he does; my nerves are not what they were, and I never dreamed that I should have trouble with the police at my time of life."

I endeavoured to reassure him.

"Mr. Morley, be at ease; fear nothing. You are the sole proprietor of your own tongue, use it to preserve silence; no one can force you to speak unless you choose."

I was not by any means so sure of this, in my own mind; but this was a detail. My object was to comfort Mr. Morley.

It was at the door of the house in Arlington Street that we parted; after all, I went with him the whole way—it was practically mine. I waited while he inquired if his master had returned. The face of the old lady who opened the door, and who I immediately concluded was Mrs. Morley, was answer enough; she looked as if she bore all the trouble of the world upon her shoulders. He had not; nothing had been seen or heard of him.

The point at which I was aiming was the photographer's. As I walked away from Philip Lawrence's house, I could not but feel conscious that every moment he remained absent made the case look blacker. What reason could he have to stay away, save one?

An assistant came forward to greet me, as I crossed the threshold of the building which housed that famous firm of photographers.

"I want you to tell me who is the original of one of your portraits."

"We don't, as a rule, sir, give the names of sitters, without their express permission."

"This is one of the exceptions to the rule. Here is the portrait—who is the lady it represents?"

I handed him the photograph which I had taken off Edwin Lawrence's mantelshelf. So soon as he saw it he smiled; looking up at me with what was suspiciously like a twinkle in his eye.

"As you say, this is one of the exceptions to the rule. I certainly have no objection to tell you who this lady is; that is, if you don't know already. In which case I should imagine that you are one of the few persons in London who does not."

"What on earth do you mean? Who is the lady?"

"You are not a theatre-goer, sir?"

"Why do you say that? I suppose I go to the theatres as often as other people."

"You haven't been to the Pandora[32] lately."

"The Pandora? I've been there three times within the last month or so."

"Then, on the occasion of your visits was Miss Bessie Moore not acting?"

"Miss Bessie Moore!"

"This is the portrait of Miss Bessie Moore, and an excellent likeness, too. She has honoured us several times with sittings, and this is about the most favourable result we have had so far. It is not easy to do justice to the lady."

Bessie Moore! The assistant was a much smaller man than I; but if, at that moment, he had given me a push, though ever such a gentle one, I believe he would have pushed me over. What an idiot I had been! No wonder that her face had seemed familiar. Bessie Moore—admittedly one of the loveliest women in town, whose name was on every tongue, who was honoured by all the world! At that moment her acting was drawing all London to the Pandora Theatre. I had seen something of theatres, whatever that assistant might suppose to the contrary, but I had never before seen such acting as hers, nor had I ever seen so lovely a woman! And it was Bessie Moore who had come through my bedroom window, at dead of night, in that plum-coloured cloak. Every moment the wonder grew.

Either the expression of my face or something else about me appeared to afford that assistant considerable amusement. In the midst of my bewilderment I was conscious that he grinned.

"You look surprised," he said.

"It is possible for persons of even ripened years to feel surprised, as you will discover when you yourself attain to years of discretion."

I fancy that it was my intention to crush that smiling youngster, though I suspect that the result of my little effort was only to increase my appearance of imbecility. At any rate, his grin did not grow less. I proceeded with my inquiries.

"What is Miss Moore's address?"

"The Pandora Theatre."

"Thank you; I am aware of that. It is her private address which I require."

"That, I am afraid, we cannot give you."

No doubt they were pestered with similar inquiries by individuals who were more or less idiots, and altogether impertinent; and, quite possibly, he took me for a member of that considerable family. I gave him my card.

"There is my name. The lady who is the original of that portrait has met with an accident. I did not know that she was Miss Moore until you told me, but it is important that I should be able to communicate with her friends at once."

"An accident? I am sorry to hear that Miss Moore has met with an accident. If you will wait a moment I will make inquiries."

The assistant disappeared; presently returning with an older man, who examined my card as he came. He addressed me:

"You are Mr. Ferguson?"

"I am."

"You say that Miss Moore has met with an accident?"

"I do."

"What is its nature?"

"That I am not at liberty to tell you. I can only say that it is of the first importance that I should be able to communicate with her friends without delay."

He hesitated, considering me attentively; then he gave me the information I required.

"Miss Moore lives with Miss Adair, who, as you perhaps know, is also acting at the Pandora Theatre. The address is 22, Hailsham Road, The Boltons, Brompton."[33]

As I sped towards Brompton in a hansom, I tried to assimilate the tidings I had just received. In vain. It may be that I am dull-witted, and that my mental processes are slow; but the more I sought the solution of the puzzle the more insoluble it seemed. It did appear incredible that the woman who had all the world, like a ball, at her feet, with whose fame London was ringing, should have come to me, at such an hour, in such a fashion, from such a scene. The mystery was beyond my finding out.

Hailsham Road proved to be a nice, wide, clean, old-fashioned street, and No. 22 a nice, clean, old-fashioned house. It was not large, but the impression which its exterior made upon me was a distinctly pleasant one. It was detached; it stood back, behind railings, at a little distance from the pavement; in the sunshine it looked as white as snow; there was a flower-bed in front, and flowers made the window-sills resplendent. My ring was answered, on the instant, by a maid who was quite in keeping with the house; she was unmistakably neat, and I have no hesitation in affirming she was pretty.

"Can I see Miss Adair? I have brought news of Miss Moore."

The maid left me in the hall—it was the daintiest hall I remembered to have seen, and very prettily papered—while she conveyed my message up the stairs.

It appeared that I could see Miss Adair; for, presently, a lady came flying down the stairs, about seven steps at a time, and all but flung herself into my arms.

"You've brought me news of Bessie? Oh, I am so glad! I've been half-beside myself; I haven't slept a wink all night. I was really just wondering if I hadn't better communicate with the police. Oh, please will you step in there?"

I stepped in there. "There" was a sitting-room. From the wall looked down on me, as I entered, a life-size portrait of my visitor of the plum-coloured cloak. The face was turned directly towards me; the eyes seemed to be subjecting me to a serious examination. I did not care to meet them; in their presence I was conscious of a vague discomfort. The atmosphere was redolent of a feminine personality. On every hand were the owner's little treasures. I pictured her flitting here and there among them, touching this, altering the position of that, dumbly inquiring of me all the time, with, in her air, a touch of resentment, what I did in her apartment.

Miss Adair perceived that I was not so ready with my tongue as I might have been. There was a sharp note of anxiety in her voice.

"There's nothing wrong with Bessie, is there?"

I stammered, like an ass, "I—I'm afraid there is."

"She's not—dead?"

"Dead! Good gracious, no! Nothing of the kind."

"Then what has happened to her? Tell me! Quick! Don't you see that I'm on tenterhooks?"

"First of all let me be certain of my ground. I take it that that is Miss Moore."

I handed her the, by this time, historical photograph.

"Of course it is. What do you mean by asking? Where is she? Who are you? What have you done to her? Don't stand there as if you were afraid to open your mouth!"

"The truth is, Miss Adair, that I am rather at a loss for words with which to express myself. But, if you will bear with me, I will endeavour to make myself as plain as I can; it is rather a difficult task which I have to perform."

It was a difficult task, nor was it made easier by the two shrewd eyes which were regarding me as if I were some curious and unnecessary kind of creature.

CHAPTER IX

THE REVELATIONS OF "MR. GEORGE WITHERS"

MISS ADAIR was a tall, commandingly built young woman, with about her more than a suggestion of muscularity. I had recognized her at once. On the stage she was accustomed to play the part of the dashing adventuress; the sort of person who could not, under any possible circumstances, be put down. I realized that she might be disposed to carry something of her stage manner into actual life. She confronted me as if I were some despised, but lifelong enemy, whose attacks she was prepared to resist at every point.

"When are you going to tell me what has happened to Bessie? In the first place, where is she?"

"She's at Imperial Mansions."

"What's she doing there?"

"She's in charge of the housekeeper—Mrs. Peddar."

"In charge! What do you mean?"

"Miss Moore is not—not herself."

"You men have been playing some trick on her. You shall pay for it dearly if you have!"

I caught her by the arm; she evincing a strong inclination to rush off to Imperial Mansions there and then.

"Miss Moore came through my bedroom window, at an early hour this morning, in—a curious condition."

"Your bedroom window! This morning! She must have been in a curious condition!"

"A man was murdered in the building about the same time that she appeared at the window. His set of chambers are on the same floor as mine; they communicate by the balcony along which she came. When she entered the cloak she wore was soaked in blood, and her hands were wet with it."

Miss Adair drew back, staring at me with distended eyes.

"Man! Are you a man, or are you a devil? Do you dare to hint that Bessie, my Bessie Moore, could by any possibility be guilty of murder!"

"I simply state to you the facts. That she was in the dead man's room there is irrefutable evidence to show; that she had anything to do with his murder I do not for a moment believe—I am as convinced of her innocence as you can be. My theory is that she was an unwilling witness of what took place, and that the horror of it temporarily unhinged her brain."

"Is she—mad?"

"No; but she suffers from entire loss of memory. Her life might have commenced with her entrance through my window; she can remember nothing of what occurred before, not even her own name. I believe that if she could be brought to recall what she actually saw take place, her innocence would be at once made plain."

"What is the name of the man who was—murdered?" I told her. "Lawrence? Edwin Lawrence? I don't remember ever having heard the name."

"She said nothing to you last night about having an appointment with him? Or with any one?"

She hesitated.

"Are you—Bessie's friend?"

"I am. At least, I hope I may call myself her friend, although I never spoke to her before last night. I do not think that there is anything which I would not do to save her from misconstruction."

She eyed me—quizzically.

"I think I'll trust you, Mr. Ferguson, though I never trusted a man yet without regretting it. I hope you won't feel hurt, but there is something about you which reminds me of a St. Bernard.[34] You're big—very big; you look strong—awfully strong; you're hairy." I involuntarily put my hand up to my beard. "Oh, I don't mean that you're too hairy, the beard's becoming; but you are hairy. You look simple; somehow one associates simplicity with trustworthiness; and now you're blushing." She would have made any one blush! "The blush settles it; I will repose my confidence in you, as I have done in others!"

Her manner changed; she became serious.

"The truth is that last night Bessie did seem worried, frightfully worried; and that's what's been worrying me. She was not like her usual self a bit; I couldn't make her out at all. I hadn't the faintest notion what was wrong; when I asked her if she was ill she snapped my head off. And for Bessie to be snappish was an unheard-of thing; her temper's not like mine, always going off, she's the gentlest, sweetest soul. She dressed herself, and walked out of the theatre, without saying a word to me; I only ran against her in the street, by accident, just as she was getting into a cab.

"I said, 'Bessie, aren't you coming home with me?'—because we always do come home together. But she answered, quite huffishly, that she was not—she had an appointment to keep. I did not dare to ask with whom, or where; though it did seem odd that she should have made an appointment, at that hour of the night, without saying a word of it to me; but I did venture to inquire when I might expect her to return. Leaning her head out of the cab, just as it was starting, she called out to me, 'Perhaps never.' I didn't suppose that she was entirely in earnest, but somehow I couldn't help feeling that, about the answer, there was something which might turn out to be unpleasantly prophetic."

"One thing is plain, Miss Adair, you must come with me at once to Imperial Mansions. Your presence may restore to your friend her memory. But, whether or not, you must bring her home, or at any rate you must take her away from the Mansions, and that immediately."

"Your manner, Mr. Ferguson, is autocratic. You don't ask me, you command; but I'll obey. That is, if you'll condescend to wait while I put a hat on."

She went upstairs. Almost immediately she had done so there came a ring at the front door. The door was opened and shut again. After it had been shut, Miss Adair called down the stairs:

"Ellen, who was that?"

The maid's voice replied, "It was some one who wished to see Miss Moore. He said his name was Withers—Mr. George Withers."

"George Withers!" I shouted.

Without a moment's hesitation I rushed out of the sitting-room, flung open the front door, and dashed into the street. I dare say that Ellen, and Miss Adair, too, thought that I had suddenly become a raving lunatic. But Ellen's mention of the caller's name recalled to me the fact that the peculiar letter which I had found in the pocket of the plum-coloured cloak had been addressed to "George Withers."

A young man was going down the street, walking rather quickly. I shouted to him.

"Hallo! Mr. George Withers!"

He stopped and turned with something of a start; then stared, as if uncertain what to make of me or what to do. I called to him again.

"I want you!"

As I spoke I moved towards him, intending, since he seemed indisposed to come to me, to go to him and then explain. But no sooner had I started than he swung round on his heels, tore off at full speed, and, before I realised what it was that he was doing, had vanished round the corner. Although I was unable to guess why he should run away from me as if I were the plague, I had no intention, if I could help it, of being run away from; so, as hard as I could pelt, I went after him.

It was a lively chase while it lasted; I must have presented an elegant figure as, hatless, my coat tails flying, I raced through those respectable streets. Fortunately, he was no match for me in pace; I had him before he reached the Fulham Road.[35] He must have been in shocking condition, for he had already run himself right out, and, gasping for breath, was panting like a blown rabbit.

Saying nothing—I felt that that was not the place in which to carry on the sort of conversation I had in my mind's eye—I took him by the shoulder and marched him back again. He, on his part, was equally mute, and made not the slightest effort at resistance. Miss Adair received us at the door.

"What on earth is the matter? Where have you been? And who is this man?"

Her trick of speaking in italics reminded me of her manner on the stage. I led my companion into the sitting-room. There I introduced him.

"This is Mr. George Withers. I fancy he can give us information on a subject on which, at this moment, information is very much needed."

"Mr. George Withers" was a mere youth, scarcely more than a boy. I was not prepossessed by his appearance, though he was well dressed and had a handsome face. He had proved himself a cur; I felt sure that he was a sneak, and perhaps something worse as well. I handed him the letter which I had taken from the lady's pocket.

"I believe, Mr. Withers, that this letter is for you."

He seemed at first reluctant to take it, as if fearful that it contained something which might disturb his peace of mind. He eyed it doubtfully; read the address; perceived that the envelope had been opened. A disagreeable look came upon his handsome countenance; he turned on me with a snarl.

"Who are you? What do you mean by treating me as you have done? And how dare you open a letter that's addressed to me?"

"First read your letter, Mr. Withers. Put your questions afterwards."

He scanned the brief epistle with looks which did not improve as he went on. Then he snapped at me as if he would have liked to bite as well.

"You stole it; you must have stolen it! I've half a mind to give you in charge; you don't know what mischief you mayn't have done."

"Is the person alluded to as 'that scoundrel' in the letter which you are holding Mr. Edwin Lawrence of Imperial Mansions?"

"What do you want to know for? What do you mean by meddling in my affairs? What business is it of yours?"

"Because, if it is, Mr. Edwin Lawrence is dead."

"Dead!"

"He was murdered last night."

"Murdered!" The fashion of his countenance changed. "Then she—she killed him."

He staggered back till he staggered against a chair. A pitiful object he presented as he perched himself upon the edge. Neither

Miss Adair nor I said a word. After a moment's interval, during which the muscles of his face twitched as if he had become suddenly possessed with St. Vitus' Dance,[36] he went rambling on, apparently not altogether conscious of what it was that he was saying.

"I knew there'd be mischief—I knew there would. I said if she would meddle in my affairs she'd make a mess of it. I told her she didn't know what she was going in for, that he was dangerous. But she's as obstinate as a mule; she never would take my advice, never!"

"Which shows that she is a lady of considerable discretion. What connection, Mr. Withers, have you with Miss Moore?"

He started forward on the chair, casting a frightened look about him.

"Is she—taken? And are you a policeman?"

"No, I am not a policeman; I have not that honour. And she is not taken—as yet. I repeat my inquiry. What connection, Mr. Withers, have you with Miss Moore?"

"Never mind! That's my business, not yours. She's got into this mess by herself, and she must get out of it by herself; I wash my hands of her. I've got an appointment which I must keep. You let me go."

He got up with a little air of bluster which was pitiful; it was such a poor attempt at make-believe.

"Listen to me, Mr. Withers—correct me if I am wrong; but you seem to be a nice young man—a very nice young man. And it's because you're such a very nice young man, always attending, Mr. Withers, your correction, that I desire to inform you that if you don't answer my questions, as truthfully as your nature will allow you, there'll be trouble. You understand? Trouble. So be so good as to tell me at once what there can possibly be in common between a lady of Miss Moore's class and a person of yours?"

"'Yours' is good. I don't see what difference there can be between our classes, considering that she's my sister."

Miss Adair interposed.

"Your sister? Bessie's your sister. Then you're Tom Moore, her vagabond of a brother, who's robbed her of hundreds and hundreds of pounds. I thought I knew your face, it's like a bad copy of

Bessie's, with all her goodness left out and your own wickedness put in.[37] You ungrateful scamp, to speak of her in that cold-blooded manner, when she has done all that she possibly could for you, and you, in return, have been to her the one trouble of her life."

He confronted the frank-spoken lady with looks which were alive with impudence. I perceived that he was a better match for a woman than a man.

"I know who you are; you call yourself 'Miss Adair.' 'Adair!' Go on! Sure that's your proper name? I know more about you than you perhaps think. And for Bessie to let out things to you about me shows the sort she is; telling a pack of lies about her only relative."

"Her only relative! It's her misfortune that she has you."

"Oh, that's it, is it? Then from this day forward she hasn't got me; tell her so, with my kind regards. As I've said already, I wash my hands of her; I cut the relationship. Willingly I'll never own to bearing her name again. It's not a name I ever have been particularly proud of, and now it's one of which I shall have less cause to be proud than ever, from what I'm told. Good-day to you, Miss Adair!"

He was now actually marching from the room. I had to give him a gentle hint in order to detain him. He winced under my touch like a hound which fears punishment.

"What was the nature of your business, Mr. Moore, which took your sister last night to Mr. Edwin Lawrence?"

"That's my business; it's none of yours."

"Answer my question."

He actually whimpered. It was beginning to dawn on me that I might be constrained to wring his neck before he went.

"Don't! You hurt! It was about some bills."

"Some bills of yours which you had given to Mr. Lawrence?"

"No, it wasn't them. Don't! It was about some bills which he got me to—to fake."

"I see. And might some of them have borne the name of Mr. Philip Lawrence?"

"Who told you? How do you know?"

"Never mind who told me. Answer!"

"It was all his fault! I should never have thought of such a thing if it hadn't been for him; he egged me on. I—I owed him a few pounds, and he said if I were to fake up some bills, with his brother's name on them, he'd let me off."

"And put the forgeries on the market, dividing the proceeds of the fraud with you?"

"Nothing of the kind, I'll take my oath to it; I swear I never had a penny. I never dreamt that he'd discount them, not for a moment! I thought it was a game he was going to play off on his brother—some sort of joke."

"Keen sense of humour yours, Mr. Moore."

"That's where he had me; he must have gone straight off and cashed the bills. Then his brother found it out, and then he came to me and threatened to tell his brother that it was I who'd done it."

"And then you went to your sister and asked her, probably on your bended knees, to save you from exposure."

"There was no bended knees about it; you're very much mistaken if you think there was. I'm not that kind. But I—I certainly mentioned to her something about it—she's my own flesh and blood."

"Being your own flesh and blood she, possibly, offered to do her best to square it for you."

"That's the mistake she made. She talked about giving him a hundred or two, as though that would be of any use. I said to her that if she'd give the money to me I could go abroad and start afresh, and it might be the making of me. But she never would take my advice, never!"

"So your sister, a young, unprotected girl, at your urgent solicitation, went alone to this man at that hour of the night, at the risk of—a good many things; and, in order to save you from the well-merited consequences of your being a cowardly rascal, offered to hand over to him her hard-won savings, and, in all probability, to pledge to the fullest extent her future earnings. And when, in the morning, he is found to have been murdered, you immediately jump to the conclusion that she killed him. With you, Mr. Moore, the sense of gratitude takes a peculiar form. In a state of civilisation in which logic prevailed, the breath would be crushed out of your body; sharing the fate of other vermin, you would not be allowed to exist.[38] Unfortunately for you, this is not a moment in the world's history in which logic does prevail."

So I shook him—gently. I did not treat him to a thousandth part of his deserts, for his sister's sake. Yet, when I dropped him back on to the floor, to judge from his looks and his behaviour, he might have been used with considerable severity. He seemed to be under the impression that I had murdered him.

"That was good!" said Miss Adair. "I feel better."

I don't know what prompted her to make such a remark, but I felt better too.*

CHAPTER X

WHERE MISS MOORE WAS GOING

IT was a relief to cease breathing the atmosphere of an apartment which was contaminated by the presence of Mr. Tom Moore. At least, that was what I felt when I was being driven with Miss Adair towards Imperial Mansions. Apparently that was her own feeling.

"Nice sort of brother that. He's a man."

"But what a sister! She's a woman."

She seemed to suspect me of a satirical intention.

"I don't fancy, Mr. Ferguson, that all women are built exactly on Bessie's lines."

"Would that they were. Miss Moore is of the stuff of which our mothers should be made."

She looked at me a little sideways; I was conscious of it, though I myself looked straight ahead.

"Are you married, Mr. Ferguson?"

I do not know why she should have asked me such a question at that particular moment, nor why the blood heated my cheeks. I answered shortly:

"No. I am not so fortunate."

"Ah! I shouldn't be surprised if you were so fortunate, a little later on."

Her tone conveyed a world of meaning; though what was its signification I could not tell. I suspected her of hinting at something which I should resent; but how to set about the discovery of what she meant I did not know. She continued:

"Suppose—I say suppose, just for the sake of argument—suppose it turns out that Bessie has killed this—man, I wonder what would happen."

"I decline to suppose the impossible."

"But how can you say that it's impossible? You're not in a position to judge; you know nothing of her character, her disposition. She's a stranger—to you."

"I know enough of her to be sure that she is incapable of anything unworthy."

"But how do you know?—my dear sir, how? From what you tell me, she hasn't said an intelligent thing to you; she's been in a condition of *non compos mentis*[39] ever since you set eyes upon her. After an hour's exchange of conversational bonbons with a lunatic woman, how can you tell what she's like when she's sane?"

"Miss Adair, if you are coming as Miss Moore's friend, be her friend; if not, I will stop the cab—you shall go back again."

She was silent for a second or two. I suspected her of stifling a smile.

"Thank you. You need not stop the cab." She looked at me, mischief in her eyes. "I believe, Mr. Ferguson, that you're a Scotchman."

There is Scotch blood in my veins; I did not see why she should charge it against me as a fault. I told her so. She laughed outright. Miss Adair was a charming woman, but I will own that I was glad when we reached our destination. She was in a provoking mood, as she showed by the remark she made as she got out of the cab.

"Now to interview this ideal conception of what our mothers should be."

I did not reply. I followed her into the lift.

"The top floor," I said.

But as we were passing the first floor, she started from her seat.

"There's Bessie!" she cried.

From where I sat, as I turned my head, I was just in time to see my last night's visitor vanish round the corner of the staircase. We were still ascending. I told the lift-man to return. When he had done so, and we were out upon the landing, the lady was already some distance along the corridor. She had passed my rooms, and was moving rapidly towards No. 64.

"Where is she going?" asked Miss Adair. "Bessie!"

Her call went unheeded. Apparently the other did not hear. She continued to hasten from us as if she were making for a particular goal, with a well-defined purpose in view. I thought it probable that the dead man's body was still somewhere in his chambers, and certainly all the plain evidences of the tragedy would have been studiously left untouched.

"Quick!" I exclaimed. "She doesn't know what she is doing; she is going to Lawrence's room, where he lies murdered. We must stop her before she gets there."

We hurried in pursuit, but had only gone a few yards when some one caught me by the arm. I had previously realised that some one else was standing in the corridor, but my attention had been too much engrossed by Miss Moore to permit of my noticing who it was. I now perceived that it was Hume. He gripped my arm with what seemed unnecessary force, his countenance betraying a degree of agitation of which I had not thought him capable.

"Ferguson!" he cried. "Miss Adair! What is Miss Moore doing here?"

His recognition surprised me, even at such a moment.

"Do you know her?"

"I believe I have that pleasure." His words sounded like a sneer, they were so bitterly uttered. "But what's the meaning of it all? I spoke to her, but she passed without a sign of recognition. What's the matter with her? She looks ill; where's she going?"

"She's going to Lawrence's room."

"Ferguson!" The increased pressure of his grasp showed that his strength was greater than I imagined.

"What's she—going there for?"

"My business is to stop her going at all, not to stand here answering idiotic questions."

I broke from him. The delay, brief though it had been, was sufficient to baffle my intentions. Miss Moore had arrived at No. 64. A policeman was standing without, seemingly acting as guardian of the portal.

"Is this the room in which Mr. Edwin Lawrence was killed?"

Although I was still at some distance from her, I could hear her ask the question with the direct simplicity of a little child. The officer stared at her as if he could not make her out.

"Yes, miss. But you can't go in; my orders are to admit no one without instructions. What's your name and your business?"

"Let me pass!"

Putting out her arm, touching him on the chest, she waved him aside with an imperious gesture, as if she were a sovereign queen. In an instant she was through the door. I was on him directly she had passed from sight.

"You idiot! Why did you let her enter?"

The man seemed bewildered.

"Let her! There wasn't much letting about it. For a lady she's about as cool a hand as ever I saw."

He perceived that my intention was to follow.

"Now then, none of that! You can't go in there! Don't you hear me say it?"

"You ass!"

I must have taken him by the shoulders more vigorously than I intended; he went spinning down the passage until the wall brought him to a standstill. Then I went after Miss Moore into the dead man's room, Miss Adair and Hume hard upon my heels.

CHAPTER XI

IN THE ONE ROOM—AND THE OTHER

EDWIN LAWRENCE was one of the most finical[40] men I had ever met on the subject of draughts. A properly ventilated apartment set him shivering, even in the middle of summer. The faintest suspicion of a healthy current of air made him turn up the collar of his coat. No room could be too stuffy for him. All his doors and windows he screened with heavy hangings. Behind the curtains which veiled the entrance into his dining-room I lingered, for a moment, to glance between the voluminous folds. Miss Moore was standing about the centre of the room. Something in the expression of her face, and in her attitude, caused me to hesitate. I checked the advance of Miss Adair and Hume, who pressed on me behind.

"Wait!" I whispered. "I want to see what she is going to do."

I would rather have been unaccompanied; Hume's society in particular I could have done without. But I could hardly induce him to withdraw without disturbing the girl within. That, all at once, I felt indisposed to do. At any and every risk I wanted light; to bring her back into the full possession of her reason. It needed but a brief glance to perceive that, in her present environment, she might pass through some sort of crisis which would bring about the result I so ardently desired. The constable had followed us into the room. He showed a disposition to require our retreat. I took him by the shoulder.

"Be still, man; you will do your duty best by holding your tongue."

He perceived that there was reason in what I said. He held his tongue, and I held his shoulder.

Miss Moore was looking round as if something in the appearance of the room struck a chord in her memory, and she was endeavouring to discover what it was. She put her hand up to her forehead with the gesture with which I had become familiar.

"I have been in this room before—surely I have. I seem to know it all quite well; but I can't think when I saw it, or how. I can't make it out at all."

She was glancing about her with bewildered eyes, as if seeking for some familiar object which would serve as a clue towards the solution of the puzzle. At last something arrested her attention; it was the tell-tale stain upon the carpet. She was standing within a yard or two of the spot on which I had discovered Lawrence lying. His body was gone, but his blood remained behind—a lurid disfigurement of the handsome floorcloth. She started at it.

"What is it?" She stooped down; she touched it with her finger tips; an odd little tremor seemed to come into her voice. "It—it's dry. Why shouldn't it be dry? What—what is it?" Still stooping, she covered her face with her hands, as if struggling to rouse her dormant memory. "It seems to bring something back to me. Something—something horrid. What can it be? Oh!"

She started upright, with a little exclamation. A new look came on her face; a suggestion of fear, of horror. She was all at once on

the alert, as if in expectation of something of which she had cause
to be afraid.

"This is where Mr. Edwin Lawrence was killed—killed!" Again
that look of puzzlement. "That means that he was—murdered!
Murdered! He fell like that."

She made a sudden movement, as if to hurl herself headlong
to the floor, which was so realistic that I started forward to save
her from a fall. It was only a feint; in an instant she was back in her
original position.

"Let me see how it was. He was here, and I was there."

She moved from one place to another, as if endeavouring to
recall a scene in which she had taken part. It seemed to come back
to her in fragments.

"I said, 'I'll kill you;' because I felt like killing him. And then—
then he laughed. He said, 'Kill me! How will you be better off for
that?' And that made me worse. I made up my mind that—that I'd
kill him."

She paused. I shuddered, clutching the curtains tighter.
Although I did not turn to look at them, I knew that there was
something strange on the faces of Miss Adair and Hume; that even
the constable was moved to a display of unusual interest. A faint
whisper reached me from the lady:

"Stop her! Don't let her go on!"

I was conscious of a weakness in my throat, which made my
voice sound as if I were hoarse, as I whispered a reply.

"I shan't attempt to stop her. I shall let her say all that she has to
say. I'm not afraid."

I felt her pull at my coat sleeve, as a dog might do to show its
sympathy.

The girl within continued. She had put her hands up to her
brow again, and seemed battling with her torpid faculties.
Through all that followed, in spite of the emotion which sometimes would grip me by the throat, I was conscious of the singular
quality of her beauty, which caused it to increase as her agitation
grew. Strangely out of keeping with the dreadful nature of some
of the things she said was the air of innocence which accompanied
them. She depicted herself as playing a leading part in a hideous
tragedy, with the direct simplicity of a little child who confesses to

faults of whose capital importance it has not the faintest notion.

"Did I kill him? Did I? Not then—no, not then. Then he came in, and it began all over again, right from the beginning; and—we quarrelled. We both said we would kill him, both of us; and he laughed. The more we said that we would kill him the more he laughed. And that—that made us worse. Then—then it came in. It! It!"

She shuddered. A look of abnormal terror came on her face. She covered her hands, uttering cries of panic fear.[41]

"Don't! Don't! I won't! I won't! You mustn't make me, you mustn't! Don't let it come near me! Don't let it touch me! I can't bear to think of its touching me! Oh!"

With a gasp, uncovering her eyes, she stared, affrightedly, at something which she seemed to see in front of her.

"What is it? I'm not afraid. Why should I be afraid? There is nothing the matter. I am not so easily frightened. I said I would kill him, but not like that, not like that. Did I say I'd kill him? Yes. And I did! I did! But I didn't mean to. Did I mean to? I don't know. Perhaps I meant to. He says I meant to, and perhaps he knows."

She stood staring in front of her, with blank, unmeaning gaze. Then, giving herself a little shake, she seemed to wake out of a sort of dream; and to be surprised at finding herself where she was.

"What is the matter with me? Am I going mad? This is the room, and yet, although I know it, I can't think what room it is. Something happened to me here which haunts me; and though I'm afraid to try to think what it was, I can't help trying. Why did I come here? It was very silly. It was because he—he told me that— Edwin Lawrence was killed here.

"Edwin Lawrence? What had that man to do with me? Lawrence? I feel as if I ought to know the name. There were two of them, and one—one was killed. Oh, I remember all! I can hear that horrid noise. I can see the knives—the knives! And I can see the blood, as he falls right down upon his face, and the hack, hack, hacking! I didn't do it! I didn't do it! Did I—do it?"

She looked about her with an agony of appeal which it was terrible to witness. My heart sank within my breast. At that moment I could not have gone to her even had I tried.

"Let me see—how did it happen? He stood here, and—the other laughed; and then there came the knife—the long, gleaming knife—and struck him in the back; and he looked round, and—I saw his face. His face! What a face! It was as if he were looking into hell. Don't look at me—not like that. I can't help you! It's too late! Turn your face away; don't let me see it; it isn't fair. It was the devil did it—the devil! It wasn't I. And then it took him by the throat with a dozen hands, and with a hundred knives cut at his face, until, before my eyes, I saw him losing his likeness to a man. And then it loosed him, and the great knife struck him from the back, and he fell on his face—what was his face, and then the hack, hack, hacking! And all the time that horrid noise."

She held up her arms in an anguish of supplication.

"Oh Lord, in what have I offended that this thing should come upon me? If I have sinned, surely my punishment is greater than my sin. That you should lay this burden on me, to bear for ever, and for ever, and for ever! Take it from me, let me wake to find it is a dream—the nightmare of a haunted night! For if it should be true, if it should be true, what is there for me but the torture fires of an eternal hell? Have mercy on me, Lord, have mercy!"

She broke into a paroxysm of sobbing. She shed no tears, hers were dry sobs; but it seemed as if they were tearing her to pieces. Then they ceased. Again a shudder went all over her, and again she seemed to come back to a curious wakefulness, out of a fevered dream.

"I'm not well; I can't be; I wish I were. It is as if I were two persons, and each keeps losing the other. Can there be two persons in one body?[42] My brain seems blurred—as if it were in two parts. When I am using one part, the other—the other's all confused. It's not as it should be. I feel sure that I haven't always been like this; something must have happened to make me so. When I try to think what it is, I'm afraid; and yet I can't help trying. I know—I know it was in this room it happened; but what could it have been? What brought me to this room at all? When was it that I came?

"There's something in my head that I can't catch hold of—it keeps eluding me. If I only could get hold of it, I'd understand— I'm sure I should.—What would it be that I should understand? I'm afraid to think! It's awful that I should be afraid of what would come to me if understanding came, especially as I want it so much to come. I seem to be haunted; is it by a vision, or by something which really happened? I wish I could sit down and quietly think it out. If I could put the pieces of the puzzle together I might know what it means. But I can't; I'm all restless; I can't keep still.

"Why is it that I am always seeing this man lying dead upon the floor? Why do I seem to be striking at his back? It is so strange. It is not a knife I'm striking with, not a common knife; it is something different—and worse. It comes out of nothing; and, all the time, there's the noise. It is not I who make the noise, no, I don't speak—I can't—I daren't—it's It. But it keeps on strike, strike, striking, and the blood all comes upon my cloak. I know I had a cloak on, I remember how it kept getting in my way. And then—he falls. And that's all—until it begins all over again, and I am standing in a room, in the moonlight, and he sits up in bed and looks at me—he, my friend."

She held out her hands in front of her, with a pleasant inflection on the final word.

"And I can't think of what took place before. I feel that I ought to know who I am, and what brought me here; but I can't quite lay my hand on it. The people are there, but I can't quite make out their faces, or who they are, or what they want with me. They all look at me, and I can hear them clapping. Then it all comes back to the man lying dead upon the floor; that's where it all seems to begin and end. I wonder if I killed him. I wish I knew. It is so strange that I may have killed him and yet not know. I know that he deserved to be killed, but did I do it?"

Glancing round, her eyes rested on the door in the opposite corner which led into Lawrence's bedroom. She crossed to it.

"What's in here?"

She turned the handle and went in. I was at the door within five seconds of her passing through it; Miss Adair, Hume, and the constable still at my heels. We must have presented a spectacle which was not without its comic side as we went scurrying across the carpet. But what I saw as I looked into that bedchamber banished from my mind all thoughts of the incongruous; it must, for the time being, have paralysed the muscles of the body; or I do not think that I should have remained for even so long as I did a silent witness of that piteous scene.

One of the first things I realised was the presence in the room of Inspector Symonds. He, in company with a colleague, was submitting the contents of the apartment to an official examination. As Miss Moore entered the two men turned and stared—as well they might. She, on her part, paid them no attention; they were at her back, in an alcove, formed by the bay of the window, in which stood a bureau, whose drawers they were ransacking. Her eyes saw one thing, and one thing only—something which lay under a sheet upon the bed.

"What's that?" she asked herself. "What's under the sheet?"

She went towards the bed doubtfully, as if uncertain as to the direction which her adventure might be taking. We watched her, silent. The officials, I take it, were for the moment too much taken aback by her appearance to know what to make of her. While for me, that was one of the occasions in my life on which I lost my presence of mind. If I had known what to do I could not have done it; my nerves were all in a flutter, like so many loose strings. She went close up to the bed; then stood still, looking down at the something whose shape she saw outlined.

"What is it under the sheet?"

She lifted up a corner, then let it fall. "It's the man I saw lying dead." I saw her tremble. A new look came on her face—half curiosity, half awe. "I wonder if I should know him if I saw him now? If it would all come back to me? I wonder if it would?"

She turned down the sheet so as to expose the dead man's head and face. She stared at him with looks of growing horror. The terror of the sight seemed to be gradually forcing itself upon her brain. Stooping a little forward, she began to move farther and farther from the bed. Her voice became husky.

"I killed him; it hacked, hacked, hacked; his blood is on my cloak and hands; the dead man lying on the floor."

She stopped. The something on the bed apparently had for her a dreadful fascination. She seemed to be in two minds as to whether or not to go close to it again, as if she would, and yet would not. Miss Adair touched me on the arm.

"Stop! Don't let her go to it! Don't!"

Her words and touch woke me from a sort of trance. I awoke to a clear realisation of the full horror of the situation—the young girl, with her poor, numbed brain, trying experiments on the man just murdered.

"You go to her," I said. "See if she knows you."

It was time some friendly hand was interposed. Inspector Symonds and his colleague showed signs of intervention on their own account, and on lines of their own. Miss Moore began to turn slowly towards the bed.

"I wonder if I could make out where I struck him, and where it hacked."

Miss Adair moved forward.

"Bessie!" she cried.

The girl turned and saw her, and appeared to struggle with the darkness which was in her brain. The contest seemed physical as well as mental; she swayed to and fro; I thought that she would fall. Then reason got the upper hand; a wave of consciousness swept over her. She drew herself upright, and she ran to Miss Adair.

"Florrie!" she exclaimed.

She burst into tears—real tears this time, not the dry sobs which, a few minutes before, seemed to be tearing her to pieces. She cried like a child.

CHAPTER XII

WHAT WAS ON THE BED

AND we—we five men—remained for a moment or two, in silence, looking on. In our breasts, I imagine, were widely different emotions. Surprise, and something else, was, apparently, the dominant feeling of Inspector Symonds and his colleague. They exchanged a few whispered words. Then the Inspector made a movement towards Miss Moore, with something in his mien I did not like. I placed myself in front of him.

"Well, sir," I inquired, "what do you want?"

He looked at me askance; then turned towards the policeman who had been placed in the passage to guard the outer door.

"What is the meaning of these people being here? I thought I told you to admit no one. Is this the way you obey orders?"

The policeman was apologetic.

"Well, sir, that young lady was through before I knew what she was up to. Then this gentleman sent me flying down the passage, and the rest of 'em got in; it was more than I could do to stop them."

The Inspector showed himself indisposed to accept his satellite's excuses.

"Tell that for a tale, my man; you will hear of this again. I will only have men with me who are able to carry out to the letter the instructions I give them." He addressed himself to me. "Mr. Ferguson, if you are not careful you will get yourself into trouble. You appear not to realise the serious nature of your conduct. It is not what I should have expected from a gentleman in your position. Surely you cannot wish to place yourself in opposition to the law?"

"Thank you for your warning; and don't you trouble yourself about my wishes. Let me advise you not to step out of the four corners of your province; men circumstanced as you are sometimes take liberties, which is a mistake."

"Stand on one side, Mr. Ferguson. I do not take my instructions from you. I wish to speak to that young lady."

"Then speak to her from where you are—though what you can have to say to her is more than I am able to imagine. She is not well, and does not want to be brought into too close contact with undesirable strangers."

"Not well? What is the matter with her?"

"I might reply by inquiring what affair that is of yours; but I don't mind informing you that she suffers from hallucinations."[43]

"Hallucinations? Oh, they're hallucinations, are they?"

There was something in his tone for which I could have knocked him down. He spoke to her across the room.

"What is your name?"

"My name? I don't know what my name is."

"Not know your name? Come, that won't do. Tell me what your name is."

"The lady does not know her name; do you not hear her say so? You will doubt the lady's word, Mr. Symonds, at your peril."

"Remove your hand; do you wish to dislocate my shoulder? You forget your own strength, as well as other things, Mr. Ferguson. If you will not tell me who this lady is, and she herself cannot, then I must detain her till inquiries have been made."

"Detain her? What do you mean?"

"This lady has forced her way into this room, and I have myself heard her, with my own ears, accuse herself, at least, of participation in the murder of this unfortunate man."

His colleague chimed in: "There can be no sort of doubt upon that point. I heard her too. She said, 'I killed him.'"

He went to the other side of the bed, and replaced the sheet over the dead man's head and face. The policeman put in his word.

"I beg your pardon, sir, but she's been behaving in the most extraordinary manner in the other room. It seems, from what she's been saying, and doing, that she was there when the gentleman was being murdered, and she's been acting it all over to herself again as it were. Struck him with a great knife, she said she did."

"You heard her admit that she struck him with a knife?"

"I did—more than once; and these two gentlemen, and that lady heard her, too. She said that she meant to kill him all along; and then she said she struck him in the back with a great knife, and he fell forward on his face; and she acted how she struck him, and how he fell."

"In face of that statement my duty's plain; the lady must be detained."

He was going on, but I cut him short.

"Then I say that the lady shall not be detained; I will save you, Mr. Symonds, from making one of the most serious mistakes you ever made in your life. Miss Adair, escort the lady from the room. I will see that no one touches her. Now, constable, out of the way."

I moved towards the policeman, who did not wait for me to touch him. He slipped aside. The Inspector interposed.

"Now, Mr. Ferguson, I warn you to be careful. May I ask you, Dr. Hume, to explain to this gentleman what are the consequences of impeding the police in the execution of their duty. You might also point out to him how worse than futile such attempts always are."

Hume was standing near the door. Now he came into the

middle of the room. I was surprised by the alteration which had taken place in his appearance since I had observed him last. He seemed to have all at once grown old. Outwardly he was cool and calm; but I, who had some knowledge of the man, perceived that he was making a strenuous effort to retain the mastery of himself in face of some most unusual emotion. He spoke with an exaggeration of his usual deliberative manner.

"You are aware, Mr. Symonds, that I am not a likely person to interfere with the police in the execution of their duty; but it happens, in this case, that I am acquainted with this young lady, and am sure that she has had no more to do with this crime than"—he paused, he drew in his lips, as if to moisten them—"I have. The account which your officer has given you of her behaviour in the adjoining room is very far from being an accurate representation. She is at present suffering from an obscure mental disease.[44] If you were to proceed to arrest her you would run an imminent risk of permanently disturbing the balance of her brain, and of driving her stark mad. The act, and the responsibility for the consequences of the act, would be yours. Let me finish, Inspector. I quite understand that if you were to allow her to pass entirely from your purview you would be assuming a weighty responsibility in a different direction. I am therefore prepared to give you my personal guarantee that she shall remain at your disposal as witness, or in any other capacity, until it has been made plain that she has had no connection whatever with this most unfortunate affair."

"First of all, what is the lady's name, who is she, and where does she live?"

"She is Miss Bessie Moore, the well-known actress, and she lives with this other lady, Miss Florence Adair, at 22, Hailsham Road, Brompton."

"I'm not much of a theatre-goer, but I have heard of Miss Bessie Moore. I wasn't aware that she was——" He finished his sentence by touching his forehead with his finger.

"I am prepared to certify that, at present, she is mentally incapable; and that to place her under arrest would be to imperil not only her sanity, but her life."

"Very good. And in the presence of these witnesses you undertake to produce her whenever she's required."

"I do."

"And does Mr. Ferguson join you in that undertaking?" I informed him that I did. "And where is Miss Moore going now?"

"To her own home."

"One of our men ought to go with her."

"One of your men will do nothing of the kind," I observed.

Hume said the same thing with a greater flow of language.

"If you give me notice of Miss Moore's being required, for any purpose whatever, I will undertake to produce her within the hour. More, if I have reason to suspect my capacity to continue that guarantee I will advise you on the instant."

"Good. On that understanding Miss Moore is at liberty to go— for the present."

We four went out of the room, the two women in front, Hume and I behind. Miss Moore had not spoken while the argument was being carried on with the inspector. When we reached the corridor she turned to me.

"Where am I going to be taken? I want to speak to you."

"You had better return with Miss Adair to Mrs. Peddar's room— for the present, at any rate. I will come to you immediately."

"You will be sure to come?"

She laid her hand upon my arm.

"Certain. I will be there almost as soon as you are."

Hume came forward.

"I also wish to speak to you."

"You? No! I don't wish to speak to you—not to you!"

She shrank from him as if he had been some leprous thing. When they had gone he turned to me with eyes in which there was a strange something, whose meaning, just then, I did not attempt to decipher; though I was dimly conscious, as my eyes looked into his, of an odd sensation of wonder as to whether the doctor himself might not be going mad.

"What is it which actuates your moves in this game which you are playing? To save your neck, do you propose to hang her, as well as Philip Lawrence?"

That is what he said to me. To save my neck! The words rang in my ears as I mounted towards the housekeeper's room. They were to me as the germ of an idea.*

CHAPTER XIII

SHE AND I

THE girl was changed. I perceived it as soon as I was in Mrs. Peddar's room. She stood behind the table, and, as I entered, turned her face away. Her attitude suggested doubt, hesitation, even shame. It was so different to the spontaneous burst of friendship which, hitherto, when she saw me, had brought her to my side.

Miss Adair was seated with her hands lying open on her knee; in her bearing there was also dubiety, and in Mrs. Peddar's as, leaning against her sideboard, she fidgeted with the fringe of her black apron. The air was so charged with the spirit of uncertainty that, as soon as I entered, it affected me. We each of us seemed to be unwilling to meet the other's glances. It was with an effort I broke the uncomfortable silence.

"I don't think, Miss Moore, that I should lose any time in going home with Miss Adair."

"Going home? Where is my home? Yes, I know I ought to know, and I do know more than I did, but—I can't just find it."

"Never mind about that, Miss Adair will see you're all right. Now put your hat on, and off you go. I'm afraid that I must hurry you."

I was thinking of Inspector Symonds down below, and how extremely possible it was that he might change his mind. She made no movement, but continued looking down on to the floor, her brow all creased in lines of pain.

"Do you think—I—killed that man?"

"I am sure that you did not."

She glanced up at me, her brow smoothed out, light in her eyes.

"You are sure? Oh? What makes you sure?"

"My own common sense. I have seen your brother, and I have heard from him what was the errand which took you to Edwin Lawrence. I can understand how your mind was strained, and what a very little more was needed to make that strain too much.

But that in what took place you did nothing of which you have cause to be ashamed, I am convinced."

"But she thinks I did it, and so does she; and—I'm not sure."

She pointed first to Miss Adair and then to Mrs. Peddar.

"You're dreaming. Miss Adair knows you too well to suppose the incredible."

"But she does think I did it. Don't you?"

In reply Miss Adair put her elbows on the table and her face on her hands, and burst into tears.

"Bessie!" she cried.

I was dumfounded.

"You see. And she thinks so too. And that man, he thinks so; he wanted to lock me up. Will he—lock me up?"

She asked the question with a little gasp, so expressive of loneliness and terror, that it cut me to the heart. I tried to speak with a confidence I did not feel.

"The police are famous for their blunders.[45] In cases such as this, if they had their way, they'd lock up every one they could lay their hands on. There's one question I want to ask you before you go—was there no one else present in that room last night except you and Edwin Lawrence?"

"Yes—you were there."

"I!"

She said it with a directness which struck me as with a crowbar.

"Yes, you were there. I thought, when I saw you sitting up in bed, in the moonlight, that I had seen your face before, and I've been thinking so all the time; and now it's all come back to me—you were there. Don't you remember that you came into the room?"

She spoke with a touch of sudden excitement. Mrs. Peddar resented her words with unusual heat.

"You wicked girl! To say such a thing, after all that he has done for you! You'll be saying next that I was there."

I endeavoured to appease my enthusiastic partisan.

"Gently, Mrs. Peddar. I am not at all sure that what Miss Moore says is not correct. I, too, suffered last night from dreams. I dreamed that I went to Edwin Lawrence's rooms, and saw him murdered; whether I saw with the actual or the spiritual eye, I cannot tell; but, in any case, all that I did see was seen as in a glass darkly."[46]

"Did you see me?"

"I cannot be certain. I saw some one who I now believe to have been you."

"Did you see It?"

"It?"

"The—the creature—the dreadful thing!"

"My vision was blurred; I saw nothing plain, it had all the indistinctness of a nightmare, but—I was oppressed by the consciousness of some hideous presence in the room. What was—the thing?"

"I don't know; I can't think. I'm afraid to try! It did it all."

"Wasn't it—a wild beast? It made a noise like one, or—was it my imagination?"

"The dreadful noise! I've heard it ever since. I hear it all the time—I hear it now. Can't you—hear it now?"

She looked about her with frightened eyes.

"That certainly is your imagination; there's not a sound. But was there no one else there in the room besides you, and Edwin Lawrence, and—I?"

"There was the other man."

"Was that other man his brother?"

"I don't just know; I can't quite think. But, if I saw him again, I should know him, I feel sure I should, as I've known you."

"Did they quarrel, the two men?"

She shook her head.

"It will all come back to me, perhaps, piece by piece; but not yet, not yet. But you were there, and you saw I did not kill him?"

"What I saw I cannot tell; as with you it was all a blur. But that you did not kill him I am as sure as that the sky is above."

"I am so glad. You have made me so happy."

"It needs but a little thing to make your happiness."

"What is your name?"

"You have heard it more than once. My name is Ferguson—John Ferguson."

"John!" Returning to her former self, she said it with the simplicity of a little child. She nestled close up to me, as if for comfort. My pulses throbbed. "Why is it that I feel safe when I am near you, and that the nearer I am to you the safer I feel?"

"God grant that you may always feel safe when you are near to me."

My voice was husky.

"I believe that I always shall feel safe when you are near; I believe I always shall."

She looked up at me with eyes in which there was something which seemed to burn into my soul. It was with difficulty I kept myself from putting my arm about her. When I spoke, it was awkwardly enough, and with a lumbering choice of ungainly words.

"The tangle is greater than I thought. It seems to be drawing us together. God moves in a mysterious way,[47] and it may be His purpose that, under this blood-red shadow, our lives shall draw closer to each other. For my part, I am content." I waited for her to speak; she was still; but she rested one hand upon my arm, and I trembled. "Don't let yourself be troubled by fantastic fears. Rest assured that your heart is stainless as are your hands. I know. Look up, the light is coming! Your innocence will be made plain to all the world, and to yourself. For it seems that of yourself you're chief doubter."

"I did doubt; I'm easier now. I don't doubt at all when you are near. I wonder why?"

"I wonder, too. But, come, there are a dozen things which I must do. You must be bundled off. Mrs. Peddar, where is this young lady's hat?"

Mrs. Peddar passed into an inner room, presently returning with a hat. While its owner was putting it on, Miss Adair came up to me. I had been aware that the two women had been watching us with wide-open eyes and gaping mouths; now one of them gave partial expression to her feelings.

"What on earth is there between you two? Have you known each other all your lives, or did you meet for the first time last night?"

"That is a question for the metaphysicians. I seem to have known her all my life."

"And has she known you all hers? Is that what I'm to think?"

"There is one thing you are not to think—you are not to think that she had any hand in what was done."

"But it's all so awful! It's all come upon me in an instant: it's taken me unawares. What am I to think after what she said, and did, in that room?"

"You are to be sure that she is as innocent as a child."

"But what am I to think? It seems now that you both were there. I have no doubt whatever that the man quite deserved being killed; if she didn't kill him, then did you?"

"God forbid!"

Miss Moore had her hat on. She made a discovery.

"I had a cloak. I feel sure I had a cloak. Where's it gone?"

"Never mind about your cloak; it's warm enough to-day, you'll be able to do quite well without it."

I caught Miss Adair's glance; plainly she remembered what I had said about the condition of that garment; there was renewed suspicion in her eye. I turned to Mrs. Peddar.

"We don't want to go through the main entrance; isn't there another way?"

"There is the service lift, and there are the service stairs."

"The very thing; show us where they are."

She showed us where they were; and we three went down the servants' staircase, through a back door, into a side street, no one saying us nay. I saw the two girls into a cab. As they were starting Miss Moore leaned her head out. She looked at me with eyes which were, to me, like magnets. Her lips formed a single word:

"John!"

As the hansom drove off, and, turning the corner, passed from sight, I felt as if something had gone out of my life.

CHAPTER XIV

HE AND I

As I returned to my chambers my whole being seemed to be a battlefield on which conflicting thoughts and feelings were fighting to a finish. I had not supposed that my nature could have been utterly disorganized by occurrences such as those which had come crowding upon me during the last few hours.

I am a hard man. My life has been lived, for the most part, in

odd corners of the world, where, single-handed, I have fought the
fight for fortune; in places where human life is not held of much
account, and where one would have thought as little of killing
such a man as Edwin Lawrence appeared to have been, as destroy-
ing any other noxious animal. I have ever been a fighter. Men have
called me "Fighting John." I have had to defend my own life, and
have not hesitated, when circumstances required, to take the lives
of others. I learnt, long ago, that there are occasions when killing
is not alone the best, but the only cure.

But I have had nothing to do with women. I have never been
on familiar terms with one of them. I have always been aware that
they are better than I,[48] and that consciousness has made me shy of
them, as of a church. But while one knows that a church is a place
for sinners, one's sense of decency tells one that evil ought not to
come into contact with a woman. So I have kept clear. Until that
night.

Now Providence alone knew what had happened. Since I had
seen her standing in the moonlight at my window, the foundations
of my life seemed to have been going under. It was absurd; yet
true. What could she care for such as I—an adventurer from the
four corners of the world, soiled with something of the grime
from each of them. What right had I to think of such as she—a
young girl, in the first fulness of her wondrous beauty, mentally,
morally, socially far above my reach; the idol of the town, with,
at her feet, some of the greatest in the land. It was midsummer
madness;[49] which, in my case, was the less excusable since, for me,
it was the time of autumn.

But she had called me "John." That was in her hour of sorrow,
of which I had taken advantage. The hour would pass, and then I
should not even be "Mr. Ferguson," but simply one of the crowd
in the street. I might take a seat at the theatre, to watch her play,
but she would not even glance to see if I was in it. That would be
a black hour for me. But with her all would be well.

But would the hour of her sorrow quickly pass? Back in my
own room I tried to think; but, like her, I was afraid. I had been
an idiot to let her return to Hailsham Road. What kind of an ass
would he be who placed his trust in Inspector Symonds. I had had
my experiences of the police. In all countries of the world they

were the same—fools when they were not knaves. If he, or any of his myrmidons,[50] laid a hand on her, what could I do? I was in a country where, even if you knocked a policeman down, it was regarded as a crime. And Miss Adair—she had her doubts. Great powers! what could the woman be made of, to have lived so long with such an angel, and yet doubt her perfect innocence! Apart from such thick-headedness on the part of a woman of common sense, it was dreadful to think of the girl living in an atmosphere of suspicion, when complete confidence was the one thing needful.

Why had I let her return to Hailsham Road? She would have been safer with Mrs. Peddar, or—God forgive me for thinking that she would have been safer still with me.

On what did the woman found her doubts? And the Inspector his? That was the mischief. On the surface the thing looked doubtful; if I were to speak of certain things, I knew they might look worse. A dozen knew now that she was present in the room. She could be dragged into the witness-box, at any rate, and then—then what might she not be forced to say. She had gone with unfriendly intentions; he had been killed while she was there; she ran away without a whisper to any one of what had been done. What deductions might not be drawn, by an unfriendly critic, from that bare statement of the facts. I dared not think of the risks she would run till all the truth was told.

"What is the truth?" I cried.

Unconsciously, I spoke aloud. Though, had I thought, I should not have hesitated, since I supposed I was alone. But, no sooner had I spoken, than my bedroom door was opened, and some one stood on the threshold, looking out at me.

"It's you, is it? Come here!"

Hume was the speaker. He spoke and looked as if I were the intruder; not he. His presence took me by surprise; so that at first, in my bewilderment, I could only stare. Then I moved towards him.

"What are you doing there?"

"Come, and you shall see."

I pushed past him into the room. As I looked round, in my amazement at the man's audacity, I was speechless. The whole place was in confusion. He had been turning my belongings

topsy-turvy—searching drawers, examining cupboards, scrutinis-
ing everything of mine which he could lay his hands upon. My
property was scattered everywhere—on chairs, on tables, on the
floor. On the rail of the bed were laid my pyjamas and a towel; and
on the bed itself was displayed, at its widest, the plum-coloured
cloak.

When I realised that he had unearthed that piece of apparently
damning evidence, it was enough.

"You hound!"

I would have taken him by the throat; but, springing back, he
pointed a revolver at my face.

"Stop that! I've had to deal with men like you before, John
Ferguson. Attempt to touch me, and I'll save the hangman his
pains."

I, also, on previous occasions had had to deal with men like
him; more dangerous men than he was, free from all the restraints
of civilisation, whom use had made handy with a pistol. There
was something in the way in which he gripped his weapon which
told me that he was not yet acquainted with all its capabilities. I
dodged; struck up; the pistol went flying through the air. I took
him by the waist; lifted him off his feet; held him tight; and shook
him. If you have the trick of it, it is surprising how quickly you can
shake the breath clean out of a man's body, or, if you wish to go so
far, by shaking him you can break his back, and make an end. My
desires were less extensive. I shook him till I had him quiet; then I
lowered him till his face was on a level with mine.

"Now, Dr. Hume, please tell me why I shouldn't kill you?"

He could but gasp, and that with pain.

"You can—kill me—if you like. You killed him. Killing's—your
line."

"And what's your line? Sneaking, like a thief, into a man's room,
and prying into his possessions like some dirty nigger?[51] However,
since you are here, we'll come to an understanding, you and I,
before you go."

I dropped him on to the floor, where he lay like a log, struggling to get back some of his breath. I picked up his revolver. It was
a natty[52] little thing, though not of the kind one carries where a
gun is one of the chief necessities of existence. There a gun, to be

worth anything, should send a bullet through an inch board at the distance of a dozen yards; it was all his would do to send a bullet through the skin of a man. I locked the door, and I waited for him to get his breath again.

"When you are ready, Dr. Hume."

I sat and watched him. He had followed me with his eyes as I moved about the room; starting as I picked up his pistol. Now he returned me glance for glance. He was getting the better of his breathlessness; and presently raised himself to a sitting posture.

"You should be in a freak museum, Ferguson."

"Indeed. Why?"

"You're a prodigy of bone and muscle."

"You should remember it."

"I've but just now made the discovery. I shall have to refurbish my faith in the labours of Hercules and the story of Samson."[53] He was, as it were, arranging himself inside his clothes. "I don't resent your physical configuration; it's educative, as showing what the strength of a man may be. It's a pity you should be a—— Are you only a fool, or are you something else as well?" He stood up, still arranging himself inside his clothes. He pointed to the plum-coloured cloak. "What's this?"

"It's what I'm going to wring your neck for."

"Is that so? I don't doubt your capacity, but why exercise it in this particular instance?"

"Then you must satisfy me that, though the heavens fall, no one outside this room shall ever learn there is such a garment in existence—and that you'll find it difficult to do."

"You wish me to tell no one of what I've found?"

"It's not an affair of a wish."

"Ferguson, you're stark mad."

"You've told me so before. You're a specialist. You should know that a homicidal lunatic is not the sort to trifle with. Label me like that."

"But you're mad in the wrong direction."

"What's the right direction to be mad?"

"That cloak's Miss Moore's."

"You're a liar."

"Let me inform you that to save her from harm I'd give my life."

"Say that again."

"To save her from harm I'd give my life. It sounds like bombast, but it's plain truth."

"Hume, I may be mad, but I'm not so mad as you think."

"You're madder, if you don't believe me. I don't know why I should make a confidant of you, of all men; but there are illogical moments in which men feel constrained to strip themselves bare. Perhaps this is such a moment in my life. Miss Moore is the only woman I ever loved. That's a line from a play, but it's true, for all that."

"Why do you say it to me?"

"What's the meaning of that cloak being in your wardrobe?"

"Why did you go to my wardrobe to look for it?"

"Man, I wasn't looking for that. I was looking for something with which to hang you. And I found this, and those. This is a towel. There's blood on it. See! The marks of bloody fingers. You wiped your hands on it when, last night, you came from Lawrence's room."

"That is what you make of it. I see."

"Those are the pyjamas which you were wearing. There are stains on them. See here, on the front of the jacket; on the breeches, too."

"What is the deduction which you draw from that?"

"I don't know. I did know. But now I don't."

His tone was one of intense dejection. He looked towards the bed. I considered for a moment. Then I spoke.

"You're quite right, Hume. The cloak is Miss Moore's."

He turned round quickly.

"Do you want to hang her now instead of Philip? Or do you want to hang them both?"

"You talk too much of hanging. I mean you and I to understand each other before you leave this room; and we shan't get there by blinking facts. I say that the cloak's Miss Moore's. You perceive that it's caked with blood."

"I see."

"I believe that blood to be Edwin Lawrence's. The proof is easy; you have only to subject it to a microscopical examination you will know. The stain on my pyjamas came off her cloak. That on the towel was where she wiped her hands, not where I wiped mine. The water in which she washed them I threw into the road. It was bright red. Not only were her hands reeking wet, there were smears upon her face as well."

"Ferguson!"

"Those are the facts. I've made it a rule of my life never to dodge a fact which I don't like; I hit at it. And it's because I hit at those facts that I know they don't mean she killed him; I know she didn't."

"How do you know?"

I laughed.

"Because I know her; perhaps you don't."

"I've known her the better part of my life."

"And I only since last night, when she came through my window with shining hands."

"But how can you know she didn't, unless you know who did? Did you?"

I laughed again.

"I did not. Lawrence sharped me; I suspected it last night, now I'm sure; but I shouldn't have killed him merely because he was too clever; at least, not like that. You're a poor judge of character if you suppose I should."

"I care nothing for you, or for your character. It's of her I'm thinking. She might have done it in a fit of temporary insanity."

"She might; but she didn't."

"Then what was the meaning of her conduct in his room just now?"

"You're a mental pathologist; you should know better than I."

"It's because I'm a mental pathologist that I—fear. Symonds suspects. I shouldn't be surprised if he arrests her within four and twenty hours. He'll hang her if he finds this cloak."

"Oh no, he won't. Nor, if Symonds is the idiot you suppose— he may be, since you're a judge of idiots—will she remain long under arrest. I shall free her."

Hume had been pacing up and down like an unquiet spirit. Now he stopped to snarl at me like an angry wolf.

"If you think brawn and muscle can prevail against the police you are a fool."

"As it happens I am not a fool on those particular lines, because I think nothing of the kind. I shall use other means to free her."

"What other means?"

"I shall confess."

"But I thought you said you didn't do it."

"Nor did I; nor did she. If Symonds must have a victim, better I than she. To go to the gallows for her sake would be heaven well won."

Hume stared. I might have been shaking him again, his breath came so hardly.

"What—do you mean?"

"My good Hume, don't you be afraid for Miss Moore. I assure you she's in no danger."

"You say you only saw her for the first time last night."

"But that's a century ago. A myriad things have taken place since, so now it's just as if I'd known her all my life."

He kept his head averted, looking at me sideways; it was the first time he had shown an indisposition to meet me face to face.

"It's like that? I see." He drew in his lips to moisten them. "A case of the world well lost for her."[54]

"You've hit it, Hume."

"Suppose, for illustration's sake, that this and that were fitted together so as to make it seem—only seem, you understand—that you actually did kill Lawrence, what then?"

"I don't know what it is, but, in this instance, something seems to be warping your natural intelligence, or I'm persuaded that you'd perceive, as I perceive, that the truth will out, and that before very long."

"Then am I to take it you'll walk away with banners flying?"

"I don't know about the banners flying, but I'll walk away."

"With her?"

"You've no right to say that."

"And what right do you suppose you have to say what you've been saying, when you know that she's to me the light of my eyes, the breath of my nostrils? when, these dozen years and more, since she was a little child in little frocks, I've waited on her will, won for her a place upon the stage I hate because she loved it, blazoned abroad her fame, because to be famous was her pleasure, although

I knew that every cry of applause took her farther from me still, and farther! And now you come and say that you saw her for the first time last night, yet talk glibly of having known her all your life, and brag of being ready to sacrifice yourself for her. Do you think if she were herself she'd accept your sacrifice?—you speak of knowing her, and yet think that? Go to!—But, see here, if you burn with a desire to make yourself a scapegoat, I am willing."

"You are willing?"

"She'll never be. But if we put together here a little, there a little, line upon line, we'll make out your guilt so clearly that there's not a jury which wouldn't see it, nor a judge who wouldn't hang you. Shall we arrange it between us, you and I?"

"You are very good."

"That she'll be in gaol by this time to-morrow is pretty positive; I shouldn't be surprised if Symonds was applying for a warrant at this moment. If you think that you will free her by merely going and saying, 'I did it, it wasn't she,' you are under a delusion. She'll not be freed like that; they'll need chapter and verse. You'll have to tell a plain tale plainly; how you planned the thing, how you did it, how you sought to hide your guilt by throwing the blame of it on her.

"Your tale will want corroboration; the support of independent evidence. I could say a thing or two, with perfect truth, which would go some way towards hanging you. Your concealment of the fact that you were in the room would look ugly, if treated well, and there's the girl who saw you flying from it as if the devil were behind you. There's the tell-tale marks upon the towel, on the pyjamas; there are a dozen things, without invention. And with— oh, we could manufacture a good round tale which would bear the strictest investigation, and which, without the slightest shadow of a doubt, would set her free for ever. Shall we set about it now?"

I was silent.

"There's some one knocking at my door."

Some one was beating a tattoo upon the panel.

"So there is; and some one in a hurry, it would seem. Perhaps it's Symonds. If so, you might make a clean breast of it at once. I'll corroborate with what I know. Then she need never fear arrest at all."*

CHAPTER XV

THE LETTER

BUT it was not Symonds. It was a messenger-boy—an impertinent young rascal.

"Mr. John Ferguson? I thought every one was out, I've been knocking for the last ten minutes."

"Have you indeed? I trust the delay has caused you no serious inconvenience. Yes, I am Mr. John Ferguson."

"No answer."

He thrust an envelope into my hand, and, turning on his heel, was about to march away. I caught him by the shoulder.

"Pardon me—one second! From whom does this communication come?"

"I say there's no answer."

He wriggled in my grasp.

"I hear you—still, if you could manage to wait for a moment, I think it might be worth your while. Let me beg of you to enter."

Drawing him into the room, I shut the door. He surveyed me with indignation.

"My orders are that when there's no answer I'm not to wait."

"Good boy! Always obey orders."

The address on the envelope was typewritten;[55] as were the sentences on the sheet of paper it contained.

"Because Edwin Lawrence is dead, don't suppose that the £1880 are paid. You have not hit on a new way to pay old debts. A knife in the back is not a quittance. You are wrong if you suppose it is. Have the money ready; hard cash—notes and gold; all gold preferred. NO CHEQUE. Edwin Lawrence has left an heir; to whom all that he had belongs, your debt among the rest. Be prepared to pay when asked. If the request has to be made a second time it will come in a different form.

"THE GODDESS."

That was what the envelope contained—an anonymous letter.

"Who sent this?"

"I don't know. I haven't read it."

"Possibly not; and yet you might know who was the sender."

"I don't see how. I'd just been on an errand right over to Finchley.[56] As soon as I came in that was given me. All I was told was that there was no answer."

The messenger spoke in a tone of resentment, as if suffering from a grievance. He was a small youth, with crisp black hair and sharp black eyes; combativeness writ large all over him.

"You didn't see who brought this to the office?"

"I did not."

"Where do you come from?"

"Victoria."[57]

"What's your name?"

"George Smith. Though I don't see what that's got to do with you."

"Then that only shows that your range of vision's limited. Because, Mr. George Smith, although there's no answer to this little communication, you're likely to hear of it again. Good-day."

The young gentleman withdrew with something like a sniff of scorn. I read the letter through again. As Hume stood watching me, his curiosity got the upper hand.

"What is it?"

"I was wondering if I should tell you. I don't see why not." I handed him the sheet of paper. He scanned it with eager eyes. "What do you make of it?"

"It is for me, rather, to put that question to you."

"I'll tell you one thing I make of it—that the typewriter, from the anonymous letter-writer's point of view, is an excellent invention. In the case of a written letter, one can occasionally guess what kind of person it is from whom it comes; but, when it's typewritten, the Lord alone can tell."

"'The Goddess.' Does the signature convey no meaning to your mind? Think."

"I'm thinking. The Goddess? I certainly don't know any one who's entitled to write herself down like that. Let me look at the thing again." He returned me the sheet of paper. "This seems to suggest that some one else is disposed to take a hand in the game—some person at present unknown."

"But who knows that you owed Lawrence £1880? And—who knows how much besides?"

"Just so. I wonder!"

Hume eyed me as if he were endeavouring to decipher, on my face, the key to a riddle.

"If some one applies to you for the money what shall you do?"

"Hang him, or her, straight off. That is, I should hand the gentleman, or lady, over to Symonds, with that end in view. Don't you see what such an application would imply? Lawrence was murdered within an hour or two of our playing that game of cards. How comes any one to know what was the amount he claimed to have won? No one saw him between the finish of the game and his death, except the man who murdered him."

"Miss Moore saw him—and you."

"Are you suggesting that Miss Moore wrote this letter—or I?"

"I see your point. You infer that whoever did write it killed Lawrence, because it discloses knowledge which could only be in possession of his murderer. There is something in the inference. But, if the thing's so plain, isn't it an act of rashness to have written you at all—rashness which is almost inconceivable?"

"'De l'audace'—you know the wise man's aphorism.[58] I don't say the thing is plain. On the contrary, I believe it's more obscure than you think. Granting that whoever wrote that letter killed Lawrence—and I fancy you'll find that is the case—the question is who wrote it. It's signed 'The Goddess.' I believe 'The Goddess' was the writer. Query, who's 'The Goddess'? There's the puzzle."

"Are you intentionally speaking in cryptograms?[59] May I ask what you mean?"

"I'm not quite sure that I know myself. I don't go so far as to say that there is anything supernatural about the business, but—it's uncommonly queer."

"Supernatural! You had better make that suggestion to the police. The English law does not recognise the supernatural in crime."

"Possibly not. You say it was a man, Symonds thinks it was a woman; I believe both of you are wrong—that Lawrence was killed neither by a man nor a woman. Who or what is 'The Goddess'? Find that out, you'll have found the criminal!"

His lips curled in an ironic smile.

"I really wonder if you think that you can successfully play a game of bluff with me."

I laughed. The man was so full of verjuice[60] that he could not resist an opportunity of squirting a drop or two in my direction. His intentions had not been over and above friendly before. Now that the shadow of a woman had come between us, I felt that he would stop at little which would help him hang me. That my innocence might be shown was a matter which would concern him not at all—so long as he had hung me first.

While I hesitated what to answer, for, though, I hoped, at the proper time, to take him by the neck and drop him from the window, my desire was, in the mean time, to treat him with the utmost courtesy—some one came rushing into the room. It was Turner, the night-porter. He seemed to have been in the wars. He held his handkerchief to his nose, and his uniform was disarranged as if he had just emerged from a scrimmage.[61]

"There's Mr. Philip Lawrence just gone down the service stairs."

We stared at him—not, at first, gathering what he meant. Our thoughts had been occupied with other themes, as, for instance, our love for one another. He, perceiving that we did not understand, went on, like a man in a rage—

"Yes, he just went down the service stairs, did Mr. Philip Lawrence, and a nice sort of a gentleman he is! I was standing in the doorway, finishing my pipe, when I saw him coming. 'Mr. Lawrence,' I said, 'this is a very sad thing about your brother. I've only just come, so I've only just heard of it;' which I had, and it had took me quite aback. He never said a word; he gave me no warning, but, as soon as I opened my mouth, he came at me like a mad bull, hit me right on the nose, and sent me crashing down on to the back of my head in the road. It's a wonder he didn't knock me senseless, I was so unprepared, and he hit me so hard. As soon as I could pick myself together I saw him rushing down the street, and tear round the corner as if he was running for his dinner. And well he might run, for a nice sort of gentleman he seems to be."

Hume and I looked at Turner, then at each other.

"Are you sure that it was Mr. Philip Lawrence?"

Turner gazed at me resentfully.

"Am I sure? Do you think I'd say a thing like that of a gentleman if I wasn't sure that it was him? Not likely!"

Hume interposed.

"Do you wish us to understand that Mr. Philip Lawrence attacked you in the manner you describe without having, first of all, received provocation from you?"

"I don't know what you call provocation. All I said to him I've said to you. I don't know what provocation there was in saying that it was a sad thing about his brother."

"You did not say, or do, anything else?"

"I didn't do anything at all—he did all the doing; and what I've said I've told you."

"Turner, I know Mr. Philip Lawrence intimately. He is not a man to commit an unprovoked assault. Either you have mistaken some one else for him, or, consciously or unconsciously, you have kept back from us something which appeared to him to be a sufficient justification for what he did."

In his surprise Turner removed his handkerchief from his nose. The blood trickled on to his waistcoat.

"Well! That beats anything! I suppose my word's worth nothing. If you ask those who know me perhaps better than you do Mr. Philip Lawrence they'll tell you I'm no liar. I say that he hit me like a coward, for nothing at all, and then took to his heels; and it was well for him he did, for if I do get within reach of him I'll perhaps give him as good as he sent, though it'll be after I've given him warning first. I'll let you know, Dr. Hume, that though I am a porter I'm not going to let a gentleman knock me about as it suits him, even though he is a friend of yours; and I don't think any the better of you for taking his part."

Going up to Turner, I clapped him on the shoulder.

"That's right! That's how I like to hear a man speak out. Don't think that I doubt you in one little jot or tittle. Mr. Philip Lawrence hit you like a coward because he was a coward. He was afraid of you; and had good reason for his fear, as Dr. Hume knows very well."

"You—you——"

Hume stopped; looking as if he were allowing "he dare not" to wait upon "he would."[62]

"Well, Hume, go on. Your friend did not give Turner an opportunity to punish him for his bad behaviour. If you behave badly, I assure you that I shall avail myself of any chance which may offer to punish you. Pray finish the remark you were about to make."

Hume said nothing. He did not even glance in my direction. But he looked at Turner, and walked out of the room.

"He looks like killing some one himself," said Turner, when he was gone.

"I shouldn't be surprised."

I wonder how much he would have given, at that moment, to have made sure of killing me—for choice, upon the gallows.

CHAPTER XVI

MY PERSUASIVE MANNER

I WENT at once to the house in Arlington Street. The door was opened by Mr. Morley.

"Have you heard anything of Mr. Philip? Is he at home?"

Mr. Morley had opened the door about six inches, peeping through the crevice as if he expected to see some dreadful object on the doorstep. The sight of me seemed to reassure him. He addressed me in a sepulchral whisper.

"Would you mind stepping inside for a moment, sir?"

I went into a front room on the ground floor. Mr. Morley came in after me, and, behind him, Mrs. Morley. I was conscious that the room was filled with old oak furniture. It is, perhaps, because I am not a man of taste that I would not have an apartment in which I proposed to live filled with that funereal wood. Old black oak furniture reminds me of an African swamp. It is dark and sombre— heavy, stiff, ungainly.

Without, the shadows had deepened; in the house it was darker still. The room was still unlighted. The figures of the old man and woman, revealed in the half light, harmonised with the ancient blackness of the furniture. As they stood side by side, as close together as they could get, with, on them both, an air of timidity which the darkness could not hide, I felt that there was a blight upon them, and on the room, and on the house; that it was a place of doom.

"I take it that Mr. Philip has not returned."

They looked at one another; as if each was unwilling to incur the responsibility of a reply. At last the husband took it on himself.

"No, sir; he's not returned, but——"

"Well, but what?"

For the old gentleman had paused. He spoke to his wife, in a whisper which was perfectly audible—

"Shall I tell him, Emma?"

"It's not for me to speak. That, Joe, is for you to say."

"This is Mr. Ferguson; he's Mr. Philip's friend."

"If he's Mr. Philip's friend——"

"Come," I said, "I see you've heard from him."

"Yes, sir, we've heard from him. That—that's the trouble."

"What is it you've heard?"

Again the reference to his wife.

"Shall I—shall I tell him, Emma?"

"I've already told you, Joe, that that's for you to say. It's not for me to speak."

Plainly Joe hesitated, then arrived at a sudden decision.

"Well, sir, this is what we've heard."

He took a sheet of paper out of his pocket, which he gave to me.

"I can't see what's on this, man, without a light! Mine are not cat's eyes; it's dark as pitch in here."

"Before I light up, sir, I'll lower the blind. There's no need for folks to see what's going on in here."

He not only lowered the blind, he drew the curtains, too, leaving a darkness which might have been felt; then started groping for a match upon the mantelshelf. When he had found one he lit the gas—a single burner. By its radiance I examined the paper he had given me. In shape, size, appearance, it was own brother to the sheet which had come to me. On it was a typewritten letter; which, however, in this case, was not anonymous.

"To Joseph Morley,
    "DEAR MORLEY,

        "I'm in a bad scrape. I can't come home. And I've no
clothes, and no money. I send you my keys. Look, you know where,
and send me all the money you can find; and my cheque-book, and
my dressing-case, and two or three trunks full of clothes. As you
know, I took nothing away with me except what I stood up in. I
don't know when I shall be able to send, but it will be as soon as
I possibly can. Have everything ready, for when I do send I shan't
want my messenger to be kept waiting. And keep a sharp look-out;
it may be in the middle of the night.

                                            "PHILIP LAWRENCE.

"Tell any one who asks that I shall be home in about a week;
and that you've instructions to send all letters on. I don't want
people to think that you're not in communication with me, or
that everything's not all right. And you're not to listen to any tales
which you may hear; and you're not to worry, or people will notice
it. You understand?"

The eyes of the two old people did not leave my face while I
was reading. So soon as I lowered the paper Mr. Morley faltered
out his question.
    "Well, sir, what—what do you think of it?"
    "That it's a curious epistle. Who brought it?"
    "That's more than I can say. There was a knock at the door, and I
saw that in the letter-box. I looked out into the street, but there was
no one in sight who seemed a likely person to have dropped it in."
    "No messenger-boy?"
    "No, sir, no one of the kind."
    "And the keys came with it?"
    "Yes, sir, in a small brown-paper parcel."
    "Addressed to you?"
    "No, the parcel was addressed to no one. There was nothing on
it at all."
    "You are sure they are Mr. Philip's keys?"
    "Of course they are. Whose should they be? Why—why do
you say that?"

"Has Mr. Philip been in the habit of sending you typewritten letters?"

"He has never done such a thing in his life before."

"In this even the signature is typed—as if he had made up his mind that you should not have a scrap of handwriting which you could recognise. I don't see why he need to have had such a letter typed at all. Is he himself a typist?"

"Not that I know of; I never heard him speak of it."

"Then to have had such a letter typed by some one else was to add to his risk. Why couldn't he have trusted you with a letter written by his own hand?"

"I can't say."

"Are you yourself sure that this letter is from Mr. Philip?"

"Not a doubt of it. I wish there were. Because it shows that he's in hiding; and what should he be in hiding for, except one thing? What—what are we to do? If—if he has his brother's blood upon his hands."

"Joe!"

"Well, Emma, if he has, he has! And where'll he find a place big enough, and out-of-the-way enough, for him to hide in? All the world will soon know what he's done, and all the world will be in search of him. He won't dare to come here—he daren't already; soon he won't dare to write to me; the police will be watching me like cats a mouse. He'll be an outcast, shunning the places which he knew and the friends who loved him—and he the most sociable gentleman who ever lived, who never could bear to be alone; with a host of friends, and not a single enemy. And—and what are we to do—the wife and I, here, in his house alone? To whom are we to look for help—for guidance—for orders? We—we're almost afraid to stop in the place as it is; it—it's as if it were haunted. We seem to see him wherever we turn; we hear his footstep on the stairs—his voice—his laughter."

"Joe!"

"Well, Emma, so we do. Our nerves won't stand it. We—we're getting all broken up; we're not so young as we were, and used to regular ways, and—and this sort of thing's beyond us. Every knock at the door starts us trembling. Who—who's that?"

As Mr. Morley was speaking, there came an assault on the

front-door knocker which seemed to shake the house. I do not think I ever heard quite such a clatter made by a similar instrument before. That the nerves of the old folks were in a curious condition was immediately made plain; the attack might have been made on them, instead of on the knocker. They drew closer together, clinging to each other for support; consternation was written large all over them. Their behaviour was not that of persons on whom I should have cared to lay the burden of a great responsibility; especially one in which coolness and presence of mind were necessary factors.

The visitor was in a hurry. There had hardly been time to reach the front door when the knocking began again—crash, smash, crash, crash, crash, crash! I really thought the door would have been broken down. The faces of the proper guardians of the house grew whiter, their limbs more tremulous.

"Hadn't you better go and see who's there? Or shall I?"

They let me go. On the doorstep I found an individual who had his own notions of propriety. With scant ceremony he endeavoured, without a word of explanation, to force his way into the house. I am not a man with whom every one finds it easy to play that kind of game. When I am pushed, I push. Placing my hand against his chest, he went backwards across the pavement at a run.

"Manners, sir! Manners!" I observed.

He seemed surprised—as a man is apt to do, who, proposing to play the bully, finds himself bullied instead. His hat had fallen off; he himself had almost fallen too.

"Who the devil are you, sir?"

"Saving a reference to any acquaintance of yours, that is the question which I should like to put to you, sir."

Picking up his hat, he came towards me, with a blusterous air.

"I want to see Philip Lawrence—at once."

"Do you indeed! That's unfortunate. You have come to the wrong place for your want to be supplied. Mr. Philip Lawrence doesn't happen to be in."

"Tell that tale to some one else; don't try it on me; I've heard it before. I'll wait till he is in."

"By all means; let me show you the way inside."

Taking him by the collar of his coat, I conducted him through the doorway, across the hall, and into the front room—where Mr. and Mrs. Morley were still clinging to each other, as if under the impression that the end of the world at last had come. The visitor was a big, black-haired man, inclined to puffiness, whose whiskers and moustache seemed to have been blackleaded,[63] they shone with such resplendence. He was clad in gorgeous attire.

"What do you mean by such disgraceful behaviour?" I inquired.

"On my word, that's good!" He was settling in its place the collar of his coat. "Seems to me that the boot's upon the other foot." He turned to Mr. Morley. "Who is this man?"

"This man," I explained, to save Mr. Morley trouble, "is a person who is competent to resent any impertinence which you may offer. So, if you have come to play the bully, you will have every opportunity afforded you to play your very best."

"Don't talk to me like that, sir, you don't know who I am. If I'd liked I might have made Philip Lawrence bankrupt four and twenty hours ago; only I thought I'd give him a chance. But I'm not going to stand that sort of thing from you."

"Pray how could you have made Mr. Philip Lawrence bankrupt?"

"I hold overdue bills of his for £5000. Some men would have made him bankrupt on the nail, and run him up a tidy bill of costs. I'm too soft-hearted; I gave him a chance. But I've had enough bother already; I'm not going to have any more. If a satisfactory arrangement isn't made before I leave this house, there'll be trouble."

"So you are the person who habitually trades in forged acceptances."[64]

"Forged acceptances! What—what the devil do you mean, sir?"

Unless I was mistaken, he increased in puffiness.

"You know. You were aware that they were forged, and by whom. You had a hand in arranging the whole matter; buying them for a song, with the intention of securing as much out of Mr. Philip Lawrence as you possibly could."

The gentleman began to bluster. Plainly he was not happy.

"I—I don't know who you are to talk to me like that, sir. Your behaviour's altogether most extraordinary. I'll let you know that I'm not going to have you speak to me like that: I'm not going to have such language addressed to me. I came into possession of these bills in the ordinary course of business."

"How much did you pay for them?"

"I paid—— Never mind what I paid for them! What's it got to do with you?" So far he had been wearing his silk hat. Now he took it off to wipe the brim. "As I say, I'm a soft-hearted man, and if it's not convenient to Mr. Lawrence to pay up all at once, why, I'm willing to do my best to meet his conveniences; but I—I'm not going to be talked to like that, certainly not!"

"Hand them over."

"Hand what over?"

"The bills."

"Against money."

"Hand over those bills."

"I haven't got them on me; they're in the safe at my office, under lock and key. Do you think I carry about with me documents of that value? You never know what sort of characters you may encounter."

This with a meaning glance in my direction.

"Hand over those bills."

"Help! Murder! Thieves!"

As he showed a disposition to make a noise, I took him by the throat. Lifting him on the big oak table, and laying him flat upon his back, I kept him quiet while I went through his pockets. As I expected, I found in the inside breast-pocket of his coat a leather case. In this were five promissory notes[65] for £1000 each, purporting to have been drawn by Philip Lawrence, and to have been endorsed by his brother Edwin. I let him get up.

"I hope I have put you to no inconvenience. Since you left the bills in your office safe, under lock and key, no doubt you will find them, still under lock and key, on your return."

"Give me back those bills!"

"They will be quite safe with me."

I put them into my coat pocket. He turned to the Morleys.

"I call you to witness that the man has robbed me, with violence! Mind, with violence!" Then to me: "You give me back those bills, this moment, or it will be a case of penal servitude for you; and I shouldn't be surprised if there were the cat thrown in."[66]

"And what will it be for you? Judges and juries are not apt to look with lenient eyes upon gentlemen who habitually traffic in forged acceptances for the purposes of levying blackmail."

"Don't talk to me like that; I tell you that I won't have it!"

"You won't have it!"

"Upon my word, I don't know who you are, but I believe you're a —— highwayman. Give me back those bills, or I go to the front door, and I call a constable."

"Call one—do. I will give him the bills, with an explanation of what they are, pointing out to him that you will presently have to stand your trial on a charge of conspiracy; and that, also, you are disagreeably associated with a case of murder."

"The man's stark mad. I never heard any one talk like he does—never!"

"Possibly you are not aware that Edwin Lawrence was murdered last night."

"Edwin Lawrence murdered?"

The man turned a greenish hue.

"Beyond doubt his death was the direct result of the crime which you incited him to commit. The whole story's known. I heard myself, this morning, a confession from the lips of the miserable tool who actually concocted the fraudulent documents. You will find him quite willing to turn Queen's Evidence. The bills will be produced in Court, when you will have an opportunity to tell your story."

He put his hand up to his collar, as if it had suddenly become tight.

"It's a lie that Edwin Lawrence was murdered last night. It's a lie."

"By the way, sir, what is your name?"

"What's it to do with you?"

"Chancing to notice in your letter-case some visiting-cards, I ventured to abstract one. We will refer to that." I produced it from my waistcoat pocket. "From this it appears that you are Mr. Isaac Bernstein, of 288, Great Poland Street.[67] Very good, Mr. Bernstein. Your bills are in safe keeping. You will hear of them again, never fear. Their history will be threshed out to your complete satisfaction—when you will be wanted again. Until then you can go."

"It's a lie that he was murdered—it's a lie."

"On that point you may be able to obtain information from Mr. and Mrs. Morley, or from the first policeman you meet in the street."

"God help us all!" groaned Mr. Morley.

Apparently there was something in the old gentleman's ejaculation which carried sufficient corroboration to Mr. Bernstein's alert intelligence. He quitted the room to presently return.

"Who—who killed him?"

"In due course that will be made plain; also your association with the motive which was in the murderer's mind, causing him to compass the death of the man whom you had incited to the perpetration of a hideous and unnatural crime."

Mr. Bernstein went out of the house without another word. When I heard the door bang, I turned to the old people.

"You see? That is the way in which to treat impertinent persons who presume upon your master's absence to traduce his name and to take liberties with the establishment which he has left in your charge."

The old gentleman shook his head. "It's easy talking, but we haven't all got your persuasive manner, sir."

It was an absurd thing for him to say, for no one knows better than myself that my manner is rude and awkward, and that I am unskilled in all those arts which go to make the master of persuasion. As I followed Mr. Bernstein out of the house, almost immediately, I had an illustration of how true that is. And again, in a more serious matter, a little later on.*

CHAPTER XVII

MY UNPERSUASIVE MANNER

As I left the house a man came across the pavement as if with the intention of knocking at Philip Lawrence's door. At sight of me coming down the steps he stopped short. It was young Moore. His appearance set the blood tingling in my veins; his hat was cocked at an acute angle on one side of his head; a cigar was stuck in the corner of his mouth. There was something in his bearing, and about the way in which he spoke, which showed that he had been drinking.

"What are you doing in that house? You answer me that! Seems to me that you've got a finger in every pie."

He addressed me in tones which were probably audible in Piccadilly.[68]

"Might I ask you, Mr. Moore, to pitch your voice a little lower?"

"You may ask, but as for paying attention to anything you ask— not me. I'm not afraid of any one hearing what I've got to say. This is the public street, this is, and if you so much as lay a hand on me—— Here, drop that! Help! Police!"

As I moved towards him, he sprang out of my reach, shouting in a fashion which could not fail to attract attention. Indeed a man, apparently a respectable artisan, who had passed us a few seconds before, turned to look at us.

"What's the matter there?"

Mr. Moore was quite at his ease.

"Nothing—at least, not yet there isn't. But there will be soon, if he so much as lays a finger on me."

The man went on.

"You seem to be a pretty sort of idiot," I observed.

He flicked the ash off his cigar with a jeering laugh.

"We can't all be as wise as you, nor as big. Size goes for something, you great overgrown monster. Barnum's museum[69] is where you ought to be, not walking about the streets."

I hardly knew what to make of him. If I had had him in a room I might have taught him manners; out in the street he had me at an advantage. He was plainly disposed to court, rather than avoid, a public scandal, while I was anything but inclined to find myself an object of interest to a curious crowd. While I hesitated he went on:

"A nice sort you seem to be, all round. A pretty lot of lies you stuffed me with this morning—Adair and you together. On my honour! Making out that Eddie Lawrence had had his throat cut, and the Lord knows what! Setting me thinking that my sister'd cut it for him—my goodness! What is your little game? I wish she had!" He burst into boisterous laughter. "Bessie cut Eddie Lawrence's throat!—that would be an elegant joke! I only wish she'd done it!

D'ye hear? I say I only wish she'd done it! You can put that into your pipe and smoke it."

He swaggered off up the street. I made no attempt to stop him—crediting him with the wild utterances of a drink-fuddled brain. I did wonder what errand had brought him to Philip Lawrence's; for that he had been going there when I interrupted him I felt sure. But that, in his present condition, I should get no information on that point, or any other, from him was evident.

I returned home. As soon as I entered the sitting-room, I became conscious that some one was in the bedroom beyond.

"If that is Hume again——"

It would have gone hard with him, if it had been; but it was not. It was Inspector Symonds and a colleague. It came upon me, with a rush of sickening recollection, that I had actually gone out without putting the room to rights, but with all my possessions lying about just as Hume and I had left them. On the bed was still that irrepressible cloak. Why had I not burnt the thing? Or torn it into rags? Or got rid of it somehow? Anything would have been better than allowing it to continue in existence. The two men were examining it minutely from top to bottom.

"What—what are you doing here?"

There was a choking something in my throat. They had taken me by surprise; and I was conscious that this was not a case in which physical force could be advantageously employed.

"Our duty, Mr. Ferguson. We are acting within the limits of our authority. I have a search-warrant in my pocket. Shall I read it to you, sir?"

"What are you searching for in my room?"

"For something that will throw light upon the murder of your friend, Mr. Edwin Lawrence. As that is an object for which you will, no doubt, be willing to do anything which lies in your power, you will be glad to hear that we have come upon what looks like a very important piece of evidence. Whose cloak is this, Mr. Ferguson?"

"Cloak? What cloak? Oh, that! That's my cousin's."

"Indeed. What is your cousin's name?"

"Mary—Miss Mary Ferguson. She was here a few days ago, and, as her nose bled very badly, she left her cloak behind."

My wits were wool-gathering. It was the first invention I could think of.

"And were these marks upon the cloak made by your cousin's nose bleeding?"

"Exactly."

"She must have almost bled to death. Did a blood-vessel break?"

"No, I don't think so."

"You don't think so?"

"That is, I'm sure. She has suffered very badly from bleeding at the nose her whole life long; some people do—as you are perhaps aware."

"How long is it since she was your visitor?"

"Oh, some days. Quite a week—if not more."

"Is that so? It's odd that the blood should have continued in a liquid state so long. Some of it is not dry yet."

"Well, perhaps it wasn't so long as that."

"So I should imagine."

"If you'll give it to me I'll pack it up and send it to her at once. I meant to have done so before."

"Let me have her address, and I will send it to her. Or, rather, I will take it to her at once. That will save both time and trouble."

"You are very good, Symonds, but I won't put you to so much inconvenience. I prefer to take it to her myself."

"You are sure that your cousin's name isn't Moore—Miss Bessie Moore?"

"What do you mean? Are you presuming again?"

"Are you prepared to assert, Mr. Ferguson, that this cloak was not worn by Miss Bessie Moore when, last night, she came out of Mr. Edwin Lawrence's room?"

"I'll swear it."

"You will have an opportunity of doing so in the witness-box. Though I warn you to consider what are the pains and penalties of committing perjury, because I shall bring trustworthy witnesses who will prove not only that she wore this cloak, but that the fact of her wearing it was well within your knowledge."

He began to roll it up.

"You are not going to take it away, Symonds—my cousin's property."

"Your cousin's property! Listen to me, Mr. Ferguson. I'm told that you've lived a good deal abroad. I don't know what may be the manners and customs in those parts, but I can assure you that, at home, you cannot do a more serious disservice to a person suspected of crime than to resist, on his or her behalf, due process of law. And I may add that, in the eyes of judge and jury, a prisoner is not assisted by the discovery that a witness has been endeavouring to bolster up his or her cause by swearing to a series of unmistakable falsehoods. I know that Miss Bessie Moore was wearing a cloak when she went to see Mr. Edwin Lawrence. Mrs. Peddar says that she had on nothing of the kind when you hid her in her apartment. What has become of it? In the interval, between her leaving Lawrence and going up to Mrs. Peddar, she was in your room. I search your room. In it I discover the cloak which Miss Moore has been described as wearing. You will do that lady a very serious injury by endeavouring to persuade me, or anybody else, that this garment is the property of a suppositious cousin, who never existed except in your imagination."

As he continued to speak in his measured, emotionless tones, I felt as if something was being drawn tighter about my throat; something against which it was vain to struggle. I endeavoured to collect my thoughts. But, somehow, all at once, I had grown stupid; more stupid, even, than I was wont to be. I could not get my ideas into proper order. They eluded me. My brain was in confusion. I could not see what was the wisest thing to do. I came to a desperate resolve, which I put into execution with sufficient clumsiness.

"You're on the wrong tack, Mr. Symonds."

"I've not said what tack I am on."

"You police are famous for your blunders. I'll save you from making another."

"That's kind."

"I killed Edwin Lawrence."

They looked at me, then at each other, smiling. The inspector's colleague gave a short, dry laugh.

"It's a little too thin," he said.

"I repeat that I killed Edwin Lawrence."

The inspector gazed at me with twinkling eyes.

"What do you propose to gain by that?"

"Gain? Nothing; except, I suppose, the gallows. But I don't care. Life has no longer any charms for me, with this—this upon my soul. His blood is on my hands. I admit it."

"With a view, I presume, to getting his blood off the hands of somebody else, eh?"

"What on earth do you mean? You seem to be some sort of monomaniac—possessed with but one idea.[70] I tell you that I am the man's murderer. You can take your prisoner. And there's an end of it."

"Hardly. What we want to know just now is, how you account for these stains upon Miss Moore's cloak."

"I know nothing at all about it."

"They are not the results of your cousin's bleeding at the nose?"

"—— you, Symonds!"

"Thank you, Mr. Ferguson. That's scarcely a matter which is likely to come within your province. You must take us for a pair of really remarkable simpletons, Gray and I, to wish us to believe that you know so much about the one thing and nothing at all about the other. It is odd."

"As you please. I have admitted my guilt. If you decline to arrest me, I certainly shouldn't be the one to grumble."

"You shouldn't be, but it seems that you are. Tell us the story of these stains. It may be that the explanation will make your guilt clear. Then we'll arrest you with the greatest pleasure."

I thought about what Hume had said about the advisability of concocting a plausible story which could hold water. I wished heartily that I had availed myself of his assistance to frame one there and then. I am one of the worst liars living. More than once, when the situation could have been saved by a lie, I have made a mess of things. I am without the knack which some men have; no one would mistake a lie of mine for truth. I felt that the two officers were watching me, with keenly observant eyes, incredulity written large all over them. I was conscious that I must say something. If Hume had only been there to prompt me! Bracing myself together, I made a plunge.

"I will tell you everything. I'll keep back nothing. What would be the use? You'd be sure to find out."

"Quite so."

"She saw me kill him. She tried to save him. She rushed forward, as he fell back into her arms, so that his life's blood dyed her cloak."

"That was the way of it—as he fell back. From the position in which he was found, the idea was that he fell forward."

"Well, it might have been forward. I—I was hardly in a state of mind to pay close attention to every detail."

"With what did you kill him?"

"With—with a knife which I brought home with me from a tribe of negroes on the West Coast of Africa."

"Might I see the weapon?"

I had an armoury of such things, but was conscious that there was nothing among them which could have been responsible for the injuries which had been inflicted on Edwin Lawrence.

"I haven't it. I took it out with me just now, and—threw it into the river."

"That's unfortunate. Because, apart from anything else, it must have been a truly extraordinary weapon—worth looking at, since the doctors were under the impression that at least fifty knives were used, of varying sizes."

"My knife had several blades."

"Is that so? All of the same length?"

"All lengths."

"But fitted into one handle?"

"Yes; but it was a peculiar handle."

"So I should imagine. I'm afraid, Mr. Ferguson, that you'll have to make a drawing of this knife of yours, in order to make the judge and jury and the doctors understand what kind of article it was. When you entered the room, was Miss Moore already there?"

"Yes; she was there on an errand of mercy."

"Indeed. Did she stop the proceedings in order to tell you so?"

"I know."

"I have already remarked that you seem to know a good deal about some things and nothing at all about others. How long was it after your entrance that the murder began?"

"I rushed at him instantly, without a word of warning."

"Describe how the crime was committed—in detail."

"He was standing with his back to me. I stabbed him before

he had a chance to turn; when he did turn, I stabbed him in the chest."

"And then in the face?"

"Yes; and then in the face."

"What was Miss Moore doing all this time?"

"She was taken by surprise. So soon as she understood what was happening she rushed to the rescue."

"I suppose, by then, you had stabbed him thirty or forty times. The corpse is disfigured by hundreds of wounds."

"I can't say."

"And, after the rescue, did you continue stabbing him?"

"I did."

"And what did Miss Moore do—nothing?"

"She tried to prevent me—she did all that she could."

"Struggled with you, for instance?"

"Yes."

"Do you say that Miss Moore struggled with you?"

"Look here, Symonds, confound you, and confound your questions! Do you know that I'm beginning to feel like killing you?"

"Steady! Keep a little farther off. You're not the sort of man with whom I should care to struggle; especially as now, for the first time, I believe you. I have no doubt that, at the present moment, you feel much more like killing me than you ever felt like killing Edwin Lawrence. No, Mr. Ferguson, I've an inkling of what you're driving at, and I'm not sure that, policeman though I am, in a sort of a way I don't admire you. But you're no hand at a game like this. You're no fictionist, it's not your line; your plots don't dovetail. We still have to find out how these stains came upon the lady's cloak."

"Aren't you—aren't you going to arrest me?"

"I am not, at present. Perhaps, when you are in the witness-box, you may succeed in inducing the judge to order your arrest; but, in that case, I'm afraid that it will be for perjury. Come along, Gray. If I were you, Mr. Ferguson, I'd let things take their course; they will, however you may try to stop them. If the lady is innocent, it will be made plain; if she is not, that also will be made plain; and, you may take my word for it, that it's just as well for every one concerned that it should be."

The Inspector went out of the room with the cloak rolled up

under his arm—I making no sort of effort to prevent him. The truth is that I was conscious that I had succeeded in making an ass of myself, and in nothing else, that the backbone had all gone out of me, and I felt as limp as a rag.

And yet that imbecile old Morley had prated of my persuasive manner!

CHAPTER XVIII

I AM CALLED

HAD I had my way, that night, Miss Moore would have sought a place of refuge, where she could have lain hidden till the cloud passed over and her integrity was made clear. Anything, to my mind, was better than that she should run even a momentary risk of a policeman's contaminating hands. But Hume would have none of it.

Some one knocked at the door, while I was sitting on the side of the bed, wondering, since I had failed to do murder, if suicide was not the next best thing. It was Hume. He gave me one of his swift, keen glances as he came in.

"Anything fresh?"

"Man, I've made an idiot of myself—an idiot."

"Ah! But what I said was, Is there anything fresh?"

I told him the story of my interview with Symonds. He kept on smiling all the time, as if it had been a funny tale. When I had finished he rubbed his chin.

"You've burned your boats, that's clear. You'll never hang for the lady. All the king's horses and all the king's men couldn't put that murder story of yours together again.⁷¹ You've managed very well, my dear Ferguson."

I cared nothing for his sneers. Other thoughts were racking me.

"I shouldn't be surprised if he's gone off to arrest her right away, and all because of my—my cursed blundering."

"I think not. The lady's safe for to-night. The police don't always move so fast as you appear to think. They'll know where to find her when they want her."

"That's it! Hume, couldn't—couldn't she be induced to go where they wouldn't know where to find her?"

"I hope she's not so foolish. To run away would be about equivalent to pleading guilty. She'd have all England hot-foot after her. Better stay and face the music. The inquest's for tomorrow. As one of the most important witnesses, you will be able to make the whole thing clear, and establish her innocence in the eyes of all men."

The inquest! I had never thought of it. And for to-morrow? The idea came with a shock of surprise. That was what Symonds had meant by his ironical allusions to my conduct in the witness-box. In my present state of mind, with my muddled head, and stumbling tongue, an expert heckler might goad me into saying anything—into hanging her with the words out of my own mouth.

I had a wild notion of flying myself, so that there might be no risk of doing her an injury by my inability to hold my own in a tongue-match with the lawyers. But I remembered what she had said about feeling safe when I was near; and I myself had a sort of suspicion that, if the worst came to the worst, I still might do her yeoman's service.[72] So, as I could not keep still at home and think, instead of going farther from her I went closer to her. After I had swallowed a hurried dinner I took a cab Bromptonwards, and hung about Hailsham Road for hour after hour.

I passed and repassed the house. A light was burning in the window of an upper room. I wondered if the room was hers. I would have given a good deal for the courage to inquire, but my nervous system was disorganised. I was as afraid of being seen as if I had been there for an improper purpose.

When any one came into the street from either direction I quickened my pace and almost bolted. Once, when some one raised a corner of a blind, with the apparent intention of peeping out into the street, I fairly took to my heels and ran.

On one point I derived some negative satisfaction—so far as I could judge, the house was not being watched by the police. The lady was free to come or go. I was the only person who was taking an obvious interest in her proceedings.

Perhaps that was in some degree owing to the weather, which was bad, even for London. There was a delightful fog, which, for some inscrutable reason, was seemingly not at all affected by a cutting east wind; and a filthy rain. I had on an overcoat; but was conscious that I was not getting drier as the night wore on. What I was waiting for I could not have told myself, until, towards midnight, a hansom dashed into the street, in which, as it passed, I saw the face of Miss Adair. I was after it like a flash, catching it just as it reached the door of No. 22.

"Miss Adair!" I cried, as the lady was preparing to descend into the mud and rain.

"Good gracious, Mr. Ferguson, is that you? Whatever are you doing here at this time of night?"

"I—I thought I'd call and inquire how—how Miss Moore was getting on."

"Well, and have you called?"

"No, I—I thought I'd wait till you came home from the theatre and—and ask you."

From her post of vantage in the cab Miss Adair looked me up and down, perceiving that I was neither so well groomed nor so dry as I might have been.

"And, pray, how long have you been waiting for me to come home from the theatre?"

"Oh, some—some few minutes."

"A good few minutes, I should imagine. And where have you been waiting?"

"Oh, I—I've been hanging about."

"In the mud, I should say, from the look of you. You are a disreputable object. So I cannot but hope that you've enjoyed your vigil. I may tell you, for your satisfaction, that when I left home Miss Moore was ill."

"Ill! Not—not really ill?"

"Really ill. This time there's not a doubt about it. She's in bed. Dr. Hume says that it's the result of the breakdown from the overstrain which might have been naturally expected."

"Hume! Has Hume been here?"

"Certainly. And another medical man."

"But—what did Hume want?"

"My good sir! Dr. Hume's a doctor; and a very clever one."

"Yes; but only in special cases. This sort of thing is not his line."

"I think you are mistaken. I should say that everything was in his line. Besides, he is a very old and a very intimate friend of Miss Moore's."

"Oh—I—I wasn't aware that he was quite—quite so intimate as that."

I felt that the woman was regarding me out of the corner of her eye. She knew that she was torturing me.

"Oh dear, yes. Not that I fancy that Bessie's very fond of Dr. Hume. Indeed, it's rather the other way. It's my belief that she can't bear the sight of the man. Though I don't know why. He's most charming—and so clever. Don't you like clever people?" No, I did not, I never did, and never shall. "Should I ascertain how Bessie's progressed since I went out, or don't you care to stay?"

"If—if you would let me know how she is!"

Letting herself in with a latchkey, she made inquiries of the maid who appeared in the hall.

"How is Miss Moore?"

"I don't think she's quite so well, miss. I sent for Dr. Nockolds, and I did think of sending for Dr. Hume."

"Hume!" I cut in. "I shouldn't send for Hume. The other man's as good, if not better."

Miss Adair turned to me.

"But, my dear Mr. Ferguson, Dr. Hume is a most skilful practitioner."

"Yes; but not—not in these sort of cases. I'm sure the other man's better. And, if you like, I'll send in a man; I—I know a most wonderful man."

"And what did Dr. Nockolds say?"

"He seemed to think she was going on all right, only a little feverish. But he sent in a nurse, who's going to sit up with her to-night."

"She'll be all right with the nurse, not a doubt of it. Good night, Mr. Ferguson. So good of you to call."

That woman showed me to the door without giving me a chance to slip a word in edgeways. I went home in the cab which had brought her from the theatre. Hume indeed! Why had I not been trained to be a doctor? If there was a more miserable man in London that night than I was, I should have liked to have seen him.

And on the morrow it was worse! They held the inquest, after the agreeable English custom, in a public-house—the Bolt and Tun—the sort of place no decent person would have entered in the ordinary way. There, in a long room, with a sanded floor,[73] the coroner sat with his jury. The witnesses hung about as if they did not know what to do with themselves. The police were very much in evidence. And a heterogeneous collection of doubtful-looking men, women, and children represented the general public.

The coroner was a man named Evanson—a Dr. Reginald Evanson. A small, thin, sharp-faced man with sandy hair, who looked as if he drank. I am very much mistaken if it was not only because he failed as a medical practitioner that he got himself elected coroner. I disliked the fellow directly I caught a glimpse of him; and I do not think that he took an inordinate fancy to me. As for his jury, he and they were a capital match; there was not one man among them to whom, on the strength of his appearance, I would have lent a five-pound note.

They commenced proceedings by viewing the body. Edwin Lawrence still lay on his own bed, so that they had a walk of a hundred yards or more. It seemed as if they enjoyed the little excursion, for two or three of them were sniggering and joking together when they returned; I should not have been surprised to learn that they had refreshed themselves with a glass of something at the bar, on the way upstairs. Then evidence was called. George Atkins.

It was Atkins and I who had discovered the tragedy. They did not keep him long. He said his say in a crisp, business-like manner, which I only hoped that I might be able to imitate when my turn came. He told how he had taken his morning cup of coffee to Lawrence's bedroom door; how he had failed to receive an answer; how he had brought my coffee to me, telling me of his inability to make the man hear; how I had gone along the balcony, looked through the window, called to him; how we had entered the room together, and what we had seen lying on the floor.

When Atkins had told them so much they let him go.

"Call John Ferguson."

It was unnecessary. John Ferguson was waiting, close at hand, completely at their service—or, at least, as much at their service as he was ever likely to be.

I stepped up to the table.

"Large size in blokes, ain't he?" whispered one idiot to another, as I passed through the little crowd.

The other idiot chuckled. I could have hammered their heads together, so sensitive was I at that moment to everything and anything, and so calmly judicial was my frame of mind, in excellent fettle to cut a proper figure on an occasion when everything—happiness, honour, life itself—might hang upon a word!*

CHAPTER XIX

I LEAVE THE COURT

As for the coroner, he was prejudiced against me directly I took up my stand at the table; he being one of those diminutive opuscula[74] who instinctively object to a man who is of a reasonable size. My height has been against me more than once. It placed me at a disadvantage then. There was not a creature present in the room who did not look upon me as a sort of raree-show,[75] and who was not prepared to enjoy the spectacle of my being put to confusion. Nor had they long to wait for the sort of pleasure they desired; I made a hash of things almost from the start.

A little fellow, who had informed us that he had been instructed by the Treasury, took me in hand. He might have been a cousin of the coroner's; he, too, had sandy hair and the same peevish countenance. His questions at first were not particularly objectionable, but ere long they became of a kind which, if I had had my way, I would have been careful not to answer in any fashion save one. He had a trick of holding his hands in front of him, fidgeting a piece of paper between his fingers. His voice was, like himself, small and insignificant; but, when he chose, it had a singularly penetrating quality, which, for some reason, reminded me of the sound of sawing wood. He kept his eyes fixed almost continually on my face, glancing hungrily from feature to feature, as if desirous not to miss the movement of a muscle. Altogether he was like some pertinacious terrier who worried, not only in the way of business, but also for sport. I should like to have taken him by the scruff of the neck and shaken him.

He wanted to know if Edwin Lawrence had been a friend of mine; how long I had known him, what I knew about him, when I had seen him last. I told him about the game of cards, but, somewhat to my surprise, he made no allusion to my loss, nor the terms on which we parted.

And here began my blundering. I wished the Court to understand that, at parting, we were on the worst possible terms, and that I was in just the proper mood for committing murder. But Jordan—that was the little terrier fellow—would have none of it. He told me to confine myself to answering his questions; and that I would have an opportunity of making any statement, on my own account, which the Court might think fit to allow, when he had done with me. I wished to make my statement then; but with him against me, and the coroner, and an ass of a foreman, who said that the jury were unanimously of opinion that I was wasting time, I never had a chance.

He had his way. Then began the real tug-of-war with his very next question. He asked me if, after I had retired to rest, I had been disturbed in the night. Then I saw a chance to score, after all. I said I had, by a dream; but when I was about to tell them of that mysterious vision, he stopped me.

"Never mind about the dream. Dreams are not evidence."

Some of the audience tittered. I have not the faintest notion what at. I should have liked to supply them with an adequate reason.

"But my dream is evidence—very much evidence. If you will let me tell it you, it will throw more light——"

"Thank you. But were you disturbed by nothing beside a dream?—for instance, by some one coming through your bedroom window?"

"I was not."

"Mr. Ferguson, take care. Do you say that no one came through your window?"

"I say that I was not disturbed by any one."

"I see. You are particular about the form in which the question is put. I will alter it. I ask you—did any one come through your bedroom window after you had retired to rest?"

"I decline to answer. It's no business of yours. I suppose I can have what visitors I choose."

"Do you suggest that the visit was intended for you—in your bedroom, alone, at that hour of the night? Consider what your suggestion implies."

"I never said that any one came."

"You as good as said so. But we will have it from you in another form. Who was it, Mr. Ferguson, who came through your bedroom window?"

Beads of perspiration were already standing on my forehead.

"I have told you," I shouted, "that I decline to answer!"

Jordan turned to the coroner.

"Perhaps you will allow me to explain, Mr. Coroner, that the police are in possession of a body of evidence which tends to implicate a particular person. This fact the witness is aware of and resents. He has not only thrown obstacles in the way of the police, but has gone so far as to assert his own guilt. That this assertion rests on no basis of truth there can be no sort of doubt. Its only purpose can be to throw dust in the eyes of the police; and, especially, to render his own evidence ineligible. His own evidence is of capital importance. And I ask your assistance, Mr. Coroner, in my endeavour to prevent a miscarriage of justice, owing to Mr. Ferguson's refusal to answer any questions which I may put to him."

"Certainly. Witness, you will answer any proper questions which are put to you, at once, and without any beating about the bush."

"I rather fancy that that's a point on which I shall please myself."

The coroner banged his hand upon the table.

"Don't speak to me like that, sir, or you'll find yourself in the wrong box. If you don't answer the questions which are put to you, I'll commit you for contempt of Court."

"Commit."

I should have liked to commit an assault upon the coroner. But he thought proper to ignore my challenge, and addressed himself to Mr. Jordan.

"Put your question again. I am amazed to find a person of the apparent position of the witness behaving in so discreditable a manner."

"Now, Mr. Ferguson. I ask you again: Did any one come through your bedroom window after you had retired to rest?"

"And I say to you, Mr. Jordan, that you have my sympathy in the position in which you find yourself. Don't you think if I were to put one or two questions to you, it might vary the monotony?"

"You hear, Mr. Coroner, what the witness says?"

"I do. And I regret to find that such conduct can be treated with levity." A titter had gone round the room. "If there is that sound again, I will immediately have the court cleared. Witness, look at me."

"If you desire it, with the greatest pleasure. Though there doesn't seem to be much to look at."

"How dare you speak to me like that?"

"No offence, my dear Mr. Coroner. A plain statement of a plain fact."

"Have you been drinking, sir?"

"That is said with an insolent intention. Is it impossible for an official person to be courteous?"

"Your behaviour is most extraordinary. You evidently cannot realise the serious nature of the occasion which brings us here. Are you aware, sir, that if you decline to answer the questions which are put to you, I can commit you to prison for contempt of Court?"

"I am not aware of any reason why impertinent questions should be answered under one set of circumstances rather than another."

"Don't argue with me. Will you answer the question which counsel has put to you?"

"My good Mr. Coroner——"

"I commit you for contempt. Officer, arrest this man."

"If the gentleman in question is wise enough to take my seriously offered advice, he will not attempt to do anything so foolish."

Hume, who was sitting opposite, rose and leaned towards me across the table.

"Are you stark mad? What useful purpose do you propose to serve by going to gaol? Or what good do you suppose you will do her by fumbling with the questions? You will have to speak out sooner or later. Speak out now! Tell the truth! That is the only way in which you can do her a service."

Jordan struck in; still twirling the scrap of paper into spirals with his fingers:

"Might I ask you, Mr. Coroner, to request your officer to refrain for a moment from carrying out your instructions? Perhaps Mr. Ferguson may be disposed to listen to this gentleman's wise and friendly counsel. Don't you think, sir, that you had better?"

I laughed.

"I do. I am prepared to answer any questions which you may put to me."

"That is more promising. I assure you that I have no desire to do or say anything to hurt your feelings. I believe I know what they are, and I respect them. But I must do my duty and you must do yours; and I do not think that you will hurt any one by doing it."

"Don't lecture me, man."

"Now, tell me; did any one come through your bedroom window after you had retired to rest?"

"No one."

"That you swear."

"Miss Bessie Moore did not come through your window?"

"Certainly not. How dare you drag in that lady's name?"

"Was she in your rooms at all that night?"

"She was not."

"Did you go up, between one and two in the morning, to tell the housekeeper that she had come through your window?"

"I did not."

"Did the housekeeper come down and find her in your room?"

"She did not."

"Did Miss Bessie Moore spend the night in the housekeeper's apartments?"

"I can't say."

"Can't—or won't?"

"Can't."

"Are you aware that you have sworn to speak the truth?"

"I am."

"Are you acquainted with the pains and penalties of perjury?"

"My good man, pray don't, even by inference, attempt to measure others' ignorance by the standard of your own."

"As you will. So long as we know that we are not dealing with one who is wholly illiterate. Have you seen this cloak before, Mr. Ferguson?"

From a bag which Inspector Symonds produced from beneath the table he took, as I had expected, the plum-coloured cloak.

"I have."

"Where?"

"In my room. And on my cousin's back."

"On your cousin's back? Not on Miss Moore's?"

"Certainly not."

"You have never seen Miss Moore wearing it?"

"Never."

"To the best of your knowledge and belief is this not Miss Moore's cloak?"

"Nothing of the kind."

"That you swear?"

"You have already reminded me that I am on my oath."

"It is necessary to keep that fact always before you, Mr. Ferguson. Then if Miss Moore says that this cloak is hers she will be stating what is false?"

"When Miss Moore makes such a claim it will be time to discuss it. Don't let us be suppositious."

"Very well. I will not put to you any more questions, Mr. Ferguson, at present; though don't suppose for a moment that I have done with you. I have to inform you, Mr. Coroner, that this witness has been uttering a series of perjuries, well knowing them to be perjuries, for the obvious purpose of defeating the ends of Justice. And I have to ask that, at the very least, a watch be kept upon his movements."

"He shall be detained."

"Detained!"

I laughed. I buttoned my coat across my chest, and I walked out of the room. The people made way to let me pass as if I had been the plague. Possibly it was because they saw something in my appearance which they did not altogether like. A constable stood at the entrance. I motioned him, with my hand, to move on one side. He moved aside. I saw that there was a key in the lock, on the outer side of the door. I had an inspiration. It was a solidly constructed door, not one of your flimsy constructions made of matchwood, but a good, honest piece of woodwork, not to be easily forced from the inside. I drew it to, locked it, and, slipping the key into my pocket, I walked down the stairs out into the street.

The Court, for all I knew, continued sitting.

CHAPTER XX

A JOURNEY TO NOWHERE

It was between three and four o'clock in the afternoon. Already the lamps were lighted. The fog still hung over the city. From the appearance of things it might have been night.

"To her!" I said to myself. I called a cab. "To Hailsham Road— the Boltons!"

I examined my possessions. Time pressed. Return to Imperial Mansions was out of the question. Of what crime I had been guilty I did not know; that there would be a disposition to make me smart for it I felt persuaded. I have lived in places where, as much as possible, a man carries his valuables upon his person, for safety. The habit has clung to me a little. As a rule I carry more money than, I believe, the average Englishman is apt to do. I had in my letter-case over £100 in notes, in my pockets nearly £20 in sovereigns;[76] a sufficiency for my immediate requirements. It was enough to take two people out of reach of the storm.

As we entered Hailsham Road I saw that a man was standing at the corner. Turning, as we passed, he closely scrutinised both the cab and me. The maidservant answered my knock. Miss Moore was in—Miss Adair out. Miss Moore was better, thank you. She would inquire if I could see her.

She showed me into the sitting-room. A bright fire was blazing. The apartment was redolent of a particular aroma, perceived of my imagination, perhaps, rather than my senses. It was an aroma I loved. I had never seen a room I liked so much. While I was considering that it might turn out unfortunately for the gentleman at the corner, should he show too pertinacious an interest in my movements, she came. With a little flutter, and a little laugh—the sound of which was good—she held out both her hands.

"Oh, I'm so glad you've come. If you'd been much longer, I should have come to you. Where have you been?"

"For some part of last night I was out in the street, watching your window."

"Out in the street! But—why didn't you come in?"

"It was too late to pay a call. Besides—I did make inquiries, and they told me you were in bed, and ill."

"I was not very well. I believe I was lightheaded. But I'm better now; my own proper self—not the person you have known."

"Indeed."

"And—I know." She drew back a little, looking down at her foot, which peeped out from under the hem of her gown, as if it were a curious thing—which it was, for beauty. "I know all that you did for me, how good you were."

"Then you know nothing."

She looked up at me with a sudden flashing in her eyes.

"I know all. I know that I didn't do it. Aren't you glad?"

"I never supposed you had a finger in the matter."

"That is strange. Appearances were all against me; you knew not what I was, or anything at all. I came into your room in—in a most disreputable way, with an impotent tale—which was none at all. My cloak was wet with blood. You have it now."

"I had it."

"You must have suspected me of at least some sort of hand in it; it would have been only natural."

"To me it seems that it would have been most unnatural."

"That's odd. I believe I'm suspected by all sorts of people; by some of the very worst. And you never doubted me at all?" She breathed a little quickly as if she sighed. "I am glad. So long as you know that it was not a murderess who came through your window like a thief, I do not seem to care what others think, which is absurd. For I had no hand in it, nor had you; nor had Mr. Lawrence's brother."

"But—who then?"

"That, as yet, I can't quite see. There was something strange about it; something like a conjuring trick, which I am not sure that I understood, even at the time. It was all done by some dreadful creature, the mere horror of whose presence drove me from my senses. I can't think what it can have been."

When, stopping, she stood before me, with shining eyes; her lips parted with a smile, so as to show the small white teeth within, I was at a loss how to enter on the subject of my errand. So, as usual, I blundered.

"Unfortunately, men are mostly fools, and blind."

There my tongue stuck fast. She looked at me a little anxiously.

"How do you mean?"

"There are those of them who cannot see the noses on each other's faces."

"Is that so?"

"It's a fact. Some of them are idiots enough to believe that—that you knew something about that scoundrel's death."

"I see." Her face lightened as if she began to perceive my drift. "You mean that they suspect me of having murdered him. That's no news."

"But I fear they go beyond suspicion."

"Beyond suspicion? Do you mean that they can prove it?"

"Miss Moore! You are severe. I mean that—they may try to arrest you."

"Arrest me! Arrest me!" She drew herself straight up, her small fists clenched at her sides. "But they mustn't arrest me. You mustn't let them."

"I won't."

"How—how can you stop them?"

"I shall be only too glad to act as your guardian, if you care to try a trip abroad until they perceive their own stupidity."

"A trip abroad—with you."

The suggestion which the words conveyed, as she pronounced them, had not entered my thick skull. I was thunderstruck.

"Or—or I could stay behind; or come on by the next train."

"I don't see what good that would do me."

"I'd take care that they didn't lay their sacrilegious hands upon you."

"I don't see how—if you weren't there."

I began to stamp about the room. I had forgotten that the fact of her being a woman made a difference in all sorts of ways. The situation was more complicated than I had allowed for.

"Miss Moore, I'm an idiot."

"Yes?"

There was something in the way in which she laid emphasis on the note of interrogation which robbed the word of its sting.

"But I'm not, in some respects, such an idiot as you might suppose."

"Oh."

This was said with a twinkle of laughter.

"Can you trust me?"

"With my life; with what is dearer."[77]

"Will you do as I tell you?"

"Implicitly."

"Go upstairs, put your hat and coat on, and some things in a bag."

"How many things? In what sized bag?"

"Enough to take you to Paris."

"To Paris? Am I going to Paris? Oh, but I'm wanted at the theatre; they're clamouring for me."

"Let them clamour. Will you be so kind as to do what I tell you? Excuse me, Miss Moore, one moment! Do you mind my bringing a man in here, and making him comfortable, till after we are gone?"

"Please explain."

"Well, there's a man in the street who, I believe, is watching the house."

"Is he going to try to arrest me? Has he a warrant in his pocket?"

"Nothing of the kind. Only he might try to follow us to see where we went, and that wouldn't be convenient."

"Do you propose to hurt him?"

"Not a hair of his head! I promise you."

"Are you going to try on him the effect of a little reasoning? You certainly have, beyond other men, the persuasive manner. You might induce him to see things in a proper light. If you think it necessary, you can try."

Her words reminded me of what old Morley had said. I thought the sarcasm was a little hard. I winced.

"There is one other thing, Miss Moore. How many servants have you in the house?"

"One at present. The cook is out."

"Could you send that one out on an errand which would detain her, say, an hour. We don't want her to know that we left the house together—or indeed anything."

"You have an eye for details. I perceive that I'm entering on another adventure. If you will take a stroll for a quarter of an hour, when you return you will find her gone. I shall have my hat and coat on, and some things in a bag."

"Good. When you are ready, go out as softly as you can, without coming in here, and without taking any notice of me at all. Leave your bag in the passage; I'll carry it. Go into the Fulham Road, and stroll towards Walham Green.[78] I'll come to you as soon as I'm able."

"You won't hurt him?"

"I'll not do him the slightest damage."

I opened the door for her to leave the room. She passed upstairs; I went out into the street. The man was still at the corner; he eyed me intently as I passed. I paid no attention to him whatever. Strolling leisurely, I crossed the Fulham Road, and, through some devious and dirty by-streets, I gained the King's Road.[79] At an oilman's shop I purchased a dozen yards of stout clothes line. Looking at my watch, I found that I had been absent nearly ten minutes. With the same leisurely gait I retraced my steps. The man was still at his corner.

He was an out-size in policemen; all of five foot ten, well set up, with a carriage which denoted muscle. Fortunately for my purpose, his face did not point to a surplus of brains; he struck me as being as stupid as I was. I marched straight up to him with an air of brusqueness.

"You're from the Yard. Why on earth didn't you give me the tip when I drove past you at first? You saw me staring at you hard enough. I've been on a wild goose chase, all because of your stupidity; you shall hear of it again!" He touched his hat. "I've just come from the court; Inspector Symonds is detained; I'm on this job at present. Has anybody come out of 22 since I did?"

"A young woman, sir."

"A young woman. And you let her go?"

"It was only the servant."

"Only the servant! Which way did she go?"

"She came out into the road here, and then got on to a Piccadilly 'bus. My instructions were to keep an eye on the young lady. I wasn't told anything about the servant."

"Oh, weren't you? Then a pretty mess you seem to be making. Come into the house; I may want you. So keep your eyes and ears well open."

I started off at a smart pace. He hesitated, then fell in at my side.

"I beg your pardon, sir, but do you mind telling me your name? I don't seem to remember your face."

I strode on, unheeding.

"Now, in you come. And mind what I told you about keeping your eyes and ears wide open."

I pushed him through the gate. The lady's wits had been on the alert; she had left the door open.

"Hallo! the door's open," I cried. "That looks suspicious. I shouldn't be surprised if the bird had flown. Servant-girl you thought she was. That'll be a bit of all right for you. Come into this room."

I led the way into the sitting-room. So soon as we were in, I began to undo the packet of rope.

"Just look out of the window and see if that's any one coming in."

He seemed as if he could not quite make me out, or the whole proceeding. But, after a moment's delay, he did as he was told. He went to the window. In buying the clothes line, I had tied a slip-knot at one end, so as to form a rudimentary lasso.[80] So soon as his back was turned I had this over his head, tightening the knot: his arms were pinioned to his sides. He struggled fiercely.

"It is a plant, is it? —— if I didn't think it was! So this is your little game!"

"This is my little game; and, if you take my advice, my lad, you'll own you're beaten. Because you are."

He was. I ran the rope about him, pulling him off his feet with a jerk. As he lay on the floor, I trussed him hand and foot. I have had some experience in the handling of ropes, and can tie a knot or two. I was prepared to guarantee that, unaided, he would never move again.

"What are you going to do to me?" he asked.

"Nothing, my good man. It's surely more comfortable in here than out in the street in such weather as this? The unfortunate part of the business is that I am so anxious that you should not make a noise that I'm afraid I shall have to take measures to keep you still."

"You are not going to gag me?"

"I fear I must. But, to prove that I regret having to subject you to inconvenience, I am going to slip two five-pound notes into the breast pocket of your coat. When you're untied you will be able to drink my health with them."

"Drink your health! My God, I will!"

"Just so. But not with so much strenuosity. Such language should not be used."

I had bought, at the same shop as the clothesline, some cotton wadding. I thrust as large a piece of this into his mouth as it could conveniently hold. Then, lifting him, I laid him carefully on the floor in a corner of the room behind a couch. As the couch hid him, and he could neither move nor utter a sound, it was possible that he might remain there for some considerable time without his presence being discovered.

I went out of the room. In the passage was a bag. Picking it up, I passed out of the house. On the pavement, just outside the door, was the lady. She was full of concern about the gentleman I had left behind.

"Have you—have you hurt him?"

"Not in the least; I have simply tied him up, so as to prevent him following us to see where we go."

I did not think it was necessary to say anything about the gagging.

"Have you tied him very tight?"

"Not I."

"Is he strong?"

"I never asked."

"But you could see. How big is he?" I told her. We were moving towards the Fulham Road. She repeated her little trick of drawing a hurried breath. "I wish I were a strong man!"

"You are stronger than any man I ever knew."

"How can you say such a thing? Am I as strong as you?"

I sighed—in earnest.

"Are you as strong as I?"

"You choose to talk in riddles. You know very well that in your hands I should be like a baby. Where are you taking me?"

"I hardly know. I hope out of the shadow into the sunshine."

"Suppose a policeman—see, there is one over the road—were to come up now, and say I was his prisoner. What should you do?"

"I should explain that he was mistaken."

"Explain!" She laughed. "But you can't explain to every one, in the same fashion, for ever."

I was startled. Her question had a little startled me. To tell the truth, I was wondering myself where I was taking her. The Paris boat train did not start till nine. It was barely five. To stay in London for another four hours would be to run a risk. By that time, too, a watch might have been set upon the boat express.

We were walking towards the Brompton Road.[81] I was just thinking of calling a cab, being only restrained from doing so by the doubt as to where I should tell him to drive us, when my attention was diverted by an exclamation from the lady.

"Mr. Ferguson! Look! There's Mr. Lawrence!"

I glanced in the direction she was pointing. In front, just far enough off to cause the outlines to be a little obscured by the mist, was a figure I seemed to recognise. I quickened my steps.

"Lawrence! Philip Lawrence!"

Although his back was turned to us, I could not but suspect that he had seen us first. Because, scarcely had I spoken, than, darting into the road, he sprang into a passing cab without troubling to stop it, shouted some direction to the driver, which I could not catch, and in an instant was away. To pursue and leave the lady there was out of the question. I waited till she came up.

"Are you sure that it was Lawrence?" I inquired.

"Certain! I have only seen him once, but then under circumstances which make it impossible that I ever could mistake him.

There is a portrait of the man upon my brain—life-size. Wherever and whenever I see him I shall know that it is he."

"It is odd that he should have run away."

I was puzzled; not only by his flight, but by the rapidity with which it had been performed.

"Yes, it is odd. What's that?"

A note of fear was in her voice. She came closer to me. I saw that her face had suddenly grown white. The hand which she had placed on my arm was trembling.

Through the mist, out there in the Fulham Road, there came the sound of a woman's laughter. It was that curious laughter which I had heard in Edwin Lawrence's room—soft, low, musical; yet within it, indefinable, yet not to be mistaken, a quality which was pregnant with horrible suggestion.

At the sound, for some cause, my heart stood still.*

CHAPTER XXI

A CHECK AT THE START

WE looked each other in the face.

"You heard it?" Her voice quavered.

"I heard something. It was only a woman's laughter. She is somewhere close at hand, but is hidden from us by the fog."

"It was That which did it. Do you think I can be wrong? It is with Mr. Lawrence. It is his shadow: it follows close behind him."

She was shivering from head to foot. Her eyes were distended, her face white; I was fearful of I knew not what. Hailing a passing hansom, I had practically to lift her into it. She seemed to have all at once grown helpless. I told the driver to take us to Victoria—fast. An idea had occurred to me. The Ostend boat train[82] left at half-past five. We might be able to catch it. Anything was preferable to inaction. The sooner we were out of London the better it would be. She was still trembling as she sat beside me in the cab. I tried to calm her.

"You are too sensitive. It was only a trick of your imagination, you let it run away with you. If you are not careful you will be ill; then what shall I do?"

She came closer to me still.

"Save me! You will save me!"

It was like the pleading of a frightened child. The contact of her person with mine set me shivering, too; it was as if I were thrilling with a delicious pain.

"At present there is nothing from which to save you. When there is, I'll not be wanting, rest assured."

"Put your arm about me." I did as I was told, wondering if she were mad, or I. "How is it that I only feel safe when I am close to you—and the closer the safer?"

"It is because God is very good to me."

"To you? God is good to you?"

"Has He not put it into your heart to feel safe with me?"

"You think so? Take your arm away. I am better now. I am not—not such a coward. You think it is God who has put it into my heart to feel safe with you. I wonder!"

"I am sure."

"You are a strange man."

"I pray that you may not always think so."

"Have you—have you had many friends among women?"

"Never one; unless I may count you as a friend."

"Oh yes, you may count me—as a friend. Do you care for women?"

"I did not know it until now."

She laughed. I was glad to have lightened her mood.

"You are odd—you are really very quaint." She leaned out of the cab. "Where are we? I have not the least idea where you are taking me."

"To Victoria; to try to catch the Ostend boat."

"Ostend? Are we going there?"

"I think we'd better."

"But—— Well, I suppose it doesn't matter, but I really was not anticipating a trip to Ostend quite so soon. Just now you talked of Paris."

"And it may be Paris after all; only the Ostend boat goes first."

"And time's the essence of the matter. I see. Between this and the departure of the Paris train I run a risk of being arrested. That is to bring it very close."

I was still, hardly knowing what to say. What she said was true; this was a case in which, at any moment, truth might decline to be trifled with. She, too, was silent. Leaning back in her own corner, as far as possible from me, she looked forward into the fog. Starting for the other end of the world at a moment's notice was a commonplace event with me. An unexpected run to Brussels was to her a thing so strange as to be almost awful. I looked at my watch; called to the driver.

"Can't you press on a little faster? We shall lose our train."

"Why such hurry? Let us lose it."

On that point we disagreed; I was not disposed to lose it. But I said nothing. The man whipped up his horse. Presently he began to insinuate his way into the station yard, which was blocked with vehicles. I saw that for him to thread his way between them would be a work of time. Moments were precious.

"Come!" I said. "Let's get out. We shall reach the pavement quicker than he will, and the train is already due to start."

We descended into the road. Picking our steps between the horses' heads, we gained the station. I tore to the booking-office, she, laughing, close at my heels, as if the whole thing were a delightful jest.

"Two firsts to Brussels!"

"Too late, sir; train's just off." As the clerk spoke a whistle sounded. "There she goes. Platform's closed; you won't be able to catch her."

The lady's face was alive with smiles.

"There! After all our hurry! Isn't that annoying?"

She didn't look as if she thought it was annoying in the least. Boys were shouting out the editions of the evening papers. Placards were displayed on the bookstall close at hand. I saw her glance at one, which had already caught my own attention.

"'Imperial Mansions Murder. Extraordinary Scene at the Coroner's Inquest.' Has the inquest been held? And what has happened there? What does it mean by 'extraordinary scene?'"

I felt as if every one was on the point of calling out, "Here's the man who locked up the coroner's court! Here's the woman he's spiriting away!" The sudden sight of that placard had got on my nerves. I was brusque, brutal.

"Bother the inquest! What we've got to think about's that train."

"Indeed? So you can be bad-tempered if you like, and civil too. I was wondering if you were always a model of lamblike decorum."

"I beg your pardon, but—the fact is, I'd made up my mind to catch that train."

"Had you? And you'd also made up your mind that I shouldn't know what was in the papers. You're very considerate, Mr. Ferguson."

I glanced round, startled. Her outspoken mention of my name took me aback. No doubt all the world was talking of John Furguson; looking for him; wondering where he was. I did not want that crowd to learn that he was in its midst. My appearance of discomfiture she seemed to find amusing.

"Might I ask you just one question?"

"You are too hard on me; you may ask a thousand."

"Did you propose to take me all the way to Ostend without giving me anything to eat? Perhaps you're not aware that four o'clock is the actor's dinner-hour. I've not had a morsel of food all day."

"Miss Moore!"

Mine was the blunder then; I could have bitten my tongue off for uttering the name. A man behind turned towards us as if he had been struck by it—or I thought so. Had he known it, he was never so near having his head twisted off his shoulders. Had he allowed a sign of recognition to have escaped him, there would have been murder done. But he was a mild-looking, grey-haired person, and the sight of the expression with which I regarded him seemed to fill him with such astonishment, to say nothing else, that he retreated precipitately backwards, as if fearful that I was about to devour him then and there. I stumbled on.

"I entreat your forgiveness, but I—I hadn't the faintest notion you were hungry."

"No—you wouldn't have."

"Meaning that I am the sort of person who never does know anything? You are right; I am. But where shall we go? I believe there's some sort of place in the station where we can get something to eat."

"The nearest, please."

"But—I'm afraid that's horrid."

"Don't you know any place which isn't horrid?"

Scarcely ever before had my constitutional stupidity been so much to the front. The missing of the train, the discovery that I had actually proposed to take my companion to Ostend foodless, and in a state approaching to starvation, the fact that the paper-boys were repeating, under my very nose, their parrot cry, "Extraordinary scene at an inquest!"—these things, joined to the confusion around, seemed to addle my brain. For the moment I could not think where I could take her to get something decent to eat. Still doubtful, I was making for the station restaurant when some one caught me by the arm. It was Mr. Isaac Bernstein. He seemed to be half-beside himself with excitement; he grasped me with a vigour which was perhaps unconscious.

"Have the goodness, Mr. Bernstein, to release my arm."

He burst into voluble speech.

"This is more than I can stand, and I'm not going to have it. Don't touch me, or I'll call for help. There are policemen close by and I'm not without protection! Even a worm will turn,[83] and now I'm going to; so just you listen to what I've got to say."

"Your affairs, Mr. Bernstein, have no interest for me. Did you hear me ask you to release my arm?"

"It's as much your affair as it is mine—every bit as much." He waved his umbrella. "There's Lawrence there."

"Who?"

"Lawrence! He's been trying to do a bolt—to Ostend or some infernal place or other, the other side of the world, for all I know—meaning to dish me as he's done the rest of you. But I was on to him. He'd have been off in spite of me only he was drunk, or mad, or something, and they wouldn't have him in the train. Now he's behaving like a howling lunatic." Releasing my arm, Mr. Bernstein took off his hat to wipe his brow. "I believe he's raving mad. That's him! Did you ever hear anything like the row he's making?"

As a matter of fact, while the excited gentleman was speaking, I had become conscious that something interesting was taking place on the platform from which the boat-train had departed. The thing was becoming more obvious every second. Apparently the railway officials were taking more or less vigorous measures to induce somebody to quit the station precincts. This person, who was the centre of a curious and rapidly increasing crowd, was announcing his opinions on divers subjects, and on the subject of railway men in particular, at the top of his voice and in strident tones with which I seemed familiar.

A sudden premonition swept upon me that matters were rushing to a head; that a few hours, a few minutes, even, would see the whole mystery made clear. Though even then I had not an inkling of the form which the explanation would take. As my eyes wandered I saw, peeping at us from out of the crowd, my companion's precious relative, Mr. Thomas Moore. For some reason the young gentleman looked as if he were half beside himself with fear; he was pasty white. When he perceived that I had recognised him he slunk out of sight like a frightened cur.

I glanced at the lady to learn if she also had observed her brother. From her bearing I judged not, though as I eyed her I understood that she also had seen the signs of the times, the shadows which coming events were casting before, and that she, too, realised that the hour, the moment, was big with her fate and mine.

CHAPTER XXII

A MIRACLE

THE hustling throng came quickly forward. In its midst some one was being propelled towards the entrance. Although he was shouting at the top of his voice, he appeared to be offering no actual resistance, but seemed rather to be regarding the proceedings as a joke. In spite of the hubbub[84] Mr. Bernstein's accents reached my ear.

"Did you ever hear anything like him? Isn't he a beauty? And that's the man who's had I don't know how much cash out of me—a hatful! And that's how he goes on!"

I was indifferent to Mr. Bernstein's lamentations. As the crowd came nearer I was beginning to ask myself if I was dreaming; if, again, I was about to become the victim of a nightmare imagining. I turned to Miss Moore.

"Hadn't you—better go? Hadn't I better—get you out of this?"

I was conscious that my voice was a little hoarse. Hers was clear and resonant. Although she did not speak loudly, it seemed to ring above the din.

"Go? Now? When it's coming face to face, the light is breaking, I'm beginning to see clear, and it's my call? No; now I'll stay and play the scene right through until the curtain drops. It was God who made us miss that train."

The crowd was drawing very close. Was I asleep or waking? Were my eyes playing tricks, my senses leaving me? What suddenly made the world seem to spin round and round? Who was it in the midst of the people—the man they were hustling—who raved and screamed? Was he a creature born of delirium,[85] or a thing of flesh and blood?

It was from the girl at my side that recognition first came.

"It's he!" she cried. "It's he!"

It was he—the wretch who had set us all by the ears; who had fooled and duped us; who had played upon us, as a last stroke, a trick whose nature, even yet, I did not understand. I strode into the crowd.

"Let me pass! Make way for me!"

They made way. It was well for them they did; the strength of a dozen Samsons was that moment in my arms.[86] I planted myself in front of him.

"How is it that you've come back—from the gates of hell?"

"Ferguson! It's you!" He broke into a peal of laughter, which spoke of pain, not pleasure. "But I've not come back! They're still stoking the fires!" He threw out his arms as if referring to the jeering mob, which pressed upon us. "Here are the attendant demons—can't you see them?"

I continued standing still, regarding him.

"It is Edwin Lawrence, as I live. Edwin—not Philip."

"Yes; not Philip—Edwin!" He laughed again. "Would you like to see the strawberry mark? It's there."

"What is this game in which you have been taking a hand?"

"It's a game of my own invention—and hers!" He made an upward movement with his hand. "It was from her the inspiration came. She named the stakes, framed the rules, started the game, watched the play—and with both eyes she's watched it ever since. Those eyes of hers! They never sleep, and never blink or wink, but watch, watch, watch all the time. They've watched me ever since the game began. They're watching now! She haunts and hounds me—into the train and out of it. She's here now—enjoying the joke. Hark! Can't you hear her?" He stopped to listen. I heard nothing out of the common, though it seemed he did. "That's her laughter!" He broke into discordant merriment. "I play the part of Echo.[87] She has me, body, soul, and spirit; and she thinks it such a jest!"

He spoke as men do in fevers. I could see that there were some about us who set him down as mad. There were those who jeered, as fools will at the sight of a man's anguish, when, in the abandonment of his shame, he trails his soul in the dust. I had seen persons in his case before. He was not mad, as yet, but on the border line, where men fight with demons. He had been drinking, to drive them back; but they had come the more, threatening, on every hand, to shut him in for ever. He knew what it was they threatened. It was the anguish of the knowledge which caused the sweat to stand in beads upon his brow.

The railway officials, I fancy, took it to be a case of incipient delirium tremens.[88] A person in authority addressed himself to me.

"Are you a friend of this gentleman's, sir?"

"I know him well."

"Are you willing to undertake the charge of him? You see he's not in a fit state to go about alone."

"I'll take charge of him."

"Then you'll be so good as to remove him from the station at once. He's already given us more than sufficient trouble."

Lawrence interposed with what he intended to be an assumption of the grand manner.

"My good Mr. Railway-porter, or whatever you may be, I will remove myself from your objectionable station without any hint from you. My destination was Ostend, and is now Pimlico.[89] This is an acquaintance of mine who owes me £1880; but I don't require him to take charge of me. There already is somebody who does that. Can't you hear her? That's her laughing."

"Come," I said. "Let's get into a cab."

"Thank you, I prefer walking. Nothing like exercise when you are liverish.⁹⁰ Are you alone?"

Miss Moore came through the crowd.

"No; I am with him."

He stared at her as if in doubt; then with sudden recognition—

"Ah! It is the sister of the brother—the affectionate relative of our dear Tom—the beautiful Miss Moore! It is like a scene out of one of the plays in which you are the bright, particular star. The ghosts are gathering round. You were there; you saw her?"

"Who?"

"The Goddess!"

"Was it—a Goddess?"

"That's a demon!"

"What do you mean?" She took me by the arm. "Ask him what he means."

Lawrence answered.

"It's not a thing the meaning of which can be clarified by words. Come, and you shall see; come together—Mr. Ferguson and you."

She looked at me, inquiry in her eyes. I questioned him.

"Where do you propose to take us?"

"To a little place of mine, where the Goddess is."

"What is this stuff about the Goddess?"

"Come, and you shall see."

I glanced at her.

"Let's go," she said.

He caught her words.

"There speaks the lady who would learn; the woman possessed of the spirit of inquiry."

I repeated my former suggestion.

"Let's get into a cab."

But he declined.

"No; I'll have none of your cabs, I'll walk. I'm cribb'd, cabined, and confined out in the open; in a cab I'd stifle. There's a hand upon my heart, a grip upon my throat, a weight upon my head; they make it hard to breathe. I'll be in close quarters soon enough; I'll keep out of them as long as I can."

I turned to the officials. "Can't you keep these people back?

I don't want to have them following us through the streets. The man's not drunk, he's ill."

"I should get him into a cab."

Lawrence, hearing what the fellow said, rushed at him in a fit of maniacal fury, repeating, in a crescendo scale—

"You'd get me into a cab! You'd get me into a cab! You'd get me into a cab! I'd kill you first." The man shrank back as if fearful that his last hour had come.

We went out of the station, a motley crowd—Lawrence with Miss Moore, and me close at his heels; behind, before, on either side, a miscellaneous assemblage of fools. I would have prevented her from coming had I had my way. I told her so at starting; but she whispered in my ear—

"I'm not afraid. Are you?"

"I am afraid for you—of these blackguards; of the mood he's in; of where he's taking us; of what may happen. I don't know what devil's trick it is he has been playing, but I'm sure it is a devil's trick, and there may be worse to come."

"I'm safe with you."

"I doubt it."

"But I am sure. The light is coming; I'd like to see the brightness of the day, for mine honour's sake, which I thought might be a consideration, perhaps, with you. Still, I'm under orders. If you bid me I will go. But—mayn't I come?"

I could deny her nothing which she asked in such a tone, though it were an apple out of Eden. But I was gruff.

"Then take my arm."

"I'd like to."

I know I was a fool, and should have forbidden her to go with us, nor have allowed her, wheedle as she might, to have run the risk of what might be to come; but when I felt her little hand upon my arm, I would not have had her take it off again, not—not for a great deal.

When we had gone a little way from the station, Mr. Bernstein, corkscrewing his way through the crowd, reached Lawrence's side. Apparently, although he had made an effort to screw his courage to the sticking point, he was still not quite satisfied as to the sort of reception which he might receive; he spoke with such an air of deprecation.

"Now, Ted, dear boy, don't be shirty,[91] it's only me. Do take my advice—be careful! Don't go too far! Be reasonable, and I'll be the best friend you ever had, as I always have been; only—do pull up before it's too late!"

Lawrence, standing still, addressed himself to the crowd.

"Gentlemen—and ladies!—because I believe there are some ladies among you—real ladies!—allow me to introduce to you Mr. Isaac Bernstein, usurer, Jew, who makes a speciality of dealing in forged bills. He keeps a school for forgers, where young penmen are trained in the delicate arts of imitating other people's signatures. He's been the cause of many a good man's being sent to gaol; where, one day, as sure as he's alive, he'll go to join them."

Mr. Bernstein stammered and stuttered.

"Don't—don't talk to me like that! The—the man's stark mad!"

"Not yet. Still sane enough to make the world acquainted with Isaac Bernstein, trafficker in forgeries."

With his open palm he struck the Jew a resounding blow on either cheek. The people roared with laughter. I turned to the lady.

"You see? I must go to him. I shall have to leave you."

"We will go together."

She kept close to my side as I went forward. I expected to see Lawrence repeat his assault. Bernstein stood looking at him, motionless, gasping for breath, as if he were on the verge of an apoplectic fit.[92] Taking him by the shoulder I sent him spinning off the pavement.

"Leave him alone. The fellow will get his deserts elsewhere."

Lawrence clapped his hands like a child.

"Bravo! Twirl him round—roll him in the mud! She enjoys it; can't you hear how she's laughing?"

He raised his hand in an attitude of attention.

"I can hear nothing."

"But I can." Miss Moore spoke from behind my shoulder. "I can hear It."

"What do you mean?"

"It which was present in the room; It which did it all; the sound which we heard in the Fulham Road just now. Listen! Can't you hear it, too?"

It might have been my imagination—probably was—but, as she spoke, I certainly did think that I recognised, as if it issued from the lips of some one who was within reach of where we stood, the woman's laughter which had in it so singular and disagreeable a quality. It had on me a most uncomfortable effect. I returned to Lawrence, fearful lest, if I was not careful, the proceedings might take a shape in which I might relish them less even than I did at present.

"Come. Let's be moving."

"With pleasure. Life is movement, and exercise is the thing for the liver."

"What is the address of the place to which you are taking us?"

He laid his finger against his nose.[93]

"That's a secret which I wouldn't divulge for worlds. There's a lady there—a goddess! And a demon! Would you have me tell all the world where she's to be found, as if she were a person of no reputation. She's with me all the time; she never leaves me for a moment alone; and yet, all the while, she waits for me at home. That's to have a familiar in attendance,[94] if you please."

I made no reply. That his words had meaning, and were not the mere ravings which they seemed, I did not doubt. I was asking myself what was the solution of the problem to which they pointed, and was still obliged to own that I had no notion. I had, also, my attention partly occupied by my efforts to keep the rabble from a too close attendance on the lady, whose little hand again caressed my arm.

Lawrence was swinging along at a good round pace, his hat a little at the back of his head; his eyes, lips, every muscle of his face were in constant motion. His arms were as if they had been hung on wires, which continually thrust them this way and that. He was not for a moment still. If not speaking aloud, he muttered to himself. Presently he began upon a theme which I would have thanked him to have avoided.

"So, Ferguson, you're a humorist—practical and actual. I've been reading the news—still sane enough to read the papers—how you locked the coroner in his court. I'd have given one of

Bernstein's forged bills to have been there to see, though it was on me that they were sitting. I thought I never should have done laughing. And she—the Goddess—she's laughing still."

The lady put a question.

"What's that he's saying?"

"He's telling about some nonsense which he saw in the papers." Lawrence interposed.

"Nonsense, he calls it! And excellent nonsense, too! Haven't you heard? Has no one told you? Don't you know? Charming sister of my dear friend Tom, to-day the coroner's been sitting on my corpse—as I live, upon my corpse! Ferguson's been there as witness. They wanted him to say, it seems, that you had killed me—yes, you, with your own two small hands; but he wouldn't. He said he'd see them—warmer first; as warm as I am now. I can't think where, at this time of the year, the heat can come from. I'm on fire inside and out. So they talked of sending him to gaol.

"But, bless their simple souls, they didn't know their man; how that he was a fellow of infinite jest. For when they talked of locking him up, he locked them up instead; marched straight out, turned the key in the lock, with them on the other side of the door—coroner and jury, counsel and witnesses, audience and policeman—the whole noble, gallant company. And so he left them, sitting on my corpse."

As might have been expected, the rabble, which still hung round us like a fringe, hearing what he said, caught something of his meaning. They bandied it from mouth to mouth.

"That's Ferguson, that there tall bloke. He's the cove[95] as locked the coroner up this afternoon, Imperial Mansions murder case. Didn't you hear the other bloke a-saying so? No lies! I tell you it is!"

While the gutter-snipes[96] wrangled, playing fast and loose with my name—with my reputation, too—the lady whispered in my ear. Despite the noise they made I heard her plain.

"So that's why you came to fetch me? Now I understand; the secret's out. It's another service you have done me! Aren't you afraid that the weight of obligation will be more than I can carry? Yet you needn't fear! They're the kind of debts I don't at all mind owing—you, since one day I hope to pay them every one."

"You exaggerate. And Lawrence is a fool."

"Yes. So are we all fools; perhaps that's why some of us are wise."

I liked to hear her voice; to feel her hand upon my arm. Yet, every moment, my concern was getting greater. The crowd was growing, both in numbers and in impudence. Any second they might make an ugly rush, then there would be trouble; and that was not a scene in which I should wish the lady to play a part. Lawrence was marching on as if he meant to march for ever. I began seriously to ask myself if he was not playing us still another of his tricks; if he was not leading us he himself did not know where. On a sudden, he determined the question by stopping before a building which, outwardly, was more like a warehouse than a private residence.

"At last," he cried, "we are arrived. The Goddess waits for us within."

"Is this your place?"

"It is—and hers. *Enter omnes!*"[97]

He threw open the door as if he were offering the whole crowd the freedom of the premises. I placed myself in front of it.

"I'm hanged if it shall be *enter omnes!* In you go." I thrust him in. "Now you and I together!"

The lady and I were across the threshold. I was about to slam the door in the face of the rabble, when some one came hurrying through the crowd. A voice exclaimed—

"Stop that! Don't shut that door! Let me in!

It was Inspector Symonds; with, as it seemed, a friend or two.*

CHAPTER XXIII

IN THE PASSAGE

THE inspector I dragged in by the collar of his coat. I slammed the door in the faces of his friends, keeping my foot against it while I shot the bolts.

"This won't do! I'm not going to stand any more of your nonsense! You let my men in!"

There was a flaming gas-bracket[98] in the passage. By its flare I eyed the inspector.

"You be so good as to understand, Mr. Symonds, that I'm going to have no more of your nonsense." He put his hand up to his mouth—a whistle between his fingers. Gripping his wrist, I pinned him by the throat against the wall. "If you are not careful, you'll get hurt."

He gasped out, between his clenched teeth, "I'll make you pay for this! You let my men in!"

"I'll not let your men in—until you and I have had an explanation."

The lady interposed. "Don't hurt him!"

"I'll not hurt him—unless he compels me. Look here, Symonds, there's been a mystification—a hideous blunder."

"I don't want to have anything to say to you. You open that door!"

His hands returned to his lips. Again I had to pin him against the wall; this time I wrenched the whistle from between his fingers.

"If you give any sort of signal, you'll be sorry."

"You've broken my wrist!"

"I haven't; but I will if you don't look out. I tell you, man, that we've been on the wrong scent; you and I, and all of us. It isn't Edwin Lawrence who's been murdered; he isn't even dead."

"Don't tell your tales to me."

"Tales! I tell you tales! Here's Mr. Edwin Lawrence to tell his own."

Lawrence was standing a few steps farther down the passage, an apparently interested spectator of what had been taking place. Symonds turned to him.

"This man? Who is this man?"

Lawrence thrust his thumbs into his waistcoat armholes.

"I'm the corpse on whom the coroner's been sitting."

"Don't play your mountebank[99] tricks with me, sir."

"I'm the murdered man."

"Indeed? And pray what may be your name?"

"Edwin Lawrence—at your service, entirely to command. Though I may mention that that's only a form of words; since, at present, I'm really, and actually, in the service of another—a lady. Bound to her hand and foot by a tie there's no dissolving."

Symonds perceived that in his manner, to say the least, there was something curious. As he looked at me I endeavoured to give him the assurance which I saw that he required.

"It is Mr. Edwin Lawrence, you may safely take my word for it. The lady can confirm what I say."

Which the lady did upon the instant. The inspector was still, plainly, in a state of uncertainty; which, under the circumstances, was scarcely strange.

"I don't know if this is a trick which you have got up between you, and which you think you can play off on me; but, anyhow, who do you say the dead man is?"

Lawrence chose to take the question as addressed to him. He chuckled; there was something in the chuckle which suggested the maniac more vividly than anything which had gone before.

"Who's the dead man? Ah! there's the puzzle—and the joke! The dead man must be me. It's in the papers—in people's mouths—it's the talk of the town. The police are searching for the wretch that slew me—the coroner and his jury have viewed my body. It's plain the dead man must be me. And yet, although it's very odd, he isn't. It's the rarest jest that ever yet was played—and all hers." He pointed with his thumb along the passage. "It's all her doing, conception and execution, both. And how she has enjoyed it! Ever since she has done nothing else but laugh. Can't you hear her? She's laughing now!"

There did seem to come, through the door which was at the end of the passage, the sound of a woman's laughter. We all heard it. The lady drew closer to me; I gritted my teeth; the inspector, with whom, as yet, it had no uncomfortable associations, treated it as though it were nothing out of the way.

"Who's it you've got in there?"

Lawrence raised his hands as if they had been notes of exclamation.

"A goddess! Such an one!—a pearl of the pantheon![100] A demon!—out of the very heart of hell!" He fingered his shirt-collar as if it were tight about his neck. "That's why she relished her humorous conception more than I have. The qualities which go to the complete enjoyment of the jokes she plays, I lack. The laughter she compels has characteristics which I do not find altogether to my taste. It gets upon my brain; steals my sleep; nips my heart; fills the world with—faces; grinning faces, all of them—like his. And so I'm resolved to tell the joke, and I promise that it shan't be spoilt in telling." This with a smile upon his lips, a something elusive in his eyes, which, to my mind, again betrayed the lunatic. He threw out his arms with a burst of sudden wildness. "Let them all come in—the whole street—the city-ful! So that as many as may be may be gathered together for the enjoyment of the joke!"

Symonds and I exchanged glances. I spoke to him in an undertone.

"If you take my advice, you will listen to what he has to say. Before he's finished, the whole story will have come out."

All the time there had been knockings at the door. Now some one without made himself prominent above the others. A shout came through the panels.

"Symonds! Is that you in there? Shall we break down the door?"

The voice was Hume's. I proffered a suggestion to the inspector.

"There is no reason why Dr. Hume should not come in. He will be able to resolve your doubts as to whether or not this is Mr. Edwin Lawrence. Your men I should advise you to keep outside. They will be close at hand if they are wanted."

He regarded me askance, evidently still by no means sure as to the nature of the part which I might be playing.

"You are a curious person, Mr. Ferguson. You have your own ideas of the way in which justice is administered in England. However, you shall have your own way. Let Dr. Hume come in. My men can wait outside till they are wanted."

I unbolted the door, keeping my foot against it, to guard against a sudden rush. The crowd was still in waiting. It had evidently grown larger. As the people saw that the door was being opened, there were cries and exclamations. Hume was standing just outside. It seemed that it had been his intention to make a dart within; but the spectacle of me in the doorway caused him to hesitate. By him were the inspector's friends. Misunderstanding the situation, they made an effort to force the door wider open. It was all I could do to hold it against them.

"Hume, you can come in. Inspector Symonds, give your men their instructions."

"Gray, are you there?"

"Yes, sir! Do you want us?"

"Not just now. I may do shortly; keep where you are. Send along for some one to keep those people moving."

"Very good, sir. Are you all right in there?"

"For the present I am. Keep a sharp lookout. If you hear me give the word, come in at once—if you have to break down the door to do it."

"Right, sir!"

I rebolted the door, boos and groans coming from the crowd as they perceived themselves being shut out from the sight of anything which there might be to see. Hume had entered. He was looking about him as if the position of affairs were beyond his comprehension.

"Symonds, what does all this mean? Ferguson, what new madness have you been up to? Miss Moore, you here! This is no place for you!"

"I think it is."

"I say it's not. You ought to be in bed. Who gave you permission to leave your room?"

"I gave myself permission, thank you. I am quite able to take care of myself. And, if I'm not, here's Mr. Ferguson."

"Mr. Ferguson! Mr. Ferguson stands in need of some one to take care of him." He turned to me. "If you've had a hand in bringing Miss Moore here, you ought to be ashamed of yourself, if you're capable of shame, which I'm beginning to doubt. Surely your own sense of decency, embryonic though it may be, ought to have told you that it is no place for her. What is this den which you have brought her to?"

"Here is some one who can tell you better than I. Ask him, not me."

Lawrence broke into laughter.

"That's it, Ferguson. Hume, ask the corpse."

Hume stared at the speaker, as if he had been a spectre; which, apparently, he was more than half disposed to believe that he was.

"Lawrence! Edwin Lawrence! Is it a living man, some demoniacal likeness, or is it a ghost? My God! is it a ghost?"

Again Lawrence laughed. He went closer to the bewildered

doctor; his eyes flaming, his manner growing wilder as he continued speaking.

"A ghost, Hume, write it down a ghost! I wonder if I could
cheat myself into believing I'm a ghost? Hume, you're an authority on madness. Look at me; do you think I'm mad? It's a question
I've been putting to myself since—she began to be humorous. I see
things—I hear things—like the men who've been—thirsty. There's
a face which looks into mine—a face all cut and slashed and sliced
into ribbons; and, as the blood streams down the cheek-bones,
which are laid all bare, its teeth grin at me, inside the torn and
broken jaws, and it says, 'After all I've done, this is the end!' I strike
at it, with both my fists, where the eyeballs ought to be, but I can't
knock it away; it won't go, it keeps on being there. I can't sleep,
though I'd give all the world to. I'm afraid to try, because, when I
shut my eyes, I see it plainer. The blood gets on my hands; the taste
gets into my mouth; the idiot words get on my brain, 'After all I've
done, this is the end!' I can't get away from the face and the words;
whatever I do, wherever I go, they're there. I seem to carry them
with me. I've been drinking, but I can't drink enough to shut them
out; I can't get drunk. And, Hume, do you think I'm mad? I hope
I am. For while I'm being tortured she laughs; she keeps laughing
all the time. It's her notion of a jest. I hope that it's but a madman's
fancy, what I see and hear; and that, when I get my reason back
again, they'll go—the face and the words. You're a scientific man.
Tell me if I'm mad."

Hume turned towards me. His countenance was pasty-hued.

"What devil's trick is this?"

Lawrence answered, in his own fashion, as if the question had
been addressed to him.

"That's what it is—a devil's trick! Hers! The Goddess's! She's
a demon! I'll—I'll tell you how it was done. She's got me—by the
throat; bought me—body and soul. But I don't care, I'll be even.
She shan't do all the scoring; I will play a hand, although, directly
afterwards, she drags me down to hell with her. Let her drag! I'm
in hell already. It can't be worse—where she has sprung from."

Taking Hume by the shoulder with one hand, with the other
he pointed to the door which was at the end of the passage.[101] He

was dreadful to look at. As he himself said, he already looked as if he were suffering the torments of the damned.

"She's in there—behind that door. But although she is in there she's with me here. She's always with me, wherever I am; she, the face, and the words. You think I'm romancing, passing off on you the coinage of a madman's brain. I would it were so. I wish that they were lies of my own invention, a maniac's imaginings. Come with me; judge for yourself. You shall see her. I will show you how the devil's trick was done."

He led the way along the passage. We followed. I know not what thoughts were in the minds of the others. I do know that I myself had never before been so conscious of a sense of discomfort. The lady slipped her hand into mine. It was cold. Her fingers trembled. Even then I would have stayed her from seeing what we were to see if I could; but I could not. It was as if we were being borne onward together in a dream. All the while I had a suspicion that, of us all, Inspector Symonds was most at his ease, while it seemed to me that Hume carried himself like a man who moved to execution.

CHAPTER XXIV

IN THE ROOM

A LARGE, bare, barn-like room. The walls were colour-washed; as seen by gaslight, an uncertain shade of grey. The floor was bare. At one end was a wooden daïs.[102] This, and a large skylight overhead, suggested that the apartment had been intended for a studio. Artistic properties there were none. The furniture was scanty. In one corner was a camp bedstead, the bedclothes in disorder. It had evidently not been made since it was slept in. There were two small tables, one at the side against the wall, the other in the centre of the room. Bottles and glasses were on both. Bottles, indeed, were everywhere; designed, too, to contain all sorts of liquids— wines, spirits, beers. Champagne appeared to have been drunk by the gallon. On the floor, in the corner, opposite the bedstead, were at least seven or eight dozen unopened bottles, of all sizes, sorts,

and shapes. Three or four chairs, of incongruous design, completed the equipment of the room; with the exception, that is, of
a tall screen covered with crimson silk which stood upon the daïs.
This screen was the first object which caught the eye on entering.
One wondered if an artist's model were concealed behind.

Lawrence placed his finger against his lips as he held the door
open for us to enter.

"Ssh! She's there, behind the screen! Listen! Can't you hear her
laughing?"

This time I, for one, heard nothing. There was not a sound.
And, since every sense was at the acutest tension, had there been,
it would scarcely have escaped my notice. Scarcely were we all in,
than a door on the opposite side of the room was opened, gin-
gerly, and seemingly with hesitation, as if the opener was by no
means sure of his welcome. Through it came the pertinacious
Mr. Bernstein, and, of all persons, young Tom Moore. At the sight
of her brother the lady shrank closer to my side. The inspector
appeared to regard the advent of the newcomers with suspicion,
as though doubtful lest there were more to follow.

"Who are these men? Where do they come from?"

Lawrence explained.

"Inspector Symonds, allow me to introduce you to Mr. Isaac
Bernstein—dealer in forged bills and patron of penmen. Surely
you have heard of Bernstein."

"Oh yes, I've heard of Bernstein. So you are Mr. Isaac Bernstein.
Who's the other man?"

"The other man is"—this with a glance towards the lady—
"merely a thief."

"I'm no thief! I'll let you know I'm not to be called thief—especially by you!"

Young Moore's disclaimer was half whine, half snarl. Bernstein
took up his tale.

"Mr. Symonds, I'm glad to meet you, sir. Our—our friend here
is fond of his joke. You mustn't take him seriously. It—it's his way
to say things which he doesn't mean. I just stepped in to say a word
to him in private—just one word; so I hope you'll forgive me if I
seem to be intruding. Lawrence, I—I came with our young friend
here along the little back passage, which the models used to use,

because I—I wanted to speak one word to you in private. Would you mind stepping on one side just—just for half a moment."

"No, Bernstein, I won't. Anything you have to say to me, you'll say in public; at the top of your voice; out loud. I'm going to say my say so that every one may hear me—she and they."

"Now, Lawrence, be reasonable, I do beg of you. Let me make to you just this one remark."

Drawing closer, Mr. Bernstein dropped his voice to a whisper. Taking him by both shoulders, Lawrence began to shake him to and fro.

"Speak up, Bernstein, speak up! Shout, man, shout!"

"Don't Lawrence, you'll hurt me!"

"Hurt you! Hurt you! If I could only hurt you as you've hurt me, you pretty fellow! Why didn't you save your skin by taking to your heels? For me there's no salvation, because of her, and the face, and the words. But for you there was a chance. Now there's none! Now there's none!"

He flung the Jew away from him, so that he went reeling half across the room. Mr. Bernstein addressed himself, with stammering lips, to the inspector.

"Mr. Symonds, he's—he's not right in his head; he's excited—he's been drinking; look at those bottles!"

Lawrence threw out his arms with a laugh.

"Look at those bottles! Evidences of a giant's thirst! I'll have another!"

Taking a bottle of champagne out of the collection in the corner, with what looked like a palette knife[103] he struck the neck off with a cleanness and dexterity which denoted practice. The wine foamed up. He filled a soda-water tumbler, emptying it at a draught.

"That's the stuff! It's got a sting in it! I like my drink to have a sting!"

Bernstein drew the inspector's attention to his proceedings.

"You see. That's how he goes on—drink! drink! drink! He does nothing else but drink. You wouldn't pay any attention to his ravings when they reflect upon a respectable man?"

"Respectable man! Isaac Bernstein, respectable man?"

He tossed the bottle he was holding towards the Jew. If the other had not ducked, it would have struck him.

"He's a liar, that's what he is; a liar to his finger-tips. No one who knows him would believe him on his oath."

This was young Moore. Lawrence pointed at him with his tumbler.

"A Solomon risen to judgment! See truth's imaged superscription on his brow."[104]

The lady stepped forward before I had guessed her intention.

"What he is he in great part owes to you—and to him!"—pointing to the Jew. "You are an older man than he, with a wider knowledge of the world. You have used him as a tool with which to save yourselves. You found him in a ditch—in the same ditch in which you were yourselves. Instead of helping him out you dragged him farther in, pressing him down in the mire, so that, by dint of standing on his body, you might yourselves reach the bank, at the cost of his entire destruction. Though he is guilty, your guilt is a thousand times as great."

"There speaks the actress. Your sentiments, Miss Moore, do you credit; though, being of the stage, they're stagey. They suppose that you can make a good man bad. I doubt it, be he old or young. All that you can do, is to bring to a head the badness which is in a bad one. Bernstein, your brother, and I, were born with a twist in us; a moral malformation; a trend in the grain which, as we got our growth, gave a natural inclination in a particular direction.[105] I doubt if we could have gone straight if we had tried. You may take it for granted that we did not weary ourselves with vain efforts. I know that I did not. The things I liked had to be, like ginger, hot in the mouth; my pleasures had all to be well peppered. Your insipidities I never relished; nor was the fact that they happened to be virtuous a sufficient sauce.

"As it happens, in this best of all possible worlds, spice costs money. And there's the rub. For I had none—or as good as none. But I'd a brother who had. An all-seeing Providence and an indiscriminating parent, had caused him to be amply dowered with worldly goods. I made several efforts with my own hands and brains to supply myself with money. Sometimes they'd succeed; oftener they would fail. When they failed, in the most natural possible manner, I looked to my brother—my only brother—to make good the deficiency. To do this he now and then objected; which was odd. Until, one day, I came upon a man named Bernstein."

The Jew, who had been listening with parted lips and watch-ful, troubled eyes, to what the other had been saying, now went forward to him, cringingly.

"Lawrence, good old friend, remember all I've done for you, and—and be careful what you say."

"I'll remember, and so shall you; you never will be able to accuse me of forgetting. This man, Bernstein, was a Jew—an usurer."

"I lend money to gentlemen who are in need of it, that's all; there's no harm in it. If I didn't some one else would."

"He negotiated loans on terms which varied—as I quickly learned. I had had some experience of usurers; but this was a new type."

"How new? Circumstances compel one to alter one's terms—it's only business."

"He lent me a little money on what he considered reasonable terms."

"And so they were—most reasonable. You know yourself they were."

"'When you want more,' he said, 'you must bring me another name upon the bill.' I asked, 'Whose name?' He said, 'Your broth-er's.' 'Do you think my brother would back a bill of mine? He'd see me farther first!' 'That,' he said, 'is a pity.' And so it was a pity. Brothers should be friendly; they should help each other; it's only right.

"'Come,' he said, 'and dine with me.' I dined. After dinner he began again about the bill. 'I'll give you £700 for a three months' bill[106] for a thousand with your brother's name on it.' 'I tell you that nothing would induce my brother to back a bill of mine.' 'If you were to bring me such a bill I shouldn't ask how it got there.' Then he looked at me, and I saw what he meant. 'That's it, is it? I've sailed pretty close to the wind,[107] but I've never got quite so far as that.' He filled himself another glass of wine. 'You say you want the money badly. The sooner you let me have the bill, the sooner your wants will be relieved.' I let him have the bill in the morning. At the end of three months there was a storm in the air."

"I knew nothing of it—he invents it all. The bill was duly met when it was presented."

"After my brother and I had come pretty near to murder, I was still, as ever, in want of money. But this time it was Bernstein who came to me.

"'I hear you're pressed.' I complimented him on the correctness of his information. 'It's no good,' said he, 'peddling with hundreds. It's a good round sum you want to set you clear.' I admitted it; and wondered where the good round sum was coming from. 'I tell you what I'll do,' he said. 'You bring me five bills for a thousand each, with your brother's name on them, and I'll give you two thousand five hundred for the lot.' I told him that it couldn't be done. I'd promised my brother that I wouldn't play any more tricks with his name, and I meant to keep my word. 'Ah,' he said, 'that's a pity.'"

"I said nothing of the kind. It is not to be believed; those who know me will tell you it is not to be believed. It is against my nature."

"'I think,' he continued, 'I know how it can be managed. I know a young fellow whom I'll introduce to you. You may find him of use. He's a first-rate penman.' 'Do you mean that he's an expert forger?' 'Lawrence,' cried Mr. Bernstein, 'you shouldn't use such words—you really shouldn't.'"

"You hear him admit it? I said, 'You should not use such words.' I have always said it—always."

"He made me known to this expert penman, getting up a three-cornered dinner for that especial purpose. The expert penman was our young friend here—Tom Moore."

"I never wanted to know you—never. I told him that I didn't."

Mr. Bernstein contradicted the young gentleman's disclaimer.

"Now, Moore, that is not so. You were always willing to make his acquaintance; why not? He was a gentleman of family, of fortune. Why should you not have been willing to know such an one?

"He didn't turn out like that, did he? Look how he served me!"

"Ah, that is another matter. We could not have foreseen how he was to turn out. We supposed him to be a gentleman of reputation—of character."

"Innocent-minded Bernstein! Ingenuous Tom Moore! After dinner Moore returned with me to my rooms."

"You invited me."

"I did—that's true; and you came. I said to him, 'I hear you're a bit of a penman.'"

"I didn't know what you meant."

"You wouldn't. I laid five bill-stamps in front of him."

"There was nothing on them."

"True again; there wasn't. I showed him my brother's signature at the bottom of a letter, and I asked him if he thought that he could make a nice clean copy of it in the corner of each stamp."

"You never said what you were going to do with it."

"Still correct—I didn't. But you said, 'How much are you going to give me?'"

"Well, you were a stranger to me; you didn't expect I was going to do you a favour for nothing?"

"Hardly. I said I'd give you a hundred pounds, which I thought was pretty fair pay for a little copying. But you said, 'I want five hundred.'"

"You didn't give me five hundred pounds, not you! You know you didn't! Or anything like!"

"Accurate as ever. I couldn't see my way to quite as much as that. I said you should have two hundred."

"That night you never gave me any money at all."

"No. But in the morning I carried to Mr. Isaac Bernstein five bills for a thousand pounds apiece, with, on each, my brother's endorsement in the corner. In exchange, Mr. Bernstein presented me with two thousand five hundred pounds, and out of that you had two hundred."

"I took it as a friendly present."

"Precisely—from a perfect stranger. Time went on. The three months slipped by. I began to fidget. Luck was most consummately against me. Two thousand five hundred pounds went no way at all; I had lost it, pretty nearly every penny, before I really realised that I had ever had it. When it was gone, I knew that breakers were ahead; a pretty nasty lot of rocks. As I say, I began to fidget. I knew my brother, and was well aware that, since last time it had been nearly murder, this time it would come as near as possible to quite. Philip's temper, my friends, Philip's temper was distinctly bad. We had had a few fights together, he and I, and out of them it had not been my general custom to come out best. Now I foresaw that the biggest fight of all our fights was drawing comfortably close; and when I asked myself in what condition I should probably emerge from it, I was not able to supply my question with an answer which gave me entire satisfaction.

"I began to hate my brother. As the days stole by, I began to hate him more and more—to fear him. The two things together, the hatred and the fear, took such a hold of me that I began to cast about in my mind how I could get the best of him, when the game was blown upon and the fight began. And at last I thought of something which I had chanced upon in India.

"It was one night when I lay awake in bed, unable to sleep. I had been drinking. The drink had been bad. Among the goblins which it brought to my bedside were thoughts of my brother. I thought of how the luck had all been his; of what a grip he had; of his bone and muscle; of how, in our quarrels, it always had gone hard with me; of how, in the next one, which was close at hand, it would go harder still. He was more than a match for me all round. In peace or war he was the stronger man. How could I get even with him? How?

"Then I thought of the Goddess. It was from herself that the first inspiration came; she precipitated herself, as the occultists have it, into my mind.[108] I suspected it then; I know it now. She had remained, till then, in the packing-case in which I brought her home. She had never been out of it, not once. I had never taken the trouble to unpack her. She might have feared she was forgotten; felt herself slighted. No; that's not her way. She knows she'll never be forgotten; and as for slights, she never will be slighted when there's need of her. She had been waiting; that was all—waiting for her time. Now her time had come. She knew it. So she reminded me that she was there.

"It struck me, at first, as a humorous idea—The Goddess. It always is her humorous side which appeals to one at first. Indeed, it is that side of her which continues to the front; only—the character of the humour changes. I laughed to think that her existence should occur to me at such a moment. And, as I laughed, she laughed too. It was the first time I had heard her laughter. The sound of it had an odd effect on the marrow in my bones. Even then I asked myself if by any possibility I could be going mad. She was in the cupboard on the other side of my dressing-room. All other considerations apart, it was an odd thing that I should hear her so plainly from where I lay.

"'I'll go and look at her,' I said. I went. As I opened the cupboard door she laughed again—a little, soft, musical laugh, suggestive of exquisite enjoyment. It drew me on. 'Why,' I cried, 'I didn't know that you could laugh. Where are you? Let's free you from your prison. If you're as pretty as your laughter, you should be well worth looking at.'

"There was the packing-case, all nailed and corded, exactly as it had been when placed on shipboard. As I touched it, she laughed again. Now that I had become more used to it, I found that there was something in the sound which braced me up; a quality which was suited to my mood. I drew the case into my dressing-room. I unpacked it. There she was inside, in the best possible condition; as ready, as willing, as happy, as on the day when I first saw her, in the place where she was born. She had borne her voyage and subsequent confinement surprisingly well; neither in her bearing nor appearance was there anything which even hinted at a trace of resentment for the treatment which she had received. As she showed me what she could do, laughing all the time, I said to myself, 'With her aid I shall be more than a match for my brother.'

"I had got her out, but, like the genie the fisherman released in the Arabian story, she was not easy to put back again.[109] Without her consent it was impossible to replace her in the packing-case. Her consent she refused to give. When I persisted in my attempts to do without it, she brought me nearer to a sudden end than I had ever been before. Whereupon I desisted. I left her where she was. That display of her powers, and of her readiness to use them, compelled me to the reflection that in her I had found not only a collaborator, but possibly something else as well. One thing I certainly had found—an inseparable companion.

"From that hour, when, in the silence of the night, and because I could not sleep, being troubled by thoughts of my brother, I took her from her packing-case, she has never left me for one moment alone. She has become part and parcel of my life; grown into the very web of my being; into the very heart of me; until now she holds me, body, soul, and spirit, with chains which never shall be broken. And to her it's such an exquisite jest. Listen! She is laughing now."*

CHAPTER XXV

THE GODDESS

I HAD been wondering, while Lawrence had been speaking, where, exactly, in what he said, was the dividing line between truth and falsehood; between sanity and madness. I could not satisfy myself upon the point; either then or afterwards. That the wildness of his speech and manner was an indication of the disorder of his mind was obvious; that in his brain there were the fires of delirium was sure; that the tale which he told was not all raving was as certain. It is probable that the life of dissipation which he had led had told upon his physical health; and that, as usual, the body had reacted on the mind.

Yet there was such an air of conviction in his bearing, and so much method in his madness,[110] that even in his most amazing statements one could not but suspect, at least, a basis of fact. And it was because this was so that we listened, fascinated, to assertions which savoured of a world of dreams; and hung, with breathless interest, on words which told, as if they were everyday occurrences, of things of which it is not good to even think as coming within the sweep of possibility.

He held up his finger, repeating his last words in the form of an inquiry.

"Hark! don't you hear her laughing now?"

I know not what we heard; I know not. We had been following, one by one, the steps which marked the progress of disorder in this man's brain, until our own minds had become unbalanced too. But I thought that I heard the sound of a woman's laughter, and it was because it appeared to come from behind the screen that I stepped forward to move the barrier, so that we might learn what it concealed. Lawrence sprang in front of me.

"Don't!" he cried. "She's there! You shall see her; I'll show you her at the proper time."

I could have thrust him aside, but there was that about him which dissuaded me. And when the lady, laying her hand upon my arm, drew me away from him, I let him tell his tale in his own fashion. He passed his fingers across his brow, as if in an effort to collect his thoughts.

"Well, the time went, forgetting to bring me ease of mind, until Bernstein wrote to ask my brother where it would best meet his convenience to have the bills presented, which were on the point of falling due."

"It was the usual custom," struck in the Jew.

"It's the usual custom, Bernstein says, and I'm not denying it. When Philip got the letter, he came red-hot to me, asking what it meant. I had had a bad day or two, and some unpleasant nights, and was feeling hipped[III] just when he came. Besides, his coming took me unawares; I was not expecting him—for the present. When I perceived what was in his voice, and in his eyes, and in the twitchings of his hands, I was afraid. I lied to him; pretending that I had no notion of what it was that Bernstein wrote; protesting that any bills which he might hold had nothing at all to do with me. I could see he doubted, but having no proof positive that what I said was false, he went, warning me what I might expect if it turned out that I had lied. It was good hearing, to know what I might expect—from him—if it turned out that I had lied.

"I went to Bernstein, to implore him to have mercy; though I knew that in him mercy was less frequent than water in a rock."

"I am a man of business! You had had my money! I am a business man!"

"He would have none. I found young Moore. I told him that certain bills had been discounted which bore my brother's name, and since he had put it there I should be compelled, in self-defence, to tell the simple truth."

"When I put it there there was nothing on the bills—not a word; I declare it. They were nothing but five blank slips of paper, on my sacred word of honour, I will swear to it. He filled them up himself; then he wanted to put it on to me."

"Yes, it was odd how I wanted to put it upon every one except myself; very odd indeed. That night I was not happy. I had some conversation with The Goddess; from which I derived comfort, of a kind, though it was not much, either for quantity or quality. The next day I had brought myself closer to the sticking point; as, I fancy, men are apt to do when they know that the music really is about to play. In the evening I had a game of cards with Ferguson. You remember?"

"I do. You cheated me."

"I did. Which, again, was odd. For it was the first time I ever had cheated at cards, and it was the last. You went out of the room believing that you would have to pay me £1880, and with, at the bottom of your heart, the knowledge that the man whom you had supposed to be your friend was, after all, a rogue. The conscious-ness that you had this knowledge was, for me, the top brick.[112] I had chosen to carry myself well in your eyes, and believed I had succeeded; yet, after all, I'd failed. When you had gone I turned for consolation to The Goddess.

"Bringing her from my bedroom, I placed her on her own par-ticular stand. I was just about to request her to go through one of her unrivalled performances when, turning, I saw in the open doorway of my room a lady. Here is that lady now."

He waved his hand towards Miss Moore. She gave what seemed to be a start of recollection.

"I remember. I had knocked at the door again and then again; no one answered. I tried the handle; the door opened; you were there."

"Which was most fortunate for me. It was an entrancing figure which I saw, in a cloak all glory; with a face—a face which would haunt the dreams of a happier man than I. It was a late hour for so enchanting a vision to pay a first call upon a single gentleman, but, when I learned that this was the sister of the ingenuous Tom, I understood; I understood still more when the lady's tongue was once set wagging, for sometimes even charming visions do have tongues. Dear Tom had told his tale on his own lines."

"It was gospel truth, every word I said to her. I'll take my oath it was."

"There's not a doubt you will. But as the tale came from the lady's lips to me, it seemed surprising. I'd no idea, until she told me, that I was so old in sin and dear Tom so young. It seemed that I had corrupted the boy's fresh innocence; that I had even taught him how to write—especially other people's names. To me it sounded odd. I had met young Tom; I was beginning to wonder if his sister ever had. I knew something of his history; one could scarcely credit that she knew anything at all. However, one was glad to learn that so fair a lady had so excellent a brother, though it seemed unfortunate that he should have such curious associates. Of one of them she was giving her opinion, to the extent of several volumes, when once more the door was opened, this time, I really think, without any preliminary knocking; for I am incapable of suggesting that the lady's voice could by any possibility have drowned even a rapping of the knuckles. My brother was the interrupter—the uninvited, unwelcome interrupter, of our *tête-à-tête*.[113]

"Then I knew that the end had come; that the game was blown upon; that the music would have to be faced. I knew this in an instant. It was written large all over him. He had a trick, when he was in a rage, of seeming to swell; as if the wind of his passion had distended him. I had never seen him look so large before. He was trembling—not with fear. His fingers were opening and closing—as they were apt to do when the muscles which controlled them reached the point of working by themselves. His lips were parted; he drew great breaths; his eyes had moved forward in his head. It did not need more than a single glance at him to enable me to understand that he had learned that I had lied, and that now had come the tug of war.

"I cannot say if he noticed that I was with a lady. He did not acknowledge her presence if he did, not even by so much as the removal of his hat. So soon as he saw me he began to edge his way into the room, with little, awkward, jerky movements, which experience had taught me were the invariable preliminaries to an outburst of insensate fury. 'I'll kill you! I'll kill you! I'll kill you!' He repeated the three words, as if he were speaking half to himself and half to me, in a husky voice, which was not nice to hear.

"My first thought was of The Goddess!"

As if he had had, from the beginning, an eye to what would be the proper dramatic effect, when he got so far, Lawrence, with a hasty movement towards the daïs, struck the crimson screen, so that it came clattering forward on to the floor. Extending his arms on either side of him, he cried: "Behold! The Goddess!"

I do not know what the others were prepared to find revealed, nor even what it was which I had myself expected. There had been in my mind a vague anticipation of some incredible horror; something neither human nor inhuman, neither alive nor dead. What I actually did see occasioned me, at first sight, a shock of surprise. A moment's reflection, however, disclosed my own stupidity. Much that had gone before should have prepared me for exactly this. Only my mental opaqueness could have prevented my seeing to what Lawrence's words directly pointed. And yet, after all, this that I saw did not provide an adequate explanation; did not, for instance, shed light on what I had seen in my dream.

The downfall of the screen had revealed an idol; apparently a Hindoo goddess. She was squatted on what looked like an ebony pedestal, perhaps a foot or eighteen inches from the floor. The figure was nearly four feet high. It represented a woman squatting on her haunches. Her arms were crossed upon her breast, her fingers interlaced. Two things struck me as peculiar. One, that the whole figure was of a brilliant scarlet; the other, that its maker had managed to impart to it a curious suggestion of life. To this fact Lawrence himself drew our attention.

"You see how alive she is? She only needs a touch to fill her with impassioned frenzy. It is for that touch that she waits and watches."

It was exactly what I had myself observed. The figure needed only some little thing to give it at least the semblance of actual life. I could not make out of what substance it was compounded; certainly neither of wood nor stone.

"As Philip came at me across the room I moved towards The Goddess. 'Take care,' I said. 'Don't be a fool! Don't you see that there's a lady here?' He did not; or if he did he showed no signs of doing so. I doubt even if he saw The Goddess. It was his way. In his fits of passion he was like some maddened bull; he had eyes only for the object of his rage. 'I'll kill you!' he kept on muttering, in a voice which fury had made husky. 'Don't be an ass!' I cried. But he was an ass. Presently there came the rush which I was looking for. He went for me as the bull goes for the toreador. And instead of me he met The Goddess. It had to be, or I should not have lived to tell the tale.

"As it chanced The Goddess was between us. I had in my

fingers this little cord—you see I have it here. My scarlet beauty was an obstacle of which he took no account at all. He made as if he would dash her into splinters and scatter them about the room. But The Goddess is not so easily to be brushed aside. As he rushed at her she leaped at him—like this."

Suddenly throwing out his arms he cried, in a loud voice, "Take me, for I am yours, O thou Goddess of the Scarlet Hands."

How exactly it all happened, even now I find it hard to say. As Lawrence sprang forward, the figure rose to its feet, and in an instant was alive. It opened its arms; from its finger-tips came knives. Stepping forward it gripped Lawrence with its steel-clad hands, with a grip from which there was no escaping. From every part of its frame gleaming blades had sprung; against this *cheval-de-frise*[114] it pressed him again and again, twirling him round and round, moving him up and down, so that the weapons pierced and hacked back and front. Even from its eyes, mouth, and nostrils had sprung knives. It kept jerking its head backwards and forwards, so that it could stab with them at his face and head. And, all the while, from somewhere came the sound of a woman's laughter—that dreadful sound which I had heard in my dream.

CHAPTER XXVI

THE LEGACY OF THE SCARLET HANDS

WE could do nothing for him. The shock of the surprise, for a moment, held us motionless. But so soon as we realised that the man was being hacked to death before our eyes, we rushed to his assistance. It was of no avail. Death had, probably, been instantaneous, so much mercy the creature showed. A sharp-pointed blade, more than eighteen inches long, which proceeded from its stomach, had pierced him through and through. The writhing, gibbering puppet held him skewered in a dozen places. To have released him we should have had to tear him into pieces. When I tried to drag him free, I only succeeded in bringing the whole thing over. Down he came, with his assailant sticking to him like a limpet.[115] Pinning him on to the floor, it continued its

extraordinary contortions, lacerating its victim with every movement in a hundred different places. It was difficult to believe that
it was not alive. Perceiving that it was not to be persuaded by any
other means to loosen its embrace, I struck it on the back, again
and again, with a heavy wooden chair.

Presently it was still; its movements ceased; it became again
inanimate. As if its lust for blood was glutted, it rolled over, lethargically, upon its side, leaving its handiwork exposed—a horrible
spectacle. A grin—as it were a smile, born of repletion—was on
the creature's face.

Later, the thing was torn to pieces; its anatomy laid bare.
Examination showed that its construction had been diabolically
ingenious. It was simply a light steel frame, shaped to resemble a
human body, to which was attached a number of strong springs,
which were set in motion by clockwork machinery. The whole had
been encased in scarlet leather, so that, when completed, it resembled nothing so much as an artist's lay figure.[116] In the leather were
innumerable eyelet-holes. Through each of these holes the point
of a blade was always peeping. So soon as the clockwork was set in
motion each of these blades leaped from its appointed place, and
continued leaping, ceaselessly, to and fro, till the machinery ran
down. In the head was an arrangement somewhat on the lines of
a phonograph;[117] it was from this proceeded the sound resembling
a woman's gentle laughter, which was not the least eerie part of its
horrible performance.

Inquiries seemed to show that the creature had originally been
intended for sacrificial purposes. Lawrence had apparently purchased it at Allahabad;[118] probably from the workshop of a native
who was suspected of the manufacture of contrivances, whose
ingenuity was almost too conspicuous, which were used in the
temples. On certain days such a puppet would be produced by
the priests, with a flourish of trumpets. One could easily believe
that miraculous power would be claimed for it; it was even likely
that, as a proof of the substantiality of these claims, it would go
through its gruesome performance in the presence of the assem-
bled congregations. Of what might have been the objects on which
it exhibited its powers one did not care to think. Some queer things
still take place in India.

Edwin Lawrence could hardly have been perfectly sane when he purchased such a plaything. It was not a possession which a perfectly healthy-minded man would have cared to have had at any price; and Lawrence must have paid an enormous sum for it, or that wily native would never have allowed such a curio to leave his hands. It was shown that the brothers had been in the habit of quarrelling their whole lives long. Edwin would do something to arouse Philip's passion, whereon Philip would attack him with unreasoning violence. The fit of fury past, and the mischief done, repentance came. In these moods Philip must have expended thousands of pounds in his attempts to soothe the feelings of the brother whom he had just been battering. One of these scenes had taken place just before Edwin's departure for India; it was the usual plaster which had enabled him to start upon his travels. That his brother's treatment of him rankled, there was scarcely room for doubt; the purchase of the scarlet puppet was, probably a first fruit of his morbid brooding.

At the very last, possibly, the crime had been the result of a moment's impulse—as he himself had said. But that it had been prepared for, as likely to happen some time, was clear. He had obtained a suit of clothes, which was exactly like those which his brother was in the habit of wearing. These he secreted in his bedroom. So soon as his "goddess" had done her work, he stripped what was left of his brother bare—an awful task it must have been. He arrayed the body in a suit of his own clothes, oblivious of the fact that they showed no signs of the cutting and the hacking, and the suit which he had prepared he himself put on.

Whether or not he saw me—or even if I was actually there to see—is not clear to this day. But either he did not notice the departure of his lady visitor, or he was indifferent to what it might portend; under the circumstances, after the tragedy had actually taken place, his movements were marked by curious deliberation. The probability is that the catastrophe finally overturned the brain whose equilibrium was already tottering. No other hypothesis can adequately explain the manner in which he retained his self-possession, expecting every moment that the alarm would be raised, and that he would be caught red-handed.

Not only did he make himself up to resemble as much as

possible his brother, but, rolling the "goddess" up in a cloth, he bore the blood-stained puppet out with him into the street. It was that which Turner had seen him carrying, under the impression that he was himself the man who was, at that moment, lying on the floor of his room, a mutilated corpse. As, by sight, Turner knew both men well, the fact that he mistook one man for the other shows that the imitation must have been well and carefully done.

No action was taken against Mr. Isaac Bernstein. Except the dead man's words, there was no evidence against him in that particular. But that the tale told of him by Edwin Lawrence was true, and that he had some sort of a conscience, after all, was suggested by the fact that a few days afterwards he disappeared from his London premises and from his usual haunts. So far as I know, nothing has been seen or heard of him since. Whether he was afraid that other shady transactions, in which he had had a hand, would be brought home to him, or whether he was haunted by memories of the dual tragedy for which he had been, at any rate in part, responsible, I cannot say. The fact remains, that so far as the police can learn, large sums of money, which at the time of his disappearance were due to him, he has never made the slightest attempt to claim.

As the two brothers were the last of their race, and no one has laid claim to Philip's estate, in due course it reverted to the Crown. It is among the large number of those for which heirs-at-law[119] are still wanting. Old Morley and his wife had not been in a good service for so many years for nothing; they would have retired from it long before had it not been for antiquated notions of fidelity. Their master's death found them comfortably off, and in the possession, as it turned out, of a little property among the Surrey hills.[120] On that property they are residing to this day. When it first came into their hands the neighbourhood was wild and rural; others, since, have discovered that it was beautiful. Building is taking place on every side; quite a town is springing up. Though this materially adds to the monetary value of their property, the old couple are a little restless amidst their new surroundings.

Hume is still unmarried. He becomes less and less engaged in the active practice of his profession. But he remains an authority on the obscure diseases of the brain. He has written more than one book upon this special subject. I have not read them—I am no reader, and such works would, in any case, be hardly in my way—but I understand that he seeks to show that we are, all of us, more or less mad, and that he goes far towards the proof of this thesis. He has not materially altered his estimate of my mental equipment. Indeed, he once assured me that he was becoming more and more convinced that men whose physical and muscular development went beyond a certain limit were, *ipso facto*,[121] mad; and, *ergo*,[122] I must be insane. However, we are tolerable friends, and he seems not unwilling to allow that I am as well out of an asylum as in.

It has been rumoured that Miss Adair intends, shortly, to retire from the stage; and the whisper is that Hume, who for some time has been her constant attendant, has something to do with her intention. In that case, they will make a well-matched pair, for in my opinion they both have tongues.

Bessie—I think that at this point in these pages I am entitled to call her Bessie—Bessie never acted again. After that hideous night brain fever[123] supervened. For weeks she lay between life and death. More than once the doctors gave her up. Fortunately, doctors are not omniscient. After all, God was merciful—to me.

Almost her first words, when the darkest hour had given place to the first glimmerings of dawn, took the shape of a question: "Where is Tom?" Her scamp of a brother! After all she had suffered for him, he was foremost in her thoughts.

"I hope that he is on the road to fortune."

Looking up at me with her big eyes, which had grown bigger, and sunk farther in her head, she asked me what I meant. I explained. I had supplied Young Hopeful with the wherewithal which would enable him to seek for gold in what was then the new El Dorado—the Klondyke region.[124] He had started on his quest. But he never found what, at least nominally, he had gone to look for. Some months afterwards I learnt that he had died; fallen at night into the waters of the Yukon river[125] and been drowned. My correspondent went on to explain that he was dead drunk at the time; which explanation I kept from his sister. I did not wish her to think that his end had been unbecoming to a man.

Bessie and I have been married just long enough to enable me to begin to realise my happiness. I am ever slow, so I will not say what is the tale of the years which that statement implies; though the sight of our youngsters is apt to give away the secret of their father's dulness. There was no question between us of courtship. I knew, as I watched by her bedside, that if she came back to life she was mine; and that in any case I was hers. And so it was. So soon as she was strong enough we were married. And we have been lovers ever since. As I sit, with her hand clasped tightly, watching her children and mine, I am sometimes disposed to suspect that our courtship is beginning. I know it will never cease.

The goodness of God has been very great in giving me my wife. By what seemed accident, but was indeed the act of Providence, I have come to have for my very own the woman of my dreams. Sleeping and waking she is mine. So true is it that some men's good fortune is out of all proportion to their deserts.

THE END

NOTES

1   *idiot*: In nineteenth-century medicine a profoundly mentally retarded person incapable of logical speech or simple tasks. This is the first occasion on which medical terminology related to mental health is used in the novel.

2   *the Trocadero, the Empire*: The glamorous, upmarket Trocadero Restaurant opened in Shaftesbury Avenue in London's West End in 1896. An upmarket variety theatre, the Empire in nearby Leicester Square had been attacked in 1894 by anti-vice campaigners as a haunt of prostitutes, forcing it to close for a short period in 1894.

3   *Imperial Mansions*: A block of this name existed in New Oxford Street, within walking distance of Leicester Square, in an area with sharp social divisions.

4   *nearly a thousand pounds*: Ferguson has lost a sum of money that would have purchased two semi-detached suburban houses at the time. A clerical salary was approximately £150 per year.

5   *electric light*: Although Thomas Edison had patented a practical electric light bulb in 1880, electric lighting was not widely used in private residences until the twentieth century.

6   *somnambulist*: Somnambulism, or sleepwalking, was seen as indicative of mental instability.

7   *imbecile*: A mentally retarded person able to perform simple tasks, with a mental age of a child.

8   *domino*: A loose, hooded cloak, often worn with an eye mask as a masquerade costume.

9   *alpaca*: Warm, silky wool.

10 *cuneiform character*: A type of writing used by the civilizations of Mesopotamia.

11 *puerility*: Something childish, juvenile, immature.

12 *lift*: Invented by Elisha Otis in 1852, the safety lift is another modern feature at Imperial Mansions.

13 *Gaiety Theatre*: Located on the Aldwych, the Gaiety Theatre was known for its music hall, burlesque and musical comedies. The fashionable, dancing Gaiety Girls were its special attraction.

14 *a pair of white kid gloves*: Gloves made of soft kid or chamois leather.

15 *Rudyard Kipling's "Many Inventions"*: Kipling's 1893 collection of short stories is a mixture of Indian and London settings, storytelling, adventure, and the supernatural.

16   *we have all of us a screw loose somewhere, and that out of every counte-
     nance insanity peeps*: Dr. Hume subscribes to contemporary theories
     that modern life was harmful to mental stability.

17   *sotto voce*: In an undertone; softly (Italian).

18   *one never knows what 'trifles light as air' may prove 'confirmation strong
     as Holy Writ'*: In Shakespeare's *Othello*, a play about civilization and
     savagery, the villain Iago uses a handkerchief to provoke Othello's
     jealousy, stating that "Trifles light as air/Are to the jealous confirma-
     tions strong/As proofs of holy writ" (III.3.323-25).

19   *eighteen shillings*: Up to 1971, the British pound was made up of
     twenty shillings, each shilling containing twelve pence, the pound
     thus consisting of 240 pence. Eighteen shillings would be ample
     pocket money, but not enough for a lady to live on for long.

20   *'Sufficient unto the day is the evil thereof'*: An invocation not to worry
     about the future, since the present day has enough trouble of its own
     (Matthew 6:34).

21   *Edgar Allan Poe's story of "The Murders in the Rue Morgue"*: Poe's early
     detective story (1841) features a series of brutal murders committed
     by an orangutan on the loose.

22   *a pathologist; a student of mental diseases*: A psychologist or psychiatrist.

23   *mnemonic intervals*: Interruptions or lapses in consciousness and
     memory.

24   *a plethoric habit*: A condition characterized by a superabundance of
     blood, leading to a florid complexion.

25   *Arlington Street*: A fashionable street in London's West End, between
     St. James's Street and Piccadilly. This exclusive address was in the
     heart of London's gentlemen's clubland.

26   *queer*: Odd, strange, wrong, improper. The word carried conno-
     tations of financial instability, with debtors said to inhabit "queer
     street." The term may have had slang connotations with homosexu-
     ality by the end of the nineteenth century.

27   *the charity which forgiveth all things*: In Psalm 103:3, God is praised as
     one "Who forgiveth all thine iniquities."

28   *bills*: A bill of sale, a legal document which transfers property
     without the said property leaving the seller. Bills were used as a
     means of raising money against a security for a limited period, with
     the seller paying back the money with interest by a specified date. In
     the nineteenth century, the bill of sale became a tool for fraud, with
     fraudsters raising money by forging signatures, while the owners
     of the securities remained unaware of the circumstances until their
     property was seized.

29 *Pall Mall*: A fashionable street approximately a quarter of a mile from Arlington Street.

30 *a Jew*: Anti-Semitism was widespread at the fin de siècle. Marsh's Jewish characters resemble "stage Jews" in their stereotyped appearance and behavior.

31 *a raving lunatic*: A lunatic, an irrational madman. Morley notes that alcohol affects Philip Lawrence's mood.

32 *the Pandora*: The theatre at which Bessie performs is named after the first woman in Greek mythology, sent by the gods as a punishment to mankind after Prometheus stole fire from them. Pandora carried a box containing misery, which she opened due to curiosity, thus releasing a range of ills into the world.

33 *Hailsham Road, The Boltons, Brompton*: An imaginary road in the wealthy suburb of Brompton, within walking distance of the West End, in South-West London.

34 *St. Bernard*: A breed of large, good-natured dogs used for rescue operations.

35 *Fulham Road*: A major road leading through Brompton and connecting the western suburb of Putney with fashionable South Kensington.

36 *St. Vitus' Dance*: Sydenham's Chorea or Chorea Minor, a neurological motor disorder characterized by rapid, uncoordinated jerking movements in the face and limbs.

37 *like a bad copy of Bessie's, with all her goodness left out and your own wickedness put in*: Miss Adair refers to contemporary theories of degeneration, which implied that families and races could regress and deteriorate over time.

38 *you would not be allowed to exist*: Ferguson borrows the rhetoric of the eugenic movement, active at the fin de siècle, which maintained that unworthy members of the human race should not be allowed to reproduce or even to exist.

39 *non compos mentis*: Not of sound mind; mentally incompetent (Latin).

40 *finical*: Fussy; particular; finicky.

41 *panic fear*: A sudden, overwhelming sensation of fear or anxiety.

42 *two persons in one body*: Bessie's questions reference contemporary concerns over duality and split personality.

43 *hallucinations*: Illusory perceptions or vivid, realistic delusions indicative of mental disorder or mental disease.

44 *obscure mental disease*: Madness, insanity; a reference to Forbes Benignus Winslow's treatise *On Obscure Diseases of the Brain and Disorders of the Mind; their Incipient Symptoms, Pathology, etc.* (1860).

45 *The police are famous for their blunders*: The police did not enjoy public confidence at the fin de siècle after their incompetent handling of the Bloody Sunday riot in 1887 and the Jack the Ripper murders in 1888-89.

46 *seen as in a glass darkly*: Misquotation from 1 Corinthians 13:12, which describes humanity as perceiving the world "through a glass darkly." Also the title of Sheridan Le Fanu's collection of psychological ghost and gothic stories, *In a Glass Darkly* (1872), which features the highly sexualized female vampire Carmilla and engages with questions of mental instability.

47 *God moves in a mysterious way*: The opening line of William Cowper's 1774 hymn.

48 *they are better than I*: Ferguson subscribes to nineteenth-century theories of women's purity and moral superiority over men.

49 *midsummer madness*: Madness attributable to warm weather; rabies. Quotation from Shakespeare's *Twelfth Night*, III.4.56.

50 *myrmidons*: Faithful, unquestioning followers.

51 *dirty nigger*: Marsh's racism and anti-Semitism were not unusual for the time of writing.

52 *natty*: Smart, dapper (slang).

53 *the labours of Hercules and the story of Samson*: Hercules, a Greco-Roman demigod known for his physical strength and for his destruction of monsters, who performed a series of physically demanding tasks; Samson, a biblical figure granted tremendous strength by God in order to perform heroic feats.

54 *A case of the world well lost for her*: The World Well Lost was the subtitle of John Dryden's 1677 play *All for Love*.

55 *typewritten*: The first commercial mechanical typewriter was patented in 1868; another modern invention.

56 *Finchley*: A North London suburb.

57 *Victoria*: The area surrounding Victoria Station in central London, approximately two miles from Imperial Mansions.

58 *'De l'audace'—you know the wise man's aphorism*: The French statesman and popular orator Georges Jacques Danton (1759-1794), addressing the Assemblée Législative in 1792, demanded "audacity, more audacity, and ever more audacity" ("*de l'audace, encore de l'audace, toujours de l'audace!*").

59 *cryptograms*: A puzzle in which a passage of text is encrypted using a cipher.

60 *verjuice*: Literally, acidic juice from fruit; metaphorically, sourness; bitterness.

61 *scrimmage*: Scrimmage, also scrum, a struggle for the ball in rugby football.

62 *Hume stopped; looking as if he were allowing "he dare not" to wait upon "he would"*: A reference to Shakespeare's *Macbeth* (I.7.44-48), in which Lady Macbeth taunts her husband, encouraging him to violence: "Wouldst thou have that/Which thou esteem'st the ornament of life,/And live a coward in thine own esteem,/Letting 'I dare not' wait upon 'I would,'/Like the poor cat i' the adage?"

63 *blackleaded*: As if drawn with a pencil; colored with black dye.

64 *forged acceptances*: Forged bills or cheques.

65 *promissory notes*: A written note with specific conditions where the issuer promises in writing to pay an agreed sum to the payee at a future date, or upon demand.

66 *the cat*: The cat o' nine tails, a multi-tailed whip used in prisons to inflict severe physical punishment.

67 *Great Poland Street*: There is a Poland Street in Soho, a central London area associated with foreigners, anarchists and the vice trade at the fin de siècle.

68 *Piccadilly*: Piccadilly, a fashionable thoroughfare, ran at one end of Arlington Street.

69 *Barnum's museum*: The American showman and entertainer Phineas Taylor Barnum (1810-1891) ran a museum in New York specializing in curiosities and "freaks" such as midgets and giants.

70 *monomaniac—possessed with but one idea*: A sufferer from monomania, an obsessive paranoia in which the patient's thoughts all focus on one topic.

71 *All the king's horses and all the king's men couldn't put that murder story of yours together again*: In a well-known English nursery rhyme, Humpty Dumpty, typically portrayed as an egg, falls from a wall, and "All the king's horses,/And all the king's men,/Couldn't put Humpty together again."

72 *yeoman's service*: Hard work; excellent, loyal service.

73 *sanded floor*: Sand was traditionally scattered on pub floors to soak in any spillages.

74 *opuscula*: Opusculum, something of little significance.

75 *raree-show*: Peep-show or rarity-show, an exhibition of pictures, objects or people viewed through a small hole, often surprising and sometimes pornographic in nature.

76 *I had in my letter-case over £100 in notes, in my pockets nearly £20 in sovereigns*: A considerable amount of money, enough for a middle-class household to live on for at least six months.

77   *what is dearer*: Bessie trusts Ferguson with her honor.
78   *Walham Green*: A new residential suburb in West London.
79   *King's Road*: A major thoroughfare running through Chelsea, approx-
     imately a quarter of a mile from Brompton.
80   *lasso*: A loop of rope used by American cowboys that can be thrown
     around a target and tightens when pulled.
81   *Brompton Road*: A major thoroughfare running through Brompton,
     connecting the West End with the Western suburbs.
82   *Ostend boat train*: An arrangement whereby a train from London
     would connect with a boat to the Continent, which would in turn
     connect with another train at Ostend in Belgium.
83   *Even a worm will turn*: Even someone who is weak or meek will even-
     tually revolt (proverb).
84   *hubbub*: Confusion; excitement; uproar.
85   *a creature born of delirium*: Delirium, a neuropsychotic syndrome that
     may result from substance abuse, is often associated with frightening
     delusions and hallucinations.
86   *the strength of a dozen Samsons was that moment in my arms*: Samson, a
     biblical figure of great strength.
87   *Echo*: Echo, a mountain nymph in Greek mythology who lost her
     voice as a punishment for her tricks and could only repeat what
     others had said.
88   *delirium tremens*: A condition brought about by alcohol abuse in
     which the sufferer typically experiences hallucinations featuring
     insects and spiders.
89   *Pimlico*: A residential district just south of central London.
90   *liverish*: Irritable; uncomfortable; bilious.
91   *shirty*: Bad-tempered; annoyed; angry (slang).
92   *an apoplectic fit*: A sudden attack which arrests the powers of motion
     and of sense.
93   *He laid his finger against his nose*: A sign of shared knowledge or
     awareness of something not commonly known.
94   *a familiar in attendance*: An attendant spirit, often in the shape of an
     animal.
95   *cove*: Man, fellow (slang).
96   *gutter-snipes*: A person of low class; a street urchin (slang).
97   *Enter omnes*: A stage direction for all (characters) to enter (Latin).
98   *a flaming gas-bracket*: A gas pipe with a burner projecting from a wall;
     a method of domestic lighting preceding electric lighting.
99   *mountebank*: Charlatan; fraudster.
100 *pantheon*: All the gods of a particular religion or people.

101 *at the end of the passage*: Rudyard Kipling's short story "At the End of the Passage" (1890) focuses on optical delusions and the horror of the experience of India.

102 *daïs*: A raised platform reserved for performers, speakers or dignitaries.

103 *a palette knife*: A flexible, blunt knife used by artists to mix and apply colors.

104 *"A Solomon risen to judgment! See truth's imaged superscription on his brow"*: Solomon, a wise biblical judge who cleverly determines the truth by tricking people into revealing their true feelings.

105 *born with a twist in us; a moral malformation; a trend in the grain which, as we got our growth, gave a natural inclination in a particular direction*: A reference to theories of degeneration and criminal anthropology. Criminal tendencies could supposedly be inherited and subsequently the heir to such tendencies was at the mercy of this bad inheritance.

106 *a three months' bill*: A note of credit which would have to be paid at the end of a three-month period with exorbitant interest. This was a common method of making money amongst loan sharks.

107 *I've sailed pretty close to the wind*: To do something dangerous or barely legal (idiom).

108 *she precipitated herself, as the occultists have it, into my mind*: According to occultists and theosophists, notes could be "precipitated" into material existence by adepts, just as messages could be telepathically "precipitated" into a person's mind.

109 *like the genie the fisherman released in the Arabian story, she was not easy to put back again*: In one of the stories of *The Arabian Nights*, famously translated by Richard Burton in 1885-86, a fisherman catches a bottle in his net. The bottle contains a hostile and powerful genie which, once released, must be tamed, and eventually makes the fisherman wealthy.

110 *method in his madness*: Quotation from Shakespeare's *Hamlet*, II.2.206: "Though this be madness, yet there is method in't."

111 *hipped*: Depressed (slang).

112 *the top brick*: The last straw (slang).

113 *tête-à-tête*: A private conversation involving two people (French).

114 *cheval-de-frise*: A defensive, often anti-cavalry, obstacle consisting of spikes or spears, in use from the Middle Ages until the nineteenth century.

115 *a limpet*: A type of shellfish that fastens itself to rocks.

116 *lay figure*: A mannequin, a jointed dummy.

117 *a phonograph*: Phonograph or gramophone, a device for recording
     and replaying sound, invented by Thomas Alva Edison in 1877.
118 *Allahabad*: A holy city in Northern India, associated in Hindu mythol-
     ogy with sacrifice.
119 *heirs-at-law*: Persons legally entitled to inherit a property.
120 *the Surrey hills*: Surrey, a rural county south and south-west of
     London.
121 *ipso facto*: By the fact itself, as a direct consequence of the action
     itself (Latin).
122 *ergo*: Therefore, consequently (Latin).
123 *brain fever*: A medical condition where the brain becomes inflamed
     and causes fever symptoms; a Victorian term for states of extreme
     agitation.
124 *the new El Dorado—the Klondyke region*: El Dorado was a legendary
     golden city in South America. Gold was found in the Klondyke
     region in Canada in 1896. There was a significant gold rush to the
     area from 1897.
125 *the Yukon river*: A major North American river which crosses terri-
     tory in Alaska and Canada.

Appendix A: Contemporary reviews and notices

In a year in which Marsh published eight volumes, *The Goddess* attracted relatively little critical attention. While the novel was occasionally reviewed, notices of Marsh's work focused largely on his rate of production.

1. "Fiction for the New Year," *Manchester Times*, 22 December 1899, 9.

BRILLIANT SENSATIONAL STORY BY THE AUTHOR OF "IN FULL CRY."

"THE GODDESS: A DEMON."

We have pleasure in announcing that we have made arrangements for the publication, in these columns, of a powerful story by Mr. Richard Marsh, whose novel, "In Full Cry," which we gave last spring, was received with much favour. Mr. Richard Marsh is extremely popular. "The Beetle: A Mystery," "The Crime and the Criminal," "The Datchet Diamonds," and other tales have been everywhere read and enjoyed. His success is not far to seek. He brings to his work gifts of a very rare order; he is a delightfully unconventional writer, and tells a story in quite a unique way. Combining something of the sensationalism of Wilkie Collins with a humorous insight reminding one of Charles Dickens, his style exhibits qualities which it owes to neither of these famous novelists, nor to any other. It is characterised by a peculiar directness and vigour which invest the narrative with fascinating interest. As for plot and incident, it is sufficient to say that in all Mr. Marsh's stories the movement is very rapid, and the reader is hurried forward with breathless interest.

"THE GODDESS: A DEMON," will be found fully equal to Mr. Marsh's earlier work.

"THE GODDESS: A DEMON," is a modern story of crime, love, and mystery. It has a remarkable opening, in which a striking dream plays a large part.

The hero, John Ferguson, dreams that he sees a friend, Edwin Lawrence, in the grip of a horrible creature, which is hacking him to pieces. As he wakes a young and beautiful lady steps from the balcony through the window into his bedroom, dressed in a cloak which is saturated with blood! With a perfectly innocent air she asks where she is and who she is. Her memory is an absolute blank.

In the morning Ferguson finds that Lawrence has been murdered.

There is a deep mystery about the crime, a mystery in which the young lady visitor to Ferguson is strangely involved.

There are many exciting developments, and the interest of the reader is fully sustained to the close.

The first instalment of "The Goddess: A Demon," will appear on Friday, January 12th, 1900.

2. "Notes on Novels," *Academy* 59 (11 August 1900), 112.

More red-hot melodrama. "The Woman Who Came Through the Window" is a charming chapter-heading. She doesn't know who she is, or where she has come from, or whether she walks in her sleep, or why she is covered with blood, or why soap and water are offered to her. There seems to be a Hindoo idol ahead. It is all capital reading for Margate.

3. "New Novels," *Athenæum* 3798 (11 August 1900), 179-180: 179.

The *dea ex machinâ* who plays so dire a part in the mysterious murder at Imperial Mansions reflects credit on the imagination of the author. The solution of the problem, which baffles Scotland Yard as well as the suspected pair who find eventual solace in matrimony, is postponed with a skill that is equally creditable. There is a good deal of naïve humour about Ferguson and his narrative, and the practical joke of locking up the coroner and his jury in the sanded parlour of the tavern where the 'quest is held is justified by its important bearing on the eventful flight of John Ferguson and the divine Bessie Moore, which brings with it the final discovery. "The Goddess" has merit as a shocker, and, in spite of some slips like "suppositious," it is fairly well written.

4. "New Novels," *Graphic*, 15 September 1900, 400-401: 401.

Mr. Richard Marsh, when he wrote "The Goddess: a Demon" (F.V. White and Co.), evidently made up his mind to go one better than Poe's story of the murders in the Rue Morgue—to which, by the way, one of his characters refers. Not that a previous acquaintance with the earlier work will be of the slightest assistance in helping the amateur detective to guess at the nature of Mr. Marsh's murder. For the rest, its combination of ghastliness and ingenuity is completely in harmony with the methods of the Master, of whom its conception is by no means unworthy. In producing the requisite reality of effect he is less successful; he is without Poe's appreciation of the value of little details, and of the still greater value of the art of omission. It is something, however, that such a comparison should be favourably suggested—much too favourably for us to risk spoiling the effect of Mr. Marsh's mystery by giving its key even the fraction of a turn.

5. H. Lush, "Scribes and Pharisees," *Judy, or, The London Serio-Comic Journal* 60 (September 1900), 430-431: 430.

The book trade is pretty dull just now; but there are some writers whose activity nothing under the sun avails to quell. For some years Mrs. L. T. Meade bore the palm for fecund invention and rapid production; her books stumbled, so to speak, on each other's heels; there was no keeping pace with them; but Mr. Richard Marsh has changed all this. And if you would keep pace with Mr. Marsh it must be to the exclusion of most other people. I regret, however, that personally I had never any desire to keep pace with Mr. Marsh. I can, therefore, do no more than chronicle the appearance—I am much too wary to commit myself by calling it the latest—of another novel from his pen.

6. "The Yarning School," *Academy* 59 (3 November 1900), 423-424.

There is one kind of novel that always justifies itself, and that is the glorified bedroom yarn. When it is fully glorified it is called

The Three Musketeers; when it is imperfectly glorified, it is called *The Mystery of a Hansom Cab*. But in either case it is the schoolboys' bedroom yarn written out with more or less reference to the facts of life—or shall we say to the labels of life? The schoolboy faculty of beginning a story anywhere and continuing without art or insight, but with reckless invention, does not require a great deal of cultivation to issue in romances which will beguile a railway journey, or even form the stay-at-home pabulum of millions. Not that we under-rate the ease with which this yarning may be developed into an income of a thousand a year. We certainly do not under-rate the faculty itself—the innate genius for telling a story; that is a fine gift. As to its practice, we are aware that the yarn must be glorified by the light of such learning and science as the crowd possesses. But we are also aware that it is precisely the prevalence of shallow learning that multiplies novelists and ensures readers. On the whole, these are fat years for the yarners. Some of them must be doing uncommonly well: and we do not grudge them their success. There is Mr. Richard Marsh: he is prodigious. The tradition current in the receiving department of this office that he publishes a new novel every Tuesday is an exaggeration. We do not believe that, working at top pressure, Mr. Marsh writes one novel a month. But that he comes near to this figure seems to be indicated by the following list (possibly incomplete) of Mr. Marsh's productions in the last eight months:

> March 3.........*Marvels and Mysteries*.
> May 5............*A Second Coming*.
> June 9............*Ada Vernham, Actress*.
> September 1....*The Seen and the Unseen*.
> October 13.......*The Chase of the Ruby*.
> November 1.....*A Hero of Romance*.
> Date (?)..........*The Goddess: a Demon*.

That is pretty good for a year of unexampled depression in the book trade. Mr. Marsh has got into his stride and he throws off a story with an abandon—we might add, an abandonment—that is refreshing. Take his story *The Chase of the Ruby*. It was published, you observe, on October 13; therefore it opens in South Africa,

where Guy Holland has a daylight vision, on the veldt, of the
death of a rich uncle. He rushes home in time to hear the will read.
And the will says that the whole of the dead man's property is to
go to Guy "on condition that he recover from Mary Bewicke, the
actress, whom he knows, my ruby signet-ring, which she obtained
from me by a trick on the 27th of this last May. . . . In default, my
whole estate, without any deduction whatever, to become the
absolute property of my other nephew, Horace Burton." This
delectable plot probably flashed on Mr. Marsh while his ticket was
being punched on the top of a 'bus. But the reader's grasp of the
issue is not too lightly assumed:

> The reading was followed by silence, broken by a question from
> Mr. Holland.
> "And pray what is the plain English of it all?"
> "The will is plain English. You are to obtain a certain ring
> from a certain lady and deliver it to me within a certain time. If
> you do so you are your uncle's heir; if you do not Mr. Horace
> is."

Mr. Marsh is at once on terms with his readers; for him the rest is
mechanics, and for them it is excitement. But this is only one type
of yarn out of many that Mr. Marsh has studied. In *The Goddess:
A Demon*, he relies on his sub-title to secure immediate attention
to certain weird happenings in Imperial-mansions; particularly the
goings on of "The Woman who Came Through the Window."
The public who will accept the solution of this story will accept
anything. It comes off in a house in Pimlico:

> How exactly it all happened, even now I find it hard to say.
> As Lawrence sprang forward, the figure rose to its feet, and
> in an instant was alive. It opened its arms; from its finger-tips
> came knives. Stepping forward it gripped Lawrence with its
> steel-clad hands, with a grip from which there was no escap-
> ing. From every part of its frame gleaming blades had sprung;
> against this *cheval-de-frise* it pressed him again and again, twirl-
> ing him round and round, moving him up and down, so that
> the weapons pierced and hacked back and front. Even from its
> eyes, mouth, and nostrils had sprung knives. It kept jerking its

head backwards and forwards, so that it could stab with them at his face and head. And, all the while, from somewhere came the sound of a woman's laughter—that dreadful sound which I had heard in my dream....

Presently it was still; its movements ceased; it became again inanimate. As if its lust for blood was glutted, it rolled over, lethargically, upon its side, leaving its handiwork exposed—a horrible spectacle. A grin—as it were a smile, born of repletion—was on the creature's face.

Later, the thing was torn to pieces; its anatomy laid bare. Examination showed that its construction had been diabolically ingenious.

This is scrumptious dormitory yarning; but is it anything else? Mr. Marsh, be it understood, has in no way presumed on his public. That we gather from an examination of other examples of the Yarning School's work. [...]

Just here we had to change for Matlock Bath. We do not know whether Guy obtained the ring; [and] what happened to the Goddess [...]. But thousands know these things, and are satisfied. And it is because these readers are so many that we take note of the crude literary fare which is supplied to them so lavishly. Doubtless, year by year the schoolmaster establishes a higher taste, and the yarning novelist will be forced—by reference to his bank account—to satisfy it.

7. "Mr. Richard Marsh's Stories," *Academy* 60 (9 February 1901), 131.

SIR,—Will you allow me to state that my story, *The Strange Wooing of Mary Bowler*, which I have just seen that Messrs. Pearson are announcing as an "important new six-shilling novel," was issued by them in 1894 at 6*d*., as No. 4 of "Pearson's Library"? As the work is not my copyright, I have no control over it.

I have been frequently the victim of this kind of thing. During the last year or two work of mine which appeared in print twelve years ago has been brought out as new. The impression has consequently grown up that I flood the market with books turned out by machinery. As a matter of fact, since I finished *The Beetle* in the spring of 1896, I have not written, on an average, one novel a year. An author can have no reasonable objection to the production of fresh editions of his books, but he has every right to protest against his old work being issued by owners of copyright as if it were new. It is unfair to the public, to reviewers, and to the writer himself.

I am, &c.,

RICHARD MARSH.

Appendix B: London, a city of darkness and fog

London suffered from heavy fogs, caused by the burning of coal, in the nineteenth century. The causes, consequences and atmospheric effects of the fogs of the late-Victorian years were a frequent topic in contemporary medical, factual, and fictional texts. *The Goddess*, like many other gothic and crime stories of the period, uses the fog to disorientate the characters and, alongside them, the reader.

1. Hon. Rollo Russell, *Smoke in Relation to Fogs in London: A Lecture* (London: National Smoke Abatement Institution, [1888]), 18-19, 21-22.

Turning to the evils which smoky fogs and a sooty atmosphere bring upon the inhabitants of large towns, there is first that most serious influence which carbonaceous and sulphurous particles, especially when in combination with a dense fog, exert upon health. Great cold in the country certainly increases the death-rate, but to a very inferior degree to the effect of cold with dark fogs in London, when the difficulty of breathing, the bronchial and other affections, cause it sometimes to advance by hundreds per million in a single week. The number of wounded is, of course, very much larger, and thousands of persons are incapacitated, for long or short periods, for active exertion. Those less affected suffer from headaches, smarting eyes, and unusual dulness and oppression. A considerable number must be the worse for the absence of daylight and the use of unscientific gas-burners during whole days. On days which are not absolutely foggy, but dismal and misty, the deficiency of light in London is very great, and on fine days the strength of the sun is very frequently less than a third of what it is in the country. [...]

The moral reaction of this atmosphere is also worth consideration. We have the strongest testimony that many who have been good housewives in the country, after an abode of some time in London give up the attempt to keep their houses clean, and become quite disheartened in their efforts to make the surroundings of their families bright and pleasant. How many windows are

kept closed for fear of blacks entering, and how worrying the ubiq-
uitous sootiness which in a few hours contaminates the whitest
linen! And the windows in poor quarters are seldom transparent,
the walls and doors are allowed to turn to that dingy colour which
alone harmonises with the dirty canopy overhead and the dirty
mud below, and ironwork rusts and scales in a manner hideous to
behold. Flowers, if cultivated, look quite out of their element on
a background of grime; and the blue sky, the most tranquillising
and universal of natural amenities, is never seen in its pure intensity. The trees and grass of the parks are steeped in the same dark
medium, and all living things fade to a sickly squalor. If smoke
were got rid of there would be a great revival of plant vigour
and human gaiety, and the dull brick walls would begin to deck
themselves with brightness. Colour is at present sadly wanting in
London. Works of art, such as the fountain in Great George Street,
where colours have been attempted, are reduced in a wonderfully
short time to the prevailing grey.

2. T. Howell Williams, *The Heating and Lighting of London by Pipe
Lines: An Open Letter to Walter Wren, Esq., L.C.C., on the Abolition
of London Fog* (London: Thomas Scott, 1890), 3, 5-7.

Both the questions of London fog and London drainage are
serious problems, which the administrative body for the metropolis must face at some early day; and it is exceedingly probable that
any further delay means not only additional expense to the community, but also a menacing danger to the comfort and health of
Londoners. [...]
Although it is true that a smoky atmosphere is the creation
of modern times, yet it must be recollected that the question has
always been of public interest. From early times the citizens of
London have been of opinion that the fumes produced by coal
combustion corrupt the air, and are injurious to public health [...];
and it may be not difficult to imagine that, with the ever-increasing
area of London, the fog nuisance will become so unbearable and
injurious that a severe punishment will inevitably be provided for
those who contaminate the already overladen air with the deleterious products of coal combustion under the present arrangements.

Theodore Hook, fifty years ago, described London as that "sink of sin and seacoal." But of late years London fogs have been becoming more intolerable and frequent. The unhappy inhabitants are compelled to grope their way too frequently amongst the darkened streets, quite unconscious of the beautiful weather which may, perhaps, prevail only a few yards above the fog, through which the rays of the sun cannot even penetrate. Fog damages the public health. It fills the lungs with choking, repulsive vapour, impedes respiration, lowers the vitality of the individual, and fills the air passages with dirt, producing the most irritating sensations. It spoils our libraries; it injures our property; it diminishes the value and beauty of our public buildings. It corrodes and destroys the appearance of our perishable articles and pictures; and the gaseous, as well as solid, impurities which are to be found in the air give a most unpleasant taste, which prevents free breathing. Added to these discomforts, there are the exhalations of human beings and animals becoming concentrated in the great blanket overlaying the huge city. The money cost of each fog must be enormous and incalculable. Traffic everywhere is paralysed by it, precious time is wasted and outdoor business practically is at a standstill. [...]

The dangerous element in fog is the smoke. There is as much fog sometimes in the English Channel as in London, but a great difference exists between the two varieties. In the Channel it is a clear, white mist; in London it becomes mixed up with carbon and other ingredients which come out of our coal fires, and on each little water particle there is a layer not only of carbon but of sulphuric acid and other choking compounds which make the "London particular" so deleterious and objectionable.

3. F. A. Rollo Russell, *London Fog and Smoke* (London: P.S. King, 1905), 10-11, 14-15.

Although dense fogs of the black, yellow, or pea-soup varieties are the most unpleasant and unwholesome products of our carelessness in burning raw coal, the less conspicuous effects which follow from it in ordinary weather should not be forgotten. We know that a dense cold London fog causes much illness, misery, and mortality, but the loss to health and spirits resulting from deficiency of light and sunshine, and the dirty discoloration covering all things, especially the fog itself, cannot be counted. With a clear air we should have had exposed to view in London many beautiful objects of art and architecture which cannot now be thought of, owing to the prevailing dirt with its solution of mordant gases. It is painful to see the really fine buildings which have been recently erected, losing in one or two years their distinction of pristine whiteness. On a fine summer day, some of these buildings have revealed to me what a magnificent city central London might have been if the stones of her palaces could have remained as white as those of Venice or Florence. There is more rather than less need of light colour in our less brilliant atmosphere. [...]

The great extension of houses over the area of land around London has diminished the number of ground fogs, and increased the number of high dark fogs covering the city at an elevation of some hundreds of feet. The higher temperature of the brick surfaces, compared with grass, and the increased effusion of warm gases from chimneys, raise the fog-cloud and relieve the streets from the dense aggregation of smoky globules which would otherwise enshroud them. The size of London is in fact now so great that in many cases the fog is unable to gain a footing, and we have, instead of a stratus cloud resting on the ground, a discoloured stratus raised to a height and forming a dark pall, either stationary or, more frequently, stalking over the country, and slowly descending as it cools by radiation.

4. R.L. Stevenson, *Strange Case of Dr Jekyll and Mr Hyde* (London: Longmans, Green, 1886), 39-41.

It was by this time about nine in the morning, and the first fog of the season. A great chocolate-coloured pall lowered over heaven, but the wind was continually charging and routing these embattled vapours; so that as the cab crawled from street to street, Mr. Utterson beheld a marvellous number of degrees and hues of twilight; for here it would be dark like the back-end of evening; and there would be a glow of a rich, lurid brown, like the light of some strange conflagration; and here, for a moment, the fog would be quite broken up, and a haggard shaft of daylight would glance in between the swirling wreaths. The dismal quarter of Soho seen under these changing glimpses, with its muddy ways, and slatternly passengers, and its lamps, which had never been extinguished or had been kindled afresh to combat this mournful rëinvasion of darkness, seemed, in the lawyer's eyes, like a district of some city in a nightmare. The thoughts of his mind, besides, were of the gloomiest dye; and when he glanced at the companion of his drive, he was conscious of some touch of that terror of the law and the law's officers, which may at times assail the most honest.

As the cab drew up before the address indicated, the fog lifted a little and showed him a dingy street, a gin palace, a low French eating house, a shop for the retail of penny numbers and twopenny salads, many ragged children huddled in the doorways, and many women of many different nationalities passing out, key in hand, to have a morning glass; and the next moment the fog settled down again upon that part, as brown as umber, and cut him off from his blackguardly surroundings.

5. J. Jackson Wray, *Will It Lift? The Story of a London Fog* (London: James Nisbet, 1888), 1-3.

It was a dull, damp, dismal evening in late November. The all-pervading fog peculiar to that month of gloom in the big, bustling, almost boundless London town, had settled thick and dark and heavy upon street and square, upon park and garden, upon court and alley, wrapping all things in its chill moist garments, hiding all things beneath its dense grey pall. It is well known that the metropolis of Great Britain is not to be equalled, much less is it to be surpassed, in the manufacture of a real downright, thorough-going article of this kind; and on the occasion to which I now refer it had produced an illustration of its skill in this direction which was quite a notability—a fog that might well be regarded as being about the most perfect of its kind. The sombre shades of night were rendered still more sombre by the dense amalgam of smoke and vapour which made the mighty city nothing more than a huge blotch beneath the leaden sky; or, let us say, a steaming cauldron in which was seething a mixture more mysterious, and, as I should fancy, more distasteful, than the startling "brew" concocted on a plain in Northern Britain by the three witches in "Macbeth."

Nowhere did the smoke counterpane lie more thick, heavy, and oppressive than in those narrow streets which lie behind the broad thoroughfare of Tottenham Court Road, and which seem to converge, as if with some design to link themselves to a region of gentility, on the once aristocratic Fitzroy Square. Very slowly and also very cautiously did the few solitary wayfarers who were of necessity abroad make progress towards the goal of their endeavour. They were eager enough to get out of the murky atmosphere, which made their eyes to smart and their lungs to ache; and yet were wisely bent on walking warily, lest they should stumble into ills they knew not of. The light of the street-lamps [...] was all but swallowed up in the almost Egyptian gloom. It was only by keeping careful and unbroken touch with walls and railings that pedestrians could make anything like safe and certain progress, and even then neither the certainty nor the safety could be at all assured.

6. Arthur Conan Doyle, *The Sign of Four* (London: Spencer Blackett, 1890), 39-43.

It was a September evening, and not yet seven o'clock, but the day had been a dreary one, and a dense drizzly fog lay low upon the great city. Mud-coloured clouds drooped sadly over the muddy streets. Down the Strand the lamps were but misty splotches of diffused light which threw a feeble circular glimmer upon the slimy pavement. The yellow glare from the shop-windows streamed out into the steamy, vaporous air, and threw a murky, shifting radiance across the crowded thoroughfare. There was, to my mind, something eerie and ghost-like in the endless procession of faces which flitted across these narrow bars of light,—sad faces and glad, haggard and merry. Like all human kind, they flitted from the gloom into the light, and so back into the gloom once more. I am not subject to impressions, but the dull, heavy evening, with the strange business upon which we were engaged, combined to make me nervous and depressed. I could see from Miss Morstan's manner that she was suffering from the same feeling. Holmes alone could rise superior to petty influences. He held his open note-book upon his knee, and from time to time he jotted down figures and memoranda in the light of his pocket-lantern.

At the Lyceum Theatre the crowds were already thick at the side-entrances. In front a continuous stream of hansoms and four-wheelers were rattling up, discharging their cargoes of shirt-fronted men and be-shawled, be-diamonded women. We had hardly reached the third pillar, which was our rendezvous, before a small, dark, brisk man in the dress of a coachman accosted us. [...] He gave a shrill whistle, on which a street Arab led across a four-wheeler and opened the door. The man who had addressed us mounted to the box, while we took our places inside. We had hardly done so before the driver whipped up his horse, and we plunged away at a furious pace through the foggy streets.

The situation was a curious one. We were driving to an unknown place, on an unknown errand. [...] At first I had some idea as to the direction in which we were driving; but soon, what with our pace, the fog, and my own limited knowledge of London, I lost my bearings, and knew nothing, save that we seemed to be going a very long way.

7. **Richard Marsh,** *The Beetle: A Mystery* **(London: Skeffington, 1897), 6-8.**

A more miserable night for an out-of-door excursion I could hardly have chosen. The rain was like a mist, and was not only drenching me to the skin, but it was rendering it difficult to see more than a little distance in any direction. The neighbourhood was badly lighted. It was one in which I was a stranger. [...] In the darkness and the rain, the locality which I was entering appeared unfinished. I seemed to be leaving civilisation behind me. The path was unpaved; the road rough and uneven, as if it had never been properly made. Houses were few and far between. Those which I did encounter, seemed, in the imperfect light, amid the general desolation, to be cottages which were crumbling to decay.

Exactly where I was I could not tell. I had a faint notion that, if I only kept on long enough, I should strike some part of Walham

Green. How long I should have to keep on I could only guess. Not a creature seemed to be about of whom I could make inquiries. It was as if I was in a land of desolation. [...]

I do not know how far I went. Every yard I covered, my feet dragged more. I was dead beat, inside and out. I had neither strength nor courage left. And within there was that frightful craving, which was as though it shrieked aloud. I leant against some palings, dazed and giddy. If only death had come upon me quickly, painlessly, how true a friend I should have thought it! It was the agony of dying inch by inch which was so hard to bear.

It was some minutes before I could collect myself sufficiently to withdraw from the support of the railings, and to start afresh. I stumbled blindly over the uneven road. Once, like a drunken man, I lurched forward, and fell upon my knees. Such was my back-boneless state that for some seconds I remained where I was, half disposed to let things slide, accept the good the gods had sent me, and make a night of it just there. A long night, I fancy, it would have been, stretching from time unto eternity.

8. Richard Harding Davis, *In the Fog* (London: Ward, Lock, 1901), 4-5.

"'You have never seen a London fog, have you?' he asked. 'Well, come here. This is one of the best, or, rather, one of the worst, of them.' I joined him at the window, but I could see nothing. Had I not known that the house looked out upon the street, I would have believed that I was facing a dead wall. I raised the sash and stretched out my head, but still I could see nothing. Even the light of the street lamps opposite, and in the upper windows of the barracks, had been smothered in the yellow mist. The lights of the room in which I stood penetrated the fog only to the distance of a few inches from my eyes.

"Below me the servant was still sounding his whistle, but I could afford to wait no longer, and told my friend that I would try and find the way to my hotel on foot. He objected, but the letters I had to write were for the Navy Department, and, besides, I had always heard that to be out in a London fog was the most wonderful experience, and I was curious to investigate one for myself. [...]

I was left alone in a dripping, yellow darkness. I have been in the Navy for ten years, but I have never known such a fog as that of last night, not even among the ice-bergs of Behring Sea. There one could at least see the light of the binnacle, but last night I could not even distinguish the hand by which I guided myself along the barrack wall. At sea, a fog is a natural phenomenon. [...] But a fog which springs from the paved streets, that rolls between solid house-fronts, that forces cabs to move at half-speed, that drowns policemen and extinguishes the electric lights of the music-hall, that to me is incomprehensible. [...]

"As I felt my way along the wall, I encountered other men who were coming from the opposite direction, and each time when we hailed each other I stepped away from the wall to make room for them to pass. But the third time I did this, when I reached out my hand, the wall had disappeared, and the further I moved to find it the further I seemed to be sinking into space. I had the unpleasant conviction that at any moment I might step over a precipice. Since I had set out I had heard no traffic in the street, and now, although I listened some minutes, I could only distinguish the occasional foot-falls of pedestrians. Several times I called aloud, and once a jocular gentleman answered me, but only to ask me where I thought he was, and then even he was swallowed up in the silence. Just above me I could make out a jet of gas which I guessed came from a street lamp, and I moved over to that, and, while I tried to recover my bearings, kept my hand on the iron post. Except for this flicker of gas, I could distinguish nothing about me. For the rest, the mist hung between me and the world like a damp and heavy blanket. [...] Although I was surrounded by thousands of householders—thirteen—I was as completely lost as though I had been set down by night in the Sahara Desert."

Appendix C: The Jack the Ripper murders and knife crime in Marsh's work

In autumn 1888, at least five prostitutes were brutally murdered in Whitechapel in the East End of London by a murderer who called himself "Jack the Ripper." The press coverage of the murders described the Ripper as a monster and Whitechapel as a gothic cityscape of darkness and immorality. Marsh was working as a journalist at the time of the murders and may even have reported on them. As testified by the extracts in this section, *The Goddess* is not the only instance of knife crime in his fiction.

1. Anon., "The Whitechapel Murder," *East London Advertiser*, 8 September 1888. Available at http://www.casebook.org/press_reports/east_london_advertiser/ela880908.html (accessed April 13, 2010).

Almost the worst feature about the two really frightful murders which have followed each other in quick succession in Whitechapel is that there are no means of accounting for them. The question of motive is in both cases a baffling one. It is particularly so, perhaps, in the second of the two crimes, the discovery of which was made by a policeman in the small hours of Thursday morning. Was it a maniac, some creature mad with thirst of blood, escaped from a lunatic asylum, who did to death the "unfortunate"—unfortunate in a double sense—Mary Ann Nicholls, with such extravagantly superfluous brutality? It certainly looks like the deed of a madman, for who, with a remnant of sense, would murder so miserable a creature for the sake of her empty purse? and not only murder but mutilate her in a manner so fiendish? The woman was found with her throat cut from ear to ear, and her body ripped open from the groin almost to the breast-bone. The whole affair is mysterious. The place where the body was found was evidently not that where the murder was committed. There were stains and pools of blood at intervals for a considerable distance from the spot where the corpse lay, and at this spot no screams or sounds of any kind were heard by the inhabitants of the street, though

a night watchman in a warehouse was at his post close by, and
there were people awake in several of the surrounding houses.
[...] Could any but a madman have done this crime? And there
cannot be any doubt that this murder and the previous one—
indeed, the two previous ones, for this is the third Whitechapel
murder since a very recent date—were done by the same hand.
If, as we imagine, there be a murderous lunatic concealed in the
slums of Whitechapel, who issues forth at night like another
Hyde, to prey upon the defenceless women of the "unfortunate"
class, we have little doubt that he will be captured. The cunning of
the lunatic, especially of the criminal lunatic, is well-known; but a
lunatic of this sort can scarcely remain at large for any length of
time in the teeming neighbourhood of Whitechapel. The terror
which, since Thursday last, has inspired every man and woman in
the district, will keep every eye on the watch. A watch should be
kept indeed behind the windows in every street in Whitechapel.
The murderer must creep out from somewhere; he must patrol
the streets in search of his victims. Doubtless he is out night by
night. Three successful murders will have the effect of whetting
his appetite still further, and unless a watch of the strictest be kept,
the murder of Thursday will certainly be followed by a fourth. The
whole of East London is directly interested in bringing the assassin to justice. Every woman in those parts goes in nightly danger
of her life as long as he remains at large. In one respect, no doubt,
the crowded character of that quarter of the metropolis provides
a certain safety for criminals of all kinds; but in a case like this
where every inhabitant is bound, from motives of mere personal
safety, to become a sort of unauthorised detective, continuously
on the alert, the chances of a murderer's escape are fewer than
they would be in a more thinly populated region.

2. Anon., "Another Murder—and More to Follow?" *Pall Mall
Gazette*, 8 September 1888. Available at http://www.casebook.
org/press_reports/pall_mall_gazette/18880908.html (accessed
April 13, 2010).

Something like a panic will be occasioned in London to-day by
the announcement that another horrible murder has taken place

in densely populated Whitechapel. This makes the fourth murder of the same kind, the perpetrator of which has succeeded in escaping the vigilance of the police. [...] Four poor women, miserable and wretched, have been murdered in the heart of a densely-populated quarter, and not only murdered but mutilated in a peculiarly brutal fashion, and so far the police do not seem to have discovered a single clue to the perpetrator of the crimes.

There is some reason to hope that the latest in this grim and gory series of outrages will supply some evidence as to the identity of the murderer. The knife with which he disembowelled his unfortunate victim and a leathern apron were, it is said, found by the corpse. If so, these are the only traces left by this mysterious criminal. [...] The fact that the police have been freely talking for a week past about a man nicknamed Leather Apron may have led the criminal to leave a leather apron near his victim in order to mislead. He certainly seems to have been capable of such an act of deliberate preparation. The murder perpetrated this morning shows no indication of hurry or of alarm. He seems to have first killed the woman by cutting her throat so deeply as almost to sever her head from her shoulders, then to have disembowelled her, and then to have disposed of the viscera in a fashion recalling stories of Red Indian savagery. A man who was cool enough to do this, and who had time enough to do it, was not likely to leave his leather apron behind him and his knife apparently for no purpose but to serve as a clue. [...]

This renewed reminder of the potentialities of revolting barbarity which lie latent in man will administer a salutary shock to the complacent optimism which assumes that the progress of civilisation has rendered unnecessary the bolts and bars, social, moral, and legal, which keep the Mr. Hyde of humanity from assuming visible shape among us. There certainly seems to be a tolerably realistic impersonification of Mr. Hyde at large in Whitechapel. The Savage of Civilisation whom we are raising by the hundred thousand in our slums is quite as capable of bathing his hands in blood as any Sioux who ever scalped a foe. But we should not be surprised if the murderer in the present case should not turn out to be slum bred. The nature of the outrages and the calling of the victims suggests that we have to look out for a man who is animated by that mania of bloodthirsty cruelty which sometimes springs from the unbridled indulgence of the worst passions. We may have a plebeian Marquis DE SADE at large in Whitechapel. If so, and if he is not promptly apprehended, we shall not have long to wait for another addition to the ghastly catalogue of murder.

There is some reason to hope that the sentiment of horror which the peculiar atrocity of the present crime excites even in the most callous will spur the police into a display of vigorous and intelligent activity. [...] As for the community at large, the panic will probably be confined to the area within which this midnight murderer confines his operations. If, however, a similar crime were now to be committed in the West-end, there would be a panic, the like of which we have not seen in our time. From that, however, we shall probably be spared; but the public will be more or less uneasy as long as the Whitechapel murderer is left at large.

3. Anon., "The Reign of Terror in Whitechapel: At the Scene of the Crimes on Sunday: Special," *Evening News*, 1 October 1888. Available at http://www.casebook.org/press_reports/evening_news/18881001.html (accessed April 13, 2010).

It would be impossible for any pen to do justice to a description of the excitement which prevailed in Whitechapel and its immediate neighbourhood all yesterday, from the time that the first news of these fresh horrors was bruited about until long after midnight. Terror and amazement were depicted in almost every face that one met in the streets of that now notorious district. I moved about the dense throngs which had grown to enormous proportions as the day wore on and whose numbers seemed to culminate in the afternoon, when people came trooping in from distant parts athirst for the latest news bearing upon these awful tragedies. Trains, trams, and omnibuses disgorged their hundreds of passengers, who wended their way to the two localities, which have, for the moment, put Buck's-row and Hanbury-street into the shade.

A TERRIBLE PANIC

has taken possession of the entire district, and its effects are to be seen in the wild, terrified faces of the women, and heard in the muttered imprecations of the men who have their homes in the densely populated streets of the East End. The very lads, ready at all times for ribald jest, and noisy horse-play, stood around in awe-struck groups, whispering to each other of the fiendish things that were happening, just as one could have supposed the people stood and talked in Goodman's Fields, near by, more than two centuries ago when the Black Death claimed some of its first victims.

"God help us," exclaimed a poor creature, whose tawdry dress and hardened countenance indicated all too clearly the wretched calling she pursued. "If the human devil who murdered all these women isn't caught, and that pretty soon, too? Why, *I* might be next! It makes my blood run cold."

She was standing, as she spoke, gazing down the alley leading into Mitre-square, and from whence could be seen the corner where the policeman had stumbled upon the body of the mur-dered woman, and at her words other women drew their shawls closer around them with a shudder at the thought of the hideous vendetta which is being waged upon their sex and class.

WHERE WERE THE POLICE?

That was the question that assailed one's ears on every hand. It seems incredible that, within the short space of twelve minutes, a man and woman should have entered the deserted precincts of Mitre-square, that the man should have murdered his victim, disembowelled her with the same unerring skill and a precisely similar result to that achieved in the case of Annie Chapman, and should have made his escape from the scene, without being seen at all. He must, when he hurried away after accomplishing his devil-ish purpose, have been reeking with blood. And yet the policeman on the beat is positive that he saw nothing of either the man or the woman within those twelve short minutes until he came upon the latter weltering in her blood.

A FIENDISH CUNNING

After having seen all that was to be seen in and around Mitre-square,

I came away more than ever impressed with the deliberate, inhuman cunning of the monster who is still abroad in our midst, and who has added those two latest horrors to the ghastly record of his crimes. Mitre-square is quite out of the beaten track, is surrounded by warehouses and shops, and would be as deserted at midnight as though it lay in the centre of Salisbury Plain. No safer place, apparently, could possibly have been selected for the commission of such an awful crime, and the murderer, whoever he is, must have been familiar with that fact. It does not seem possible that accident could have led him to a spot so pre-eminently suited to his deadly purpose. The police, moreover, declare that they have never known the place used for the purposes for which these wretched women court secrecy.

THE CROWD IN BERNER-STREET

Making the best of my way through the dense mass of people wedged in the narrow space of Duke-street, Houndsditch, I strolled along to Berner-street.

I found the street literally packed with people of both sexes, all ages, and nearly all classes. Clubmen from the West-end rubbed shoulders with the grimy denizens of St. George's-in-the-East: daintily dressed ladies, whom a wondering curiosity had drawn to the spot, elbowed their way amid knots of their less favoured sisters, whose dirty and ragged apparel betokened the misery of their daily surroundings. Policemen were there in great numbers, jealously guarding the approach to the yard in which the murdered woman was found. I may mention that the same thing (the number of police on duty) struck me in passing Mitre-square, reminding one irresistibly of the old adage about locking the stable door after the steed has been stolen.

"It's a pity some of you fine chappies wasn't about 'ere larst night," said a morose individual who had been ordered to move on. "You'd a-done a deal more good than shovin' innercent folks hoff the pavement this arternoon." Then, in a jeering tone, "When do you expect you'll ketch the murderer, sonny?"

"Ketch the murderer?" laughed another dilapidated onlooker.

"Not till they puts a 'bobby' to sit upon hevery doorstep in Vitechapel. And then 'alf on 'em will be asleep."

These taunts, and the manner in which they were received by the crowd, show how utterly the poor creatures in that neighbourhood have lost confidence in police protection. I shall never forget the aspect of that street, yesterday afternoon. The intense excitement, the vast swaying throng of eager, and, for the most part, terrified faces, the murmur of the hundreds of voices, the frantic struggles to get as near as possible to the scene of the sickening tragedy, all made it utterly impossible for one to realize that it was the afternoon of a Christian sabbath in the capital of the most civilized and religious country in the world.

4. Anon., "A Thirst for Blood," *East London Advertiser*, 6 October 1888.   http://www.casebook.org/press_reports/east_london_ advertiser/ela881006.html (accessed April 13, 2010).

The two fresh murders which have been committed in Whitechapel have aroused the indignation and excited the imagination of London to a degree without parallel. Men feel that they are face to face with some awful and extraordinary freak of nature. So inexplicable and ghastly are the circumstances surrounding the crimes that people are affected by them in the same way as children are by the recital of a weird and terrible story of the supernatural. It is so impossible to account, on any ordinary hypothesis, for these revolting acts of blood that the mind turns as it were instinctively to some theory of occult force, and the myths of the Dark Ages rise before the imagination. Ghouls, vampires, bloodsuckers, and all the ghastly array of fables which have been accumulated throughout the course of centuries take form, and seize hold of the excited fancy. Yet the most morbid imagination can conceive nothing worse than this terrible reality; for what can be more appalling than the thought that there is a being in human shape stealthily moving about a great city, burning with the thirst for human blood, and endowed with such diabolical astuteness, as to enable him to gratify his fiendish lust with absolute impunity? The details of the two last crimes make it morally certain that they were committed by the same being who took the lives of the other unfortunate women. The victims belonged to the same class—wretched wanderers in the streets of the lowest type; they were killed under circumstances of a similar nature, and although mutilation did not occur in the case of the woman who was first killed, there is good reason for supposing that this was only because the murderer was interrupted in his ghastly task. It is owing to this fact, in all probability, that a second murder was perpetrated on the same night. Stopped before he could gratify his fiendish mania, and with fierce desire coursing through his veins, the ghoul slunk off to find another victim. When everything is shrouded in such impenetrable mystery it is impossible to advance a theory which can bear examination.

5. Anon., "The Whitechapel Murders: Eight in Twelve Months and More to Follow," *Pall Mall Gazette*, 10 November 1888. http://www.casebook.org/press_reports/pall_mall_gazette/18881110.html (accessed April 13, 2010).

We publish the following complete list up to date of the murders which have been committed in the last twelve months in a comparatively narrow area in the East-end. The first two do not appear to have been by the same hand as the last six. The murderers are still at large:—

No. 1—Impaled with an Iron Stake

The first of the so-called Whitechapel murders took place at Christmas, when an unknown woman was found murdered near Osborne-street, Whitechapel. How she came by her death no one could say, but a certain grim horror distinguished it from ordinary murders by the fact that an iron stake was thrust into her person. It is necessary to mention this, because in the lists that appear in the morning papers she is confused with the victim of Easter Tuesday, Emma Smith, whose death was not caused by an iron stake, but by repeated outrage of the worst kind.

No. 2—Outraged to Death by a Gang

On Easter Tuesday, Emma Smith, "unfortunate," was passing

Whitechapel Church at half-past one in the morning, when she was accosted by some men who seized her money and then outraged her in succession. She was picked up dying, but lived long enough to tell her story. The gang seem to have been animated by plunder and passion. They stayed long enough to kill the woman by every imaginable atrocity, but not one of them has been identified. The incident attracted little attention and no arrests were made.

No. 3—Stabbed, with Thirty-nine Wounds

Early on the morning of August 7 a woman, supposed to be Martha Turner, aged thirty-five, a hawker, lately living off Commercial-road E, was discovered lying dead on the first-floor landing of some model dwellings known as George-yard-buildings, Commercial-street, Spitalfields. The woman when found presented a shocking appearance, her body being covered with stab wounds to the number of thirty-nine, some of which had been done with a bayonet. How the body came to be here is a mystery which the police as yet have not solved. It is a singular coincidence that the murder was committed during Bank Holiday night, and is almost identical with another murder which was perpetrated near the same spot on the night of the previous Bank Holiday. The police, said the coroner, would endeavour to bring home the crime to the guilty party. No one was arrested for this crime and it also passed unnoticed.

No. 4—The First Disembowelled

Early in the morning of September 1 Mary Ann Nichols was murdered under circumstances of a most revolting character in Buck's-row, Whitechapel-road. The body was found lying on the footpath against the gates of the yard. Police-constable Neil was walking along Buck's-row between four and half-past in the morning, when he noticed the body on the footpath, and a very brief examination revealed the fact of her murder. Her throat was cut from ear to ear, and her body had been ripped up from the abdomen almost to her breast bone, while a second cut gashed the left thigh. The coroner, on September 23, 1888, said that she was last seen endeavouring to walk eastward down Whitechapel. She said she had had her lodging money three times that day, but she had spent it; that she was without money; that the lodging-house deputy refused to trust her; that she was going to look about and get some money to pay her lodgings; and that she should soon be back. What her exact movements were after this it is impossible to say. At all events, in less than an hour and a quarter after this she was found dead at a spot rather under three-quarters of a mile distant. [...]

No. 5—The First with a Missing Portion

On September 9, at five minutes to six o'clock on Saturday morning, a man named John Davis, living at 29, Hanbury-street, Spitalfields, discovered the body of Annie Chapman in the yard at the rear of that house; the body had its clothes so disarranged as to show that the lower part of her body had been horribly mutilated. The throat had been cut so deeply that the head was nearly severed from the trunk. The surgeon said he had no doubt that the throat was first cut and the stomach subsequently mutilated. The body had been ripped up from the abdomen to the breast bones, and then hacked and gashed until the entrails protruded; portions of the flesh hung in shreds, and some of the viscera were on the shoulders. On examination it was found that the uterus had been removed.

Nos. 6 and 7—Two in One Night

On Sunday, September 30, two murders were committed. The first was on Elizabeth Stride, in Berner-street, opposite the "International and Educational Club." The woman's head was nearly severed from her body, and her blood streaming down the gutter. The body when found was quite warm. In one hand was clutched a box of sweets, and at her breast were pinned two dahlias; she was respectably dressed for her class, and appeared to be about thirty-five years of age. Her height was 5 ft. 5 in., and her complexion and her hair were dark. On the same date shortly

before two o'clock, Police-constable Watkins (No. 881), of the City
police, was going round his beat, when, turning his lantern upon
the darkest corner of Mitre-square, Aldgate, he saw the body of
a woman, apparently lifeless, in a pool of blood. The woman's
throat had been cut from the left side, the knife severing the main
artery and other parts of the neck. Blood had flowed freely, both
from the neck and body, on the pavement. Apparently, the weapon
had been thrust into the upper part of the abdomen and drawn
completely down, ripping open the body, and, in addition, both
thighs had been cut across. The intestines had been torn from the
body, and some of them lodged in the wound on the right side of
the neck. Her clothes were thrown up on to her chest. Both hands
were stretched by her side.

No. 8—The Latest and Worst

On Friday, November 9, Mary Jane Kelly hacked to pieces at
No. 26 Dorset-street, Spitalfields.

6. Anon., "The Mysterious Atrocity in Whitechapel," *East London
Advertiser*, 17 November 1888. http://www.casebook.org/press_
reports/east_london_advertiser/ela881117.html (accessed April
13, 2010).

HORRIBLE MUTILATION OF THE VICTIM

Early on Friday morning another shocking murder was perpetrated in the East-end of London, the crime being carried out in a
most horrible manner. This is the seventh which has occurred, and
the character of the mutilations leaves very little doubt that the
murderer in this instance is the same person who has committed
the previous ones. The scene of this last atrocity is at No. 26, Dorset-
street, Spitalfields, about 200 yards distant from 35, Hanbury-street,
where the unfortunate woman, Mary Ann Nichols, was murdered.
Although the victim, whose name is Mary Ann (or Mary Jane)
Kelly, resides at the above number, the entrance to the room occupied is up a narrow court, in which are some half-a-dozen houses,
and which is known as Miller's court; it is entirely separated from

the other portion of the house, and has an entrance leading into the court. The house is rented by John M'Carthy, who keeps a small general shop at No. 27, Dorset-street, and the whole of the rooms are let out to tenants of a very poor class. Nearly the whole of the houses in this street are common lodging houses, and the one opposite where this murder was enacted has accommodation for some 300 men, and is fully occupied every night. [...]

HOW THE MURDER WAS DISCOVERED

At a quarter to 11, as the woman was 35s. in arrears with her rent, Mr. M'Carthy said to a man employed by him in his shop, "Go to No. 13 (meaning the room occupied by Kelly) and try to get some rent." The man did as he was directed, and on knocking at the door was unable to obtain an answer. He then tried the handle of the door, and found it was locked. On looking through the keyhole he found the key was missing. Through a broken pane of glass he could see the woman lying on the bed naked, covered with blood, and apparently dead. The police were sent for, and Superintendent Arnold, having satisfied himself that the woman was dead, ordered one of the windows to be entirely removed.

A HORRIBLE AND SICKENING SIGHT

then presented itself. The poor woman lay on her back on the bed, entirely naked. Her throat was cut from ear to ear, right down to the spinal column. The ears and nose had been cut clean off. The breasts had also been cleanly cut off and placed on a table which was by the side of the bed. The stomach and abdomen had been ripped open, while the face was slashed about, so that the features were beyond all recognition. The kidneys and heart had also been removed from the body, and placed on the table by the side of the breasts. The liver had likewise been removed, and laid on the right thigh. The lower portion of the body and the uterus had been cut out, and the thighs had been cut. A more horrible or sickening sight could not be imagined. The clothes of the woman were lying by the side of the bed, as though they had been taken off and laid down in the ordinary manner. The bedclothes had been turned down, and this was probably done by the murderer after he had cut his victim's throat. There was no appearance of a struggle having taken place, and, although a careful search of the room was made, no knife or instrument of any kind was found.

7. Bernard Heldmann, "A Couple of Scamps," *Union Jack*, N.S. 1.26 (27 March 1883), 413-414.

The door was opened, and three men came in. I shuddered at their appearance. They were villains of the deepest dye. Crime was stamped upon their countenances as the sun upon the sky. [...]

They were of different ages; they might have been, they probably were, grandsire, son, and grandson; their relationship there was no mistaking; they were so strikingly alike that one was almost apt to forget the difference of their ages in the face of the many points of resemblance. What was it which struck the eye at once with a sense of likeness? It was difficult to tell—were they the same man? Unconsciously I asked myself the question; was not each the double of the other? What was it that made them seem so strange? [...] [O]ne, I saw, had blood upon his hand; it was the youngest of the three, and the hand on which it was he held up, so that the others saw.

"See," he said, "it is a famous stain."

"It is," said they, "a famous stain."

And one said, his father, as it seemed,—

"It will stain your hand for ever."

Whereat the youngest laughed, and said,—

"For ever, until I wash it with fresh water, and then it will be gone."

But his father said,—

"Not all the water in the world shall wash away the stain."

On which the youngest one [...] slipped up his sleeve, and said,—

"Now see, when I put my hand into the water, the stain will there and then be gone."

And he put his hand into the water, and the stain was exactly as before, save that it seemed brighter and plainer to be seen. And a cloud came over his brow, and his father and the old man laughed to see it was not gone.

"Bring me some soap!" he cried [...]. And he made a lather, and with it began to wash his hand. But it was all in vain, for, though the lather was so thick you could not see the flesh beneath, the crimson of the stain was easy to be seen. It stood outside the soap, upon the top of it, and stared him in the face; and brighter was it even than of yore. And the oldest said,—

"Grandson, it will stain forever. Not all the lather and the soap will take it from your hand."

And he leaned back his head, and laughed both loud and long.

And his father said,—

"It is like a curse which clings to you. Do I not know? for have I not curses clinging to me?"

And the son's brow was heavy, and on his face was woe, and he said,—

"Not so, not so, for I will brush the stain away." [...]

[The brush] was hard, and worn, and tough, and he put it in the water, and, covering it with lather, commenced with it to scrub his hand. But it was vain, for scrubbed he never so hard, the stain was brighter than of yore. And to see him scrub! and to see his face while he scrubbed! the fury of the scrubbing! and the anguish that was on his face! And all the while his grandsire and his father laughed. And the stain grew in brightness more and more, till it became wet blood, and all the soap grew bloody, and, falling, crimsoned the water too. And in his agony he cried, to see his hand thus stained with gore,—

"Oh!—oh! my hand!—my hand! How shall I take this stain from off my hand?"

And in the passion of his woe, he [...] waved his hand round his head, and in so doing, some of the blood thrown off his hand went into the faces of his grandsire and his father. And when they felt it spatter them, and knew that it was there, instantly they ceased to laugh, and cried out,—

"You have stained us too. [...] Why have you done this thing? why have you stained us too?"

But he did nothing but cry out, and gaze upon his hand, and, seeing how it streamed with blood, in a paroxysm he seized a chopper from beside him on the floor and laying his hand upon the iron bowl, with a single blow with the chopper, he severed it just at the wrist, so that nothing but the stump remained. But though his hand was gone the stain still stayed, for there it was upon his arm above the wrist; and again he seized the chopper, and struck off his arm just at the elbow, and immediately there was the stain upon his arm still higher up. And with a cry so bitter that none so bitter ever yet was heard before, with his left hand he seized what of the arm remained, and, wrenching it from the socket, flung it on the floor, and instantly there was the stain upon his shoulder blade.

And seeing then that this thing would be, and must be, and could not be by any means prevented, he flung himself upon the floor, and cried, and wailed, and threw himself this way and that, as though he had gone mad.

But the two elder ones still stood up, and each looked upon the other's face, and the grandsire said unto his son, pointing to the stain upon his cheek,—

"How came that there?"

And the father said,—

"He flung it off from him; it is the way with stains; one has it, and, though not willingly, he gives it unto others, so that many have it in the end."

Then the oldest said,—

"No son of mine shall have a stain upon his face." [...]

Then the grandsire stretched out his hand, and laid it on the other's cheek, on which there was the stain, and tore it from his face, and immediately the stain appeared upon his brow.

Then the son said,—

"See what you have done; you have made it worse instead of better; some stains there are, and the stain of blood is one, which shall never be taken from the person of him on whom it shall be found." [...]

Then the oldest said,—

"Then let us die."

And the others cried,—

"We will."

Then straightaway the son and grandson took their skewers and ran them through their bodies, through and through, so that they came out the other side, and immediately they fell dead. But the oldest took his skewer, and put it up his sleeve, and did not harm himself at all. And when he saw the others dead he laughed unto himself for five minutes, and he threw the water out of the bowl, and filled it again with fresh, and washed the stain from off his face, and it was gone.

Then he sat down beside the dead, and filled his pipe, and smoked, and said, "There are no fools like the young."

8. Richard Marsh, *Mrs. Musgrave—and her Husband* (London: Heinemann, 1895), 32-33.

It was murder—and the verdict was, "Wilful murder." The medical theory was, that Dr. Byam had been kneeling on his bed when he had been stabbed, from the front, and from below, and had reeled over onto his back, dead—the transition from life to death having taken place in less than an instant of time. The weapon used must have been a curious one, probably something of the nature of a bodkin—the Shakespearian "bare bodkin"—very long, very finely pointed, and very thin. It had only pricked the skin. It must have been wielded by a cool hand and a steady wrist; by one having some acquaintance with the vital parts, for the point of the weapon had been driven almost through the dead man's heart—it had fairly "skewered" him.

There was no evidence of any sort to point to the criminal; as they said in Fleet Street, it was a "beautiful" mystery. It made copy which went off like red-hot cakes! The doctors had it that the crime had been committed between two and three in the morning. The press said that this suggested a woman. They declared that the probabilities were in favour of a scandal. The doctor had admitted a woman into his room, and that woman had done him to death. This, of course, was "romance"—of a most popular kind!—and, from the evening paper point of view, made the affair more "beautiful."

The Musgraves remained in the hotel during the inquest. Mr. Musgrave offered himself as a witness. When the police heard all that he had to tell, they did not see what his evidence would prove. So he was not called. On the afternoon that the verdict was returned—"against some person or persons unknown"—the husband and wife shook the dust of Worthing from their feet. While engaged in the pleasures of packing, Mr. Musgrave, in a fit of absence of mind, opened, by mistake, a handbag of his wife's. Until he had done some rummaging among the contents he did not discover the error he had made. While rummaging he came upon a long, slender instrument of fine steel, scarcely coarser than a knitting-needle, but with a point of marvellous keenness. It was set in a heavy iron handle,—so heavy that one had but to drop it, point downwards, to drive it, up the hilt, into the floor. This he did not replace in the bag. And that night, while crossing the Channel, he dropped something into the sea.

9. Richard Marsh, "A Member of the Anti-Tobacco League." In *Under One Flag* (London: John Long, 1906), 179-195: 179-180.

Sunday morning. A cold wind blowing, slush in the streets, sleet drizzling steadily down. For the moment the market was deserted. Not because of the weather, wretched though the weather was, but because of the excitement which was in the air.

A crowd buzzed about the entrance to the court. A crowd which grew every second larger. A crowd which overflowed from the street itself, so that its tributaries streamed into the network of lanes and of alleys. An excited, a noisy, a shouting crowd. An angry crowd. A crowd which gave utterance to its opinions at the top of its voice, in language which was plain-spoken to a fault.

Jim Slater caught sight of a friend. He twisted himself round to shout at him.

"Wot yer, Bill! That's another one he's done for—that makes seven!"

"It is true then? He 'as done it."

"Done it! I should think he 'as done it! Found the pore gal just as he left 'er, lying up agin the wall, with 'er clothes over 'er 'ead, and 'er inside, wot 'e'd cut out, lying alongside—a 'orrid sight!"

"I'd like to 'ave the 'andling of 'im !"

"'Andling of 'im! My Gawd!" A volley of expletives from Jim. "If I 'ad the 'andling of 'im once I wouldn't want it twice. I'd cut the —— up for cat's meat!"

There was a chorus of approval from those who had heard. A woman's voice rose above the hubbub; she shook her fist at the police who guarded the entrance to the court.

"What's the good of you p'lice? You lets a chap carve us women up as if we was cattle, and you never don't trouble yourselves to move a finger! I'd be ashamed."

She was supported by a lady friend, a woman with a shawl over her head, her hair streaming down her back; a woman who, evidently, had risen hastily from bed.

"You're right, Polly! If a pore bloke steals a 'aporth o' fried fish, they takes jolly good care, them slops, they runs him in, but a —— can do for as many of us gals as he —— well chooses, and they don't even trouble themselves to ketch 'im. Yah-h! I'd like to see him do for some of them, I would—straight!"

From the crowd another loud-voiced chorus of approval. Jim Slater formed a speaking-trumpet with his hands, and yelled,—

"Why don't yer ketch 'im?"

A hoarse, husky murmur from the throng, rapidly rising to a roar,—

"Yes, why don't yer?"

The enquiry was repeated over and over again, each time more angrily. The people began to surge forward, pressing towards the entrance of the court, where the police were standing.

Appendix D: Modernity and mental instability

At the end of the nineteenth century, medical men argued that the experience of modernity was conducive to mental instability. They diagnosed an alarming increase in mental illness, attributing this in particular to modern urban existence.

1. Forbes Winslow, *On Obscure Diseases of the Brain, and Disorders of the Mind: Their Incipient Symptoms, Pathology, Diagnosis, Treatment, and Prophylaxis* (London: John Churchill, 1860), 173-176.

The subject of latent and unrecognised morbid mind is yet in its infancy. It may be said to occupy, at present, untrodden and almost untouched ground. [...] How much of the bitterness, misery, and wretchedness so often witnessed in the bosom of families arises from concealed and undetected mental alienation! How often do we witness ruin, beggary, disgrace, and death result from such unrecognised morbid mental conditions! It is the canker worm gnawing at the vitals, and undermining the happiness of many a domestic hearth. Can nothing be done to arrest the fearful progress of this moral avalanche, or arrest the course of the rapid current that is hurling so many to ruin and destruction?

This type of morbid mental disorder exists to a frightful extent in real life. It is unhappily on the increase, and it therefore behoves the members of the medical profession, as guardians of the public health, as philosophers engaged in the loftiest and most ennobling of human inquiries, as practical physicians called upon to unravel the mysterious and complicated phenomena of disease, and administer relief to human suffering, fearlessly to grapple with an evil which is sapping the happiness of families, and to exert their utmost ability to disseminate sound principles of pathology and therapeutics upon a matter so intimately associated and so closely interwoven with the mental and social well-being of the human race.

These unrecognised morbid conditions most frequently implicate the *affections*, *propensities*, *appetites*, and *moral sense*. In many instances it is difficult to distinguish between normal or healthy irregularities of thought, passion, appetite, and those deviations

from natural conditions of the intellect, both in its intellectual and
moral manifestations, clearly bringing those so affected within the
legitimate domain of pathology. [...] The phases of mind of which
I speak are necessarily obscure, and, unlike the ordinary cases of
mental aberration of every-day occurrence, they frequently manifest themselves in either an exalted, depressed, or vitiated state of
the moral faculties. The disorder frequently assumes the character of a mere exaggeration of some single predominant passion,
appetite, or emotion, and so often resembles, in its prominent features, the natural and healthy actions of thought, either in excess
of development or irregular in its operations, that the practised
eye of the experienced physician can alone safely pronounce the
state to be an abnormal one. I do not refer to ordinary instances of
eccentricity, to idiosyncrasies of thought and feeling, or to cases in
which the mind appears to be absorbed by some one idea, which
exercises an influence over the conduct and thoughts quite dispro-
portionate to its intrinsic value. Neither do I advert to examples
of natural irritability, violence, or passion, coarseness and brutality, vicious inclinations, criminal propensities, excessive caprice, or
extravagance of conduct, for these conditions of mind may, alas! be
the natural and healthy operations of the intellect. These strange
phases of the understanding, *bizarreries* of character, vagaries of
the intellect, singularities, irregularities, and oddities of conduct,
common to so many who mix in every day life, and pass current
in society as healthy minded persons, present to the moralist and
philosophical psychologist many points for grave contemplation
and often suspicion. Such natural and normal, although eccentric
states of the intellect, do not, however, legitimately come within
the province of the *physician* unless they can be clearly demon-
strated to be *morbid results*, and positive and clearly established
deviations from cerebral or mental health.

2. Henry Maudsley, *Body and Mind: An Inquiry into their Connection
and Mutual Influence, Specially in Reference to Mental Disorders; Being
the Gulstonian Lectures for 1870 Delivered before the Royal College of
Physicians* (London: Macmillan, 1870), 41-43, 61-62, 64-65, 75-76.

Mental disorders are neither more nor less than nervous

diseases in which mental symptoms predominate, and their entire separation from other nervous diseases has been a sad hindrance to progress. [...] In a great many cases—in more than half, certainly, and perhaps in five out of six—there is something in the nervous organization of the person, some native peculiarity, which, however we name it, predisposes him to an outbreak of insanity. [...] Multitudes of human beings come into the world weighted with a destiny against which they have neither the will nor the power to contend; they are the step-children of nature, and groan under the worst of all tyrannies—the tyranny of a bad organization. [...]

It certainly cannot be disputed that when nothing abnormal whatever may be discoverable in the brains of persons who have a strong hereditary tendency to insanity, they often exhibit characteristic peculiarities in their manner of thought, feeling, and conduct, carrying in their physiognomy, bodily habit, and mental disposition the sure marks of their evil heritage. These marks are, I believe, the outward and visible signs of an inward and invisible peculiarity of cerebral organization. Here, indeed, we broach a most important inquiry, which has only lately attracted attention—the inquiry, namely, into the physical and mental signs of the degeneracy of the human kind. I do not mean to assert that all persons whose parents or blood relatives have suffered from nervous or mental disease exhibit mental and bodily peculiarities; some may be well formed bodily and of superior natural intelligence, the hereditary disposition in them not having assumed the character of deterioration of race; but it admits of no dispute that there is what may be called an *insane temperament* or *neurosis*, and that it is marked by peculiarities of mental and bodily conformation. Morel, who was the first to indicate, and has done much to prosecute, this line of inquiry, looks upon an individual so constituted as containing in himself the germs of a morbid variety: summing up the pathological elements which have been manifested by his ancestors, he represents the first term of a series which, if nothing happen to check the transmission of degenerate elements from generation to generation, ends in the extreme degeneracy of idiocy, and in extinction of the family. [...]

I have sketched generally the features of the insane

temperament, but there are really several varieties of it which need to be observed and described. [...] One group might consist of those egotistic beings, having the insane neurosis, who manifest a peculiar morbid suspicion of everything and everybody; they detect an interested or malicious motive in the most innocent actions of others, always looking out for an evil interpretation; and even events they regard as in a sort of conspiracy against them. [...] Another group might be made of those persons of unsound mental temperament who are born with an entire absence of the moral sense, destitute of the possibility even of moral feeling; they are as truly insensible to the moral relations of life, as deficient in this regard, as a person colour-blind is to certain colours, or as one who is without ear for music is to the finest harmonies of sound. Although there is usually conjoined in this absence of moral sensibility more or less weakness of mind, it does happen in some instances that there is a remarkably acute intellect of the cunning type. [...]

It is an indisputable though extreme fact that certain human beings are born with such a native deficiency of mind that all the training and education in the world will not raise them to the height of brutes; and I believe it to be not less true that, in consequence of evil ancestral influences, individuals are born with such a flaw or warp of nature that all the care in the world will not prevent them from being vicious or criminal, or becoming insane. [...] No one can escape the tyranny of organization; no one can elude the destiny that is innate in him, and which unconsciously and irresistibly shapes his ends, even when he believes that he is determining them with consummate foresight and skill.

3. Andrew Wynter, "The Borderlands of Insanity." In *The Borderlands of Insanity and Other Allied Papers* (London: Robert Hardwicke, 1875), 1-73: 1-5, 8.

That there is an immense amount of latent brain disease in the community, only awaiting a sufficient exciting cause to make itself patent to the world, there can be no manner of doubt. [...]

There is, in fact, no such thing as sudden insanity, or at least it is of the rarest possible occurrence. [...] [E]very one who has studied the human mind must be aware that it is not constituted like a piece of cast iron, which snaps suddenly under the influence of a sudden frost-like emotion.

The grey fabric of the brain, before it gives way, always affords notable signs easily capable of being read by an accomplished psychological physician, of a departure from a state of health.

It happens oftener than we imagine that impending lunacy is known to the individuals themselves before any sign is made to others. There is a terrible stage of consciousness in which, unknown to any other human being, an individual keeps up, as it were, a terrible hand-to-hand conflict with himself, when he is prompted by an inward voice to use disgusting words, which, in his sane moments, he loathes and abhors; these voices will sometimes suggest ideas which are diametrically opposed to the sober dictates of his conscience. In such conditions of mind, prayers are turned into curses, and the chastest into the most libidinous thoughts.

It does not necessarily follow, because a man is haunted by another and evilly-disposed self, that he has reached the stage of lunacy, if his reason still retains the mastery. [...] It is indeed strange what wayward and erratic turns the mind will take even in robust health. [...] [W]e are often haunted by an air of music, or some voice will repeat itself with such obstinacy as to annoy and destroy the mind, and often to prevent sleep. These curious phenomena are not symptomatic of brain disease, but they are singular examples of transient conditions of mind, which, when persistent, are clearly allied to insanity. When, therefore, this persistence does arise, a man may be sure then that he requires the attention of his physician, and that there is some cause at work, which is breeding mischief; and unless he attends to the significant warning, the probability is that disease will take a more serious turn, and that the voices believed to be internal will appear external, and lead the unfortunate sufferer to desperate courses.

Possibly the stage of consciousness is the most terrible of all the conditions of mind which lead the way to insanity. The struggles with the inward fiend, which the reason finds it cannot exorcise, must be far more appalling than a condition of absolute madness, in which, very often, the mental delusions are of a pleasing character. [...] In such cases the demon in possession seizes those very moments in which the enjoyment of other men is to be found.

4. Andrew Wynter, "'Hallucinations and Dreams." In *The Borderlands of Insanity and Other Allied Papers* (London: Robert Hardwicke, 1875), 257-290: 270-272, 274-275.

The use of haschisch in the East produces the most delightful visions. It is a preparation of Indian hemp, a very powerful narcotic, and one which is coming into use in this country. The fact, that by the use of drugs we can artificially produce hallucinations for a very short period, such as are persistent in the really insane, is very curious, and proves that in the latter case there is an exaltation of the brain, the product of a morbid condition, produced probably by the blood. It must be confessed, however, that the visions and delusions produced by the use of drugs are different in kind to the true hallucinations of the insane. The mind sees with the inner eye as it were, and the figures or visions partake more of the nature of those which appear in a dream. When the person under them has recovered from their effects, he is conscious that what he has seen was the product of his own excited brain. [...] In all such cases of brain excitement the senses, for the time, are preternaturally acute, the hearing and the sight are marvellously exalted, and the memory for past events and scenes is very vivid.

The scenes that pass before the mind in sleep may be likened to those produced by narcotism. Whilst they are passing like a panorama, they seem to be veritable objects, and we believe in them most implicitly. The most extraordinary events occur without in the least appearing strange to us, indeed, the sense of surprise and comparison seem for the time suspended; judgement is also wanting; in short, we seem to be quite as satisfied of the naturalness and truth of the most extraordinary and contradictory scenes and actions, as do the insane with respect to their own ideas. Indeed, the waking dreams of the demented are in many respects the counterparts of those which we experience in our healthy slumbers; the only difference is that the sane do not act upon them. But in the case of the somnambulist, there is not even this point of difference. Persons in this condition are continually walking in their sleep—generally without harm to themselves, but sometimes they walk through open windows and are killed. [...] It is a remarkable characteristic of the state of dreaming, that the mind often assimilates, in the train of ideas it is pursuing, any chance sound that may strike upon the ear. [...] The bodily movements, again, which take place in sleep, set the mind upon a new course of adventure; the excitement which takes place in the different organs suddenly colours the misty action of the dream, and no doubt the extraneous sights and sounds are accountable for many of the sudden distractions which we all experience in the visions we have in the night.

5. Victor Parant, "Persecution, Mania of." In *A Dictionary of Psychological Medicine Giving the Definition, Etymology and Synonyms of the Terms Used in Medical Psychology with the Symptoms, Treatment, and Pathology of Insanity and the Law of Lunacy in Great Britain and Ireland*, edited by D. Hack Tuke. 2 vols (London: J. & A. Churchill, 1892), II, 925-935: 927-928, 930.

Of all hallucinations the principal one is that of hearing; it is of such importance that most authors following Lasègue, consider it as the only one essential to persecution-mania. [...] [A]t first hallucinations consist of simple noises, and [...] are elementary; afterwards they become more defined, and the patient begins to hear voices, which, however, are still at some distance and confused so that the patient does not easily understand the words; in addition to being distant, they are also uttered in a deep voice. Rapidly they seem to be nearer, and become more distinct. At first the patient hears only isolated words which are abusive, insulting and obscene; the patient hears himself called murderer, assassin, drunkard, or similar epithets. Then the isolated words become framed into more or less lengthy sentences, which are all of the same character, and in which accusation, insults and threats always predominate.

These auditory hallucinations are heard by day and night, but they are generally most intense at the beginning of the night. [...] They may come from all directions, through the ceiling or the

walls, and through the chimney, or out of cupboards and ward-
robes; sometimes they come from underneath the ground, and are
then heard not only with the ears but by means of a transmission
of the vibrations by the whole system. [...]

At the moment, the patient believes that he hears clearly and
well-articulated words; he also believes he recognises the voice of
a certain person whom he considers as the originator of all the
persecutions of which he himself is the victim; the voice of this
individual, who is the cause of all misfortune, harasses the patient
incessantly. [...] [S]ome patients greatly troubled by the voices
which they believe that they hear, identify these voices so completely with their own thoughts that they finally believe that they
are no longer masters even of their own ideas. They are actually
possessed by what Baillarger describes as psychical hallucinations.
The patient believes that people read his own mind, that somebody steals his ideas, and that the voices which he hears immediately transform his ideas into words. [...] After this it may also
happen that the patient feeling that his ideas escape him, and are
known to every one when he would rather conceal them, imagines that he has in himself two separate individuals. He experiences
an actual doubling of his personality, and in addition to this he is
quite prepared for other modifications which may occur at a later
period. [...]

Lastly come the more serious attacks, namely, murderous
assaults. The patient generally does not reach this stage all at once,
but passes through a long period of hesitation. His ideas however
drive him on, and seeing no other way out of such a deplorable
situation, he commits some frightful deed. Some become hom-
icides in the hope that they will have peace after their persecutors are dead; others, because they hope to be given over into the
hands of justice, and that on the day of the trial they will be able to
denounce their persecutors, to cleanse themselves from all impu-
tations they believe to be made against them, and to have their
innocence publicly proclaimed.

6. D. Hack Tuke, "Demonomania." In *A Dictionary of Psychological Medicine Giving the Definition, Etymology and Synonyms of the Terms Used in Medical Psychology with the Symptoms, Treatment, and Pathology of Insanity and the Law of Lunacy in Great Britain and Ireland*, edited by D. Hack Tuke. 2 vols (London: J. & A. Churchill, 1892), I, 352-354: 352-353.

We have seen men labouring under the delusion of demoniacal possession, whose agonies were of the most terrible description, and who answered in every respect to the descriptions given of those unfortunate self-accusing wizards or witches who were burnt at the stake, firmly believing that they were what their judges charged them with being. Some patients, constantly dwelling on the frightful idea, have it reflected in their countenances, their physiognomy suggesting an uncanny personality, which would have inevitably sufficed for their condemnation in the old days of witchcraft. [...]

The *crisis* or fit is signalised by the occurrence of sudden yawning, when the patient is perfectly calm, pandiculations, sudden starts, and jerks of a choreic character in the arms; this is followed by rapid movements, as if from a succession of discharges; the pupil is by turns dilated and contracted, and the eyes sympathise with the general movements of the body. At this moment, the patients, whose aspect has first indicated fear, pass into a state of fury, which becomes more intense, as if the idea which dominates them caused two almost simultaneous effects—depression and excitement. The patients strike the furniture with violence, begin to speak, or, rather, to vociferate, the same word being endlessly repeated. If the spectator speaks to them, they reply to his remarks, but without escaping from their ruling idea, that they are lost souls in hell. And as it is always a demon of which they are the mouthpiece, the imaginary spirit sometimes recounts what he did on earth, and what he has done since he left it for the infernal regions. Their physiognomy is expressive of their mental excitement, the neck is swollen, the face injected, with some; it becomes pale with others; the lips are often covered with saliva, which gives the idea that they foam at the mouth. The movements, which at

first were limited to the upper extremities, extend to the trunk and
the lower limbs; the respiration becomes rapid; the patients, redou-
bling their fury, are aggressive, displace the furniture, hurl chairs,
stools, or anything they can lay hold of at anybody who stands by;
assault them, whether relatives or strangers; throw themselves on
the ground continuing their cries; roll about, striking their hands
on the earth, beating the breast, stomach, the front of their neck,
and try to tear out something which incommodes them in this
region. They bound hither and thither. [...] This crisis lasts from
ten minutes to half-an-hour, according to the exciting cause.

7. Henry Maudsley, *The Pathology of Mind: A Study of its
Distempers, Deformities, and Disorders*. 2nd edn (London: Macmillan,
1895), 32-33.

One thing we may feel pretty sure of, that if insanity be on the
increase among civilized peoples the increase is due more to their
pleasures than their pains—to idleness, luxury, and self-indulgence
more than to work, thrift, and self-denial. [...] At the present day it
is the fashion for men to pity themselves and to be pitied because
they have to work hard for a livelihood. Craving leisure to cultivate
their higher or indulge their lower natures, they despise the real
discipline and self-denial involved in hard work well done, the self-
discipline by which their uncultivated forefathers made a strong
nation. To shirk work or to do it badly in order to have time to
practise self-culture is a new method of going to work to make
virtue by a process of unmaking it. When such strain of self-indulgence pervades all the classes of a nation in all the relations of
life, it marks a decay of those hardy virtues by which a sound and
strong social fabric was built up; the corruptions which then ensue
and spread will not fail to show themselves in manifold degenera-
cies of individual vice, crime, and madness, and, inasmuch as individuals make the nation, in its corruption and decadence. Neither
for nations nor for individuals is it well when, waxing fat and doing
what they lust, they are deaf to the eternal lesson of renunciation
which is the hoarse-sounding refrain of the human hours.

Appendix E: Alcohol and personality

The end of the nineteenth century saw extensive medical debate over the impact of alcohol abuse on personality. These extracts chart the very real anxiety felt at the time.

1. Edgar Sheppard, *Lectures on Madness in its Medical, Legal, and Social Aspects* (London: J. & A. Churchill, 1873), 19-21.

We turn from the moral to *the physical causes of insanity*.

Without doubt the most frequent of these is *intemperance*. [...] Every additional year of experience confirms me in my belief that it is filling our madhouses with its subjects. I cannot tell you by it how many homes are broken up—how many hearts are broken down. It is a gigantic evil parturient of gigantic misery, committing its terrible havoc not only upon the first, but upon "the third and fourth generation of them that hate Me."

Yet it is to be noticed that even here an element of great uncertainty is introduced. A renowned French psychologist, M. Moreau, says: "Drunkenness is regarded as one of the most frequent causes of insanity. But it is equally certain that drunkenness, or rather *the taste for drink*, is as often, and even more frequently, a first symptom (the effect, therefore, and not the cause) of disease." [...] Esquirol long since gave utterance also to something like the same truth when he wrote, "If the abuse of alcoholic liquors is an effect of mental depravity, of educational vices, and the force of bad example, men sometimes give way to it by reason of a morbid impulse which they have not the power of resisting."

Another French psychologist (Morel) also observes: "It is not necessary to create a monomania of which the chief characteristic is an irresistible tendency to fermented liquors. That tendency is most frequently only the *symptom* of a principal disease, especially when it is suddenly developed in persons who previously had given no evidence of such a propensity."

Dr. Anstie, who has made alcoholism a special study, is clearly of opinion that of all depressing agencies it has "the most decided power to impress the nervous centres of a progenitor with a neurotic type, which will necessarily be transmitted, under varied forms and with increasing fatality, to his descendants."

2. Andrew Wynter, "The Borderlands of Insanity." In *The Borderlands of Insanity and Other Allied Papers* (London: Robert Hardwicke, 1875), 1-73: 49-51, 54-56.

Among the more special forms of moral perversity, or, as the alienal physicians would say, insanity, which are transmitted by an insane parent, [...] may be mentioned [...] Dipsomania, or thirst-madness [...]. That an individual should in all other matters appear to be of sound mind, but that at certain seasons he should be seized with an irrepressible desire [...] to reduce himself below the level of a beast by means of drink, seems to the unprofessional under-standing quite incomprehensible; and the common view—taking this bare aspect of the case—is the right one. There is indeed no such thing as simple thirst-madness [...]. Those who have watched such cases with professional knowledge and experience, observe that the whole moral tone of the individuals so afflicted is, so to speak, below par. They suffer from a paralysis of the moral sense; invariably they are untruthful, very commonly full of impure thoughts, and always eccentric both in thought and action. They have long belonged to the Borderland of Insanity, in the opinion of those who know them best; but it is only the last supreme act which, in the eyes of the world, takes them over the frontier into the domain of the insane. [...]

To the ordinary observer the dipsomaniac is nothing more than an utterly reckless person, who is determined to obtain drink, regardless of consequences. He is confounded with the ordinary drunkard, and his infirmity is looked upon as a simple vice. But, in reality, the two cases are utterly unlike. Whilst in the case of the ordinary toper drink is only the accompaniment of the festive board, in the dipsomaniac it is a secret vice. He will, indeed, avoid drinking in company, and assume the virtue of temperance, all the time that he is madly looking for liquor; and when he cannot obtain it, will drink even "shoeblacking and turpentine, hair-wash, or any-thing stimulating," says Dr. Skie. There is one feature in the dipso-maniac which is very observable; he is invariably good-tempered when not suffering from the physical depression which follows the indulgence of his desire. [...]

When the attack is over, the patient is overwhelmed with remorse at the disgrace he has brought upon himself; and this remorse and swinish bestiality alternate until every worldly prospect is ruined, and the poor patient dies in a fit of delirium or is transferred as "a boarder" to the custody of an asylum.

3. M. Legrain, "Alcoholism." In *A Dictionary of Psychological Medicine Giving the Definition, Etymology and Synonyms of the Terms Used in Medical Psychology with the Symptoms, Treatment, and Pathology of Insanity and the Law of Lunacy in Great Britain and Ireland*, edited by D. Hack Tuke. 2 vols (London: J. & A. Churchill, 1892), I, 62-74: 64-65, 67, 69.

Individuals who poison themselves with alcohol unintentionally are very numerous. In analysing the different ways in which they poison themselves, and trying to find out by which psychological process they become intemperate drinkers, we shall prove that their brains are imperfect and act irregularly.

In the *first group* we may place those individuals in whom the moral sense is only feebly developed or completely obliterated. These are the *morally insane*. In these the instincts are perverted or predominant; they are no longer in accordance with the normal requirements of human nature, with the intellectual functions and with the conventional principles of morality as adopted by civilised nations. The higher faculties no longer exercise any control over the instincts. This group comprises the drunkards properly so-called, to whatever social class they may belong, united by one common band: *the predominance of the instincts over the higher faculties.*

To the anomalies of the instincts we may oppose *the anomalies of proclivity*. The intemperate of this class form a *second group*. [...]

In a *third group* we shall range the intermittent drinkers, known under the name of dipsomaniacs, men with still weaker brains than those beforementioned, who at ordinary times do not show any anomalies of instinct or of tendencies, but whose will is periodically subject to complete paralysis. [...] The patients of the first group, deprived of all moral sense, *never strive* against the temptations; those of the second group are able to strive and do *strive sometimes*: those of the third group are unable to strive successfully, although they are *always striving*. [...] These considerations establish one fact—viz., *that the great majority of drinkers are predisposed, disordered and defective*. [...]

One of the first effects of alcohol is the *dis-equilibration of the intellect*, and this is much easier in a predisposed individual, whose mental equilibrium is already unstable at ordinary times. Consequently, alcohol *creates an abnormal opportunity* of revealing the innermost nature of the patient to the outside world in a most striking manner; the slightest defects of the mental state are exhibited; the dominant feature of the character becomes exaggerated; the instinct, desires, and tendencies, no longer subject to the regulating control of the higher faculties, have free course; the animal nature is set free. [...]

The two principal attitudes of the drinker, sadness and gaiety, give rise in a predisposed individual to two well-defined forms of drunkenness, *melancholy and maniacal drunkenness*. In the former as a short attack of melancholia we find the elements of that psychosis: imaginary accusations, depression, scruples, ideas of unworthiness, and attempts at suicide. In the second form we find an attack of mania of some hours' duration, with the symptoms peculiar to that derangement: exaltation of the faculties, disorder, and incoherency in words and actions. In both forms even hallucinations have been observed. [...]

At first, all the elementary symptoms of the period of incubation, as insomnia and fearful nightmares, are of great importance. But what becomes still more characteristic is *the tendency of the patients to interpret their sensory illusions*, and to make them the basis of so many delirious conceptions [...].

A patient in sub-acute alcoholism is *very often suffering from persecution mania*, but his ideas of persecution are not steady and not well connected together; they are never systematised. The patient is gloomy, sad and restless. It seems as if the nocturnal tragedies at which he is present continue to impress him during the day, and that he seeks in his surroundings for their explanation. Jealous and timorous, he is afraid of and suspects everybody—his wife, his children, and his masters. Often he believes himself to be the object of the special attention of the police. All sorts of ideas of persecution may be found, and all of them are characterised by great *changeableness*, not being continuous, but *constantly interrupted by lucid periods*, and remarkable for producing on the part of the patient, in consequence of his continual alcoholic excitation, *violent reactions*, outrages, and even homicide. It is not rare to observe some hallucinations, especially during the night (of hearing and vision), towards the end of this period, but on the whole illusions are predominant. It is characteristic of the derangements of intellect caused by alcohol, that they are of a painful nature, and it is therefore not astonishing if the superadded delirious ideas of the period of incubation are those of depression.

If predisposed individuals do not become deranged, they nevertheless have periods of intellectual excitement; they show themselves loquacious and obscene, but their talk has always a lugubrious character. They like to talk of battles, slaughter, blood. Others give themselves to debauchery, begin to lead a disorderly and expensive life, and refuse to work.

4. M. Legrain, "Delirium Tremens." In *A Dictionary of Psychological Medicine Giving the Definition, Etymology and Synonyms of the Terms Used in Medical Psychology with the Symptoms, Treatment, and Pathology of Insanity and the Law of Lunacy in Great Britain and Ireland*, edited by D. Hack Tuke. 2 vols (London: J. & A. Churchill, 1892), I, 340-345: 340-342.

Break-down of the intellectual equilibrium, progressive mental instability, quickness in the production of ideas and excessive flow of the latter, rapid transformation of conceptions, all these are so many characteristics of this bubbling up, of this cerebral pruritus, which one finds at this period under the influence of an incessantly renewed stimulant. Sometimes it might seem as if the ideas follow each other with the rapidity of the fibrillary agitation of trembling muscle. The cerebral exaltation shows itself also in a great susceptibility of the character; in sudden passion and anger without cause, which often lead to violent actions on the part of the inebriated person, which he regrets the more, as they are brought about impulsively before the intervention of the will has time to prevent them. We see already the eminently sad character of the conceptions, altered under the influence of alcohol. The individual is aggrieved, misanthropic, and restless; he has uncertain fear and vague suspicion. Too much occupied with himself, and in some way troubled by this transformation of himself, which he perceives instinctively, he only cares for himself; his moral affective sensibility is diminished; one finds a tendency to absurd interpretation of the simplest facts. The absence of stability in his ideas and the diminution of will-power explain his attitude: he often changes his place, does not finish work he commenced; and is grieved with his unfitness and unskilfulness. At the same time, one may observe a disorderly activity, and an intense neuro-muscular excitability, which causes the patient to walk incessantly, to move from one place to another, and to give out much strength for nothing; fatigue is never perceived. Conscience is not completely extinct, but it is visibly altered. Rarely are the patients able to judge their own state rightly. The rapidity of the conception is so great that the conscience does not receive any durable impression, and therefore is a bad judge.

There is one singular and constant symptom: all these troubles become exaggerated with the beginning of the night. The vague uneasiness increases, and becomes an inexpressible anxiety; the fright grows; if the patients are very much troubled they are unable to get rid of that fear, and to define their uneasiness. The fall of the day incites the thoughts to new activity, or, to express it better, the patient, who during the day had his attention distracted and his senses calmed down by manifold impressions from all sides, begins again to consider his own condition, as soon as he leaves off work and returns home, there being nothing more to distract him.

The nights show truly characteristic symptoms. The drinker does not get any rest; and especially the hypnagogic phase, in which the fantastical conceptions of dreams are produced, is of great moment. It consists of myriads of painful thoughts, of fearful nightmares, and dreadful visions, so that the patient prefers not to sleep at all rather than undergo this frightful punishment of the nightmare, which troubles him so vividly. One must have heard the tales of drinkers to know the great moral anguish they suffer.

The slightest sensorial impressions, especially of hearing, which in normal sleep are simply stored away, or form the starting-point of an association of insignificant ideas, are here the germ of the most terrible scenes; battles, slaughters, punishments, incendiarisms, robberies, crimes, and all sorts of outrages follow each other or are mixed up in one picture. The patient plays an active part in these fantastical dreams, which escape the control of the intellect, and he awakes out of breath, bathed in perspiration, and sometimes sighing loud, at the moment when he falls down a precipice, or is to be devoured by a lion. Towards the end of the night only the patient, exhausted by sleeplessness and also by abundant perspiration, enjoys a little sleep, but dull and not deep it only lasts a few hours, leaving the patient more exhausted than before; in this way the resistance diminishes from day to day, still more lessened by fresh excesses in drink. With the arrival of the day the fantastical dreams of the night disappear, and the patient again takes up his occupation.

The prodromic period is also remarkable for its *sensorial illusions*, which are numerous and precede the hallucinations of the next period. The excitability of the cortex is not yet great enough, and the conscience is not yet troubled enough, to make the illusions so many hallucinations. *The prodromic stage is the period of the illusions, that of actual delirium the period of the hallucinations*.

The illusions affect all the senses, but preferably those of vision and hearing. They possess the patient visibly, and augment his anguish. They are predominant at the end of the day and *especially during the night*, when, in consequence of the surrounding quietness, the brain is susceptible to the slightest impressions, the intensity of which is increased tenfold. Often the unfortunate alcoholists have to strike a light in order to put to instantaneous flight these terrible scenes, from which they were not able to withdraw their attention. Every sensation is interpreted: a ray of light, the shining of the fire in the fire-place, or a star, take the proportions of a great fire; a murmur, or an unusual noise, produces the effect of the discharge of a pistol, of a stroke of the clock, of the tolling of the funeral bells, &c. The patient feels vertigo, dizziness, and, even with his eyes closed, swimming of the head; he imagines himself falling, to be removed from his place, and to be carried through the air. A frequent and characteristic illusion of vision is the *displacement of objects* with more of less considerable rapidity. [...]

After a few days the illusions have become more frequent and sleep has entirely disappeared; the tremor is very intense; the troubles of the intellect are no longer nocturnal only, but continue in the daytime. The patient has given up his occupation. Trembling and frightened he lives in a perpetual nightmare. Conscience has been gradually extinguished, and the delirium is continual. The patient is a victim of *panophobia*; he is the sport of all his senses, producing myriads of hallucinations, which follow each other with a frightful rapidity, leaving the brain no respite and no intermission, keeping the patient constantly in alarm, and maintaining the delirium. [...]

The patient sees the most frightful and awful scenes defile before his eyes with extraordinary rapidity. These are on the whole the same scenes which unrolled themselves before him in his nightmares during the prodromic period, with the difference, however, that now he is himself an actor as well as a spectator; he is in these tragedies the principal personage and believes in their reality. The succession of the scenes is as rapid as in a kaleidoscope; scenes of slaughter, murder, and incendiarisms; the patient sees funerals pass by, assists at an execution, or sees his wife and children killed; he sees grimacing figures; the objects take on other colours, appear transfigured, &c. The most typical visual hallucination, however, is the *vision of animals*, real or fabulous, monsters and chimeras, of objectionable and repulsive animals, as spiders, rats, mice, &c. They are mostly aggressive; the patient sees them rushing up to him and showing him their teeth. What augments his fright is that all these objects are gifted with motion; the animals run about and climb upon his shoulders; the objects change their form, grow or become smaller, and finally vanish, to reappear or to make room for others.

5. Henry Maudsley, *The Pathology of Mind: A Study of its Distempers, Deformities, and Disorders*. 2nd edn (London: Macmillan, 1895), 308-311, 492-493.

A mania of persecution is not always of gradual growth and

chronic. When the disorder has a definite cause in alcohol, or sexual abuse, or extreme mental trouble, it may come on in periodical attacks, subacute or acute, which are characterised by great mental excitement, acute apprehensions, numerous hallucinations of sight and hearing, and much confusion of mind, all which pass away in due time. [...]

Such persons are prone to be dangerous at one period or another of their malady [...]; for they are always liable, when despairing of help and out of sorts bodily, perhaps worn out by restless days and sleepless nights, to be so maddened as to lose self-control and to make a desperate assault on some innocent person who, incurring their suspicion, attracts the discharge of their explosive fury. [...] It is all the worse when they make fatal use of a revolver or other deadly weapon which they buy and carry for their protection. [...] [T]hose who suffer from alcoholic and hypochondriacal mania of persecution are especially dangerous; they are prone to fix on a particular person whom they believe to be the cause of their sufferings and to discharge their accumulated fury against him. They have also mind enough to feel bitterly their miserable state, to plan deliberate revenge, and to carry a desperate resolution into desperate effect; managing their delusions, if necessary, to the extent of dissembling or denying them for the occasion, and even of concealing them methodically for a purpose. [...] [T]he alcoholic patient is acutely fearful, keenly anxious and agitated, believing himself to be menaced by, and in tremor of apprehension of, what *will* happen to him; his emotion is more acute, definite and consistent [...]. Moreover, the intellectual delusions are less and the hallucinations more marked in the alcoholic patient, who is prone to see strange animals and persons about him, perhaps corpses in the room, ceilings open and shut, flames of fire, and the like; the hallucinations, which are fleeting, changing and incoherent, being both of sight and hearing, whereas they are chiefly or entirely of hearing in ordinary mania of persecution. [...]

The attack of *delirium tremens* is usually preceded by a very unquiet depression: lowness of spirits, apprehensive anxieties, gloomy forebodings and suspicions, extreme nervous agitation, nausea and loss of appetite, unrest and sleeplessness; the little sleep obtained being disturbed by a succession of frightful dreams out of which the patient wakes in terror, panting and bathed in perspiration, and because of which, though he longs for sleep, he dreads to fall asleep again. His troubles are worst in the night season, when he is at the mercy of himself, for the impressions and incidents of the day help to distract him from himself. Upon this depression follows mental excitement with delirium, the delirium characterized by acute fear and trepidation and accompanied by terrifying hallucinations and extreme restlessness. [...] Most common are the visions of rats and mice, snakes, beetles and other creatures running and crawling on the floor, walls and bed, of bats flying about the room, and the like, but sometimes they are the more alarming spectres of dead persons, of thieves, of assassins.

Appendix F: Women, nerves and sexuality

The nineteenth century saw the diagnosis of insanity, particularly
hysteria, as a "female malady." Women and nerves were associated
with each other, with decisive, bold women particularly liable for
accusations of "moral insanity." Female sanity was, according to
contemporary medical commentators, linked to female sexuality.
It was argued that women were liable at the "critical periods" of
life to suffer from excessive emotion and irrational impulses, and
that their sexuality should be carefully monitored at these times.
Thus, the menstrual cycle was seen as inextricably linked to female
sanity.

1. E.J. Tilt, *On the Preservation of the Health of Women at the
Critical Periods of Life* (London: John Churchill, 1851), 31, 34-37, 41.

We constantly hear parents talk of "bringing girls forward,"
but all my observations, reading, and meditations on the subject,
confirm me in the opinion which I have long entertained, that the
art of educating girls in order to bring them to the full perfection
of womanhood, is *to retard as much as possible the appearance of first
menstruation.*

If there be any possibility of effecting this purpose, it must
be by maintaining in its integrity an essentially English institution—*the nursery.* The nursery, in the usual acceptation of the
term, means rational food, rational hours of rest and of rising,
and rational exercise at judicious times. It means the absence of
sofas to lounge on—the absence of novels fraught with harrowing
interest; it means the absence of laborious gaiety, of theatres, and
of operas—the absence of intimacies which are of a too absorbing
nature, and a wholesome subjection of every minute to rule and
discipline.

This institution is essentially English; for in other countries,
girls from the cradle sit at their father's table, and mix in the society
to be met with at their homes; and *this national institution is, in my
opinion, the principal cause of the pre-eminence of English women, in
vigour of constitution, soundness of judgment, and still more, in their*

rectitude of moral principle. Under all circumstances, girls should, as long as possible, be kept under this restraint; but when there exists any constitutional weakness—any very painful performance of the menstrual function, a girl should be kept in the school-room much longer than the usual time—by those, at least, who wish to build up power for the future, and who think their daughter's health preferable to a life entirely devoted to excitement or to disease. [...]

With regard to the government of the mental faculties, I have little to say, except that one ought not to be developed at the expense of another; they ought to be kept in a regular state of counterpoise, so as equally to improve the reasoning powers, and by more completely occupying the time and thoughts, to keep in check the too sudden development of those sentiments [...] which, in girls of the higher classes, often assume a wrong direction, attain a morbid intensity, and are productive of the most deplorable consequences. [...]

The proper direction of the affections is one of the most sacred duties of a mother; and if I touch on a subject so delicate, it is because, in accordance with woman's destiny, her moral and mental conditions effectually re-act on those organs which direct the periodic flow that critically determines the measure of her health. For a mother, in attempting to perform her duty towards her daughter, to deny the validity of this principle in its highest earthly manifestations, would be folly: it should be admitted, and directed by a mother's experience and that of well-chosen associates, and not injudiciously developed by frequenting too much balls, concerts, theatres, and operas, or by the habitual reading of hair-uplifting novels.

This excessive development of the nervous system, the predisposing cause of so much disease, can be produced by an undue stimulation of all those nervous expansions which, underlaying the whole surface of the body, render it capable of sensation, and principally by the prolonged and exaggerated exercise of those portions of the body where nervous substance and nervous energy are concentrated to become senses, for the appreciation of special qualities: for the senses, and more particularly the ears and eyes, are the mysterious portals through which mind and emotion enter a material structure, to place themselves in communication with the mind and emotion of another being. Therefore the skin, by the habitual stimulation of heat; the palate, by luxurious feeding; the nostrils, by the indulgence in "soul-dissolving scents;" the ears, by a superabundance of musical vibrations, may give an undue activity to the nervous system, can awaken the dormant powers of imagination, and by increasing the energy of the human passions, may react on the organs which they call into action. [...]

At this critical period, girls should be treated with that happy, even mixture of firmness and mildness, oftener met with in the mother than in one of the sterner sex [...]. It is not wilful wickedness that often afflicts girls at this important period, but it is a transient want of self-control, in consequence of a new influence obscuring for a time the clearness of the moral principle. Until Nature assert her sway, gentle means, and a soothing treatment, to keep in check all eccentricities, added to the firm assertions of the rights of reason, blended with the tenderness of a mother's affection, without which all reasoning would be powerless, seem to me parts of the best plan to be pursued; for harsh treatment might, and probably would, give a permanent warp to the yet unformed character.

2. H. Sutherland, "Menstruation and Insanity." In *A Dictionary of Psychological Medicine Giving the Definition, Etymology and Synonyms of the Terms Used in Medical Psychology with the Symptoms, Treatment, and Pathology of Insanity and the Law of Lunacy in Great Britain and Ireland*, edited by D. Hack Tuke. 2 vols (London: J. & A. Churchill, 1892), II, 801-803: 801-803.

Esquirol has said that the derangements of menstruation form one-sixth of the physical causes of insanity, and Morel exactly agrees with him. [...]

In mania, it is agreed by Esquirol, Greissinger, and Morel that increased excitement is observable at the catamenial period. On the other hand, we occasionally find instances in which mania is associated with more or less suppression of the menses. The mischief in these cases may be due either to congestion of the brain in consequence of the blood usually discharged by the normal channel being retained, or the amenorrhœa may be due to the general condition of anæmia which often accompanies an attack of asthenic insanity.

It cannot fairly be stated that in cases of recovery from mania the return of the catamenia always precedes the cure of insanity in cases where the discharge has been suppressed. Frequently the order is reversed, the patient becomes sane and is discharged from the asylum, but the monthly flux does not occur regularly for some weeks or months afterwards. A reappearance, however, of the catamenia cannot but be regarded as a favourable sign during an attack of insanity, and in many cases is followed by recovery. In puerperal insanity also the outlook becomes brighter on the return of the menstrual flux.

In insanity with menorrhagia, erotic actions and obscene language are frequent accompaniments.

Out of one hundred and sixty-two cases of mania, no less than ninety-nine, or about two-thirds of the total number had attacks of excitement which could be distinctly referred to the catamenial period.

Of these ninety-nine, in eleven instances the maniacal excitement was observed to occur at periods varying from one day to a week before the accession of the catamenia. In the remaining eighty-eight, the mania appeared to occur, and to be at its worst, during the period of the catamenial discharge.

An increase in the number of fits and maniacal excitement occurred in many epileptics at the monthly periods. [...]

The importance of avoiding all emotional disturbance at the menstrual period has been insisted on by the authors of all ages. [...]

The medico-legal aspect of the effects of menstruation upon the emotional centres cannot be over-estimated. Krugelstein says: "Amongst all the female suicides it has been my lot to see, the act was committed during the catamenial period."

Dr. Icard truly says: "The menstrual function can by sympathy, especially in those predisposed, create a mental condition varying from simple psychalgia, that is to say, a simple moral malaise, a simple troubling of the soul, to actual insanity, to a complete loss of reason, and modifying the acts of a woman from simple weakness to absolute irresponsibility. The tribunal cannot appraise with any certainty the disposition of a woman who is the subject of menstrual disturbance."

The following morbid mental phenomena have been observed by Icard to occur at the menstrual periods: Kleptomania, pyromania, dipsomania, homicidal mania, suicidal mania, erotomania, nymphomania, religious delusions, acute mania, delirious insanity, impulsive insanity, morbid jealousy, lying, calumny, illusions, hallucinations, melancholia; of which he reports cases at great length in his admirable work.

3. Edgar Sheppard, *Lectures on Madness in its Medical, Legal, and Social Aspects* (London: J. & A. Churchill, 1873), 87, 90-91, 98.

It does not appear that, as our psychological and pathological researches are extended, we have any clearer ideas than formerly of that derangement to which Dr. Pritchard gave the unfortunate name of *moral insanity*—defining it to be "a morbid perversion of the natural feelings, affections, inclinations, tempers, habits, moral dispositions, and natural impulses, without any remarkable disorder or defect of the intellect, or knowing and reasoning faculties, and particularly without any insane illusion or hallucination." [...]

Your sensational experience in the perusal of the daily press has already made you acquainted with the fact, that what is termed moral insanity at times derives great and spasmodic interest from its association with great crimes. [...]

The characteristics of this temperament are, for the greater part, vanity, restlessness, capriciousness, impulsive action, with general eccentricity of thought and feeling, and not unfrequently a singularly inharmonious physiognomy. [...] Sometimes moral insanity is characterized by a great and shameless depravity [...]. Women of good social position and education will manifest an utter disregard of all the decencies of life. Spasmodic intemperance and sensuality will for a time destroy all the proprieties which are ordinarily regarded as having imperious claims. Often allied with some form of neurosis, such as hysteria or epilepsy, this distressing malady will give scandal and notoriety to a neighbourhood. Its subjects will break all the commandments of the Mosaic law, and many others (not written upon tables of stone) which society has set up for her protection. In the sex endowed with a child-bearing organ exacerbation takes place at the menstrual periods, and erotic symptoms are very marked. Impulses of depravity will manifest themselves in the exposure of the person, in disgusting language, and in various acts of indecency which need not be particularized. So also impulses of violence and destructiveness will be evidenced by broken windows, torn clothes and bedding, and even self-mutilation. At such times women will introduce foreign bodies into the vagina, swallow pins, eat and drink the excretal residua of previous eatings and drinkings, and disclose endless varieties of vitiated taste and feeling. [...]

"The act of violence," Dr. Maudsley writes, "whatever form it may take, is but the symptom of a deep morbid perversion of the nature of the individual of a morbid state which may at any moment be excited into a convulsive activity, either by a powerful impression from without producing some great moral shock, or by some cause of bodily disturbance—intemperance, sexual exhaustion, masturbation, or menstrual disturbance. There are women, sober and temperate enough at other times, who are afflicted with an uncontrollable propensity for stimulants at the menstrual period; and every large asylum furnishes examples of exacerbation of insanity or epilepsy coincident with that function."

4. Robert Brudenell Carter, *On the Pathology and Treatment of Hysteria* (London: John Churchill, 1853), 20, 31-33, 35-36.

The power of judgment against emotion is most strikingly illustrated by an extended comparison between the sexes, in whom the general predominance of reasoning and feeling respectively, is universally acknowledged, although, probably, not to the extent in which it actually obtains. A recent writer in the *Edinburgh Review* has well described this "organic difference," which he regards as subservient to the office of maternity; and the author would propose the contrasted proclivity of the male and female to hysteria as a measure of its degree, believing that the range of emotional instincts in woman is very large indeed, and that it includes many actions apparently volitional. [...] [U]nder certain circumstances, an hysteric paroxysm may be produced in a perfectly healthy woman, who is not the subject of any special proclivity to it, and upon whose system no appreciable influence has been exerted, excepting that of strongly-excited feeling; which, in the absence of all evidence to the contrary, must be received, in such cases, as the cause of the subsequent phenomena. [...]

Speaking with reference to the female sex only, the most common of these feelings is terror; and the most violent is the sexual passion. [...] The attack does not usually commence until the first apprehension has in some measure yielded to a feeling of security, and consequently it is most apt to occur, either where the fear has been out of proportion to the danger, or where the danger itself has been only momentary. [...] [I]n the female, a hysterical attack is sometimes seen after escape from very perilous situations, and especially after the exhibition of considerable (so-called) presence of mind, which, in such cases, is probably purely instinctive [...]. There does not appear to be any *à priori* reason for supposing that any individual, whether male or female, is totally exempt from liability to primary hysteria; but in considering the circumstances which are most favourable, or most opposed to its development, our attention is at once arrested by a strongly-marked difference between the sexes; a difference so great that the disease was named, and long thought of, as if peculiar to women. Indeed, among the ancients, it is very likely to have been so; but the advances of modern civilisation and refinement have nurtured and increased many feelings in man to which he was almost a stranger in rude and barbarous times. The circle of masculine emotions having thus been manifestly widened, it is not unreasonable to suppose that some evident effects have resulted from the change; and that as the feelings become more vivid, the physical organism has been more and more subjugated to their influence.

If the relative power of emotion amongst the sexes be compared in the present day, even without including the erotic passion, it is seen to be considerably greater in the woman than in the man, partly from that natural conformation which causes the former to feel, under circumstances where the latter thinks; and partly because the woman is more under the necessity of endeavouring to conceal her feelings. But when sexual desire is taken into the account, it will add immensely to the forces bearing upon the

female, who is often much under its dominion; and who, if unmarried and chaste, is compelled to restrain every manifestation of
its sway. Man, on the contrary, has such facilities for its gratifica-
tion, that as a source of disease it is almost inert against him, and
when powerfully excited, it is pretty sure to be speedily exhausted
through the proper channel. [...]

The greatest difficulty which has hitherto presented itself to
writers on the disease under consideration, has depended upon
its distinct association, in the majority of cases, with the sexual
propensities of the female, and with derangements of her sexual
organs, while, at the same time, it cannot be connected with any
one kind of derangement rather than with others, or with desire
rather than with loathing, except in the usual numerical proportion which exists between the different states. [...]

This being so, it is evident that any circumstances which direct
attention to the reproductive system, will tend to increase materially the proclivity of persons exposed to them, and to establish
trains of thought of the kind most likely to originate the disease.
Such conditions are furnished by all morbid conditions of the
uterus, whether they only excite sensations, or whether they are
fixed upon the mind of the patient in consequence of medical
treatment. Faulty menstruation, whether local or constitutional,
will have a similar effect; and it will be found that, although affections of this kind often arise consecutively to hysteria, still that
women suffering from them are more liable than others, *cæteris
paribus*, to be the subjects of that disorder.

Women of strong passions, who are separated from their hus-
bands, either permanently or for a time, are especially liable to hysterical attacks. This is well instanced by the wives of sailors, or other
men, who are constantly taken from home by their occupation.

5. Henry Maudsley, *Body and Mind: An Inquiry into their
Connection and Mutual Influence, Specially in Reference to Mental
Disorders; Being the Gulstonian Lectures for 1870 Delivered before
the Royal College of Physicians* (London: Macmillan, 1870), 79-80,
82-83, 87-88.

[W]e might in like manner make of *hysterical* insanity a special

variety. An attack of acute maniacal excitement, with great restlessness, rapid and disconnected but not entirely incoherent conversation, sometimes tending to the erotic or obscene, evidently
without abolition of consciousness; laughing, singing, or rhyming,
and perverseness of conduct, which is still more or less coherent
and seemingly wilful,—may occur in connection with, or instead
of, the usual hysterical convulsions. [...] Loss of power of will is
a characteristic symptom of hysteria in all its Protean forms, and
with the perverted sensations and disordered movements there
is always some degree of moral perversion. This increases until
it swallows up the other symptoms: the patient loses more and
more of her energy and self-control, becoming capriciously fanci-
ful about her health, imagining or feigning strange diseases, and
keeping up the delusion or the imposture with a pertinacity that
might seem incredible, getting more and more impatient of the
advice and interference of others, and indifferent to the interests
and duties of her position. Outbursts of temper become almost
outbreaks of mania, particularly at the menstrual periods. An
erotic tinge may be observable in her manner and behaviour; and
occasionally there are quasi-ecstatic or cataleptic states. [...]

The slight shades of this kind of morbid influence we cannot
venture to trace; but it is easy to recognize the most marked
effects. Take, for example, the irritation of ovaries or uterus, which
is sometimes the direct occasion of *nymphomania*—a disease by
which the most chaste and modest woman is transformed into a
raging fury of lust. [...] We have, indeed, to note and bear in mind
how often sexual ideas and feelings arise and display themselves
in all sorts of insanity; how they connect themselves with ideas
which in a normal mental state have no known relation to them;
so that it seems as inexplicable that a virtuous person should ever
have learnt, as it is distressing that she should manifest, so much
obscenity of thought and feeling. [...]

The monthly activity of the ovaries which marks the advent of
puberty in women has a notable effect upon the mind and body;
wherefore it may become an important cause of mental and physical derangement. Most women at that time are susceptible, irritable, and capricious, any cause of vexation affecting them more
seriously than usual; and some who have the insane neurosis

exhibit a disturbance of mind which amounts almost to disease. A sudden suppression of the menses has produced a direct explosion of insanity; or, occurring some time after an outbreak, it may be an important link in its causation. [...] There is certainly a recurrent mania, which seems sometimes to have, in regard to its origin and the items of its attacks, a relation to the menstrual function, suppression or irregularity of which often accompanies it; and it is an obvious presumption that the mania may be a sympathetic morbid effect of the ovarian and uterine excitement, and may represent an exaggeration of the mental irritability which is natural to women at that period. The patient becomes elated, hilarious, talkative, passing soon from that condition into a state of acute and noisy mania, which may last two or three weeks or longer, and then sinking into a brief stage of more or less depression or confusion of mind, from which she awakens to calmness and clearness of mind.

6. H.B. Donkin, "Hysteria." In *A Dictionary of Psychological Medicine Giving the Definition, Etymology and Synonyms of the Terms Used in Medical Psychology with the Symptoms, Treatment, and Pathology of Insanity and the Law of Lunacy in Great Britain and Ireland*, edited by D. Hack Tuke. 2 vols (London: J. & A. Churchill, 1892), I, 618-627: 619-620, 622, 625.

The subjects of hysteria are, in a very large proportion, of the female sex, the symptoms most often appearing at or soon after puberty. Children, however, even when quite young, may suffer from it, the sexual distribution being much less unequal in the earlier years; and marked cases occur not infrequently in men. The typical subject of hysteria, however, is the young woman; in her organism and her social conditions the potential factors of hysteria are present in a notable degree. Apart from whatever fundamental difference of nerve-stability there may be between the sexes, and this is probably very great, the girl usually meets with far more obstacles to uniform development and consequent nervous control than the youth. The stress of puberty, marked in both sexes by a great increase in the complexity and activity of the organism, is more sudden and intense in the female; the sexual organs which undergo these great changes are of relatively greater importance in her physical economy, and consequently involve a larger area of central innervation than in the male. The nervous balance is thus in especially unstable equilibrium. With this greater internal stress on the nervous organism there are in the surroundings and general training of most girls many hindrances to the retention or restoration of a due stability, and but few channels of outlet for her new activities. It is not only in the educational repression and ignorance as regards sexual matters of which the girl is the subject that this difference is manifest, but all kinds of other barriers to the free play of her powers are set up by ordinary social and ethical customs. "Thou shall not" meets the girl at almost every turn. The exceptions to this rule are found in those instances where girls and women of all conditions, owing to the influence of good education or necessity, or both, have regular work and definite pursuits. [...] Among the activities thus artificially repressed in girls, it must be recognised that the sexual play an important part, and, indeed, the frequent evidence given of dammed-up sexual emotions by both the special act of masturbation and numerous extraordinary vagaries of conduct, have led many to regard unsatisfied sexual desire as one of the leading causes of hysteria. [...] There are clearly other stresses which render women especially liable to hysteria. The periodic disturbance of menstruation, the times of pregnancy and parturition, and the numerous and multiform anxieties of home life, have their influence in contributing to the number of sufferers. There are, perhaps, as many or more instances of neurotic women commencing hysterics after marriage, as there are of hysterical girls showing greater nervous stability with the same change of condition. [...]

Motor disturbances in hysteria are legion [...]. The commonest and most fundamental example of hysterical spasm are laughter and weeping with comparatively inadequate cause, symptoms which obviously connect hysteria by invisible links with the normal neurosis underlying all human emotion. Lastly, we have numerous examples of spasm of limbs and the voluntary muscles generally, transient or of long duration, often simulating the organic forms of spastic paraplegia and other diseases in various degrees. The most chronic instances of this affection are known as contractures;

sudden recovery may occur in any case, but some become permanent with visible nerve-changes. The most familiar example of spasm is the hysterical fit, which constitutes the essence of what is vulgarly known as hysteria, and attacks a very large number of hysterics [...]. The hysterical fit is generally preceded by various kinds of emotional display, such as laughter or crying, by globus, and disorders of general and special sensibility; and its spasms usually lack the regular process and distribution which mark true epilepsy. It takes place but seldom at night, perhaps never when the patient is alone, and is generally without the signs of complete unconsciousness. There is a purposive appearance of many of the wild and disorderly movement which mark the fit, even at its height, when ordinary sensibility is certainly largely in abeyance, and the facial expression is not lost, as in epilepsy, but is one of varied emphasis, and the eyes are generally closed. The paroxysm may last much longer than any single epileptic one, and ends not in coma, but, as it began, in emotional display. [...]

On the vulnerable nervous material of the hysterical subject many exciting agents work to produce disorder. Prominent among these are great and sudden emotions, such as fear in all its forms—a notable element in the hysteria of childhood; disappointment; forcibly repressed desires, especially sexual; enforced mental overwork; nervous shock, as, *e.g.*, the result of railway accidents, earthquakes, &c.; traumatism of all kinds, including surgical operations; general exhausting conditions, such as hæmorrhages, anæmia, the menstrual periods, pregnancy, parturition, poisoning by alcohol, chloroform, mercury, &c.; diseases such as enteric and other fevers, pneumonia, malaria, syphilis; organic nervous disease, as tumour of the brain, disseminated sclerosis, tabes dorsalis, and especially paralysis agitans; and local affections of the generative and other organs; though it is to be observed here that marked disease of the uterus, such as cancer, is not a frequent exciting agent in hysterical display.

7. J.M. Charcot and Pierre Marie, "Hysteria Mainly Hystero-Epilepsy." In *A Dictionary of Psychological Medicine Giving the Definition, Etymology and Synonyms of the Terms Used in Medical Psychology with the Symptoms, Treatment, and Pathology of Insanity and the Law of Lunacy in Great Britain and Ireland*, edited by D. Hack Tuke. 2 vols (London: J. & A. Churchill, 1892), I, 627-641: 630.

The convulsive attack may present very diverse modifications. [...] In a complete typical attack one may distinguish three periods: *First*, the *epileptoid*, characterised by initial agitation of the limbs, falling backward with loss of consciousness, suspension of respiration and swelling of the neck. Most often the lips are covered with foam free from blood, after a slight sound of expectoration; also, as in ordinary epilepsy, the hands are pronated, and the forearms and legs are stretched out violently (tonic phase); then these same parts become subject to short and violent oscillations which soon spread over the remaining part of the body and especially the face and neck; respiration, suspended before, recommences with pain, and the whistling and jerking respiratory movements are interrupted by hiccough. Gradually these symptoms subside: this is the phase of muscular relaxation; the patient lies on the back, the head most frequently inclines to one side, the face is still congested and slightly puffed; the eyes are closed, the respiration, more regular but violent, is accompanied by stertor. The duration of this period, which, as we see, well deserves the name "epileptoid," varies from one to five minutes. Each of the phases however presents, with regard to duration and intensity, numerous variations.

Secondly, the scene changes; after lying down of the bed the patient begins again to stretch out the limbs, but this time no longer in a purely tonic manner, an immobile position. On the contrary, a period of disordered movements commences, which generally begins with the phenomenon called a "segment of a circle" (*l'arc de cercle*) [...]: the body rests on the feet and occiput only; the trunk is raised, and according to the expression of the patients forms a kind of "bridge" on the bed [...]. The duration of this position is naturally very variable, and it often gives place to the "salutations," in which the patient,—the trunk having fallen back flat upon the bed—passes alternately from the lying to the sitting posture, and thus bending forward seems to salute; sometimes also the patient leaning backwards raises his feet in the air, and thus executes *"sauts de carpe"* on his bed. The movements are sometimes such that the name of *clownism*, given to this condition, is not exaggerated, and one is sometimes surprised to see weak girls practising such gymnastics. The duration of this period is a little longer than that of the preceding one, and, although extremely variable, may be said to be on the average from five to ten minutes.

The *third* period presents quite a different aspect. Hitherto the symptoms observed were purely convulsive, but now the psychical element begins to play the first part in these morbid phenomena. The patient begins to give himself over to expressive mimicry, indicating the sentiments or series of sentiments which move him; pleasure, pain, fear, even fright, love, hatred, &c.; not unfrequently this sentiment and mimicry are in relation to a vivid impression or an emotion formerly experienced by the patient, which often has played a part in the explosion of hysterical symptoms. [...] This period of *"attitudes passionelles"* marks in some patients the end of the attack; the patient comes to, and the attack is over, or another attack supervenes.

8. Pierre Janet, *The Major Symptoms of Hysteria: Fifteen Lectures Given in the Medical School of Harvard University* (New York: Macmillan, 1907), 93-95, 98-99, 101-103.

All the preceding examples—the study of monodeic and polydeic somnambulisms, the study of fugues and of double existences—showed you the considerable importance assumed by somnabulisms in hysteric neurosis. We should still have many forms of the same phenomenon to consider. But to-day I wish only to dwell on certain elementary and, in some manner, degraded forms of somnambulism, because they are common, because they are to be met with every day, and because it is necessary, in order to understand them, to be able to connect with the more typical somnambulism, of which they are only inferior forms. You will understand the interest of this study, if you notice that it first applies to two phenomena very important in practice,—convulsive attacks and fits of sleep. [...]

Convulsive attacks, which we have first to attend to, are exceedingly frequent phenomena [...].

At first sight, the patients, who seem to have become unconscious, and writhe in disorderly convulsions, appear to be very different from the somnambulists we have just studied. Complete somnambulism was evidently characterized by a great number of intelligent manifestations; the subject expressed his idea, his dream, by his adjusted movements, which usually are to our mind the expression of reasonable thoughts. The first and clearest of these expressions was speech, and we had no great merit in guessing the subject of such dreams, since the patient expressed it himself by language. When he did not speak, he had expressions of the physiognomy, attitudes, and especially acts, the interpretations of which was very clear; he was seen to get up, to walk, to seek for objects in a drawer, to make the gesture of holding a revolver and pulling the trigger, to struggle with phantoms, etc. In a word, the outer expression of the somnambulic ideas was as clear as possible. There is nothing of the kind in convulsive attacks, in which the subject seems to writhe in great, irregular, apparently meaningless movements.

Yet it is easy to prove that, from many points of view, these convulsive attacks approach somnambulisms. These accidents, though apparently constituted by uncoördinated movements, have the same moral causes as somnambulisms; they begin, like them, on the occasion of particularly affecting events, genital perturbations, sorrows, fears, etc. [...]

You would perhaps find it more difficult to recognize the same law if you considered attacks, the starting-point of which seems to be the touch or excitation of a point of the subject's body. You know that formerly great importance was attributed to such points, which were called *hysterogenic points*. [...] It was admitted that the fit began with a pain or strange sensation situated at such and such a point of the body; the most frequent points with women were the lower region of the abdomen, called the ovarian region, on either side. [...] In fact, this sensation of uneasiness, which often begins in the lower part of the abdomen, seems to ascend and to spread to other organs. For instance, it very often spreads to the epigastrium, to the breasts, then to the throat. There it assumes rather an interesting form, which was for a very long time considered quite characteristic of hysteria. The patient has the sensation of too big an object, as it were, a ball, rising in her throat and choking her. [...]

Let us now return to the facts constituting the fit itself. They are at first meaningless movements. The patients grow stiff, then seem to try still to exaggerate this extension by throwing back the head, by raising the abdomen, by "making a bridge," according to the usual expression; the head is agitated in one direction or the other, the eyes closed, or open with an expression of terror, the mouth distorted. Now the patients grind their teeth, but without biting their tongue; now they open their mouth and utter piercing cries in every tone. The arms are agitated in every direction; they strike at haphazard on the surrounding objects or on the breast; the fists alternately close or open. The breathing is loud, irregular, the heart beats quickly, the face is congested, without, however, being violet-hued, as in the epileptic fit. It all seems very disorderly and unintelligible. [...]

It is easy to verify the assertion that this crisis is in fact an ensemble of emotional manifestations. In many cases it is even possible to distinguish and recognize the particular emotion being manifested. Certain patients plainly manifest anger, they strike, scratch, bite, and their cries are menacing; others evidently have crises of grief and despair, their tears and moanings have quite another meaning than the cries of the former. It is not very difficult to recognize erotic crises with the latter, for they play certain scenes in a remarkable manner. With the former, on the contrary, much oftener you have crises of fear; the bewildered expression of the eyes, the movements of defence of the arms stretched forward, the drawing back of the body, are quite characteristic. [...] These phenomena are almost somnambulisms, analogous to the preceding ones, but less perfect.